Critically Endangered

By NS Austin

Contents

Prologue..5

Chapter 1: The Beginning 19

Chapter 2: A+ 2, First Day Out.............................23

Chapter 3: A+3, More of the Same.......................34

Chapter 4: A+14, Metamorphosis.........................37

Chapter 5: A+22 Attitude Adjustment 44

Chapter 6: Mabel...49

Chapter 7: A+42, Change Can Be Good...............55

Chapter 8: Thomas...65

Chapter 9: A+43, Idaho 72

Chapter 10: A+62, Beauty Shop...........................78

Chapter 11: A+87, Mike 84

Chapter 12: Jed..103

Chapter 13: A+88, What Do You Want to Do? 114

Chapter 14: A+89, Twins.....................................120

Chapter 15: A+90, The Gifts................................133

Chapter 16: A+92, The Ruse................................139

Chapter 17: A+93, Sylvie 142

Chapter 18: A+94, Gas Station 152

Chapter 19: Mike and Katie.................................158

Chapter 20: A+94, Ranch Style Welcome.............163

Chapter 21: A+ 96, Home Base 167

Chapter 22: A+97, Home Base Gathers Friends....172

Chapter 23: A+95, Nothing Looks Better at the Ranch 176

Chapter 24: A+98, The Tribe at Home Base 183

Chapter 25: A+97, The Ranch..............................187

Chapter 26: A+99, Oregon 196

Chapter 27: A+101, Karen Meets Enlightenment 212

Chapter 28: Jack 222

Chapter 29: A+103, The Home Team 224

Chapter 30: A+110, Bad Meets Worse at the Ranch 231

Chapter 31: A+114, Home Base Gets Some News...................................248

Chapter 32: A+114, The Ranch and I Hate Snakes 252

Chapter 33: Jack and the Wild Dogs 261

Chapter 34: A+116, White Knights to the Rescue 263

Chapter 35: A+115, Bugs and Bodies 271

Chapter 36: A+116, The Ranch Meets a Hard Place 277

Chapter 37: The Ranch, Before Dawn 281

Chapter 38: Stable Reunions 299

Epilogue 311

Thanks! 316

Prologue

My name is Karen, and today is my 113th birthday—177th if you count the years before the change. My title is Founder Mother for the New Washington Enclave. I don't care much for titles—they don't mean a whit to me. It was "awarded" by the enclave counsel after they voted me out of office—probably because they felt guilty.

My granddaughter, Chrystel, ran against me for Enclave Mayor. If she'd asked, I would have gladly stepped down since I was sick of dealing with people's petty problems anyway. But she didn't, and I got hurt and stubborn and, well, you know how that goes. It doesn't matter; I lost. It took a year or so to repair our relationship, but I love that little girl like crazy. She is such a spitfire, and she makes me laugh.

My fifth son, Geronimo, is giving me the evil eye over my shoulder as I write. He's been nagging me for ten years to write about my experience before and after the change to document our history. He thinks I'm already off topic. Yesterday he said, "Mom, you have to do it before you're too feeble to remember." Sometimes Geronimo isn't very tactful. We finally struck a compromise: I'll write what happened in the two weeks or so leading up to the change, and he'll write the rest of the story. That way, no one will worry about me forgetting my name during the telling. LOL, as we used to say.

Some of you may ask, "How can she remember what happened 113 years ago?" I think that's the biggest problem with trying to write it down. I remember it more vividly than anything else in my 176 years of life. Each time I begin, I'm thrown back to that time and grieve the loss all over again. So much loss. Unfathomable loss…

I've given Geronimo license to embellish his part of the story; no one much likes a dry statement of facts. He has my spotty journal, and he's heard the tales from me and his father and his adopted aunts, Katie and Rachael, more than a few times. Since he just brought me coffee, one of the most precious commodities in the Northern Hemisphere, and hugged me before saying, "Get on with it," I won't explain how he got his name. He plans to write our history for the last hundred years, and maybe Geronimo will share that funny anecdote himself.

So, here it goes. March 16th was like any other day except I woke up with a huge pain in my neck. As with most of us baby boomers, a stiff neck was not usually a huge concern. On a long list of aches and pains, having to tilt my head at an awkward angle to avoid stabbing jolts was not in the top ten symptoms that required a doctor's visit. I booted up the computer, visited my favorite news and social media sites, checked email, and turned on the TV news for background noise.

In hindsight, I still don't know why I turned on the news at the beginning of each day. It was rarely uplifting and often downright depressing. But like a moth drawn to a flame, I did it anyway. March 16th was no exception. We were still waging battles around the world against crazed jihadists, and there was talk of global warming and how to get people back to work. Walking past the TV I noticed a red banner flashing across the screen that said "10 HOSPITALIZED IN MARYLAND WITH SPIKING FEVERS." Great! Last year's Egyptian Flu making its debut again this year.

In the previous year, forty or so otherwise healthy adults had died in the U.S. from The Egyptian Flu before we'd gotten it under control, but not before the stock market had another mini-crash and people started wearing gloves and masks to work. Some enterprising group even made designer plastic ensembles to sell on eBay and Amazon. I think they lost their shirt, or rather their plastic-draped and gathered muted-tone hoodies, because the whole mess was over before they really got into production.

By 4:30 that day, the outbreak was all over the news. Sporadic social media postings told of loved ones and friends that had fallen ill, lightly strumming my freak-out nerve. "Keep the faith" memes competed with fear, anger, blame and wild-assed theories regarding the end of days.

I rubbed my eyes and stepped away from the computer. My original plan for the day included trying a new recipe for Hungarian beef paprika soup. Deciding a good meal always makes the day a little brighter, I laid ingredients on the kitchen counter and had the TV turned up so I could listen and glimpse while I worked. Reports from across the eastern U.S. told of sick people with spiking temperatures. As much as I tried to keep my perspective on over-hyped news reports, that freak-out nerve was seriously resonating and my gut did a somersault in time with the vibrations. This didn't sound like the flu.

A leggy blonde in a short skirt, standing in front of a small hospital in New Hampshire, was trying to interview a young man who was shaking and sweating profusely. *Why wasn't she wearing the doomsday designer hoodie?* The young man's bloodshot eyes and inability to stand totally erect didn't stop him from wanting to get his minute of fame on national news.

"Excuse me, sir, I can see you appear to be sick. Can you tell me what happened?"

The camera zoomed in on the sick man. Trembling, he said, "I don't know, dude. I woke up this morning with a really stiff neck and started feeling hot. I was supposed to go to work at eight but I couldn't do it. I'm probably fired, and I needed that job."

"Sir, can you give me your name and tell me if you know anyone else who has become sick lately?"

"Pete Crowe, and no, I don't know anyone else who's been sick. I work at a distribution warehouse entering shipments into a receiving database—no one is sick because they fire your ass if you don't show up. This is the kind of job that my 100K college education bought me. Can you believe that crap?"

"Pete, do you think it's Egyptian Flu again, or something else?"

At this point poor Pete started to shudder and convulse. The startled reporter dropped her microphone when Pete leaned into her and grabbed her waist with both arms for support. You could hear her scream to the cameraman, "Get this guy off me!!"

I turned the channel. Greta, always the consummate professional, stared into the camera and announced, "Breaking news: four deaths have been reported from the baffling illness that started in Maryland earlier today. We cannot confirm the deaths, but the head of the CDC will be making an announcement in one hour regarding the new contagion, if that is what it is. I have Dr. Freelove, an expert on infectious diseases, as my guest. Dr. Freelove, do you believe this is the Egyptian Flu or perhaps Ebola?"

"Good afternoon, Greta. It's impossible to say at this point, but I would think it highly unlikely for this to be either Egyptian Flu or Ebola. The spiking temperatures are similar to those diseases, but from what we have learned, patients exhibit additional early symptoms like a stiff neck. The accelerated rate of symptom progression and spread are not at all synonymous with either contagion. Even airborne transmission would not account for the speed with which people are falling ill. In the early stages of disease transmission, there exists a geographical dispersion pattern which allows us to trace the source. In this instance, cases are, if you will, all over the map. Perhaps we missed the early warnings, but my CDC source said that was not the case. Very perplexing. Perhaps it is something other than a disease."

The camera panned back to Greta, and even her heavy make-up appeared faded. "This just in: unconfirmed deaths have been reported in Washington D.C., Virginia, and New York. There are also reports of people flooding emergency rooms throughout the Midwest, particularly in Chicago."

Holy crap! I had a stiff neck this morning like the unfortunate Pete Crowe!! My gut performed another gymnastic event, this time a double back flip with a half twist. Before I really started to panic, I calculated my ability to survive the apocalypse. As a lover of science fiction, I was well read regarding most possible scenarios. Not a couple of months before, I had told my husband Don that I was beginning to believe somehow humans would destroy themselves. He had recommended I start reading something other than science fiction.

Sure, since the kids moved out and I semi-retired, I'd had more time on my hands. And yes, I understood that meant I had more chances to obsess over weighty issues that I hadn't given the time of day when I was working and had two school-aged kids. But all my personal quirkiness aside, I still couldn't shake that feeling of impending catastrophe. *Is it possible the collective psyche of so many authors and Hollywood producers had been on to something?*

Also, I trust my instincts. From very early on in my life, I had just known things. I was right about what would happen in the future so often, I sometimes scared myself.

So yes, I had purchased the multi-canned chicken packs from a warehouse store, but I'd tucked them away so no one saw my possible craziness. And yes, I had inventoried our weapons, ammo, matches, batteries, flashlights, and bottled water stock so I could protect and survive in a pinch. But most of those things are also necessary in the event of earthquakes on the West Coast. Just saying…

I needed to call my husband and kids, but I didn't want to alarm them. I started with Don. His cell phone bleated in my ear.

"Hey, babe, when are you going to be home?" I asked.

"I'm about halfway home now."

"Did you hear about that crazy illness everyone is getting?"

"Heard something from our office admin lady as I was leaving. I had a meeting for most of the afternoon over upcoming labor negotiations. Totally useless, by the way. John Demming was leading it. Nice guy but boring. Couldn't get to the point and wasn't organized. We sat there for almost three hours trying to build a strategy for taking away benefits. It almost seems a bit unfair. Hey, I know these guys are paid well, but they have families too. And—"

I had to cut him off. "Don… this illness, or whatever it is, sounds sort of serious. Why don't you turn on the news? Also, can you stop by the grocery and get another pack of bottled water?"

"Thought we had plenty, but sure. Should be home in twenty minutes or so."

"OK, see you soon. Um, I had a stiff neck this morning. One of the worst I've had in a while," I added nonchalantly.

"Really? I had one too. Weird."

Crap, crap, and holy crap. I didn't want to waste time watching the news, although I figured it might be important later to see if any dead sprang back to life since apocalypse scenarios often involved reanimated dead. Both the kids were still at work, so I decided to wait a couple of hours to call. Anne's fright-meter would be pegged because she had something of a germ phobia. Nathan was probably clueless. He usually plugged into a game as soon as he walked in the door. They talked to each other in those games, though, so maybe he would hear something about it from his gaming partners.

I did a checklist of our doomsday items and inventoried my stash. Anne arrived home at 7:30. She blasted in the door, and the dogs began their normal boisterous welcome as she yelled from the foyer. "Mom, where are you?!"

Running down the stairs, I could see she'd been crying. The stark fear written across her face dislodged my denial-by-preparation routine. We hugged, and I whispered the reassuring words all mothers whisper to their children even when they know or suspect they aren't true. Glad she chose to come home, I reassured her we could stay here safe and together. She brightened a bit and asked if we had anything to eat.

Intelligent, self-aware, and totally without guile, Anne possessed an abundance of natural gifts that only served to make her lack of confidence more frustrating to me. The art history degree she had earned only qualified her to work at the better customer service jobs. She lived in an old house with four other early twenty-somethings trying to get a toe-hold in a less than forgiving economy. Poor as a church mouse but still wanting to do it on her own, she came home to do laundry, eat, and "borrow" stuff.

As a child, Anne developed anxiety issues and intermittently visited counselors. She was one of the all too many children who fell on the fringes of what is considered "normal" by her peers. She either couldn't or wouldn't pretend to be anything other than what she was. Still, she wanted to be like everyone else. I thought she was brave and unique; she saw herself as different and a loser, a view reinforced by mindless youngsters. Her teenage years were hard and a struggle for all of us. We avoided the worst results, such as drug and alcohol problems, and arrived out the other end of adolescence only somewhat bruised. More than anything else, I had wanted to see her blossom.

I tried calling, texting, and messaging Nathan, to no avail. If I didn't hear from him by tomorrow, I would take a drive over to his apartment. After a quick dinner, the five of us (we count our dogs as family members) cuddled in front of the TV in the master bedroom listening to different news broadcasts. There was nothing hopeful. It appeared that those people plagued with spiking fevers died within the first 12 to 18 hours. A whole lot of guessing was going on about what had happened, ranging from biological warfare to a random virus mutation to the always possible alien invasion. Bottom line: they didn't know shit! Cases were popping up around the globe except for North Korea. An expert on North Korean affairs proposed the North Koreans had accidentally dispersed a biological weapon. This was immediately refuted by another expert who reminded audiences that most people in North Korea did not have power at night, much less communication via the net. If they were off the grid at night, it was normal and not an indication they had succumbed to a bio-catastrophe.

The President was expected to make an announcement at seven the next morning. That was less than reassuring, as it seemed these days Presidents of both political persuasions had a knack for being a day late and a dollar short, saying whatever people most wanted to hear.

I commented to Don, "I sure hope he doesn't make an announcement for everyone to stay home after they've all already left for work. Remember when we were in D.C. and they released everyone at 10 a.m. in the middle of a blizzard? I thought I'd never get home. Couldn't believe the idiots who left their cars in the middle of the road and starting walking! Speaking of that, is there any possibility you could call in sick tomorrow?"

"I can't. Even if they do tell people to stay home, I'm pretty sure our outfit will be designated as emergency workers."

"Oh please, if they tell everyone to stay home you really think anyone will be riding light rail? Don, this isn't just another snow day. People are freaking dying!" My voice did that high-pitched quaking I hate, which made Anne start crying. The commotion roused the dogs from sleeping on the floor, and they got up to take part. If there was food or a walk involved, Tilley and Raider didn't want to miss their chance. Any time the humans got worked up, they were hopeful. "Don, you just can't pretend tomorrow will be a normal day—it won't be. I am afraid if you leave it'll be hard to get home. Please, just once, listen to me and trust my instincts. You—we— are safer here if we haven't already been exposed."

After a moment to collect his thoughts, Don said, "OK, I will see what it looks like in the morning and then make a decision."

How could this be happening? I searched Google before I went to bed about the spread of viruses. Nothing in the literature said it could happen this quickly. You can't put anything in the air or water that will disperse worldwide almost instantaneously. None of it made any sense, and I was scared.

Don and I made love that night. It was both passionate and tender—not the "go through the motions, done it a thousand times" kind of sex. Anne crawled into bed beside me sometime during the night. We held each other trying not to think about what the next day would bring. It was a fitful, restless night. Each time I would almost nod off, my thoughts would turn to Nathan. *Was he sick?*

We were up by six the next morning. Anne made coffee with a local designer blend. My clunky brown mug topped-off, I turned on the TV hoping the news would look different. It didn't. The reporting was so confused that it was difficult to determine if the outbreaks were concentrated in any specific areas or everywhere all at once. The only thing common to every report was that there were no survivors, at least none that anyone knew about. One announcer said within 12-18 hours of fever, everyone was dead, end of story.

Don walked into the kitchen carrying his work cell. I implored another time, "Don, what is the point of going to work today? Just call in sick. You have about a thousand sick days. Besides, God only knows what the traffic will be like. Wait and see if things are any better tomorrow."

"I just got a text message. They want everyone in to come in and close things out just in case. They will probably let us go home early."

I knew my husband was going to feel he had to be a part of it, so I got what could. "Will you stop at Nathan's apartment on the way? It will only take you an extra ten minutes. I'm worried about him. Text me if he's there, okay?"

"Yeah. I promise I'll be home as soon as I can. Do we have enough food to last a few days around here?"

"I think so—if the electricity stays on."

Sighing, Don said, "Karen, I think the media is overplaying this. Truth is we don't really know anything yet. I'll let you know what I find out and keep you updated. I'll be home as soon as I can. I promise."

I reached up and hugged him for all I was worth. The man was like an extra arm. It doesn't really fit on my body and sometimes it's impossible to coordinate a willful third appendage, but without it, I would be lost.

After sending three more text messages to Nathan, I sat down with Anne to eat cereal. We were still waiting for a message from the President, the CDC, or anyone who might know something on the TV. They announced that the Presidential press conference had been postponed until 11a.m. Eastern Time. Once again, I envisioned every working person in the country fleeing to their homes from work after an announcement was made to stay home. I said a short prayer that for once our leaders would use some common sense and tell people not to report to work tomorrow.

At 8:15 Pacific time, the Vice President stepped behind the podium. He did not explain where the President was other than to say, "He is currently meeting with his cabinet." I turned to Anne and her wide eyes found mine. "He's either sick or dead," she flatly intoned.

Just once before everything went to shit it would be nice to hear the truth, the unvarnished truth. Like, "Hey, we don't have a clue what's happening. You may all die, but then again some of you will probably make it—be prepared for the worst, and best of luck to you." Instead, the Vice President spewed less than reassuring political platitudes meant to keep the masses from rioting. "We have it under control and there is no need to panic. The CDC Director has identified a pathogen, and they are working on a treatment now. State National Guard elements and most of the Department of Defense are on alert to assist where necessary with emergency efforts. For your safety, unless you are identified as an essential emergency worker, everyone should return to their homes immediately and stay there until notified that the crisis has ended." Traffic Armageddon was all they had to offer us, just as I'd feared.

By nine that morning, I received a text from my husband that Nathan was at home getting ready to report to his National Guard unit and should be there by now. He also said he would leave by noon for home. Traffic reports indicated utter and complete gridlock—people were leaving their cars on the road to walk.

I never heard from my husband or son again. Anne and I took turns calling their cell phones, but the system was so overloaded all we got was recorded "try back later" messages. We busied ourselves baking cookies and pies while we watched the TV and internet with horror as the world crumbled around us. As hours turned into days we talked about searching for Don, but both of us knew that finding him would be nearly impossible. If we left, it would probably mean we would never get back to our little sanctuary, and thus far, we were safe. Looting and chaos in major metropolitan areas was broadcast live in a continuous loop on TV.

I didn't want to leave the house. When we turned off the TV and computers at the end of the day, I could somehow convince myself that if we hunkered down long enough, everything would blow over. Don and Nathan would walk through the door and we'd all share our interesting apocalypse stories. Silly, I know. My SUV tank was just a little over half full, so on the third day after it all started, my better instincts prevailed and I decided to fill-up while there was still gas to be had. Also, I needed to know what was out there. Leaving a note that I would be home soon, I stealthily crept out while Anne was still sleeping so she wouldn't worry.

I opened the back door for Raider, who refused to be denied a ride that morning. We set off to the closest gas station. At the first major intersection, a man and teenager, not 100 yards to my left were running along the side of the road toward some unnamed emergency with rifles slung over their backs. Concerned but not deterred, I continued down the road at an accelerated pace.

My fingers clenched the steering wheel as brake lights ahead blocked the gas station entry. Not wanting to behave like the panicked masses Anne and I had been watching on TV, I sat behind the car in front of me, talking to Raider to pass the time. "Raider, do you think this is the line to the pumps?" To which he cocked his head as if to say, *maybe*, *probably*, or *beats me*.

After fifteen minutes of a one-way conversation, I slid a jazz CD into the slot hoping to calm my frayed nerves. Ten minutes later, my patience snapped. It seemed important to remain with the car and Raider, so I got out and stepped on the front bumper of my SUV to the hood, then crawled on hands and knees over the windshield and stood on the top of the cab.

From my elevated vantage point, I had a clear view of the surrounding chaos. A hastily prepared fabric sign billowed from center poles supporting the pump weather overhang and read, "OUT OF GAS!" Two women, yelling and wrestling over something were on the ground in the grassy area between the station and the road. A pimple faced, adolescent boy exited the payment and convenience store with an overfull and obviously heavy black trash bag carried precariously on his head and neck. Broken glass from shattered store windows was strewn around the building. There were enough deserted cars and trucks crowding the station blacktop to prevent entry or escape.

Resigned, I jumped down and walked to the car to my front, knocking on the window to share the situation at the gas station. An elderly woman sat ramrod straight in the driver's seat, mouth open and car still running, totally lifeless. Choking on a scream, my legs back-pedaled of their own volition. Raider had his paws on the dash waiting nervously for my return and sat back on the seat as I leaped into the SUV, giving me a questioning stare. "Raider, we're too late. It's a mess out there." He very inappropriately wagged his tail and gave a happy yip in reply. After a clean maneuver to get out of the imaginary gas line and pointed home, we drove back to the house in silence.

I pulled into the garage and sat in the SUV, screaming, cursing, and pounding the steering wheel as Raider huddled forlornly in the back seat. It took almost an hour to collect myself enough to let my daughter see me.

The electricity went off on the morning of the sixth day. Anne started feeling ill right after lunch. My poor little girl was so terrified that she sat trembling and moaning on the overstuffed chair in the living room, refusing to let me touch her. "Don't, Mom," she warned whenever I reached out. "You'll get it too!"

Trying to reason with her, I replied, "Anne, we've been together in this house for the last few days. I've already been exposed. Please let me help you. Why don't you lie down while I get some cool rags to help with the fever?"

She pursed her lips and shook her head no. I think she was afraid that crawling into bed would be an admission that she was sick. We sat together for several hours in paralyzing fear, frittering away scarce time. I began to talk about Don and Nathan and some of the wonderful and funny times we'd spent on family vacations. This soothed Anne and, laughing, she joined in. "Do you remember the time we were in Las Vegas and Nathan let a big stinky one rip in that glass elevator filled with people? He just stood there looking straight ahead like nothing had happened while everyone else was glancing around trying to figure out who was responsible." Anne laughed that special, low rumbling sound that I loved with every part of my being.

"Yeah, and because you started laughing everyone thought it was you!"

Anne's smiling face changed abruptly and she wrapped her arms across her belly, gulped air, and then started to shake from fever. "I think I'm ready to lie down, Mom."

I helped her to bed and spent the evening and night in shock, trying to make her comfortable. During her last lucid moments, she said, "Mom, do you realize this pathetic scene is probably playing out in millions of homes right now?"

I saw my precious daughter, flushed and frightened, her beautiful face searching my eyes for hope. I tenderly brushed hair from her damp forehead.

"I love you, Mom. I know I haven't been easy. By the way, you aren't the easiest mom either, but I've always known you'd be there for me no matter what."

I couldn't hold it together after that. Sobbing, I hugged her fevered body in my arms and told her she was my greatest gift. I lay down beside her and held her until she became too uncomfortable, and I had to use cold rags again to keep her fever down. She lost consciousness at about 2 AM and was gone before the sun came up. Just like that, the snap of a finger, my amazing, insightful, and unique baby girl was gone. I would never hear her laugh again.

In the morning, I buried Anne in the yard. I should have thought harder about where to place the grave, but honestly, at that point I wasn't doing much thinking. The soil was damp from rain but filled with dinosaur egg-sized rocks that clanged every time my shovel hit one and then had to be worked out of the dirt. By the time the hole was large enough to discourage animals, my muscles quivered from the unusual exertion and tears and sweat stung my eyes.

The dogs seemed to know now was not the time for play and sat silent a few feet away, watching me dig. I wrapped Anne in her favorite childhood blankie, which I'd kept stored in a closet, and a quilt I'd made for her twelfth birthday. I don't remember making a cross by nailing two boards together and engraving her name and the date with the rechargeable Dremel tool Don had bought for some project. I only know that I must have done it because it's still there, in that same place, even now.

My teeth rattled with chills. Whether it was grief, exhaustion, or sickness I wasn't sure, so I took my temperature. 102 degrees; I was done for. There was nothing I wanted more than to just lie down and go to sleep, but I still had my fur children to contend with. Everything ached from digging, the fever, and a greater, undefined pressure in my chest. If I was going to die, I needed to do the best I could for the dogs; it didn't appear canines were susceptible to whatever had taken hold of humans.

Our home was a completely fenced two-acre parcel with a gate. I felt safety the first time I'd seen it even though the house was unusual. Most people didn't even know it was there. Located somewhat back from a forested ridge, the opposite boundary was owned by a family of environmentalists that refused to sell or develop. As such, it was country living in the middle of a mostly suburban area.

I stared at the fence and thought about the dogs. If I opened the gate would they survive? They were pampered pooches; their idea of hunting was raiding the trashcan in the pantry or stealing goodies off the kitchen counter. But if I confined them inside the gate would they starve? I didn't want to visualize what the coyote pack we heard on occasion would do to domestic dogs, so I opted to leave them inside the closed gate. Placing buckets and bowls everywhere outside to catch rain, I left a twenty-pound bag of dog food in the middle of the kitchen floor, and I opened the front door. For good measure, I put some thawed steaks that didn't smell too bad on the front porch, which they immediately consumed.

By this point I was full-out shivering. I no longer cared about my temperature. All I wanted to do was rest. Finally, I lay down on the bed and closed my eyes.

Chapter 1: The Beginning

Karen opened her eyes. She wasn't sure where she was. This was obviously her room, but everything felt so different. *What day is it?* Tilley the goldendoodle, on the bed next to Karen, jumped up on all fours, stuck her nose in Karen's face, and started whining before providing a full facial bath with her tongue. Rapidly swishing her tail and dancing on the bed, Karen heard Raider the terrier launch himself to the bed for a side attack. He planted himself in the middle of her chest.

Her mouth felt dry and cottony. She rolled Raider off her stomach, padded into the bathroom, and leaned on the sink, drawn by an overwhelming thirst. When she twisted the faucet, an air explosion, sputtering, and knocking pipes sounds was followed by a trickle of water plopping in the sink. *What the heck?* Karen walked down the hall to the kitchen, trailed by Tilley and Raider, and noticed the open front door. *Why is it open?*

Karen's stomach clenched in a tight knot as an electrical shock jolted her memory. *My God, no!* The day before she went to sleep flashed behind her eyes. Scenes of Anne, restless and sick as she sat helpless and more terrified than she could ever describe. Moaning, Karen thrust her hand forward to the nearest wall, as she folded to the floor. With her back against the wall, Karen placed her hands on the side of her head and pressed while an unearthly keening poured from her lips.

Tilley and Raider sat curious and slightly afraid in front of Karen as she sobbed and questioned a God who would take everything, again. If it wasn't for an all-consuming thirst, Karen might have remained curled in a ball against that wall as day turned to night. Finally spent, she whispered to the dogs, "Everyone is gone" and pushed herself up from the floor.

Other than a gathering of fruit flies hovering over apples in a bowl on the counter, everything was as it was when Karen had last entered the kitchen. She opened the refrigerator to get bottled water and was assaulted by rotten food smells. "How long have I been out anyway?" Karen mumbled as she grabbed two 16-ounce bottles of water, slammed the door shut, and guzzled both.

Munching on a fiber bar from the pantry, Karen stepped outside to see if there was water in her collection of bowls and buckets left for the dogs. It must have been raining; they were all full. *Probably best to use the outside water for washing and save the bottled water for drinking.* Taking the closest bowl, she dumped it in a pan and used the grill on the back deck to boil some water for washing. Noticing the butane was only half full, she made a mental note to get some more.

As she carried her pan of warm water, Karen cautiously stepped into the bathroom, trying not to spill the overfull vessel. She turned away from the mirror as she dipped a washcloth in the liquid to take a sponge bath. There was a day when Karen would have said she was pretty. With striking green eyes, good bones, and a face that in total fit well together, her reflection used to inspire confidence. Now, well, the best she could say was "I look good for my age." Her skin, a walking advertisement for the effects of being outside too much without sunscreen, was etched with a collage of joy and disappointment that comprised her life. Mirrors were no longer Karen's friends; their use was closely guarded, preferably in dimmed lighting, and only to apply make-up evenly or check for food wedged between her teeth.

Risking a glance as she brushed her teeth, Karen gasped in surprise. Turning her face right and then left, she pulled at her skin. "Good grief, what's up with that?!" After a battle with an unknown plague, Karen expected her face to be a parody of death warmed over. Instead, somehow, she looked . . . better. Her color was great, and some of the age spots along the sides of her face were gone. *Very, very strange.*

Freshly sponged, she grabbed another bottled water and sat in the home office, a corner of the master bedroom. Willing herself not to panic, Karen considered the most important question: *why am I alive?* The contagious virus research she'd Googled when people started dying made it clear that a naturally occurring virus wouldn't kill everyone. Also, she'd seen the effects on her daughter—Karen wondered what had happened after she fell ill and went to sleep.

Either she was immune or it was just a simple flu bug. Could she still get it? There were several signs she'd been unconscious for some time, which didn't happen with the flu. Since she seemed to have slept for more than just a night or a day, most likely, she'd somehow survived the virus or whatever it was. And it would follow that if she was alive, so were others.

Karen pulled her almost fully charged tablet from the desk shelf and changed the settings from Wi-Fi to cellular. She held her breath. No bars, no internet. "Damn." She tried anyway, clicking to a couple of her favorite sites in the vain hope some errant signal might magically connect, but nothing. The tablet clock, which continued to march forward without internet said March 26, 10:05 AM. She had been unconscious for three days and four nights. "It wasn't a simple flu—I survived."

Karen checked her email—Outlook opened but there were no new emails in the last few days. Scrolling down, she saw an email from her son the same day Anne had fallen ill. She'd been so busy taking care of Anne, it had never occurred to her to check email.

Dear Mom and Dad, I hope you get this. I have a fever. Everyone here is either sick or dead. It sure sucks they made us come in because we didn't even have a mission; people starting getting whatever this is before we could do anything. I wish I could be home with you guys. Please give the dogs a hug and say goodbye from me. I love you. See you on the other side. Love, Nathan.

Karen slid from her chair to the floor and hugged the dogs. She cried into Tilley's ruff for a long time as Raider sat on her lap licking her hand. She beseeched her companions, "Ten days... tell me how in ten days everything can be gone?! My family gone! Water, power, phone, internet—all history. Who the fuck did this!?" Their gentle, sympathetic eyes offered up nary a clue.

Karen's face mangled in grief and rage, she admitted to her canine family that Don and Nathan would probably not return. "They would have come home by now if they were okay," Karen moaned. She imagined their mortal bodies lying in a ditch or a car, unclaimed and alone. Her stomach contracted, attempting to expel its contents through her throat. When it seemed she could no longer endure the pain, Karen folded into the fetal position, hands together between her knees; Tilley and Raider nestled against her, witnessing her grief.

Karen woke up later, her teeth chattering from the chill inside the house. *Damn, it's so quiet.* She put on her warmest robe over sweat clothes and then wrapped herself in a blanket. She fed the dogs and then waited by the door in a daze for them to finish their business outside. After gulping another bottle of water, she headed to bed, calling Raider and Tillie to get in with her. Sleep took a long time.

All the sounds of the modern world—a heater turning on, faraway road noise, the almost imperceptible hiss of electronics—were gone and replaced by nature's rumblings. As she lay wide-eyed, Karen thought she could hear a squirrel racing across the roof. She knew everything was different, but the more germane question now was, how different? *How many people are left? I must get out tomorrow.*

Chapter 2: A+ 2, First Day Out

Karen woke the next morning feeling a little better. Once she'd finally drifted off, she'd slept hard for over eight hours. She was vaguely aware that her joints didn't pop and crackle as she shuffled to the door to let the dogs outside. *Hmm, maybe all the time sleeping has been a good thing.*

She heated water from her outside stock of water bowls, cleaned up, and grabbed a brush to put her hair in a ponytail. Glancing in the mirror for the second time, Karen was amazed to see her skin appeared tighter— damn, she thought, my face is almost glowing.

Throwing on jeans, athletic shoes, and a long sleeve tee, she debated taking the dogs. Karen didn't want to admit it, but she was frightened by what she might find outside the gate. Tilley and Raider would serve as an early warning system for squirrels or rabbits, but it was far more likely they would rather greet strangers than act as guard dogs. Still, she didn't want to go alone.

Karen loaded a shotgun and her .38 revolver in preparation for her outing. After her last foray into this new world, she thought, it was better safe than sorry. The first order of priority was a generator, medical supplies, weapons, and ammo. If she exited the gate and there were survivors and/or some sort of organized emergency system, she would change the list to food and water.

She grabbed the dogs' leashes, which was their cue to run to the SUV. Karen opened the back door and they jumped in. Tilley leapt over the center hump, scrambling for space on the front passenger seat, and turned a couple of times until she was comfortable. She sat erect looking at Karen in anticipation. Karen shook her head and sighed as she dropped into the driver's seat. "Tillie you're supposed to be in the back seat. But screw it, I'm not in the mood for a fight. Okay, guys, listen up, I'm going to need your help. Please save your barking for important notifications. If I'm attacked by a zombie… oh, wait I forgot a long, pointed object." Karen ran back inside and retrieved a garden hoe she'd tucked away behind the entryway étagère, and wasting no time, returned to the SUV at a jog.

The survivor team was ready to go. Karen started the engine, placed her foot on the brake, yanked the shift into reverse, and then pushed it back again to park. "I think I need something to drink." She left the vehicle running as she exited to take a warm diet soda from the dead garage refrigerator and settled in the driver's seat.

Karen sat for a moment, sipping her drink and staring at the garage wall. "Part of me really doesn't want to know what's out there," she said to the dogs. "The other part, says we gotta go." Karen rubbed her eyes, breathed deeply, and placed the SUV into reverse once again. "Now, as I was saying," she continued to the dogs, "if I'm attacked by zombies, please do not attempt to assist me. I don't believe canines fare well against biting zombies. Otherwise feel free to help when necessary." Raider's ears were pointed forward and alert to process the instructions. Tilley pressed her nose to the window with her tongue hanging out, excited for a new adventure.

Nothing could have prepared Karen for the world outside her gate. Everything looked the same, and yet felt eerily different. There were no smoking ruins laid waste by a tremendous battle or people running frightened through the streets. She could almost imagine it was any other workday—except where normally she would see someone walking their dog or a couple of guys doing yard work, the neighborhood was utterly devoid of human activity. The large orange truck that had recently been installing new telephone poles was parked alongside the connecting street, empty and immobile. Karen cracked the window so she could listen for sounds of other people or cars. Even the dogs, normally bouncing from seat to seat for a better viewing experience, sat confused, quietly staring out the window.

She arrived at the local strip mall a mile and a half from home without seeing one other person. The grocery store included a small pharmacy where Karen thought she might find some antibiotics or pain meds. Cars were still in the parking lot, but not in an orderly way. Backed into the front of the store, just outside the doors, sat a red delivery truck parked as if ready to load something quickly. A white Toyota had broadsided the truck and was half on the sidewalk. Someone was in the Toyota, slumped over the steering wheel.

She parked 50 yards from the grocery and away from the other cars. Moving the seat back, Karen reached for a vintage 80s Army green web belt with shoulder straps. It was the last of her Army gear. Somehow, it had never made its way to a donation site or garage sale because she kept thinking it might have a use. She smiled a sad smile and said out loud to no one in particular, "Who would have thought I would need it for the apocalypse?" The holster on the belt encased the loaded .38. Snapping it in place at her front, Karen wedged the hoe on the left side under the strap and hoped she wouldn't stab herself.

"Tilley, you're coming with me. Raider, you guard the SUV."

Together, and tentatively, Karen and Tilley moved toward the store. The smell from the crashed car told Karen there was no need to check on the Toyota driver. One side of the store's glass doors was shattered, but there were no broken bits or chunks on the ground. Amid the chaos, some enterprising individual had probably decided broken glass was a danger to customers and had swept the debris from the sidewalk.

It didn't seem possible, but the aroma in the store was even worse than the smell emanating from the unfortunate driver: a mixture of rotting meat and something else. Tilley whined, hugging close to Karen's side. Luckily, the front store windows provided enough light to see inside the grocery store. There had been looting; as they moved through the aisles toward the pharmacy, the only items left on the shelves were gluten free products and other tasteless healthy stuff. One rack had tipped over, spilling canned goods and boxes in a pile. Decomposing stench wafting from the pile was the most likely the reason the food had not been carried off.

The pharmacy window in the grocery had a steel half door padlocked to the counter. Karen decided she was going to need a bolt cutter to get in, which she hadn't thought to bring.

"Tilley, let's go check the drugstore across the way since we're already in the neighborhood." Getting no argument from Tilley, they jogged outside, two shops down to the drug store, through the wide-open doors, only to find this pharmacy padlocked as well. They turned as one and headed to the car at a trot. Raider scream-barked at their arrival as if they had been gone for a day rather than ten minutes; guard duty at the end of the world can be stressful. Karen's heart was pounding, but she noticed her knees and ankles weren't hurting from their dash. Putting her hands to her knees, breathing hard and chuckling, Karen pictured herself, a 64-year-old short woman with vintage field gear, a gardening hoe, and a guard doodle scared shitless raiding empty stores. "I really need to get a grip."

Next stop was the home warehouse store. Karen wracked her brain for something smaller that might stock tools and a generator. She shuddered thinking about a large, dark, and empty warehouse—worse yet, not so empty. Both dogs started barking and climbed over each other to the right passenger window to acknowledge three mutts running along the sidewalk. Karen momentarily thought to stop; she often stopped to help strays, but their returning barks didn't sound friendly. They were the first live creatures she'd seen in almost four miles, which was only slightly comforting.

Karen spied the familiar orange warehouse sign ahead. The access road was scattered with deserted cars and a collision that might have been more on purpose than by accident. A sedan and a minivan were smashed against each other, front bumper to front bumper, in the middle of street. How or why would forever remain a mystery. She crept around the abandoned vehicles. From the far side of the parking lot, Karen caught a flash of movement in her peripheral vision. She turned and studied the area directly. Two people were near the half-open sliding front door; one face down and one sitting up. "Wait! I was right. There is movement," she yelled.

Pressing the accelerator, she drove more quickly through the lot keeping her eyes on the two people. She steered right at the frontage road and stopped close enough to get a better view. The people shapes were not moving but undulating—horrified, Karen realized it was rats writhing on top of the poor souls, devouring their remains. "Ah, no!" Karen shrieked. She opened her door slightly, leaned out, and puked on the parking lot.

After wiping and spitting and taking several deep breaths, Karen turned to the dogs, "Forget the big box store. Cashiers wouldn't be handing out dog treats anyway. Let's just drive around and see if we can find something else—I should have enough gas."

Over an hour and hundreds of side streets later, Karen panicked. "How is this possible? How can I be alive and no one else? There has to be somebody!" She stopped in the middle of the road, pummeled the steering wheel, and in total frustration, honked an earsplitting soliloquy. Tilley and Raider woke up and jumped to an alert.

If not for the meltdown, Karen might not have noticed the small store set back from a drive-through oil change station across the street, creatively named "Tools." The light-up sign was off and difficult to see. As a matter of fact, Karen was surprised that she could see it at all, given her poor long-distance vision. She wondered if her vision was improving after a few days of sleep and no computer.

They pulled into the tiny parking lot. Bars on the windows made front access impossible, but just in case, Karen jiggled the door handle. Locked. Rising to her toes peeking inside the window, Karen could see just the right types of tools. Determined, she shouted to Tilley and Raider, "We are getting in that store!"

They walked around to the back. A rectangular window without bars, probably a bathroom, was eleven or twelve feet off the ground in the back corner. Karen and the dogs got back in the SUV. "Tilley," she explained, "we're going to drive the SUV to the back corner under that window as close as possible. There's a big tree on the side that might be a bit close, so please watch and bark before I hit anything."

Karen had to back in. A brick wall flanked the rear of the store, separating it from a residential area and making it impossible to turn around. Sliding the gear shift into reverse, she straightened the SUV, aiming between the tree and the side of the building and nervously pushed the accelerator.

When her back end was just past the tree, the SUV slowed as crunching metal on both sides angrily shook the vehicle. Tilley and Raider started barking. "Guys, you were supposed to warn me before I hit it—lot of help you are. If we get stuck we're screwed." She pressed the gas harder. The SUV burst through with a lot of grinding and almost smacked into the brick wall behind the building.

Karen got out and climbed on top of the car with the garden hoe in one hand and a towel that she always kept handy for muddy paws in the other. The window was just around the corner in the back of the building. Reaching out with her right arm, her body balanced on the corner of the building, she broke the window glass with her zombie defense tool. She banged the edges to remove glass from the window frame, wrapped the towel around her hand to push fragments inside, and then hung the towel over the edge. She couldn't reach the far side of the window to remove that glass so she'd need to be careful. Still balancing on the corner, she placed her right foot on the window ledge but couldn't gain leverage or a handhold to get her body up through the window.

Climbing back down, Karen's brow furrowed as she studied the situation. "Any ideas, furry friends?" Apparently not. Tilley was now in the back seat, her right leg twitching madly, scratching at something while Raider, perched on the console, was intently studying a fly buzzing around his head. "Hmmm, well maybe." Karen opened the passenger door. Its outside edge clanked against the corner. After checking how much room she had left to back-up, she climbed in, started the vehicle and crept backwards until she heard a tap of the SUV meeting the wall.

The car door, now fully open was almost directly under the window. She climbed on the top of the SUV, again, and very carefully stepped down to the door edge and stood up, placing her hands on the wall. Karen inched along on top of the door using gymnastic balance beam skills she'd never possessed while using the back wall to stabilize herself. The car door shook with her movement.

At the far end of the door, the window ledge was still more than a foot above her head and a foot away. Bending slightly and tensing her thigh muscles, Karen sprang while grabbing for the ledge. For a fraction of a second, Karen thought she wouldn't be able to pull herself up from a dead hang and that she'd fall instead to her death, impaled on a car door, a less-than-fitting end for an apocalypse heroine. She heaved and grunted, pushed with her feet against the wall and had enough momentum to get her shoulders over the window sill. Using the balls of her feet on the wall and her elbows planted, she pulled until her tummy was balanced on the window sill and she could see inside.

"Ah hell. Nothing's ever easy, is it?" She would have to clear a standing sink directly underneath as she attempted to ninja like, drop into the store. Tilley and Raider concerned with their master's machinations, had exited the vehicle and were barking at Karen from underneath the window. They could have been barking to say, "Come on you can do this," or more likely, "What the in the world were you thinking?" Karen wasn't sure but either way, she was going in.

"Could you guys hold it down please? I'm thinking," Karen huffed as she gazed at the twelve-foot drop. She played in her mind a wall facing hang drop trying to clear the sink and a forward facing leap with a PLF or parachute landing fall on hard linoleum. She'd never had a good reason to jump from a perfectly good airplane while in the Army. Her only real experience with the PLF was from a bar stool to the carpet after at least one too many shots of tequila at a party with Army friends. And that was a very long time ago. Still, the chances of catching on the sink in a backwards hang and breaking bones or cracking her head upon landing seemed too risky.

As if they knew what she was thinking, the dogs were frenetically barking and running back and forth under the window. Before she could lose her nerve, Karen scooched and twisted to get her feet under her into crouch on the window frame, her head now fully in the building. "I can do this. In for a penny, in for a pound." She visualized the place she wanted to land and how she would keep her knees soft and together and then allow her body to roll over on impact onto her cushioned and less fragile side. She did her best steely-eyed stare and jumped.

At landing, the sound of Karen hitting the floor sent the dogs into a full-on frenzy. It hurt more than she thought it would. That first touch-down felt like a drop from more like fifty feet. She exhaled an ugly sounding "uugh" as her feet hit the floor. She kept her wits about her though, pressing her knees together, allowing them to fold to protect her legs and spine. For a first effort, she'd executed a rather impressive side roll, from legs to side to shoulder. Karen sprawled on the floor not feeling any broken bones and began to giggle. The giggle turned into a laugh and just for a moment, the dogs stopped their incessant barking to curiously listen.

The store was just what they needed. Best of all, two new generators sat in boxes in a storage area. Too bad she only had room for one—Karen decided she was going to need a big truck. She found a four-wheeled dolly to move the generator to the SUV, but lifting the unwieldy thing enough to slide it in through the back door was a struggle. Actually, Karen was surprised at her strength—where did that come from? Piled next to the generator was a giant sledge hammer, large bolt cutters (euphemistically known from her time in the Army as a master key), a glass-cutting kit, and a long, sharp, pointy thing she didn't know the name for but would nevertheless be useful for zombie or vampire close-in fighting.

Everything loaded, Karen did a one last look around and made sure the back door was unlocked, planning to return later for the second generator. She froze in her tracks, Tilley and Raider on her heels, as she stepped through the door. A beautiful and extraordinarily large German shepherd had entered the open SUV and was sitting regally on the folded-down back seat in front of the loaded generator. Another slightly smaller, darker version of the regal dog was outside the car sniffing around the tires. Both dogs stopped when Karen did. Tilley and Raider moved directly behind Karen's legs as if she was going to protect them from charging monster dogs. Raider started a high pitched, rapid-bark warning, to which Karen replied, "Hush, Raider!"

It was a Mexican standoff. Seconds or minutes, Karen wasn't sure, passed while no one moved. Karen loved dogs. She'd grown up with dogs big and small. She loved their smell, the feel of their fur, and the way they leaned into you when they trusted you—but she wasn't stupid about them. A white German shepherd had snagged her in a butt cheek many years ago, the only time Karen had been bitten. Running from big, strange dogs wasn't a smart move.

Karen crouched, turned to the side, and lowered her eyes. Slowly reaching into a jacket pocket, she gently threw a dog treat into the vicinity of the darker shepherd. Drawing the dog closer by repeating the treat throw, Karen held the last morsel from her stash in an open palm with her arm extended, eyes down and away from the dog. The darker shepherd casually walked over and sat, facing Karen.

"Do you want it, pretty baby?" Karen asked. The dog wagged its tail, gave a short snuffle, and took the treat from her offered hand. Regal dog continued to sit in the car, unfazed. "Sorry, but I don't have any more," The female dog (at least Karen thought it was female), realizing no additional food was forthcoming, turned and jumped into the car with its friend or brother or father—no telling. Both dogs had collars with tags and were the picture of healthy canines— a good sign. But now what?

She turned to Tilley and Raider, who appeared perplexed with recent developments. "OK guys, here's the deal. I don't think I can get them out of the car, and I'm not sure I want to. You are both, sorry to say, worthless in the personal protection business. We could use their help. I am going to close the back door of the SUV and open the front. You can both sit in the front seat with me."

Karen used her best unthreatening walk to stroll to the SUV. She heard the thwack of a gently closed SUV door as she pushed it shut and corralled the shepherds in her vehicle. They didn't seem to mind. They sat patiently waiting and watching for whatever came next. Karen opened the front passenger door and called to her pampered pooches. Raider jumped in, but Tilley sat rock still in the store doorway as if to say, "You've got to be kidding me!"

A highly intelligent dog, Tilley learned things quicker than most, but her goofball antics made her smarts almost unnoticeable. The thing that truly stood out about Tilley, besides a remarkably gentle and playful nature, was how stubborn she could be. If she decided she didn't want to do something, no amount of sweet talk, firm voiced commands, coaxing, or treats would move her. Sans treats, Karen tried the first three approaches, then sighed and scooped Tilley's four legs, carrying 60 pounds of doodle to the car.

Raider stood on the center console glancing at the shepherds in the back seat while they mostly ignored him. Tilley hugged the passenger door, melting along the edge to make her profile as small as possible. Karen gingerly entered the SUV and turned on the engine.

Conventional wisdom says dogs don't make associations of their reflection or other objects in a mirror. As Karen looked in the rearview mirror, she saw the big male's chocolate brown eyes returning her gaze and was entirely certain he was appraising her worthiness.

She wasn't used to the constant adrenaline rush of this changed world. Exhausted from her first trip out, she only wanted to sleep. She chose a different route on the return trip home with the same result—not one live human being in a car or outside. The gas light came on as they pulled into the driveway and came to a stop.

The shepherds happily jumped from the vehicle as she opened the SUV doors. Karen stepped inside to grab treats from the canine canister and lured the shepherds near the front porch. They appeared to be satisfied with their new lodging arrangements, and allowed Karen brief greeting pats. Hanging from their collars was some sort of government-issued dog tags; a bar code was stamped on the back. Their names, Jack and Jill, were prominently embroidered on the blue collars.

"Well, hello, Jack and Jill. I am so glad to properly meet you. SIT!" Both dogs sat, and Karen handed them treats. "HEEL." Jack and Jill padded behind Karen and sat in formation on her left side. Karen moved toward the house, and both dogs walked by her side, meeting her stride. When she stopped, they stopped and sat. "Hmmm, what is the command to set you free? GO!"

Nothing.

"RELEASE."

Nothing.

"FREE!"

At that Jack ran to a water bucket and drank in huge gulps, his tongue spilling water in every direction. Satiated, he flew to the fence in only three strides to mark the new territory. Raider followed Jack, trying unsuccessfully to meet his urine stream pee for pee.

A light drizzle started to dampen hair and fur. Tilley went into the house first, probably to pout, as Jill followed Karen inside. Realizing she didn't have the energy to figure out how to get the generator inside, much less learn to set it up and make it operational, Karen plopped on the couch with a moan.

She was handy, a jack of all trades and master of very few. This whole "new world" you're completely on your own thing was a serious wake-up call. She really didn't know how to accomplish much of anything from start to finish. Don took care of the mechanical projects around the house, and he'd been good at it, so there wasn't reason to spend time learning. Besides, YouTube videos were available to guide the uninformed in the use, diagnosis, and repair of equipment from bombs to pasta makers. All she had left was her woefully inadequate memory and what was left of her wits.

Tears formed and then turned to sobs. She was totally alone and not at all prepared to survive on her own, physically or emotionally. "I have to keep moving," Karen whispered to herself. It was too overwhelming to stop and consider her predicament. She fed the dogs, ate peanut butter on crackers, and placed blankets in the foyer for the new guests. Finally, Karen put on heavy sweatpants and a sweatshirt and crawled into bed.

Chapter 3: A+3, More of the Same

In those foggy moments before waking, Karen dreamed of running down a street yelling for someone to help, not knowing what was chasing her and seeing no one. She knew she needed to run faster, but her legs were stuck together and her feet sank into the road with each step. She had been bitten by something. She couldn't move her hands to scratch the itch, and a mournful howl could be heard in the distance.

Karen's eyes bolted open to daylight, her heart pounding with a half scream stuck in her throat. She tried to sit up, but Tilley was lying across her feet. Turning to her side, Karen lifted her arm to scratch the underside and saw cracked and flaky skin. The other arm was likewise mottled. "Well if that isn't just adding insult to injury!"

Jumping out of bed, the dogs cheerfully greeted her and bounced to the front door for their morning constitutional. Karen could barely get the door open for all the wiggling and tail wagging of four dogs who didn't grasp or care that it was the end of the world.

Karen brushed her teeth with bottled water and stopped at the lower front portion of her mouth. "Oh no, this can't be." She studied her reflection in the mirror, leaned in closer over the sink, pinched one of the lower teeth between her fingers, and moved it. "No friggin' way!" She grabbed a couple of other bottom teeth and confirmed they were loose. Karen's scrunched her face and stomped her feet. "What the hell, I can't lose my damn teeth—not now!"

A close inspection of her skin showed scaly red and dry patches on her arms, legs, torso, and back. And they itched! The inflammation was particularly pronounced on scar tissue. Her cesarean scar and a long scar on her right elbow, received from a slightly inebriated early 20s skateboarding accident, were both inflamed. Pushing it out of her mind, Karen rubbed some poison ivy itch relief on the worst spots, swallowed a couple of ibuprofen dry, and tried to organize a survival plan for the next several days. At least her shoulder and knee pain seemed to be in remission.

After everyone was fed, Karen's top priorities were to set up the generator, get gas for the SUV, and begin the process of bringing Jack and Jill into her family. On a normal day, Karen would organize tasks for optimum efficiency. If she had errands, she would map them in her mind for the quickest route. Hard or challenging projects were saved for the afternoon when her brain and body seemed best able to work in harmony. Dogs first, Karen said to herself with a smile.

She took tennis balls out to the back of the house and played fetch with the shepherds. Tilley didn't like to play fetch—she liked to steal. Easily bored by running after a stupid ball and bringing it back, she preferred instead to intercept the flying object or wait for other canines to drop the ball. Then, like an inexperienced shoplifter, she did a grab-and-go, hoping to be chased. Karen was a little concerned when she saw Tilley waiting on the sidelines for her chance. Raider ran happily behind the shepherds, making no attempt to get in the way of their play.

Jack was an amazing animal: strong, athletic, and graceful, with eyes that could convey both fierceness and an affable disposition. Underestimating the distance since he probably wasn't accustomed to the lackluster throw of a 64-year-old woman, Jack watched as the ball bounced behind him and leaped to catch it as it ricocheted off his snout. Tilley took her cue, ran, and grabbed the ball. Lightning fast, Jack was there, planting his feet by Tilley and giving her a look. Tilley's eyes drifted down and away from Jack while demurely dropping the toy at his feet, as if that was her intent all along. And then an amazing thing happened: Jack towered over Tilley and rather than take the ball back, gave the universal dog signal of play by crouching in the front with his hindquarters in the air.

Tilley scooped up the tennis ball and ran for all she was worth; the other dogs gave chase. Somehow, smart, crazy Tilley had managed to turn the game in her direction. The dogs ran around the yard three times until Karen yelled for them to heel. Jack and Jill were there first. Seeing the shepherds respond appropriately, Tilley and Raider, who knew heel but were inconsistent in their obedience, followed suit. Karen smiled and said, "Good dogs! I think this is going to work out."

The rest of the day was spent getting the generator onto the front porch, out of its box, and reading the godforsaken operation manual. She postponed the gas mission until the next day after she tried to syphon from her daughter's car and couldn't get any flow. She found Anne's keys and checked to see if the tank was empty but it was almost full. "This could be a problem," Karen said to Tilley who'd climbed into the car and was sitting in the passenger seat, hoping to go for a ride.

After dinner, Karen spent time in the mirror searching her body for any other unnoticed changes. So far, no extra toes, fingers or eyes were taking root from unusual places. "Well that's a good thing, I think," she said to Raider who was watching from his vantage point on the edge of the bed. "Raider, it seems like, and I know this is impossible, but my eyes are a brighter color."

Raider didn't seem to care. He jumped down and picked up his favorite squeaky toy, chomping up and down to make as much noise as possible. She tightly closed her eyes, then opened them wide, peering into the mirror—they still looked different. What the hell is going on?

Chapter 4: A+14, Metamorphosis

Karen named days like the Army used to do when there actually was an Army. Today was A+14, short for Armageddon plus 14 days. That morning, two of her lower front teeth fell out, and most of the rest were loose. Other than obtaining a really cool juicer and food processor from the neighbor's house in the event she spent the apocalypse toothless, she did her best to ignore the problem. There didn't seem to be a damn thing she could do about it anyway.

Karen felt the gap where her teeth used to reside and wasn't sure but thought there was something coming in to replace her perfectly good but worn originals. "Well, that's interesting." A brief mental flash of some fangs sprouting from empty gum holes made Karen shudder and she reminded herself to stay away from science fiction novels.

The terrible itching skin had finally abated. As the scabs and flakes fell off, the skin underneath was pink and new without the thin buckling that usually meant a scar had formed. In fact, Karen's scars were completely gone. Her eyesight was nearly perfect as well; she'd tested herself before she went to bed the previous night. Best of all, her knees, ankles, neck, and hands—sometimes stiff with varying degrees of arthritic pain—had become flexible and pain-free. Karen assumed there was some relationship between her illness, subsequent survival, and the changes to her body and was simply glad they were positive thus far—except for her teeth, of course.

It was a bit cooler that morning, so Karen pulled on her stretchy jeans. Sliding her feet into shoes, she tugged the bottom of the jeans to cover her exposed anklebone, but there was no give. She stood up, went to the mirror to study her reflection and huffed, "That can't be." The jeans were shorter. "How the heck is that possible?" As a petite person her entire life, except for a year when she started her growth spurt early, Karen had learned to shorten pants to exactly the right length. Since she'd reached her full height nearly 51 years ago, Karen considered herself to be something of an expert at having the right fit.

Suddenly, like being kicked in the head, the too short jeans situation made sense. "Oh my God, I'm getting taller! Tilley, Jack, Raider, Jill, Zoe, come here and look!" Thinking there was a treat involved, the dogs gathered around to view the spectacle. Less than impressed but excited that their human was happy, they vied for a pat as Karen danced around the room. "No wonder my shoes felt tight," Karen said. "I'm getting bigger! Zoe followed Karen as she pirouetted through the room, trying to dance along with her.

Their latest pack addition, Zoe, was a sweet brown Labrador dog that had become part of the family when they found her on A+5, barely alive in the doctor's house down the street. Obtaining pharmaceuticals had been difficult because the drug stores Karen visited were locked up tighter than banks guarding gold deposits. Thankfully, Americans believed in guns and drugs; there was no shortage of either in homes around the neighborhood. The doctor's house was a huge score. She found a drug glossary as well, which helped decipher the names of medications and their purpose.

As she'd entered the doctor's house, Karen put on her mask. Most people, it seemed, had made it home. It was incredibly sad to see two, three, or even four people curled together on a bed. Karen learned to shut bedroom doors before she accidently viewed the scene inside. Family photographs on dressers and walls were reminders of families that used to be, so she simply diverted her eyes and went about her work in an organized way. The smell in the doctor's house was particularly daunting; it was a combination of decomposition and poo.

They'd found Zoe whimpering under a table in the corner of the kitchen. Jack barked and growled, which terrified the poor animal. Karen commanded Jack to heel and sweet-talked Zoe until she crawled out. She'd obviously run out of food and water and could barely walk, requiring Karen to carry her to the new extended cab truck she had stolen from a local car dealership. There were so many dogs running loose and only so many Karen could care for. She wondered how long it would be until domesticated dogs became so desperate they turned into feral packs—at that point, she would have a very large problem.

Karen knew dogs and humans shared a need for routine. Some people claimed they lived in the moment and supposed dog experts said living for the now was the beauty of the canine species. Karen thought that was all total BS. Go to any lunchroom or classroom in the world and watch as people chose the same seat, day in and day out. As for dogs, their internal clock regulated everything they did, from waiting for their owner to arrive home, to sitting at the food dish when it was time for a meal to be served. Change an arrival time, move the food bowl, or sit in someone else's seat and watch how restless and agitated the aggrieved party became.

By the fourteenth day of the new world, as best as possible, Karen had created a routine. An hour in the morning was devoted to eating, cleaning, fur-brushing, and organizing. After that, dog training for a half hour and another half hour of dog play. Training was followed by Karen's exercise hour consisting of running around the yard and driveway with a weight circuit routine she'd devised. The dogs considered this another hour of play, following her around the yard with balls in their mouths, sometimes nipping at her heels or licking her face when she dropped to the push-up position. Karen ate lunch with five pairs of eyes hoping for a morsel before she set out for scrounging expeditions in the afternoon. In ten days, Karen had accumulated at least a year's supply of food and water, four operational generators, filled gas cans, tools, instruction manuals, and most of the medical supplies she needed.

In hindsight, her hoarding probably didn't matter. Since there was no one left but her, getting what she needed was a cakewalk at the thousands of deserted homes in the area. Today's mission was to begin a search in earnest for a shortwave radio, the one thing she hadn't found. Karen didn't know how to operate one and wasn't sure where to find one, but she knew it might be her only chance to locate other survivors. So far, as she extended her search parameter to 30 miles out, she hadn't seen one other living human being.

Karen called for Jack, Jill, and Tilley to get in the truck. Not wanting to be bested by the shepherds, smart Tilley was now almost as good at following commands as they were. She zoomed around Jill to be the first to jump in.

Since she'd read once in a science fiction novel that pawnshops were a good place for radios, Karen carried a list of pawnshop addresses in her pocket. The day was beautiful, with crystal clear skies and temperatures somewhere in the mid-50s. Spring was beginning to assert itself, and the season's first rhododendrons and tulips were already in bloom. She inserted a Credence Clearwater Revival CD, turned up the volume, and they were on their way.

Post-apocalypse American highways near major cities were in total gridlock, so Karen was forced to stick to side streets. The news before the lights went out made that fact very clear, and the corridor from North of Seattle to just south of Olympia was living proof the news reports were accurate. She'd tried to use the highways but they were jam packed with deserted cars, trucks, trailers, RV's—the whole shebang. If Karen wanted to find survivors, she'd have to do it via secondary roads. The interstate was impassible.

In an older part of town, searching for Pete's Pawn and Fishing Store, Karen caught movement out of the corner of her eye. As one, Jack, Jill, and Tilley started barking. She wasn't positive, but it seemed like the front door had closed on a home they'd just passed.

She did a quick U-turn and pulled into a short driveway that led to a detached garage. Stepping out of the truck, three dogs and one lonely woman searched for signs of life. The yard was neat but the grass needed cutting; the house was completely dark. Karen and her companions climbed up four concrete steps to a wide entry porch and looked in the front window. There was a sofa, large TV, and recliner in the small living area. Beer bottles and an overflowing ashtray sat on an end table next to the chair. She could see a kitchen table covered with stuff through a narrow view into a kitchen. "Okay, guys, I think we need to check it out just to be sure. Stay close in case there is an animal inside." Not realizing how prophetic those words would be, Karen knocked on the door and waited.

Getting no response, she tried the door, found it unlocked, and pushed it open gently. Karen called out, "Hi, I'm Karen Henry. Anybody home?" She took a step into a small foyer and felt the hair on her arms stand up. Close at her side, Jack and Jill were wary, and a rumbling growl was coming from Jack. As usual, Tilley was out of harm's way directly behind Karen, hugging her heels. "Sorry to just barge in—is anyone home?" Total stillness greeted Karen and the dogs. Other than lingering cigarette odor, there were no dead body smells in the house. But there was something else—something nasty tickling her nose. Totally creeped out, she decided it wasn't worth the effort and was just about to turn to leave when a huge man jumped out of the hallway, standing a mere ten feet from her. One second no one was there, and the next he appeared. He was close enough that Karen could smell his pungent odor.

In milliseconds, Karen's senses collected thousands of different stimuli. He must have been lurking or hiding quietly in the hallway of the dark house. Dangling at his side in his right hand was a hatchet. Karen had carelessly left her weapons in the truck. Very big, maybe 6'3", and well over 200 pounds, the man's eyes gleamed with intelligence but there was something about them that wasn't quite right. He was wearing a frightening smile, and absolutely nothing else except boots. He'd also lost a few teeth, but it was hard to tell whether they'd been lost before or after the apocalypse. All of this was complemented by some knobby bumps on his forehead and chin. Karen's small brain processed the information and spit out a conclusion in about a second: RUN!!

She was backing out the door when her leg got caught on Tilley. She fell hard over the dog, twisted, and landed on her back and right elbow. The man lunged toward Karen as the shepherds jumped at him, grabbing an arm each trying to pull him to the ground. Karen heard the big man's bone snap as Jack brutally twisted, and the hatchet fell out of his hand. As Karen tried to use right hand for leverage to push up from the floor, pain shot up her arm from her elbow landing.

Even with almost 200 pounds of dog hanging off his arms, the man kept coming. He lifted his big boot to stomp on Karen, but she rolled out of the way just in time. The man was howling as he kicked at the dogs. Tilley, probably shocked into action, locked on to one of his legs from behind, pulling with all her might, and the big man fell forward on top of Karen.

Pinned under him, his stinking breath was gag inducing and, of course, as in all apocalypse scenarios, he tried to bite, wetting her face with big drips of saliva. To pull him back, Karen folded her fingers in his hair with her good hand and had to weave and bob her head to keep away from the man's mouth.

In shock, she called out, "Jack, help me, Jack…" Jack released the man's arm and jumped on his back. Grabbing the strange man's neck with strong jaws he planted his front paws into his upper back. Jack violently shook and pulled. Blood exploded all over Karen, Jack, and the man. The man grabbed his neck with his hands screaming—blood still pumping through his fingers. Karen watched from the floor without breathing until his eyes went empty and his body fell limp.

She wiggled out from underneath the man and sat clutching her knees, rocking as her teeth began to rattle. The dogs looked to Karen, panting and hoping for a sign they were not bad dogs. She surveyed the carnage. His arms were almost completely severed; only exposed bone holding them together. Tilley had taken a pound of flesh off his calf. Blood blanketed everything, and the coppery odor of it hung in the air. "Good dogs, good dogs, good sweet dogs," Karen whispered. On legs that felt like rubber, Karen stood up, stepped away from the mess, called the dogs to heel, and walked out of the house.

It had all happened so fast! Freaked out and crying, Karen stripped off her t-shirt and jeans by the truck tailgate and threw the bloody clothes into a trashcan beside the house. "My arm or elbow must be broken," she lamented. Every time she moved her arm or tried to grasp with her right hand, it hurt like a son of a bitch. She doused herself with a gallon jug of water and used one of the towels in the truck to wipe blood from her face and hands. She had another full quart water bottle and attended to Jack, the bloodiest dog, wiping as much of the blood from his fur as possible. To Karen's horror, she saw Tilley and Jill licking blood from their paws and flanks.

"Oh my God, what have I done? I just killed maybe the only person alive besides me!" Karen moaned. More than anything else in the world, what Karen wanted right now, this very instant, was a working cell phone to call someone and tell them to come get her. To hear another human voice, any voice, express concern for her plight. To have Don arrive in front of the house in his little green car, run to her, and hold her in his arms until she felt safe again. Instead, she'd just killed possibly the only other living person in the whole world. Karen had no idea how long she stood behind the truck in her panties and bra. Jack moved his head under her hand, and Jill laid her head on Karen's foot, pulling her out of her descent into shock. Karen swallowed, gritted her teeth, and said, "I wish I could bury him, but I can't with this screwed up arm. As soon as I'm better, we'll come back and dig a grave. Let's just go home."

At the sound of "home," her companions rushed to truck doors, wanting to split this joint as quickly as possible. Karen put on an extra shirt in the cab of the truck and drove carefully to their sanctuary. Her brain started to function again as the body- shaking bouts subsided and they neared the safety of their home. What had made him like that? Is the same process that's changing me, doing something different to everyone else alive? And more frightening, are there more like him?

Chapter 5: A+22 Attitude Adjustment

Karen kept replaying the scene with the strange guy over and over in her mind and searching for a different outcome. Maybe he was just scared and reacted badly when she'd tried to run. With Jack and Jill locked on his arms, what else could he do? "But Karen," she told herself, "He did have a hatchet in his hand. Were you really willing to take a chance on his good intentions?" On and on, the battle raged inside her head—and it always ended with blood spurting from the crazy man's neck, Jack looking at her wild and ferocious from his stance on the man's back, and then finally, the shine from strange guy's eyes flickering off like a used-up light bulb.

She'd never killed anything larger than a good-sized Washington slug. Hell, she'd never even aimed a weapon at a live breathing human—only at targets. She would have gladly killed a snake if she had seen one when her grandpa took her on hunting expeditions in the Michigan wilds. Karen loathed snakes, but, it was normally cold when they set off on their trips and the few snakes that were around had gone to ground.

After their run-in with Crazy Man, killing the only other survivor she'd seen, Karen refused to leave the safety of the house and fenced yard. She had convinced herself there really was no need to leave because they had everything they needed right there. What would be the point? No one else was out there anyway.

She alternated between sadness and fuming anger that the gods of fate had left her alive but alone. During those dark days, she spent more than a few hours crying at her daughter's grave and taking naps during the day, often waking from bad and unsettling dreams. Karen told herself she had a right to be this way; who wouldn't? She was supposed to be enjoying her retirement right now, travelling the world with Don to see all places they had yet to visit or spending long luxurious hours painting to her heart's content.

Her dreams, her hopes, her family, her friends—all were gone, snuffed out in an instant. What kind of sick joke was it to leave just one person alive? Even Tom Hanks, marooned on an island in *Cast Away*, knew people were still out there if he could just get off that damn island.

Yeah, okay, Karen had to admit, five dogs were preferable to a volleyball as far as companionship goes, but still…

On that terrible morning, day A+22, Karen did not want to get out of bed. She woke up several times and forced herself to sleep longer. Sensing her malaise, the dogs hung around endlessly. Wedged on the edge of the bed, Karen faced away from the scratching and snoring Raider, Zoe, and Tilley, who were taking up most of the usable bed space.

For the first time since the apocalypse, Karen considered doing what everyone else had done: just go to sleep forever. She opened her eyes to find Jack standing at the side of the bed staring at her, completely still. In his eyes, Karen saw compassion, love, and some sort of innate knowledge that transcended what a dog was capable of understanding. Absolutely sure that Jack knew what she was thinking, in that moment Karen saw God's hand. Some force had sent Jack to her, a wonderful dog, the truest friend, companion, and workmate humankind had ever known. He put his paw to her arm and whined.

She was so stuck in her own pity party, Karen hadn't considered what would happen to her dog family if she wasn't around. Jack and Jill could probably learn to hunt and survive, but crazy Tilley, sweet Zoe, and little Raider making a go of it—not likely. They needed her as she much as she needed them.

Karen had a long talk with herself that day. Since she had no one else to talk to, she played the role of both patient and counselor. When her life had gone to hell on a couple of occasions, Karen had visited a counselor or two to get through the rough patches. She remembered the annoyingly leading questions they asked. Today, playing both roles, she had a session. Karen talked out loud since there wasn't anyone to overhear and judge her as totally off-her-rocker, as indeed, she might well be. It went something like this:

"So Karen, it seems you've decided to give up. Can you tell me a little bit about that?"

"It all seems kind of pointless. I don't want to live the rest of my life alone."

"Okay. Why do you think you'll be alone for the rest of your life?"

Karen rolled her eyes. "Duh, because there aren't any other people, except of course the one I killed, and he didn't look like my kind of guy!"

"How do you know there aren't any other people?"

"I have driven around a city of 300,000 or so and there are none."

"There may not be any in this city. How do you think *you* survived?"

"I don't have a clue. Probably I had some sort of immunity or genetic makeup that allowed me to survive the disease, if that is what it was."

"So far you and a nut case survived—that's 2 in 300,000 that you know of, correct?" Counselor Karen asked in a monotone.

"Yeah, I suppose."

Exasperated, Counselor Karen said, "Karen, you are way smarter than this. Do the math. If there were seven billion people in the world, and the sample here holds true, how many other survivors are out there?"

"2,000… no, wait, 20,000, but half of them are really different!"

"So, the question is: do you want to find them?"

"Of course, I do, but how? That's 20,000, or actually 10,000 normal people—but spread across the world. I can't go from town to town and have any real hope of finding someone. It would be like ships passing in the night. I'm not sure what the population of the U.S. is, but let's assume it's 5% of the world. That makes only 500 non-crazy people in the entire U.S."

"I believe you had the answer before you got stuck in a PTSD-like feedback loop. Also, there may well be some additional survivors that are totally alone and segregated. Say, for instance, people in a submarine. I read that in a book somewhere, so I know it's possible."

"I don't have PTSD! But, okay, I really do need that radio."

"Exactly. So why aren't you looking for it?"

"I'm afraid."

"What are you afraid of?"

"Dying."

"Really? That's interesting. You just had a thought about ending it all, and now you're afraid of dying?"

"Funny, you got me there. And for the record, a thought is not a plan. I think maybe I'm afraid of not being up to this and then dying."

"And who will you disappoint if you aren't up to it?"

"Just me."

"And you'll be dead, right?"

"Oh, screw it," Patient Karen said. "I hate arguing with myself. I will look for the damn radio!"

"Outstanding idea! And Karen, don't forget, you are alive when so many others are gone. Whatever the reason you survived, you are now the standard bearer for your family and the human race. What would your family want for you? What does the human race need from you?

"Okay, okay, I get the idea. You don't have to be so dramatic. I can almost hear the music crescendo in the background. Now if you will please leave my head, I have work to do."

That afternoon, Karen and crew were back on the road in search of a shortwave radio. She also hoped to find her son Nathan at his last known location—the National Guard facility in Seattle.

She was mostly certain her right elbow was broken; it was swollen and hard to move. Karen took 800 milligrams of ibuprofen and kept her .38 revolver with her at all times, surmising she could still shoot a small weapon with her left hand.

Nathan's body wasn't at either the National Guard Center in Seattle or at his apartment in Tukwila. That was both a good and a bad thing. Good because in her wildest fantasies, Karen could continue to imagine he and her husband were still alive. Bad because they were most likely dead and alone, their bodies being consumed by insects or wildlife with no chance for her to say a proper goodbye. Karen didn't believe you ever found closure when a loved one was ripped away from you horribly or suddenly. It was a tragic wound that eventually healed, leaving memories and scars. Scars that remained to remind you of the loss. Scars with the capability to wake you in the dark of night. But, somehow the act of honoring their mortal bodies made a difference. It was the chance to yell to an incomprehensible universe that this person was important and special! This person was loved by me and they were never alone.

Travelling on side roads Karen thought Don might have taken on his return from work, she didn't see his car. It was still painful to imagine what might have happened to them. Probably always would be.

Dogs, cats, and the occasional deer, now free to safely run in the streets, were the only other life forms out and about. Beyond abandoned and not-quite-so-abandoned cars, Karen added wildlife to the list of things that required more caution when driving.

Chapter 6: Mabel

He almost passed her by. Mathias used secondary two-lane roads through Salt Lake City as he made his way back to the ranch. At the end of the world, too many people left their cars in blockade fashion on major interstates around cities. Not that he cared. This was his chance.

Out of the corner of his eyes, he saw the woman sitting in front of a one-story, sprawling building. A building that somehow managed to communicate, to even a casual observer, that it was an institution for the old. He pressed hard on the brakes and looked out the window again to make sure she wasn't a mirage. A short-haired woman smiled a fetching smile and waved to him. Bold. Just what I need!

Mathias backed up to the paved drive. It was flanked by three-foot-wide nearly barren landscaping beds that appeared designed to keep visitors off the once-manicured lawn that was already sprouting weeds. He slowly drove toward the building, stopping parallel to the woman sitting on a ratty lawn chair in the grass. Before getting out, Mathias checked his perfectly coiffed hair in the rearview mirror and pulled his cuffs and collar to straighten his shirt.

Mabel watched his arrival with interest. She hadn't entertained a guest in what seemed like a lifetime. Her granddaughter Shelly had stopped by once or twice a week, but she was always in a hurry to leave. Shelly had two jobs and three kids—her schedule didn't leave a lot of time for visiting with ancient relics like Mabel. Of course, Mabel sighed, Shelley was gone now, like everyone else. The nurses and doctors were always in a hurry too. They said the obligatory, "How are you doing today Mabel?" and then got on to business, poking and prodding and otherwise disturbing her peace. Even the other inmates, a steady stream with whom she shared a room, were generally unable to carry a conversation.

Mabel studied his bulk as he uncurled from the older sports car he was driving. She didn't know what kind it was but it seemed pretty darned impractical given the end of the world and everything. Tall and well built, the man's gait as he walked toward her reminded Mabel of her son Jimmie, who always had trouble coordinating his limbs to accomplish even easy athletic tasks. Nice head of hair though, Mabel thought.

He stopped a little too close and peered down at her. "I'm Mathias Dedington. Glad to make your acquaintance. And you are?"

Mabel flashed a grin without rising from her chair. "Mabel. And how are you on this fine day Mathias?"

He seemed to flinch from Mabel's casualness. "Very well. Thank you for asking. I'm a little surprised that you have no fear regarding my arrival."

"Should I?"

"Should you what?"

"Have fear?"

Mathias gave a small shoulder shrug. "No, not at all. I just find it unusual."

"How so?"

"Most attractive women, totally alone, will have difficulty trusting any strange men that land on their doorsteps."

"I can't say about most women and don't want to. And good lord, you just called me attractive." Mabel gave a wry smile. "Just a couple of weeks ago, I was lying in bed at that old folks' home behind me, barely able to walk, just waiting for my time to end. Now look at me! I'm so happy to be alive and moving again, I don't figure I'll waste any more time on being afraid."

"If you don't mind me asking, how old are you?"

"98!"

Mathias's eyes widened. "That's amazing. What a gift."

"Well, it is for those of us that lived. How many people are out there…still alive?"

"I have been searching for others since I woke up and I've only met one other woman, Carlotta, and a man who didn't fare well as a result of the change."

"That's it?! Good Lord, I knew it was bad but…."

"Yes, I'm sorry to say, that is all. If you will indulge me, we could stand out here and chat all day, but I was hoping you would consider a proposal. I would like to invite you to join us at my ranch in Idaho. I was organizing a retreat before all this, and I believe now is the perfect time to set it in motion. The idea is to establish a community of like-minded individuals that could learn to live together in harmony. To create a more true existence with open communication and feedback. When we're successful, I'm convinced, we can avoid a reoccurrence of a catastrophe like the one that has befallen this world.

"Is it like a religious thing?"

"No, not at all, dear lady. Just the opposite. We want to encourage the individual to achieve their best selves and be free to enjoy that freedom with others."

"Hmmm, sounds too good to be true. I don't know much about harmony. Haven't seen much of it outside my marriage. Even then, there were times…"

"Exactly! Can you imagine the wonder of it? Very different people living in complete peace and fulfillment." Mathias smiled for the first time.

"Yes, indeed I can imagine it. Just have a hard time believing in it. How you reckon you're going to make it happen?"

"I am glad you asked. I have a doctorate in behavioral psychology. That means I am a doctor."

"Really? An old country gal like me would have never figured that out if you hadn't said."

Mathias wasn't sure if she was pulling his leg or was just slow as he'd first believed. He plowed on. "I have developed a new interpersonal group technique which guarantees improved relationships and overall feelings of well-being. I did some initial testing before the world's collapse and the results were very promising. I never had the chance to publish my findings or conduct a more robust experiment, but I am excited to offer the process to any survivors desiring a better life."

Mabel gazed at Mathias through narrowed eyes. He certainly sounded sincere. More than likely, he truly believed everything he just said. "And if I decline your proposal?"

"Then I shall bid you good day and let you return to whatever it is you were doing in this place."

Mabel sat and thought some more about it as Mathias shifted from foot to foot. His ideas sounded a little beyond the pale to an old woman from the hills of Tennessee. If what he said was true, that there wasn't anyone left, it might be some time before anyone else came along. She didn't have anywhere to be, that's for sure. And, it was a good sign when he said he would leave if she didn't want to go with him.

Finally, "Okay, two conditions. First, you let me drive to Idaho. They took away my driver's license seventeen years ago and I miss driving. And second, I don't get any grief from you or anyone else, if I decide to leave because I am not *like-minded* enough.

"Deal!"

Mabel loved driving, especially now that she could see the road again. Mathias spent most of the trip talking about himself. When Mabel would add something about her life, Mathias had a way of bending the conversation back to him. She was just beginning to think maybe she should have stayed where she was or headed in another direction when they arrived at a beautiful piece of land. Mathias puffed up his chest and announced, "This is my ranch!"

The first two weeks were strange but still manageable. The others, and particularly Mathias, treated her like a child—go there, do this, Mabel. As if she didn't have any sense at all. *Well*, she thought, *it isn't the first time someone underestimated me*. Still, something was off. It was like they all had a big secret they were keeping from her because she was too simple to understand. Once she caught Mathias, with two of the others, Carlotta and Dave, whispering in a huddle as she came around a corner. They stopped abruptly when she said "Hey", as if they were talking about something they shouldn't be.

Mathias and Carlotta frequently left to seek out other survivors. Mabel remained at the ranch and was assigned to take care of a deformed man locked in a cage and to operate the short-wave. Mabel didn't feel right about either job. It wasn't right to keep a man locked in a cage for no good reason, and she didn't think she should encourage others to join a place that might not be all that it was cracked up to be. Her heart wasn't in it. Mabel was glad when they replaced her with Eric, one of the new men, as soon as he arrived.

Carlotta and Dave, were reprehensible people. Mabel recognized them for what they were from the get go. Maybe it was the cold eyes or the way they were quick to laugh at the expense of others. She saw them taunting the strange man in the cage for no reason. Mabel only knew they oozed malevolence from every pore. Also, and this was kind of strange, their smell reminded her of her drunken daddy when he would walk in the house wild-eyed, looking for someone to beat on. Funny, she thought, she didn't recall ever smelling that odor since, until now. She'd always thought it was the alcohol she smelled, but maybe it was something more. Mabel was thinking more and more each day about pulling up stakes and leaving.

She sat on a folding chair and waited for another of their silly enlightenment sessions to begin. Mathias, always the last to enter, dimmed the lights and stood in the middle of the circle taking time to study each participant. His deep soothing voice was the only sound in the room. "It is time for us to disrobe our true selves. I would like each of you to shed your clothes, everything. Show yourselves to the group in your most basic form so that you may be comfortable and free from embarrassment with each other."

Mabel, normally quiet, spoke up. "Mathias, that's just plain ridiculous! I wasn't raised to parade around strangers in my birthday suit."

He gave her a cold stare. "Mabel, that's the point. When you bare your real form, you will no longer be a stranger."

"Sorry, but I believe I'll just take a pass on this group exercise." She frantically searched the room for a *like-minded* individual and found none. Dave sat leaning forward clenching his fists with a hideous smirk on his face.

Carlotta came and stood behind Mabel's chair. She had a knife in her hand and laid it flat against Mabel's arm. "Do what he says. Walk around the room and then you can put your clothes back on if you feel that damned uncomfortable with your own body."

Mabel gave a moment's thought to making a run for it. She didn't know if they would hurt her, but she wasn't sure they wouldn't, either. The others were already getting naked, and Mabel did as she was ordered. When it was her turn, she walked around the room hunched over, with her arms across her chest, to the leering stares of five other ranch dwellers. Carlotta cruelly laughed, "Show those titties, Mabel. They aren't any big deal." Mabel picked up her clothes and headed directly out of the meeting area when she was done. It was the single most humiliating moment of her long life.

She waited until the session was complete and then went to see Mathias at his office. "I plan to go tonight and don't give me any guff, just like you promised."

"As you wish Mabel. I am disappointed it didn't work out for you." Mabel turned to leave and as she was almost through the door, Mathias said, "And Mabel, you are free to go but we can't afford to provide you any transportation."

Mabel ran blindly in a rage to the vehicle parking area, searching desperately for one with keys inside. Mathias' sports car was the only choice. The keys were lying on the front seat. The car door screeched as she yanked it open. Mabel glanced up as Dave came out of the darkness like a steroid-amped linebacker and heaved her to the ground before she could climb in. With a closed fist, he hit her in the face.

As her tears mixed into the dusty ground, Mabel rediscovered fear. She had always avoided getting herself in a pickle like this since she'd watched her drunken daddy beat her mama nearly a century ago. "I got cocky with my new found youth," she whispered to herself. "Now that I'm not at death's door, I got something to lose. I won't make this mistake again."

Chapter 7: A+42, Change Can Be Good

Days are starting to run together and still no one else, Karen thought. The verdict was in. She wasn't imagining it; she was changing. Standing with her back to the wall, she used a pencil lying flat on her head to mark her height. Karen marveled when she realized she was almost three inches taller. Unfortunately, her teeth were in total disarray. Most of Karen's front teeth were gone, but the bottom row had rallied and a new set was growing in quickly. The rest were in varying degrees of looseness. For the first time in what seemed like a very long time, her waist had returned. The roots under her color-treated hair appeared a darker, richer color than she remembered. But then Karen said to herself, "It's been so long since my hair color was totally natural, I'm not sure what color it was." She was sure there was no grey in the new growth.

Karen realized with no small amount of awe that she looked 20 to 25 years younger. Her cheekbones were more pronounced now that she'd lost the basset hound sagging under the chin and around her nose and mouth.

Most incredible, physical improvements ranging from strength and speed to hearing and smell helped to make the lonely days a little bit brighter. Karen made a game out of timing her exercise regimen. It wasn't unusual to improve her speed by 15 seconds each day. And it wasn't only speed. In the beginning, Karen was able to finish 20 to 25 pushups; 75 push-ups were now a breeze, more than she had been able to pull off even at her most fit when she was young and in the Army. And she did them with most of the weight on her left arm because her right arm was still not right from her encounter with the deranged survivor.

Karen and the dogs ran around the neighborhood on a one-mile loop four times, often logging in at under 28 minutes. "Hot damn!" Karen would yell after they completed their run. "Seven-minute miles—totally awesome!"

And the smells! The aroma of newly budding lilacs sent Karen into a different time and place. Food tasted great, even canned stuff, and she couldn't seem to eat enough, even though she was losing weight and gaining lean hard muscle.

She also needed more sleep. Karen thought it was probably a combination of things. Without the internet, late night voyages online, linking to and reading anything that sparked Karen's interest, were impossible. To conserve fuel, she only used the generators for a few hours in the evenings for meals, small appliances, and heat as necessary, but she could not adjust to reading by gas lamp light after dark. It felt a lot like her teenage years when she needed ten or twelve hours of rack time. Physical changes most likely required more rest.

Karen was thrilled with the bevy of positive physical changes she'd experienced, but she still spent too much time crying. The melancholy grabbed her without warning; a smell, a song, or a past memory would sweep her up and drop her into a deep hole. She thought if she'd survived a zombie apocalypse instead of this last woman standing version, it might have made the whole apocalypse thing easier. You just can't spend a lot of time emoting or feeling sorry for yourself when every waking moment is devoted to running for your life. Her lot was comfortable. She had plenty to eat and was peeling years off her age. The thought of her singular survival and improving physical condition only added a healthy dose of survivor's guilt to the emotional morass.

Her tear ducts appeared to have a limitless supply of salt water. Worst of all, there was no one around to judge or say, "Girl, you need to get it together!" Karen had never been keen on regrets or ruminating on what could have been; she viewed that as a monumental waste of time. Yet, here she was, spending far more time thinking about the past than looking forward to a future.

Sifting through her psychological tool chest, Karen pulled out two proven techniques. The first was discipline. Her grandfather and to some extent the Army had demonstrated how practicing something every day, even if just for a few minutes, guarantees you will get better at it. Karen decided she would only allow an hour total per day for crying. Then as she improved and not crying became easier, she would constrain it further.

The other technique, one that was probably even more important, was what Karen called the *pretend* approach. She would pretend she was excited about the future. Her "in-head" counselor smirked with disdain at Karen and said out loud, "Karen that is just silly!"

"So you say!" Karen scoffed. "This has worked for me before. If you pretend to be something long enough, with a little luck you become what you are pretending to be. I think it's a lot like those self-help books that have you visualize what you want and then somehow wish it into existence—or something like that. Anyhoo, I used to pretend I had my shit together and after enough pretending, I actually did."

Counselor Karen rolled her eyes. "I don't suppose it had anything to with experience. Whatever works for you. We can both agree something has to be done. You're still kind of a mess."

"Well thank you ever so much for that rousing vote of support. Who asked for your opinion anyway? And good God, I'm talking to myself again."

Karen's plan to *pretend* a bright future was working out quite nicely. Day A+42 was the best day yet. Besides whittling away at her height impairment, she found not one but three shortwave radios! Karen could not have imagined it would take this long to find a working radio. If the internet were still alive and helping people find what they needed, it would have taken one day, two days tops. Karen was stuck with only the collection of memories and facts stored in her grey matter, and, as she was fast learning, most of that information was not very specific. Her picture of a shortwave radio was of a computer-sized desktop box with plentiful lights and knobs, most likely collected after viewing an old science fiction movie.

Having thrown away paper telephone books, she stopped in the local library only to learn hard copy indexes no longer existed and the computer-powered indexes were without power. Karen walked out of the library after a couple hours with a stack of interesting fiction novels but nothing that would help in her search for a shortwave radio.

Karen tried all the local stores that carried electronics; most were completely trashed. It appeared that at the end of the world some people had decided it was their best chance to get that amazing cell phone they always wanted for rock bottom prices. Any radios that may have been on the shelves were long gone.

She focused on trucks and boats and had finally found a shortwave on A+26 in a large cabin cruiser boat at harbor in the Puget Sound. She couldn't find an instruction manual or transmission mic, and after getting the thing out of the brackets and unhooking the cable and wires, she took it home and connected it to her generator. It didn't work.

But on that day, A+42, in a small pawnshop close to Seattle, she scored the mother lode. Not just one but three radios, extra parts, antennas, and instruction manuals were prominently displayed in the storefront window. Luckily, they were clearly marked "Shortwave Transceivers" or she might have missed them completely since they were much smaller than her mental picture.

The pawnshop, Joe's Marine Emporium, specialized in marine equipment. The shelves were full of depth finders, unusual fishing nets, and rods. Fresh fish sounded pretty darn good, so after axing through the door and gathering the radios, she took her time to shop for nifty fishing stuff.

As Karen was studying lures in a glass case, Jack padded around a table on wheels and hit the mobile junk receptacle with his body. A white foam life preserver secured with heavy rope slid on top of Jack. All four paws left the floor at one time. Jack did a dog scream and circled madly, attacking the inanimate object with great vigor. The crazed circling helped to entwine Jack in the rope. By the time Karen and other dogs reached Jack, he was on the floor with the rope wrapped around him, thoroughly humiliated. Tilley, being the brat of the pack, snorted.

Karen extricated Jack from his predicament as he growled satisfaction at having bested a life preserver. Then, as one, all the dogs alerted and began a serious barking session. Glancing up, Karen could see a Doberman and a spotted white pit bull mix outside on the street in front of the shop.

Jack, Jill, and Tilley ran out the front door and positioned themselves just outside. Tilley surprised Karen because she seemed every bit as aggressive as the shepherds with their fighting posture, growling, and bared teeth. Karen pulled out her 9mm Glock. She had swapped her .38 for something more substantial after going toe to toe with Crazy Man. Aiming through the window away from the dogs in the street, she fired two shots. During training sessions, she'd worked with her dogs to eliminate reactions to shots fired. Karen's dogs remained in place; the street dogs decided it wasn't worth it and ran off. Hoping the escaping dogs didn't have any friends nearby, Karen quickly grabbed a couple of lures, finished loading, and everyone except Jack jumped in the truck.

"Jack, come!" Karen bellowed. He came out of the shop, his strong jaws holding the nautical rope and dragging the life preserver behind him. "Did you find a new toy, Jack boy?" Jack swished his tail a few times and then pulled his cumbersome booty into the truck.

Feeling a sense of accomplishment, Karen determined now was the time to bury the poor man torn apart by her friends. It was an easy stop on their way home. Karen couldn't un-ring the bell on how he met his demise or her part in it but, she could offer this one measure of human decency. Leaving him there in a pile had weighed on her conscience. She intuitively knew his craziness had something to do with the plague and probably not a purely evil nature. He'd been another survivor, just like her—only he got the worse end of the deal.

As they drove into Crazy Man's driveway, the dogs became agitated, clearly sensing where they were. Karen stepped out, shovel in hand, leaving the dogs in the truck but carrying the Glock. She decided that a flowerbed was likely to have loose soil and would be the easiest place to dig. The smell smacked her in the face as she entered the house. Gagging, Karen held her breath and took in the scene. It was worse than she had remembered. It had been about a month since their truly unfortunate encounter, and most of the flesh had rotted off, turning Crazy Man into a liquefied goo. "Oh, shit!" Karen yelled and then gritted her teeth (at least the ones that had grown back), and said out loud, "You can do this Karen!"

Counselor Karen was yakking at her as she went back to the truck. "You should have known, Karen. You've seen enough bodies since this whole thing started. Sometimes I think you set yourself up for agony."

Determined, Karen ignored that little voice and dug around in the truck for a face mask, leather gloves, and the heavy wool blanket. Tilley looked offended when Karen rolled her off the blanket, but Karen's expression said she was in no mood to be questioned.

Karen walked into the house, donning a face mask and gloves, and pulled the hinge pins from an interior door. She maneuvered the door right beside the man's remains and spread the thick blanket on top what was left of his body. "Now the tricky part." Kneeling on the door, she leaned over the body and began to scoop with the blanket, rolling the entire package onto the door as she slid back out of the way. His boots, feet still inside and skull partially clad with hair, didn't get scooped so Karen picked them up and carefully placed them with the residuum.

Dragging the makeshift travois outside, down the steps and next to the hole, in one fast move, Karen flipped the door so the man went in first and the door landed atop his remains. Karen wiped her hands in an all done motion after mounding dirt on the door, which happened to resemble a casket. She said a few words over the grave and walked to the trash can to discard the reeking gloves and paper mask. She noticed slimy crud on her clothes, made a face, then stripped them off and threw away her jeans and tee as well. In the car with only her bra and panties, Jack, Jill and Tilley subdued, they wasted no time leaving. Ironically, Karen thought, other than accomplishing a good deed rather than a bad one, it was very much like their last departure from this place.

When Karen got home, she decided to celebrate the new cache of shortwave radios and completion of an unpleasant responsibility. She opened one of her favorite bottles of wine from the well-stocked garage wine collection, started two generators, and began dinner. Karen had become accustomed to generator engine noise and compensated by raising the volume on her mini sound system. Smells of Spam chili on the butane stove and a fresh loaf of bread baking in an electric bread appliance meant her companions gathered in the kitchen hoping for any dropped tidbits. She sat on a stool at the eat-in bar and studied the radio and radio manual in front of her. Karen ate, put everything away, and unplugged unnecessary appliances before completing connections for the plug-in shortwave.

Two of the radios were small portable battery-powered devices. Karen thought the larger electric radio would be more powerful and chose to try that one first. She installed the antenna as pictured in the book.

"Okay, dog friends, this is the moment of truth," Karen muttered as she pressed the power switch. The radio came to life with roaring loud static, causing Raider to leap in the air barking. At his outburst, the rest of the pack chimed in, and Karen turned down the volume. "Hush!" she commanded. Holding her breath, she started slowly pushing the next button to scroll through channels, listening intently. After just a few clicks she heard someone talking in what sounded like Japanese. Almost choking on her wine, she pressed "transmit" on the mic and said, "Hello, this is Karen from Washington State, do you read me? Over."

Momentary silence followed and then to her relief she heard, "Hello, Karen! This is Shiguru Hotoke from Osaka, Japan."

"Hello, Shiguru! You are the first live voice—no, live *person* I've heard in nearly six weeks!" Are you a survivor? Are things in Japan like they are in the United States? Most everyone is gone here."

There was silence for a while. "Karen, my English is no good. Please slow talk. No one in Japan; all dead. Eleven people I meet in Osaka. Eight people I meet from Japan on radio. Five people in Osaka crazy."

That got Karen's attention, especially since she had just buried Crazy Man. "What do you mean by crazy, Shiguru?"

"Uh, very big, big bone on top of eyes, many hair, and what is word… hmmm, aggress?"

"You mean aggressive?"

"Yes! Aggressive and not right, no talk."

"I ran into one like that. It wasn't pretty. Have you heard anyone on the radio from the United States?"

"Yes, yes, some people in U.S."

"Shiguru, if you don't mind me asking, how old are you? Did you get sick and have you changed?"

Shiguru chuckled, "Yes, yes, Karen. I get sick. I am 86 years and now I am young."

"Wow! It happened to me, too. Do you have any idea why this happened?"

"No! Japanese here think Americans do it." Shiguru chuckled again. "One doctor say impossible disease kill so many so fast. We do not understand. Please tell us if you know."

"Sorry Shiguru, I have no idea. Honestly, I'm just a normal person and don't know anyone but you right now. Not sure how we'll ever find the answer. If this is a man-made thing, it's likely anyone who knew is dead. You said you heard Americans on the radio. Do you remember when or what channel?"

"We most concerned with Japanese. I know others on radio from the world but cannot say where on dial. I will in future write it for you. We talk on radio every day in Japan at this time. Please talk with us."

"Thank you Shiguru. I will! It means a lot to know there are other survivors. "

"Yes, Karen. Not enough people. We must help each other."

Ecstatic to hear another human voice and discuss all the questions that had haunted her for the last six weeks, Karen stayed on the channel to shoot the breeze until Shiguru politely mentioned the Japanese group had some important matters requiring his attention.

"Sure Shiguru. Thanks for talking with me. I wish you all the best and will check back in later." *What a nice man*, Karen said to herself. She wished the internet was still alive so she could look him up. Shiguru had proudly mentioned he was a prominent Japanese architect.

Karen rotated her stool around and hollered to the assembled dog observers, "Thank you Lord! We are not alone!" as she pumped both fists in the air. There was some confusion from the dog audience on a correct response to her outburst. Jill and Zoe jumped up and wagged their tails, Tilley tucked her tail as if guilty and Jack and Raider continued their naps.

Refilling her wine glass, Karen resumed her journey through the mystical air waves. She bypassed what sounded like a Slavic language and finally landed on an Aussie group. She listened to their discussion about meeting in Sydney before breaking in to say hello.

Karen was on her fourth glass of wine and was giddy with excitement hearing their plans for the future. *Actually*, Karen thought, *I may be a tiny bit drunk*. "Hello, this is Karen Henry from Washington State. I am so happy to hear about survivors. I have not seen anyone where I live except one man that was not right. Do you happen to know of any American groups or survivors?"

"Good day, Karen," a female voice chimed in. "Welcome to the world of the living! I know of at least two different groups, one from the American East Coast and one from the West. Jake, could you check the log and see the number and time? Karen, Jake is our record keeper. So how are you doing? Are you a recluse or survivor? Over."

"If by survivor if you mean did I get sick, then yes, I did get sick."

"My name in Annette, by the way. How much have you changed?"

"I've grown four inches, my skin sort of molted off, and my teeth are falling out and growing back in. I feel great physically."

Annette chatted about her change experience and then Jake came on and gave Karen two times in the morning and dial numbers for American groups. They exchanged some pleasantries. Only individuals who had no contact with others, whom they called recluses, hadn't changed. They were not sure whether recluses could now be infected because it had not been tested. Each of those who had been sick were physically changing for the better and seemingly getting younger. They had not run into any deranged people and were glad Karen had shared that information since it was a new wrinkle. Jake was a doctor, Annette a physicist, and two others in the group were highly educated. Karen thought the large percentage of educated survivors was beginning to form a pattern. She was at a total loss on what that pattern meant.

Karen asked, "Do you have any idea how this happened?"

After a long silence, Jake answered, "No. We rather thought the Americans had something to do with it. They are the most advanced in terms of genetic research. Perhaps a retrovirus or some form of nanotechnology that changed us. I can't imagine this was a naturally occurring phenomenon. I have analyzed our blood and don't see anything unusual, but then I am not a researcher or specialist. I plan to keep looking. Please keep in touch if you learn anything, and I will do the same."

Karen signed off after receiving an offer to join the group whenever she needed some company. "Interesting about the numbers", Karen said to Jack who was watching, head erect from a Danish modern leather chair. Karen rifled through an end table drawer and pulled out a calculator.

"Hmm, let's see. Shiguru said there were 2.6 million people in Osaka and 11 survivors that he knew of." She entered numbers and frowned at the result. "Jack that means, even assuming there are a few more survivors Shiguru doesn't know about, the survival rate is .0000042. Good God Jack, that's only 1 in 236,000 or .00042%. It's about as close to extinction as you can come! Did someone or some group try to kill us all?!" Jack's expression reflected the right sentiments; his ears tilted back, and there was fear and perhaps a dash of sadness in his eyes.

Chapter 8: Thomas

Thomas pulled the lid from the glass canister and inhaled deeply. "Now that shit is nice!" He'd been smelling tea for nearly a half hour. Normally, his olfactory sense would be burnt after just a few sniffs, but since the change, hell, he had a nose like a damn dog. "Ghost, I might be almost as good as you!" Ghost was laying on the floor of the Tea Store and lifted her head slightly at the sound of her name. Recognizing quickly it was only a rhetorical statement, she dropped her head back to the floor and resumed her nap.

Thomas had never liked coffee. His preference for tea was cause for an unending ration of shit from his buddies. Like clockwork, his mom would send him his monthly quota of tea. Since the Army didn't provide for his more discriminating tastes, he carried little baggies around in a pocket like a drug stash. Before a mission, he would begin the calming ritual of brewing a steaming cup with his special tea equipment and then poured one packet of sugar, no crème into the mix. He'd stir, clinking the spoon on the cup, when he had the luxury of a real one, to get a rise from his squad. It never failed. Dead Eyes or Petey would yell, "Tea time," followed by jokes and laughter not meant for polite company. Thomas's moniker was *Tee*.

He missed those guys. He missed everybody. He'd been riding around Seattle on a bike for three days hoping to run into someone. Anyone. Thomas refused to believe he could be the only person left alive. He just wasn't that special. Special yes, that special no.

He was so huge now that finding a bike that could be adjusted for his height and weight wasn't easy. Thomas gave up his truck on the outskirts of town and improvised with the bike. Seattle city center streets were bad on a good day. Post-apocalypse Seattle traffic wasn't going to move anytime soon. Ghost raised her head again and this time followed with her body, barking a warning at the tea shop door.

Thomas checked the front windows. A lean woman was running, seriously running, on the sidewalk across the street, black hair streaming behind her. He noted that her running form was as near perfect as you could get. "That would be our cue, Ghost."

Thomas didn't think he needed to hurry. He could catch her on his bike. They came out onto the street and as Thomas went to mount his ride, he saw what the beautiful lady was running from. This other two-legged individual had an unusual loping running style but was every bit as fast. There was something very wrong with the face and he—or she?—needed a good body wax. Other than the eyes, nose and forehead, fur or maybe hair was covering every other inch of exposed skin.

"A damsel in distress then. Better do this on foot, Ghost." Thomas bee-lined across the street, dodging through cars and buses. He was running hard by the time he hit the sidewalk. He could still see the black-haired woman up ahead, but her pursuer was gaining on her. She looked back once (never a good idea in a foot race) and then took a right at the intersection. He yelled out to whoever would listen, "Hey, hey, stop!" When that didn't work, Thomas focused on his breathing and his stride, pushing hard to pick up speed. As he closed the gap, he used his arms to increase momentum. Thomas was puffing through what was left of his teeth as he got within range.

Ghost ran up alongside the creature-person and barked; four legs are better than two no matter how fast you are. It slowed momentarily, as if totally unaware that it was being chased until it saw Ghost. The distraction was just enough to allow Thomas to perform a leaping tackle from behind. The hairy two-legged anomaly was propelled forward, Thomas hugging its back. Both bodies flew to a crash landing on the street where the running woman had just made a quick right turn. "Find the woman Ghost. Find," Thomas wheezed, since the impact and sprint had left him gasping for air. Ghost acknowledged the command, even though she was hesitant to leave, and then took off down the street.

Thomas didn't have a plan, but he knew he didn't want to hurt the creature-person if he didn't have to. There'd been enough dying. It was alive, but apparently shocked into stillness by his tackle. "I'am not going to hurt you. Just lie still." Thomas sat on its back and pulled wide green tape from the pack that he'd taken to wearing at all times. The tape came in handy for oh so many things. He bit off a piece to wrap the hairy monstrosity's hands behind its back. Before he could begin, the creature let out a blood-curdling screech and went up on hands and knees.

Thomas reached around its neck in a choke hold, trying to push it back on the ground, and planted his feet to keep it from rolling.

"Stop fighting!" Thomas yelled. The creature was incredibly strong and pushed back against Thomas's nearly 275-pound body until it was able to get on its knees. "Jesus Christ" Thomas heaved, realizing how dangerous this creature thing might be if it could push him back. Thomas grimaced as he struggled to maintain the choke hold. "Goddamn it. Quit fighting!"

Its hands now free, the creature grabbed Thomas' arms to pull them off its neck, digging long fingernails into the skin and crushing the flesh. Thomas tightened the choke hold; he knew if he let go he'd have a significant problem. The creature thrashed and twisted, never letting go of its grip on Thomas' arms. One last time, Thomas begged, "Please stop. Please don't fight me."

Thomas couldn't take the chance this thing would best him. He squeezed harder, his face tense from the effort. The pressure from the claws in Thomas' arms finally gave way. The creature-person shuddered and then dropped to the ground. Thomas released its neck and rolled it over to check for a pulse. There was none. Thomas started CPR. He couldn't have explained why he was trying to save something that might have destroyed him except that he didn't want the thing to die. Other than the face, the hair, and its strength, it looked mostly human. The creature had breasts so it was definitely female.

He'd been performing CPR for a long time when Ghost came back to his side and whined. Sorrow written on his face, Thomas stared at his friend and stood. "Did you find her?" Ghost barked twice and started to run back the way she'd come when Thomas stopped her. "Come Ghost, you can show me later."

Thomas dragged the female creature into a restaurant and covered her with a table cloth. He made an apology to the woman and wondered what had happened to make her this way and whether there were more like her in the area. He inspected his arms, already bruising and bloody from the nail depressions. "Don't think it's anything life threatening. Just a nasty bruise and some holes I'll need to see to. Let's go, Ghost."

He followed Ghost down the street for almost a mile to an apartment building. The glass front doors were locked tight. "No need to scare the poor woman any more than necessary. I can be a bit intimidating." Ghost and Thomas smiled at each other. "We'll just hole up in the building across the way and wait."

He didn't think she would come out right away, so they went back to the tea store to collect his bike and pack—and, of course, choose some tea. Thomas and Ghost found a spacious third-floor apartment with good access and a view of her building. They made themselves comfortable sitting in in front of the windows eating, watching and waiting.

Thomas didn't mind waiting. When he first started in Special Forces he was surprised by all the waiting. Waiting for a bad guy to appear or for someone to do something for hours on end. Waiting through the discomfort of shitty weather. Waiting for the command to go. He learned to focus where he needed, often creating stories in his head or reliving the better parts of his life, which often involved a hot woman.

Thomas found a baseball in a glass case in the apartment. He pulled it off its pedestal and realized it was signed by none other than Randy Johnson. "Shit, Ghost, this is signed by The Big Unit. He was a radical dude." Thomas savored the feel of the leather ball in his hand. "You know, if I'd been the man I am now, then, I might have been a big unit myself. Hmm, well, maybe not. I was good but probably not that good."

Thomas held the ball and positioned himself to throw facing the windows. He spit on the floor and then let his muscles guide his body through a slow motion fastball, stopping at the last minute without throwing. "Maybe when everything settles down . . ." Thomas had to smile at himself. There wouldn't be any coming back or settling down from this. Besides, he loved baseball, but it was only a game. It didn't give him what he needed. He hadn't known that until he found something that did.

Still, he often wished he'd applied himself at baseball instead of crazy partying in college. After achieving a 1.5 out of 4.0 total grade point average at the end of four quarters and not particularly impressing anyone with his dedication to baseball training, Thomas was politely informed his scholarship was null and void.

Thinking he would try a walk-on gambit for the major leagues, Thomas had been to two tryout camps and got some attention but no contracts. If he was going to be successful, Thomas had to get serious about training before tryouts the next summer. He was heading to his best friend's Darius' apartment after finishing the night shift security job he held at his uncle's used car dealership. He'd tried to be a used car salesman but kept telling the customers the truth when they were about to buy a piece of shit. His Uncle Stan had clucked and sighed when he'd sat Thomas for a "talk". "If I send you home, your mom will give me hell. We could use someone around here at night. How about lot security?" Thomas readily agreed. Other than the fact that it was monumentally boring and most nights he fell asleep on the floor of the showroom listening to tunes, it paid the bills.

Four times a week, he and Darius would work out and then Darius would help Thomas practice. They'd been friends since grade school days in Milwaukee. Together they'd helped their high school baseball team win the state championship—Thomas as pitcher and Darius an excellent left-handed hitter and second baseman. Both had received full rides to college but Darius took it way more seriously. Even after an injury his junior year and unable to play truly competitive baseball, he graduated with a business degree.

One morning, Darius took a long time to answer the door. He peeked nervously through the blinds at Thomas, then popped off the chain and motioned him in. "Man, come in quick, you got to see this."

Thomas followed Darius, who was standing in front of the couch facing the TV. A loop replaying airplanes crashing into the sides of skyscrapers was accompanied by shocked and sometimes hysterical newscasters. "What the hell is that?" Thomas asked.

"They're attacking. Those Middle East motherfuckers are attacking us! They crashed planes into the World Trade Center. Both buildings are on fire!"

Even though it was morning, Thomas grabbed two beers from Darius' refrigerator and sat on the couch with his friend, watching with building rage. They watched like the rest of the world, mouths agape, as the two buildings collapsed into a pile of rubble. By the time a plane crashed into the Pentagon and news of terrorist hijackings clarified the cause, something shifted in Thomas. Thomas and Darius decided that day, on the couch drinking beer, like thousands of other young men and women, they couldn't let it stand. They went together the next day to a local recruiting center and joined the Army. Thomas was still pissed that they gave the Bin Laden mission to the Navy Seals. "The fucking Navy" was a common refrain among his elite band of brothers.

Thomas stared out the window to the street and wondered if there was any chance Darius had survived. It was starting to get dark. He turned to talk to his last remaining friend, "As scared as she looked, I'm thinking she isn't going to come out to play after dark. Let's get some shut-eye and get up at dawn." Thomas didn't have to convince Ghost, who was already snoring comfortably with her feet sticking in the air. Thomas climbed on the huge couch and set his watch for 4:30 am. He was asleep seconds after nestling into the memory foam couch pillow.

It was mid-morning before she made an appearance. She stood behind the closed glass apartment doors, glancing right and left, and maybe debating the wisdom of leaving at all. Thomas watched her indecision and then announced, "Go time." They flew down the stairs. She'd already made her move by the time they came out the building. She stopped and stared at them from her side of the street.

Thomas couldn't help but notice what a fine-looking woman she was. Long black hair, now pinned back, framed scared almond eyes. She was slender and tall but still had meat on her in all the right places. Thomas wondered how he must look to her, a massive, bald, behemoth of a man—*at least Ghost looks nice*, he thought. Thomas made sure not to move and send her skittering away. "Hey, I'm Thomas. Sorry to stake you out, but you're the first person I've seen in a long time. I just want to talk."

Her eyes narrowed. "Leave me alone!" She glanced behind her probably wondering if she could make it back to the safety of the building and then decided instead to run. She took off at a blistering pace in that fluid movement Thomas had admired the previous day.

Thomas and Ghost looked at each other. "I'm thinking with a lot of effort we could catch her, but then what? I sure as hell don't want a repeat of yesterday's fiasco. She's scared and being chased by me isn't going to improve that situation. Not one bit. We are going to have to divert to Plan B." Ghost seemed curious as to what Plan B might entail.

Thomas got on his bike and pedaled to the Glass Gardens. He'd been there once with a girl he was dating and was surprised at how much he enjoyed it. As he dismounted, Thomas started to explain the plan to his true friend. "Ghost, the one thing the ladies really like, besides something beautiful, is that you have given it some thought. They want to know they are as special to you as the gift you bring them."

When Thomas saw the mess in the museum and broken glass everywhere, he ordered Ghost to wait outside. It took some effort to find just the right piece, since what hadn't been carried off was mostly shattered. But as he had learned the hard way, determination pays off in the end.

He carried the ten-inch glass tulip carefully in one hand while he steered his bike with the other hand. They stopped at a boutique card shop where he found a beautiful hand-crafted card. He opened a package of fancy pens and sat on the floor to take his time writing a note to the latest girl of his dreams that he had yet to meet. Thomas told her who he was, what was important to him, what he'd done with his life, and a little about his family. He closed by saying he would gladly come back to get her if she needed him for anything. He left a short-wave radio frequency and told her where he would be. In his P.S., he complimented her on her running form. "All we need now, Ghost, is a pot for this flower."

They found the right clay pot after a search of several stores and left the note and the flower on the doorstep of her apartment building. Thomas and Ghost arrived back at their truck a little disheartened but ready to continue their search for other survivors. At least now they were sure there were other survivors. The next stop was   Bellevue. The short-wave came to life just as Thomas slid on his sun glasses. "Thomas, this is Sara. Do you hear me, Thomas? I'm the runner."

Thomas smiled, pounded the steering wheel and then laughed, his deep base roar shaking the truck windows. "I told you, Ghost. The *what* is far less important than the *how*."

Chapter 9: A+43, Idaho

Karen was up and pleasantly satiated with caffeine when she turned on the generators and radio and set the dial for the 8 a.m. east coast broadcast. She was over-stimulated after listening to static for an hour. She went up and down the channel finder in case the Australians had given her the wrong channel. Nothing. The next time window for the west coast group wasn't for another hour. Too amped up to accomplish anything else, Karen gathered some dog toys and played with her companions in the driveway to pass the time.

At 9:30 she gave a little more of her life to listening to dead air space on the radio. Perhaps they had the times wrong, Karen thought. Rather than waste the day, she decided to go about her daily routine and try again in the evening. For reasons Karen couldn't explain, she felt a deepening sense of anxiety. "Maybe I drank too much coffee, or I'm disappointed," she explained to Jack.

Karen and crew spent the afternoon fishing on a pier in the Puget Sound and playing ball in the water. Unlike Jack, Jill, and Raider, Tilley and Zoe loved swimming to catch sticks and balls. The non-water-loving dogs waited impatiently on the rocky shoreline, trotting back and forth and then harassing the swimming dogs as they emerged from the water. Tilley liked to get as close to Jack as possible before shaking the salt water from her curly coat. Jack would stand, incensed, his eyes blinking shut, waiting to steal whatever Tilley had retrieved from the sound. The chase game followed until Karen threw something else into the cold water. Karen loved watching them. Of all the things her dogs had done to help her survive, getting her out of her head and into life may have been the most important. Karen laughed a full throttle laugh as Tilley proudly leaped from the pier into the sound with the coveted stick still in her jaws.

With two small fish in a bucket, she realized that she was running low on gas and stopped to siphon some from a dilapidated old truck left at the pier parking lot. Karen discovered she couldn't siphon from newer vehicles and guessed they had some sort of one-way valve near the gas tank. Just one other little thing to make life more challenging, Karen thought.

She was sucking on the siphon tube when the dogs began to bark. Karen could hear their nails digging into asphalt as they charged across the parking lot. After spitting out gas and placing the hose in her gas tank, Karen ran toward the ruckus and slowed to a walk when she saw her dogs swirling around a big mutt under a maple tree. The strange dog seemed to be enjoying the attention. *Dog communication is an amazing thing*, Karen thought. After nearly six weeks with only canines as company, Karen was beginning to truly understand their signals. How they positioned their tails, stood, or directed their eyes to or away from each other could all convey a different meaning. After considerable checking each other out and butt sniffing, Jack bounded back to Karen and the rest of the pack followed, including the new dog.

The new dog was male and appeared to be a puppy of anywhere from ten to twelve months. He was sturdy and already big, maybe 90 pounds. His short brown fur highlighted muscular haunches and shoulders. "Judging by your ears, you may have some scent hound in you big boy," Karen said, reaching to pet him. He licked her hand and moaned with delight while his back-end twisted hither and yon. The very last thing Karen needed was another dog to care for, much less a puppy to train. She gazed down at his pleading eyes—eyes that studied her with what could only be described as adoration. Her heart couldn't walk away. "Okay, you had me at hello. I give up. We'll call you Maple. You do realize cleaning up dog crap in the yard is becoming a full-time job, don't you?" Maple wagged his tail wildly, barked twice, and then there were six dogs; two German Shepherds, one Labrador, one Golden doodle, one Cairn terrier, and one tree-like, Heinz 57. Six wiggling, wagging, panting dogs made her extended cab truck start to feel small.

Despite the distraction of adding to her canine family, Karen's sense of dread increased through the afternoon into the evening. Her stomach was in knots by the time she began her radio search. She waited on the east coast channel for a half hour and then switched to the west coast site for another half hour, worrying the entire time that it was all a big ruse. Could they have changed their meeting times or worse yet, already met with some calamity? She expelled the air in her lungs. It felt like she'd been holding all her breath all day. Then at 8:10 p.m. on A+43, she heard the first American survivors. A soft-spoken, melodious male voice was leading the discussion. Karen decided to listen before announcing her presence.

"Sylvie, it's your turn. How was your day? Any significant changes you would like to share with the group?"

"Hey, Mathias. My day was fine, nothing extraordinary, which I consider a good thing. I did start a journal of physical changes as you suggested. I'm also trying to document any emotional changes that correlate to my physical metamorphosis, but I have to say it's difficult to isolate feelings that are simply reactions to my current situation from any change pattern."

Mathias replied, "Yes, Sylvie, that is in essence the problem, very astute. My thought is that over an extended period, if you continue to document all changes, physical and emotional, some pattern may emerge. We really don't know what we are dealing with, and the more we know about ourselves and how the continuing changes affect us, the better we will be at using and developing any enhancements that occur. Also, when you compare your changes with others, we may find some significance. I am glad your day was good. Have you given anymore consideration to joining us in Idaho?"

"Still thinking on that, Mathias. Regardless, I need to wait until the mountain passes are clear. I can't really leave until June or so, depending on the weather."

"Sylvie, we could probably help you with that. I'm sure I could arrange an escort to facilitate the journey."

"I'll think about it, Mathias. That's all I have."

Mathias said, "Eric, your turn."

Karen waited for three people to describe their day, document the changes, and report on any plans to join Mathias. The last to speak, one woman and two men already located on Mathias's ranch in Idaho, described what they were doing and how much fun they were having at the ranch. There was an obvious comradery that had developed between the ranch dwellers.

Now is the time. "Good evening, this is Karen Henry from Washington State. I just listened to your evening meeting and was hoping to join you."

Mathias piped up, "Welcome, Karen! It is so good to hear from another survivor in the great Northwest. You are the first to join from the state of Washington. How are you doing? By way of introduction, as you have probably heard, my name is Mathias Dedington, and I'm 69 years old. I had three children and am a divorcee. I'm not sure what happened to my ex-wife. By trade, I am a PhD in behavioral psychology and am, or was, an adjunct professor at two universities. I live on a large working ranch in Idaho and am grateful to be alive. Will you share something about yourself?"

Karen was a hands on/do it kind of person. University professors often seemed a little too disconnected from real things for Karen's taste, particularly those in social sciences. Thinking she needed to keep pre-judgment in check, Karen responded, "First, I'm excited and relieved to finally meet other American survivors. I've been really lonely and recruited six dogs to help me keep my loneliness at bay. I am, or was, married with two grown children. I had several career changes but for the last twenty plus years I worked as a demographer. Recently, I cut back on working hours and had been enjoying semi-retirement. I'm 64, chronologically anyway, and like probably all of you, my family is gone. I've run into one other person, but he wasn't right."

"Demographer! That is a rather unusual field of study isn't it?"

"If by unusual you mean there aren't a lot of us, then yes, that would be true. And, I'd have to admit, most people look dazed and yawn a lot, when I try to explain what I do. I found it very stimulating. Studying populations and cultures from a data perspective and then determining trends can be invaluable information."

Mathias gave what sounded like a derisive snort. "Educated guessing then?"

Karen's voice took on a steelier tone. "Better an educated guess than an uninformed one, I suppose. Particularly when it can mean success or failure of a substantial project or policy. If you don't mind, I have a few questions more pressing to my current situation."

"First, does anyone know how or why this happened? Also, I heard from an Australian gentleman there was also an east coast group—do you know if that's true? Finally, is there a way to speak to members of the group individually—as a way of getting to know them better or just as a resource if I have a question?"

Mathias responded again. *Doesn't anyone else have a voice?* Karen wondered. "The answer to your first question is no, only theories. We can talk about them later. I do not know of any other groups. As far as contacting individuals directly, everyone can do what they want. I believe everyone benefits from those questions, and we have allowed time at the end of our sessions for individual conversations."

A man (or kid?) from California named Jed cut in, "Dude, I think it would be a great idea to allow more time for one-on-ones!"

Mathias sighed, "Do whatever you wish."

Karen spent some time getting to know the people in the group. Jed was a tech nerd in Silicon Valley and only 31 at the time of the plague. He said he was working on gathering some technology that would be helpful to survivors but was cagey about giving any details. Carlotta from Flagstaff, Arizona, said she was Deputy Sheriff in a small town on the border of Arizona and New Mexico. Hailing from Las Vegas, Eric worked as a structural engineer who updated huge casinos, but he'd started out as an EMT. With only two exceptions, the remainder of the group, mostly from large cities, consisted of educated professionals, with ages ranging from eighteen to over ninety. Sylvie lived the closest to Karen in Bend, Oregon. Karen liked Sylvie and Jed immediately. Neither was too serious. After everything that happened at the end of the world, it took amazing strength to find humor and grace. Sylvie had a deep, throaty voice which she used to deadpan what Karen thought was tongue-in-cheek statements. Jed said he was short and wiry before the change and after suddenly gaining muscle bulk, spent way too much time gazing at himself in the mirror. He thought he might even try shooting hoops, a skill he always dreamed of mastering.

After almost two hours of gabbing, Karen said her goodbyes until tomorrow's meeting. She had a sneaking suspicion Mathias listened to everything said during that last hour without saying a word. Regardless, the low-grade anxiety Karen experienced throughout the day finally relented. She poured a glass of wine, turned on her favorite gas reading lamp, and curled up with a book and her dogs in bed. Karen slept well but an unusual and disturbing dream woke her.

She was strolling on a path littered with snakes. As the snakes began to slither and hiss, Karen jumped over them and darted down the path. Her heart was racing as the number and frequency of snakes meant she could no longer avoid them. In a panic, she stopped running. They twisted and crawled to encircle her. She couldn't breathe, immobilized as a particularly large snake raised its head from the ground, its entire snake-body rearing up. The repulsive creature linked eyes with hers. This snake had a human face with an abundant head of hair. But the eyes—the eyes were still that of a snake, cold and reptilian. It opened its mouth as if to speak. Its fangs were dripping venom and then it struck. Karen bolted up in bed gasping for air. Her pulse was racing and it was several long seconds before she realized the snake was only a figment of her sleeping imagination. She wondered if the dream was trying to tell her something. And if it was, what was it trying to say?

Chapter 10: A+62, Beauty Shop

"Yowza!" Karen yelled. Just over six inches in two months. "Now that's some growth spurt," she commented to Maple and Zoe, the only dogs currently awake. Her overall proportional body shape remained mostly the same. Karen had always been athletic, with a curvy figure that was more muscle than actual frame curves. It now seemed she had both. If it was possible, her hips appeared to be wider, matching her always-strong shoulders. Likewise, her breasts had more heft. Karen laughed when she considered the possibility that it was simply an illusion since the effects of gravity and time meant her breasts had pointed in a different direction before the change.

No doubt about it now: Karen's hair was no longer a mid-range brown. She wasn't sure exactly what to call the color of the two-inch roots underneath her untrimmed mop. Maybe auburn or extremely dark red. Karen resolved to cut it herself as soon as she found some decent hair cutting scissors. Sporting a style, recently termed an ombre or two different color sections, she was suddenly sad remembering when she first heard the term. Karen had seen Anne's hair growing out in two different colors, natural dark brown for four inches and dyed red blonde on the remainder. Karen had offered to pay for a trip to the beauty shop. "Mom," Anne had said indignantly, "that's an ombre and it's very in right now." Remembering her family still resulted in an almost physical pain. As tears formed in her eyes, Karen sat down to have a brief cry. She still had fifteen minutes left in her daily cry quota.

She'd kept a promise to herself to reduce the amount of time she spent immobilized by grief, but it was a hard promise to keep sometimes. Zoe tried to sit on Karen's lap. Failing, she stood and licked Karen's chin to wipe away the tears. Karen knew she needed other people in her life—more than just voices over a radio—to move on and begin to live again. Also, it was dangerous to live totally alone; if she had an accident or got sick, she was screwed. The problem was that she didn't trust Mathias.

For the last couple weeks, Karen had dutifully tuned in to the nightly west coast meeting. Minutes or sometimes hours before the broadcast, her stomach would protest and release annoying butterflies for no apparent reason. After the hour-long session, always hosted by Mathias, she enjoyed free-flowing discussion among the circle of people. By the time it was over, she was happy again—or at least as happy as she allowed herself to be these days.

Mathias asked individuals to join him nearly every night, even as the numbers at his ranch increased by two. Maybe that was the problem: Mathias's insistence that they join him along with his complete confidence that everyone would be happier on the ranch. Karen's life experience said that anyone totally certain about what would make someone else happy was either a politician or a person with an ulterior motive. Karen realized he'd never specifically asked about her plans or whether she intended to relocate to Idaho. She wasn't entirely comfortable with him knowing too much about her location or plans. She very simply didn't trust him. Then Mathias casually asked during one nightly broadcast, "Karen, where are you exactly in Washington?"

Karen quickly lied, "I live in Olympia, about a mile north of the state capitol building."

She was certain Jed was attempting to contact her. He'd hinted there were other pockets of survivors and described the square footage of his remarkable home in Santa Cruz, using a number that Karen guessed might be a frequency range. Playing with the radio, she found that there were more people in the U.S. "short waving," a term now used commonly like "surfing the net"—but she couldn't find Jed. The stories she heard over the radio were similar everywhere and mostly heartbreaking.

The highs and lows of this new world were a form of emotional whiplash. One moment Karen was plunged into the depths of despair from a memory of her family triggered by a smell or item found in a drawer; the next moment she was jubilantly playing ball with the dogs on a beautiful spring day, happy that she not only survived but had a chance to replay her youth. And then, like a train running on an exact schedule, the guilt of surviving when so many perished consumed that momentary indulgence.

It didn't help that Karen's libido was accelerating faster than she could process. The regeneration of her body had been replete with hormonal changes and the resulting desires of a younger woman. Before the world went to hell, Karen had been sloloming the downhill side of her lifecycle. She'd mostly ignored the very gradual effects of aging, at least until her deterioration reached some tipping point when she'd see herself in the mirror and ask, "When the hell did that happen?" What she was living through now was the opposite of gradual. This change was a full-scale assault on her senses. The combined effect of an urgent, young woman's need and knowing there wasn't a soul around to fill the gap, maybe ever, was exasperating and a heavy burden.

Today's plan for survival enhancement included working with the dogs on hiding, being quiet, and alerting to the right things. The truck only had an eighth of a tank of gas; gas, a couple more propane tanks, and sharp hair scissors were the order of the day. The normal crew and Maple on his maiden voyage set out about noon.

Karen left the dogs in the truck, leaving the windows down about a third of the way. She smashed the door window of a local beauty shop with the butt of her Mossberg and reached in to unlock the door. Rummaging through drawers, she found haircutting scissors in different shapes and sizes, grabbed a handful, and dropped them into a to-go bag left on a rack by the counter. To make the theft worthwhile, she added haircare products to the bag. As could be expected, it was eerily quiet in the store, but what wasn't expected was the sudden fit of hysterical barking coming from her truck.

Karen pulled the Mossberg 12 Gauge off her shoulder, leaned against the edge of the door, and peeked outside. She was already regretting her decision to leave the dogs in the truck for this quick stop.

Jack, fighting mightily, had his front paws and head outside the window, but he couldn't wedge the remainder of his body through to jump out. Three dogs were stalking Karen, arrayed in a semi-circle around the front door of the shop. They glanced warily at the truck filled with Karen's growling canines. She didn't want to shoot a dog and was afraid that with three animals, the other two would come at her anyway if she tried.

She slammed the front door shut, fired a shot out the window at a store across the street, and watched for their reaction. If anything, the shot made the feral dogs more determined. They were lean, hard, and menacing, creeping closer to the beauty shop entry while low hung heads were baring sharp teeth.

Jack backed away from the truck window, and Jill took his place. She tried to squeeze through the small space. Maple's head was completely stuck in the back window, the whites of his eyes bulging as he whined. Tilley knew how to roll down a window by pressing her foot to the button in the door, but the truck wasn't running, and Karen had the keys in her pocket.

Karen decided the best course of action was to wait out the free ranging dogs, thinking that with time they'd move on to greener pastures. That strategy probably would've worked if Jill hadn't shimmied free of the window and jumped down to the ground in an aggressive posture just like the marauding dogs. The dog closest to the truck leaped at Jill, and Karen thought Jack might break the truck window with his herculean effort to get out. Karen ran through the front door, aimed, and shot the middle dog while moving to the truck with her shotgun pointed at the third dog.

She couldn't help Jill; the two fighting dogs were a mass of savage biting, saliva and flying fur, so instead Karen slid quickly to the truck and opened the door. In one leap of maybe fifteen feet, Jack joined the fray. Within seconds, he'd grabbed the neck of the dog fighting with Jill. The third dog ran for his life, just as Tilley also jumped out of the truck and chased after the escaping dog.

Two dogs were dead and one had made a getaway. Karen could see Jill's confusion as she wobbled on her feet, hurt and panting. She dashed to Jill's side and gingerly ran her hands over her body. Pulling her t-shirt off, Karen wrapped it around the worst wound, a bleeding tear on Jill's front neck. Unable to tighten the shirt without strangling her, Karen scooped Jill in her arms, and laid her out as gently as possible in the back of the truck. She called to Jack. When he jumped in next to Jill as commanded, Karen placed his paw on the wound area and directed him to stay. Jill was still breathing freely, so Karen extricated Maple from the window and called for Tilley, who thankfully came back immediately.

Karen quickly drove home. During the drive she considered what she had at home to treat Jill. Perhaps her pre-planned scavenging would come in very handy. Always squeamish about doing anything medical that might hurt someone, if Don was around, Karen had always allowed him to clean cuts or pick a sliver out of the kids' fingers. Even cutting the dogs' nails made her nervous. Serving as a sort of supervisory nurse, Karen had performed diagnoses and recommended treatment in the family but preferred to let someone else do the work. She reviewed her Army basic lifesaving training and continued her mental inventory of supplies. Glancing back at Jack, he remained perfectly still, holding his position even as she made turns.

The short drive home seemed to take way too long. After laying a clean sheet on the dining room table and pulling out the chairs, Karen carried Jill in. She placed pain pills in the back of Jill's throat and dripped water in her mouth to make her swallow. Flying around the house, Karen gathered antiseptic, alcohol, injectable lidocaine, anesthetic cream, super glue, tape, wound dressings, disposable shavers, and a needle and thread.

Jill was quiet and still breathing. Karen pulled the t-shirt from Jill's neck. "I can do this," she reminded herself. "Crap," Karen said to Jack seated next to the table looking very concerned. "I can't see anything other than a bleeding gash." After a taking a deep breath and steadying herself, Karen pulled the skin back to examine the tissue underneath. She couldn't see any torn arteries or veins, but it looked like a muscle had been sliced open. Jill did not seem to mind her ministrations thus far. Karen told Jack, "Keep her attention, Jack," and for the first time in Karen's life, she pressed a needle into flesh near the wound to inject the lidocaine. Jill jumped as the stinging sensation hit, nearly causing Karen to lose her grip on the shot. She talked to Jill, calmed her, and began again.

Fearing she would make matters worse if she tried to do anything with the torn muscle, Karen cleaned the area as best as possible and used super glue to bind the outside skin. With the new hair scissors, she cut the fur around the wound and then shaved what the scissors didn't get. Surgical tape was applied over the superglued wound. Having dressed the worst area, she moved on to the next.

It took nearly three hours to finish. Karen had a new respect for surgeons after she was done; running a marathon would have been much easier. At the end of the surgery, Karen once again placed pills in the back of Jill's throat, this time antibiotics, and tried to get some water into her using a dropper. Karen carefully carried Jill and placed her on blankets in a collapsible cage to keep her immobilized.

She and Jack kept vigil all night; neither slept. When Jill tried to stand, Karen climbed into the cage to pet her, talking to her softly. Jack crept outside the cage near Jill's head and comforted her with his nearness. *There really is something almost magical about Jack's ability to understand what to do*, Karen mused.

Chapter 11: A+87, Mike

Cross-legged beside her daughter's grave, Karen's tears dripped from her chin as she talked to her child. "Anne, I think I need to leave you. I don't think I'll make it if I stay here alone. Eventually something will happen. I'm not afraid of dying anymore and made a choice to live . . . but I don't want you to be alone."

After the incident with Jill, Karen started thinking seriously about joining Mathias's group. She didn't like or trust him, and he gave her the creeps, but the ranch was the only group within a reasonable driving distance. She just wished there was another way. Besides, she was comfortable where she was and had, against all odds, staked out a way of life here with her dogs.

The nights convinced Karen she needed to find other people, even if the cost was leaving her home. The loneliness and fear snuck up on her in those quiet evenings when she listened to the plaintive calls of coyotes that had seemed to get closer and louder during the passing weeks. Also, Sylvie's constant pressure for Karen to join her at the ranch had finally weakened her resolve. She'd agreed to meet Sylvie in Oregon in five days to finish the journey together.

Karen squinted into the sun to let the warmth seep into her skin and dry her tears. It was warming up nicely today. Suddenly, as if a UPS delivery man had arrived to leave a package at their address, the dogs went wild. Their necks rigid and tails up, rapid fire barks blasted in a cacophony of warning. Giving the command for quiet, Karen listened for sounds of danger. It took another minute, but she was sure she heard a vehicle. "Hide, and quiet," Karen hissed to the dogs while running into the house for her Mossberg.

Karen hid under the bushes 40-feet from the gate with her shotgun sighted on the road. For the second time, she growled from gritted teeth at Raider and Tilley, "Dammit, hide and stay!" Raider crawled behind a large rock and lay down, and Tilley dove into a clump of Photinia and was quiet. After one too many apocalypse novels, Karen wasn't about to be raped and mutilated by a group of bandits.

The engine noise got louder as it came down the street. Karen saw a small RV rounding the corner toward the cul-de-sac. Not believing it was truly happening, the RV stopped directly in front of the gate. Karen whispered "Quiet" one last time to the dogs. The reflection of the sun on the windshield made it impossible to see who or what was inside. The empty world was filled with the sound of the engine shut-off and emergency brake engagement.

A spectacular and somewhat familiar man stepped out of the RV. He had shoulder-length dark wavy hair and a short beard; a rifle was slung over the wide shoulders of what looked like a young slim hipped athlete. Karen realized he could be any age at all. "Damn, I sure hope he isn't a bandit," Karen whispered to herself.

The man walked to the gate, scanned the area and yelled, "Don, Karen, you here? It's Mike McCollough."

"Oh . . . my . . . God, Mike!" Karen screamed. Fearing he would leave, she launched herself from the ground, and in her excitement the toe of her left boot caught on a tree root. What Mike saw from the gate was a woman flying from a bush with substantial velocity, landing face first on the ground, several feet away from where she launched. Karen felt the whoosh of lost breath as she landed. Thinking their human was hurt, the dogs broke the stay and quiet commands, with Zoe and Raider checking on Karen and the remainder heading to the fence to protect their home.

Mike backed off a few feet and stood quietly observing four dogs demonstrate their ownership of the land behind the gate. Karen calmed herself until she could breathe again, and using what little was left of her dignity, stood up, brushed herself off, and strode toward the first normal human being she'd seen in almost three months.

All Mike could focus on was those legs and the feminine strength of Karen. She walked with a purpose and called to the dogs in a commanding voice to sit and stay. Mike remembered Karen as a very attractive and compelling woman; the woman he was staring at now made his knees a little weak. He reminded himself to button up those feelings as he was certain Karen had been through a different version of the same hell he'd experienced.

Gaining control of her pack, once Karen had the dogs in a quiet stay, she glanced up at Mike and said "Hi" as she unlatched the fence. Sliding through the opening she closed it, leaving six curious dogs alone in the fenced yard. She stood in front of the gate, arms crossed over her body and looked at Mike in astonishment as he looked back at her in the same way.

Karen always wished in moments of significance that she could find the exact right thing to say. That she would somehow know the correct words and tone. This was one of those moments. As was normal, however, the words were stuck somewhere in her head, impossible to access. Later, on reflection, the exact right phrase would come to her. For now, Karen stood with her mouth open, eyes probably wild, unable to express the myriad of feelings causing her heart to pound out of her chest. What came out instead was a fallback banal statement she would've used on any other normal day. "What are you doing here, Mike?"

Mike, not being a guy who talked a lot anyway, and just as surprised to find someone alive, was lost for words. He also went with a familiar refrain. "Well, I was passing through the area and thought I would stop by. Is Don…?"

Karen pressed her lips together and shook a no. "Missy?"

Mike returned a similar head shaking reply and studied his feet.

For the three longest months of Karen's life, she'd been deprived of simple, life affirming human touch. Her body reacted and her mind stayed wonderfully silent as she ran to Mike and threw her arms around his neck.

Almost knocked over, Mike grabbed her and hugged tightly. Karen was shaking and holding on, sharing all the trauma, pain, fear, and joy of this changed world. She could smell his musky masculine scent, and the feel of his strong lean torso and hard shoulders felt safe and unsettling, all at once. Thank you so much for stopping by," Karen mumbled into his chest.

Before the water works started, she released Mike and gazed up at him. Taller than before, Mike had a confident stillness that had always drawn her in and at the same time made her nervous around him. Mike smiled in that unassuming and slightly quirky way Karen remembered.

"You are welcome, Karen. I'm truly glad I did." Mike looked down and pressed his thumb and first finger on the sides of his nose as if he was clearing out his own tear ducts. His gaze bored into Karen's eyes, "I didn't expect to actually find anyone. I was on my way back to the east coast and was planning to stop and look for everyone I ever knew, just in case."

"You might want to call first, next time," Karen said with a grin. I could have shot you. I didn't recognize you with all the changes. You looked familiar, but not."

"Yeah, quite a few changes. Also with you too, I see."

Karen shrugged. "They're calling it *the change* on the radio. That's a fairly apt description. Hey, let's not stand around out here. There are dogs everywhere, some not as nice as mine. You hungry? I'm making canned chicken and noodle soup. Why don't you come in and meet the gang?"

"Yeah, I could eat. But, I don't know," Mike replied. "Will one of those shepherds eat me for lunch instead?"

"Naw, they're pussycats. You just got to get to know them."

Karen opened the gate a crack to keep the dogs inside and gave them a sit and stay command as she and Mike entered the protected property. Mike was still tentative about Karen's herd of dogs. She advised him to hold her hand and simply act like he belonged. Tilley was first to greet Mike, jumping on him to say hello and maybe get in a lick. Zoe was so excited about a new friendly human that she peed, wetting Mike's shoe. Milling around, the others tried to smell his feet or get his attention. Only Jack hung back, watching Mike's movements to make sure he meant no harm to his human woman.

"He's obviously the king, and I'm not sure he likes me," Mike said as they entered the house.

"He may be a little bit jealous. As long as you don't show any aggression toward me, Jack will follow my lead."

"He's a beautiful animal. When I was in Afghanistan, I saw several of them training with the MPs. Amazing, the attachment their handlers have with them."

Karen smiled, "I totally understand that connection. He is way more to me than an animal. Jack saved my life a few weeks back. The only live person we've seen happened to be totally whacked out . . . came at me with a hatchet. Jack is nearly clairvoyant. It's like he can read my mind. He reacts before I tell him what to do. He's truly a gift."

Mike responded, "Nothing negative intended with the animal comment, it's only I've never lived with dogs. My father didn't care for them, and Missy was allergic. We had cats on our farm growing up, but no dogs."

Showing Mike around her house, Karen pointed out the food storage room, the parts and tools area, and medical supplies, fuels, and batteries in an outside shed. Coming back through the garage, she proudly pulled the sheet off her expensive wine collection, or at least it would have been had the world not ended. During the entire tour, Mike was followed by a curious dog entourage as he warily glanced over at Jack.

"Have a seat, Mike," Karen said when they arrived at the kitchen. "I'm going to whip up some chicken noodle soup and boxed cheese grilled with homemade bread."

A not entirely comfortable silence followed as Karen placed the meal on the table and sat with Mike. She realized she didn't really know much about him. He was an Army friend of Don's from the first Gulf War. Don and Mike had stayed in contact while both were living in the D.C. area. They had dinner with Mike and his wife Missy on a few occasions, met up once in Hawaii by accident, and then three years ago the couple stopped by when they were in Washington visiting relatives. Mike's wife was nice but a little boring for Karen's taste, so there wasn't a mutual friendship developed between wives.

"You almost missed me, Mike. I agreed to meet this woman from Oregon and then join a group at a ranch in Idaho in five days."

Mike swallowed and appeared unfazed. "I thought I might swing by there on my way across the States anyway."

"You know about the ranch and Mathias!"

"I found a shortwave before I left Fairbanks. I've been listening to several groups for a few weeks. I tuned into the ranch early on and got irritated with Mathias's style so quit listening. I never heard you though."

"It took me awhile to find a shortwave. I had a few setbacks in the beginning."

Mike stared at Karen wondering what sort of setbacks she might have experienced. When she didn't volunteer, he figured she didn't want to talk about it yet. "I've also been talking to a man in California who's trying to get some satellite communication gear together. By the way, I can fix your antenna so you'll get more range from your shortwave."

"Is the guy's name Jed? And what were you doing in Fairbanks?"

"Yeah, Jed. Knows a lot about tech stuff. He's helped me out. I'd been in Prudhoe Bay visiting my son and his wife when everything happened. They just had a baby girl." At that Mike stopped and stared at his plate. Karen could see him take a deep breath to gather himself. "I have brain cancer—or more than likely, *had* cancer. I think it's gone. Doctors gave me three to six months. Missy and I wanted to spend some time with our son and his family while I was still doing okay. My son Tony is, or was, a petroleum engineer working in Alaska." Mike leveled his green brown eyes directly at Karen and said, "It really sucks, you know. It's such a miracle that I'm alive and healed, and yet everyone else is dead."

All Karen could say was, "I know." They sat in silence for an extended period until Karen couldn't bear anymore. "Hey, how about a drink? Or even some pot. Don bought some when it became legal in Washington, but we never tried it."

Mike laughed. "If you have a beer that would be great, and only if you'll have one with me."

They drank and laughed, shared some old Army stories, and talked about people they knew in common. Finally Karen asked, "Where have you been all this time, and how did you end up on my doorstep?"

Mike said with a sad smile, "Now that's an interesting story. We thought we'd be safe since not many people were living in Prudhoe Bay. Missy and the baby got sick within a week after hearing news of the illness, and then Tony and my daughter-in-law two days later. I still can't understand how a virus, if that is what it was, could be in Alaska at the same time it was everywhere else."

"I wanted to bury them, but the ground was frozen solid so I did my best at cremation and made a mausoleum of sorts out of some landscaping bricks Tony had in his backyard. By the time I went into town to get supplies, I only found two people alive and they were both sick. All the stores had been raided so I gathered what I would need to travel, cold weather gear, and a snow cat from nearby homes."

"I went back to Tony's house to box some pictures and say goodbye. It was lucky I did, because I started feeling ill. I'm pretty sure I would have frozen to death if I had started out and been on the road somewhere when I got sick. It was already below freezing in the house when I began to shiver from fever, so I climbed into Tony's arctic sleeping bag and woke up sometime later. I'm still not sure how long I was out. What about you?"

Karen's expression was grim as she thought about Mike alone in a home with his dead family. "Pretty much the same thing happened to me. From what I could tell, I was out for three days."

"Hmmpf," Mike nodded. "That's close to what I thought. I was terribly thirsty when I woke up. Anyway, after I drank a gallon of water, I loaded up and headed south. Everything was going fine. With a map left in the cab of the snow cat, I was able to locate stops for fuel for just over 350 miles. Then the damn thing broke down between Coldfoot and Livengood in the middle of nowhere. I hoofed it to Livengood, which was almost a hundred miles away. Had to stop and build shelters at night. Luckily, I had the right kind of gear with me and the weather wasn't too bad. Other than a brief run-in with a bear and some terrible itching as my skin molted, mostly I was worried about frostbite. When I got to Fairbanks, I was bone tired and hungry so I stopped for a week to rest up and make a plan."

"I decided to head to D.C. I figured if anybody knew what was happening, they would be there. Figured I could stop on my way, at every location where I knew someone, just in case. Borrowed a four-wheel drive truck from a car lot and left for Anchorage. In Anchorage, I looked for other survivors—spent a little over a week there. Ran into one person very much like the one you described who was crazy. He chased me a short distance and then gave up. I found an RV and loaded it with food and other essentials. Stopped at every town along the way to Vancouver. Met a lot of pets and wildlife but absolutely no one else.

"You were my third stop. My uncle and his wife were in Seattle. They were in their home when the thing hit. I buried them as well. So here I am. I come bearing gifts. I got some beef from a dairy farm north of Seattle and a wild turkey along the way. Both are in my freezer."

"Wow, that's quite a story. And to think all I've been doing is hanging out and collecting dogs," Karen smiled. Mike didn't want to stare but he just couldn't take his eyes off Karen. He told himself she was going to think he was creepy if he kept taking glances at the swell of her breasts, but it was difficult to stop. Even with the unusual hairstyle she was stunning. The change had been very kind to an already attractive woman. "Total eye candy" as one of Mike's young IT employees had described a particularly attractive client.

But she was more than just eye candy. He knew something of her resume. Karen had earned a spot at West Point as an enlisted soldier in the very first group of women to attend. After graduating, she did her five years and had a promising career but decided to get out. It was the demography stuff where she'd made a name for herself. From what Don had told him, she was making big bucks working for companies in new product introductions. Don had bragged that the CEO at one large corporation had called her a soothsayer.

I'm hungry.

Mike looked around thinking he heard a male voice. "Did you say something?"

Karen puckered her lips and said, "No, why?"

"I thought I heard someone say, 'I'm hungry.'" Perplexed, Mike saw Jack sitting by the table staring at him. "If I didn't know better . . ." He handed Jack the last piece of his sandwich, which Jack happily ate.

Mike helped Karen clear the table and clean up. Facing the sink with her back to him she said, "Hey Mike, you have any idea how long you might hang around?"

Mike stepped next to her and put his hand on her shoulder. "Is that an invitation or a gentle prodding for me to move on down the road?""

Karen chuckled and turned to him. "Uh, that would be an invitation."

They looked into each other's eyes for a few moments until the tension became too much. Mike put his hands on the counter, leaned down and stared out the window as he started talking. "From everything I can tell, there aren't many people left alive."

Karen nodded. "From my calculations, somewhere from 1 in 150 to 250 thousand."

"I hadn't put a number to it but that sounds about right. Anyway, the odds that I would meet someone alive, someone of my generation, someone that I already know? Astronomical. You are here, and I don't have anywhere else to be."

Karen stepped back, put her hands on her hips, and with a half-smile on her lips mimicked, "Because I am here and you don't have anywhere else to be? That's a notch below faint praise."

"Oh, crap," Mike replied, flustered, scratching his head. "That isn't at all what I meant. What I meant to say was you, or at least I, or maybe you too, darn it…let me start again. I have never been very good at saying the right things to women. And frankly, lately I haven't had much opportunity to practice. I like you, Karen. I'm glad I found you. I would love to stay around for a while if you will let me. How's that?" Mike looked at Karen with such sincerity from his leaning position, her heart did a little double beat.

"Okay, that works. I would also like to hang out." Karen giggled and then Mike joined in. "Actually," Karen said, her face more serious, "I understood what you meant and was just giving you a hard time. A few hours ago, I was thinking about leaving my home to travel to a place I've never been, to live with people I don't really know, some I don't particularly trust so that I wouldn't be alone. The last three months, well, I've had a good taste of what a life lived totally alone feels like and it isn't much of a life. For me it's a devil-you-know situation."

Mike did a caricature version of Karen's incensed, hands on the hips position. "Oh! So now I'm just the devil you know, huh?" Mike grinned.

They stood in the kitchen laughing while the dogs milled around the dining and kitchen areas tilting their heads, curious about this human behavior.

Karen shook her head and gave Mike a light punch in the arm. "I am going to tune into the nightly ranch meeting soon. You want to join me?"

"Would love to. Let me fix your antenna set-up first. And, at least for tonight, don't mention I am here."

Cocking her head, Karen asked, "How come?"

"I want to get the lay of the land with this group. I wasn't paying a lot of attention to the individual players when I listened in before. It would be better to hear how they relate to you and your Oregon friend first."

Karen hugged Mike then backed off. "Thank you . . . and you need to show me what you do to the antenna."

"I think that's an excellent idea. It's important we share knowledge. You can teach me a few things, too!" Mike gave Karen a huge grin and ran out to the RV.

Karen was wondering what Mike meant by that last statement as he was walking back carrying some radio accessories. He fiddled with the shortwave and made three trips outside to the roof while Karen watched as he explained what he was doing. Karen noticed the precision of his movements as he cut and rewound wire. He had amazing man hands, large and strong with long square fingers. Veins in his forearms bulged as he gripped tools. Just watching him move was an almost erotic experience for Karen; she smiled inwardly, thinking about how three months alone and a recent infusion of hormones had impacted her view of the world.

Finished, Mike demonstrated the additional frequencies now available because of the antenna.

"Thanks, Mike, that's amazing. Hey, a question: do you know why I can't siphon gas from new cars?"

He shrugged at Karen like she needed to ask more difficult questions. "Of course; it's a safety feature. There's a check valve on the fuel tank so if your car rolls in an accident, it won't leak gas everywhere and explode. There's a way to get around it by using the fuel rail in the engine and tricking the fuel pump. The car has to start, though. If you want, I'll show you tomorrow."

"Absolutely, first thing if you could. I've had a couple of tense moments when I was out on missions and had trouble finding an old vehicle."

"My schedule is wide open," Mike replied and extended his arms fully out.

They were only five minutes late to the start of Mathias's daily broadcast. It went as usual, going around the various participants to explain how they were doing. The discussion after the formal portion centered on the best routes people could take to arrive at the ranch. Mathias did not give his exact location and instead made plans for group members to meet along major highway intersections at specified times to be led to the ranch.

Karen chatted with Jed and Sylvie after the formal session and asked Sylvie if she was ready for the journey. Sylvie sounded like she couldn't wait. Signing off, Karen shifted her eyes to Mike. He'd sat preternaturally still for the entire hour of the broadcast, never giving away any emotion or reaction. "What are you thinking, Mike?"

"I am thinking something doesn't feel right, but I'm not completely sure. Regardless, kiddo, this whole new world set up is ripe for the truly power hungry. We need to be smart whatever we decide. Also, if we decide not to go, I think we need to go get Sylvie. Uh, I keep saying 'we.' I would be most honored if you would keep me around for this undertaking."

"I agree. At the very least, I owe it to her to meet and give her a choice. And you have no idea how much I would appreciate your help."

"I need some time to think about it, and I'm pretty tired. I've been up since 5 AM. I'll sleep in the RV and we can game plan tomorrow."

Both disappointed and relieved, Karen said goodnight and grabbed Mike's hand. "I'm so glad you are here."

He gestured like he was tipping his hat and replied, "Glad to be here, ma'am. Steak and eggs in the morn at 8, in the RV, if you're interested."

"Eggs? Where did you get eggs?"

They both smiled, and he was gone. As Mike walked up the drive to the RV with Jack as an escort, he could have sworn he heard a male voice whisper, *Good man gone.*

Karen's mind was whirling from the day. Lying down and opening her book, she found it impossible to concentrate on the words. She wished the internet was around so she could look up the name of that feel-good chemical that floods your brain when you are smitten by someone. Come to think of it, the last time she remembered feeling a little this way had to do with Mike.

Karen had driven to Don's office to give him some paperwork that needed to be signed immediately. Not finding him at his desk, she'd sat down in his office to wait. Mike peeked in the doorway, seeing a woman he didn't know. He introduced himself as Don's boss. "Oh, you must be Karen."

Karen stood up to shake his hand. "Colonel McCollough, it's great to meet you."

"Sit down, sit down." Mike grabbed the chair next to Don's desk and talked to her for ten minutes until Don returned. She couldn't say exactly what it was about him; from the minute he grabbed her hand to shake it and their eyes met, some part of Karen felt like he had reached into her heart. Maybe it was his earnestness or his centered confidence. Or perhaps, as one friend proposed many years ago, we are all energy and some people are simply on the same frequency. Whatever the reason, Karen had pulled those feelings into a locked room and resolved to keep her distance.

What were the odds that this particular man was among the very few survivors, much less that he happened to be away from home visiting Alaska and then stopped by her house only five days before her planned departure? Astronomical, as Mike would say. She felt as if she had won some great cosmic lottery. Karen's previous life was about earning her way; very little luck was involved.

Karen's parents were their own special brand of dysfunctional. Her first memories were of loud, red-faced arguments between Judith, her biological mother, and Danny, her flawed father. It would start with an unkind comment, what Karen would now call snarky, and quickly escalated to top-of-the-lung rants, door slamming, and the heaving of small items. The best sound was when Karen heard gravel scooped from the driveway and then the screeching of tires which meant one of them was leaving.

Karen would tiptoe to her room and sit on the bed with her coloring books. For the most part, they left her alone to wonder why they were so mad. Even at five, Karen understood that this wasn't right. When she went to her friend Kelly's house next door, her mom made them cookies and let them sit in the kitchen with her while she worked. Karen spent most of her day and evening at her friend Kelly's. Mom and Dad never asked her to come home. Mrs. Edwards would simply say, "Karen, I think you need to go home now," with a sad expression on her face. Karen would quietly enter the back door of her house and try to make it to her room before the fireworks started again.

She still remembered coming home from her first day of school, excited about school and all the kids. The house was silent. On the table was a note from her mom that Karen could barely read. She had spent so much time alone in her room with the picture books her grandfather sent that she could understand enough to get the general idea. Judith was gone.

Her dad came and got her, unannounced, the second week of school, which was tremendously embarrassing for a six-year-old girl. He told her they were moving from Detroit to live with Grandpa. Everything was packed and in the car. Karen had never met her grandfather, but she liked the books he sent. *Maybe things will get better*, she thought to herself. She argued with her father to let her say goodbye to Kelly and Mrs. Edwards, but all he would say is no. She cried in the car for an hour until her dad told her to shut up.

Things were better at Grandpa's house. There weren't any other kids around, but he never yelled and he let her play with his dogs. Dad helped out with the tree farm during the day and then took off in the evenings. Every so often, Danny would stumble in when she was still up, sitting with grandpa in the crook of his arm as he read to her. "I'll put you to bed, little girl", Danny said in a too loud voice. This annoyed the heck out of Karen, and Grandpa would sadly shake his head.

She got under the covers and begrudgingly listened as her father leaned over her with his stinky alcohol breath and told her how unfair the world was and how worthless Judith turned out to be. Even at that tender age, Karen remembered thinking she had a better grasp on the world than her angry father.

At 10, she was watching a scary show on TV with Grandpa, one of their favorites, when the police came to the door. Danny was gone. He ran off the road into a tree, most likely inebriated, they said. Grandpa thanked them for making the drive out and asked where he could collect Danny's remains. When they left, he hugged Karen tight and kept saying, "Don't worry my little shiny star (his pet name for her that she didn't understand but liked anyway). Everything will be fine." Karen believed Grandpa and only felt bad because she wouldn't miss Danny.

Judith came to the funeral. Karen crept under the screened window to listen to her grandfather and her biological mom outside by the side of the house. It was the only time Karen ever heard Grandpa raise his voice. "But she's your daughter," he growled indignantly. When they came in, Karen was waiting, sitting at the table in front of a tuna noodle casserole. With no regard to all the people there to pay respects, Karen said in her best imitation of a firm adult voice, "I do not want to go with her. No matter what the adults think, I am better off here with Grandpa."

Her grandpa's eyes welled up and Judith smirked and said, "I told you so, Gene."

Life on the southern edge of Michigan's Upper Peninsula with Grandpa was good. It was lonely and bone-chilling cold sometimes, but good. He gave Karen her very own Beagle puppy for her twelfth birthday and then showed Karen how to train her dog on their hunting trips. The only reason Grandpa allowed her to hunt was that Karen begged him relentlessly until she finally wore him down. Grandpa said, "If you are bound and determined to come along, you need to know how to shoot and have respect for weapons." Karen smiled sweetly and agreed to his terms. Not wanting to kill an animal, she never actually used the rifle Grandpa had bought for her. Eventually Grandpa got the idea and quit bringing it along.

Karen didn't truly enjoy hunting or the Michigan cold. What she loved was her grandpa, the dogs, and their conversations out in the woods. He wasn't a motor mouth like Karen, but something about the solitude of the forest and crisp snow crunching under his boots opened him up. He shared funny stories about the people he'd met during World War I and her grandma, who he said Karen favored. He would talk about the Vietnam War, the tree business, how to pick out a good dog, the cycle of life in a forest . . . you name it. The best part of it all was that he asked her what she thought and truly listened and considered her opinions.

Karen had plenty of chores and never resented having to pull her weight. As a teenager, as long as the chores were done, Grandpa let Karen come and go as she pleased. When she didn't have school activities or a date, they would hunt and fish or drive into town to eat steaks at Tom's, the local diner.

One day Grandpa saw some of her drawings in a book by her nightstand. The next day he brought home an art set, actual drawing pencils, and some blank paper and laid it on the table. "I appreciate all you do around here Karen. But you need to do more than just work and school. You need things in your life you do for yourself. I spent a pretty penny on this stuff, so don't waste it. I expect you to practice at least a half hour a day. That's the only way to make talent useful."

Karen was seventeen the second time she lost everything. Dolly, Grandpa's best retriever, ran into the house barking insistently, begging Karen to listen. Karen followed her to the trees and found her best friend, her hero, and her parent figure all rolled into one, deathly still next to his chainsaw. Grandpa had suffered a massive heart attack. It was all a blur in the weeks to come when Danny's brothers and sisters explained that they had to sell the property and Karen would have to come live with one of them. She was shuffled off to Illinois to live with Aunt Mary, which was better than going to live with Judith who had remarkably, offered to "take her in."

Aunt Mary was a nice lady. Other than having to sleep in a dank basement in a converted storage room, it wasn't too bad. Karen's plan was to get a job, save for a year, and then try to get a scholarship to college. Grandpa had left her a little bit of money, but it wouldn't be nearly enough. One year turned into three as Karen moved from waitress jobs to store clerk positions, always falling just short of earning enough to live on her own and go to college, even with a small scholarship.

On a windy spring day, she took the bus to the downtown area to apply for a bank teller position—a friend had mentioned it paid better than waitressing. As Karen rounded the corner to Main Street, she almost knocked over a good-looking young guy in a uniform standing on the sidewalk smoking a cigarette.

"Oh, excuse me." Karen said.

"No problem", he replied with a beguiling smile. "Where are you going in such a hurry?"

"Actually, looking for a job in the bank down the street."

"Why would you want to do that?"

Karen scrunched her face in an "are you out of your mind", expression. "To get a job that pays more than bupkus."

"How old are you anyway?"

"Twenty", Karen answered growing suspicious.

He threw his cigarette on the ground, snuffed it out with his shoe, then picked it up and placed it in the standing ashtray propping open the door. "If you want to see the world, I may have a job for you. He stuck out his hand to shake Karen's and said, I'm Sergeant White, an Army recruiter. Glad to meet you. And you are?"

"Karen Henry, but I'm really not interested in the Army."

"Understand, understand. It's kind of a slow day for me today. Why don't you just give me fifteen minutes and I'll tell you what we can offer. Take a break for a few minutes and gather yourself before you interview for a boring bank job. What have you got to lose? You look like the kind of young woman who would like to go college, am I right?"

Karen chuckled, "You're pretty good at this".

"I'll take that compliment. But what if I was to tell you we would pay for your entire college education, provide the technical skills for a decent job and you could go to a really cool place. Ever been to Europe?"

Now Karen was laughing. "Make that really good at this. Oh hell, what can it hurt? Fifteen minutes, not a minute more."

"You got it! Now if you will please step into my office", Sergeant White said with a flourish of his arm.

Sergeant White made good on most of his promises. She landed an assignment to Germany. What he failed to mention was that she would be part of a humongous experiment. She joined the Army at the cusp of its transition to recruit women. Government decision-makers saw women as the winning solution after realizing they were falling well short of recruitment goals to fill the empty ranks of an unpopular post-Vietnam institution. Besides, they reasoned, the narrative fit well with the growing bra-burning feminist movement. The people in the Army, almost all men, were not as sold on the idea.

Karen wanted to do her time, get some technical education and experience, and then make a quick exit to attend college. To her great surprise, she enjoyed most of the people and the work. A senior non-commissioned officer who had a daughter about Karen's age took her under his wing, protected her from unsavory characters even though Karen was quite capable of handling herself, and gave her significantly more responsibility than the average specialist.

One day Master Sergeant Yelm walked up to Karen's desk and said, "Specialist Henry, you are going to West Point!" He then dropped a huge application on her desk.

"Well, what if I don't want to, Master Sergeant? I don't have time to fill that thing out with all the damn work you've given me," Karen said with a mischievous smile.

"Not an option," MSG Yelm returned sternly. He plopped himself in the chair next to her desk, put his elbow on the corner, and stretched out his long legs. "Look, Karen, I hate to lose you. You do everything faster and ten times better than most of the dirt bags around here. I saw this over at the Education Resource Center, and it's a great opportunity. You will do well, and the only thing I need from you is the chance to give you your first salute. I'll get the officers in the Brigade to write letters of recommendation."

"Awww, you like me." She smiled.

"Like's got nothing to do with it! Just get that thing finished by Friday." With that, he stood up and hustled off.

Yet another experiment in the integration of women in the Army, Karen was accepted at West Point with history's first class of women. She passed the entry tests with flying colors and was soon learning the political intrigue associated with 4500 competitive young men and women sequestered in an unreal world. At graduation, now Sergeant Major Yelm attended and gave Second Lieutenant Henry the salute he had promised.

The Army was a hard place to grow up for a young woman, but the rejection by both parents early in her life served her well and reinforced her true belief that for every bad in life, there's a good that can come out of it—if you could just find it. It didn't bother Karen that many of her contemporaries, the soldiers placed in her charge and, most particularly, her superiors, didn't want her around. Karen would simply shake her head in frustration, prepare herself for the challenge, and then get to work.

She did well. It was more of a surprise to Karen than to her Army family. She often felt like a fraud, only pretending to be a capable military officer. She couldn't run as fast, carry as much, compartmentalize her feelings as well, or even mimic the part of a steely-eyed leader. Those qualities were left to her male colleagues. Seriously, how can a woman just a smidge over five feet tall and 100 pounds do that? Instead, she used the one skill unique to her that those around her couldn't quite grasp. Call it female intuition or prescience or refined logical reasoning, take your pick. Karen very simply always knew when trouble was lurking around the corner. If the shit was going to hit the fan, Karen was ready for it. She didn't make big mistakes.

As she began to drift into sleep, Karen wondered if maybe it was all random events strung together and any bit of control she thought she had in this life was merely an illusion. How else had she managed to ride the tide, waves thrashing and cresting on the beach where she washed-up into this new world, alive? She had survived it all, and Mike, a man who made her heart flutter in a way she couldn't get a handle on, was in an RV outside her gate. What else but dumb luck can explain it?

As she gave in to confusion and sleep pulled her deeper into its nest, Tilley rolled over and smacked Karen in the face with her scratchy paw. Karen grumbled, "Maybe I should have asked Mike to stay".

Chapter 12: Jed

Jed couldn't explain the muscles appearing on his legs and arms. For most of his life, or at least since the first time someone called him bird-legs, he'd refused to wear shorts. In sunny California, avoiding shorts was no easy feat. He looked at his naked body in the floor-to-ceiling mirrors of his ridiculously large master bath one last time. Other than an hour or so playing hoops outside the garage each day, he hadn't done anything special to make the muscles grow. It had to be some sort of DNA change.

"Stereo and lights on," Jed said as he walked into the ultra-modern gathering area of his home. Since he didn't need to impress women anymore and June his housekeeper was long gone, Jed had made a few adjustments to the décor. The sumptuous furniture and stuff his decorator had recommended was mostly piled against one wall. He left his favorite chair and gaming console across from the wall screen but otherwise, the room was filled with tables where he could work.

Stripped-down weapons covered one of the tables. Jed had never used a real weapon before the apocalypse. His doctor parents wouldn't allow one in the house. He'd killed hundreds of thousands in video games, but that cred wouldn't help him defend himself. Without an internet, there was only one way to learn: trial and error. First, he took the weapons apart. He studied the simple but deadly mechanisms until he fully understood what made them work. After that, he put them back together and began target practice from the back deck of his home.

Jed sat at the gun table and set his watch. He picked up the parts for the Colt AR-15 and assembled it. He loaded the weapon, placed it under his chin, aimed at the chimney of the house below his and said, "Bang!"

"Not too shabby, 59 seconds. I'm ready." Jed knew there wasn't a need to put the weapon back together each time, but he liked doing it and it made him more comfortable with the feel of it. The feel of it was the hardest part. There wasn't anyone around to show him the best way to carry a weapon. He experimented by rapidly responding to threats while holding it in different ways until he found something that worked. As it turned out, playing video games was good for something—it made learning to sight, point, and shoot easier. Real weapons were more precise, but the aiming thing came naturally.

He had to get to LA for the thorium generator specs and satellite phones and it was nearly 700 miles from here to there. More important, he had to get there in one piece. He couldn't risk something happening to those plans or to him. If this totally hosed planet was to have any hope of pulling itself out of the very deep hole it was in, the world would need the thorium technology.

After he woke from the great dying, the first thing he did was head to Tallmark's primary testing facility only ten miles away. He'd hoped to find some of his colleagues alive and already safeguarding the prototype generator, batteries, and drones. He shouldn't have been surprised when no one was there, but he was anyway. Like a mantra, Jed kept saying to himself, *some of them will be alive*, even as he drove the thirteen-mile congested path without seeing anyone else. His first sign that all was not well was an unlocked front entry. Tallmark took security seriously. Particularly since this non-descript building housed the most important technological advance since the internet. Arguably, even more important than the internet.

Toblinsky, the lead fusion scientist, was lying on the floor next to the generator. The putrid smell of Toblinsky's body and incessant buzzing of flies industriously working on his corpse sent Jed fleeing outside the room.

That was the moment when it occurred to Jed that the world as he understood it was truly, unalterably different. His old life was safe; a life where you got the idea of dead bodies from video. You didn't really have to smell them or fight off flies to recognize a face. He sat against the wall on the floor wondering how he'd lived for more than thirty years and could still be so unprepared for, well, really bad shit. He wasn't without the ability to imagine. He wasn't naive. Everyone said he was one of the best minds in the world. But even so, Jed put his face into his hands and cried like a baby.

It might have been reassuring to know that almost every other survivor had at some point huddled in a corner or against a wall crying their eyes out. But he didn't know that. Jed told himself to quit being a pussy. With red puffy eyes, he found a dolly and loaded the technology into a company van and drove it home.

He set up the drone computer and satellite links and then flew the drones up and down the I-5 corridor of California. There were no words, at least none Jed knew of, that could describe the dread he felt as he viewed the human emptiness of a once thriving land. He flew the drone to his ex-girlfriend's house, to his friend Trevor's apartment, and to his parents' home all the way in New York. In all that time, he only saw three people, and one of them could best be described as a gorilla man.

For Jed, technology had become an extension of himself. He explored and engaged the world from multiple portals as naturally as a child learned to swim. No task was so small that it was unworthy of replacement by an innovative application or an auto-remote button. Now that he couldn't connect online, most of his technology was useless junk. He grieved the loss. Isolation and aggravation finally drove Jed in search of a low-tech solution. He found a shortwave radio in a specialty tech shop.

Small groups were just beginning to form on the radio. Jed talked with everyone. A lot like the dating apps he'd once used, he tried to read between the lines on which people offered the most promise. The only difference was that instead of texting they were talking. Oh, and the fate of the earth might hinge on his ability to make a good decision. No pressure. He needed to be part of a group, and it had to be one that could be trusted with the technology. The stakes were too high.

Too much could go wrong if he tried to make it cross country. He would choose between groups on the west coast and southwest. The ranch guy, Mathias, was a pompous pseudo-intellectual; for a real scientist there was nothing worse. Having travelled in the circles of some of the greatest scientific minds on the planet, Jed could spot a fraud. Another group in LA, with three members, was worth checking out when he took the trip south. And then there was Mike. Mike had an appealing hands-on common sense about him. He was the kind of dude that was confident enough that he didn't need to prove it to anyone. Jed couldn't explain why, but when he talked with Mike he felt that rare quality that tapped you on the shoulder and said, *Follow me and I won't screw you over*.

It was smooth sailing to Los Angles. Jed had mapped out traffic detours before he left. There were two items on his agenda: he wanted to meet in person with the LA group gathering on the shortwave and swing by to get the plans and specs for the Thorium generator from Tallmark Corporate Headquarters. He loaded the generator and drones in the van for the trip because he wanted to ensure they were safe.

Finding the meeting place for the first address without a GPS was more of struggle than he'd imagined. It was not easy to navigate alone with a paper road map while driving. Jed had hoped since satellites were still circling the earth, an old-fashioned car mounted GPS device would work—but that wasn't the case. *There must be earth-side infrastructure required or a satellite failsafe because of the atomic clocks. I will have to work on that problem later.*

He parked away from house and curious eyes and then walked a mile up a winding canyon road. He kept the Colt hanging from his shoulder on the hike even though it still felt odd to be lugging around a gun. The house was a lot like his own: jutting corners that hugged the landscape, plenty of glass, and mega money. Jed rang the doorbell. When that didn't work, he knocked.

A man peeked through the side glass and mouthed the question, "Jed?" Jed smiled a half-smile and nodded. The man opened the door and stood with a wide toothy grin, his hand out. "Jed, so glad you could come! And, I believe you're a little early. I'm Scott. Come in and meet the others." They shook hands, and Scott clasped Jed's hand with both of his.

Scott was only medium height. *He must have been really short before the change*, Jed thought to himself as he followed him through an opulent entry to a massive room. Glass windows showcased the view of LA and the ocean beyond. One other woman and a man sat on furniture that looked tiny and isolated in the cavernous space.

"Jed, this is Millie and Stan." Millie might have been a model or an actress. Long blonde hair surrounded a perfect face with soft brown eyes. Stan the man had a rough edge. He stared at Jed like he was an insect that needed to be squished. "Jed, can I get you something to drink before we begin?" Scott asked.

"A cup of herbal tea or a cherry coke would be good if you have it."

"I can do the tea. Please sit and get to know everybody."

Huh. This feels like an interview, Jed thought. I was supposed to be interviewing them. The whole world has crashed, and these folks are dealing with it by having business meetings.

Millie started. "So what did you do, Jed? Please tell us about yourself."

"Ah, um, I'm sort of a technical kind of guy. I worked in IT and scientific development, that sort of thing. I'm originally from New York, but I'm living in the San Jose area now."

"That's interesting," she replied, clearly not interested.

Stan continued the penetrating stare. Jed thought he must be the one assigned to ferret any exaggerations to his resume. "What type of scientific development?"

"Mostly energy related stuff like new energy sources and improving efficiency of existing technology."

"Hmmm, that could be very helpful to our cause."

"And what exactly would you say *is* your cause?"

Before Stan could answer, Scott returned. He set down the tea he was carrying, but kept a folder that looked to be paperwork clutched to his chest. Scott hitched his pants and sat across from Jed, plastering another smile on his face. He had close cut curly dark hair and deep-set eyes. Everything about him screamed lawyer or salesman, possibly both.

"So, where are we?" Scott asked.

"Stan was just about to tell me about your *cause*."

"Really? I'm not sure we have totally agreed upon a cause per se. At this point, we are talking with prospective group members. As I'm sure you're aware, Jed, things are rather dire right now. I am, well, *we* are trying to round up survivors that could help build a new community here in LA. We want to be sure each new member is invested in the group. It wouldn't serve anyone to be fighting amongst each other for turf. I know you're a scientist, and we could certainly use some of that. What we have to offer to our first seven members is a buy-in bonus."

"A buy-in to what?"

"Glad you asked. Let me show you." Scott smiled as he expansively pulled a map from his folder. We have divided the LA region into seven areas. I have the largest area since it was my plan, but as you can see, the rest are very evenly distributed. As a founding member, you would receive one of these areas and preside over any survivors that you can roundup."

"So let me get this straight, you are dividing up LA, even though it isn't yours to divide?"

"Well, I wouldn't put it that way. Son, let's talk facts here." Jed hated being called "son," but he continued to listen. "People are shit, and they're greedy as hell. As soon as they figure out they can take areas and people by force, they will. Our thought was to form a conglomerate and set up a secure system before that happens."

Scott reached into folder and pulled out a contract, smiling like it was his first born child. "Here is the contract we would all sign. It provides a working document for basic government, trade, and mutual protection of all areas within the conglomerate. We would help each other develop our respective areas. You would get your pick of the four remaining sections. Millie and Stan have already signed and selected theirs."

Jed sighed. There was a weird, twisted logic to their approach. "I'm guessing you are a lawyer, Scott. You must understand this contract isn't worth the paper it's written on without a legal system or government to enforce it, right?"

"I am a lawyer, and of course I understand that. It isn't enforceable now, but it will be as soon as we get going. That's the point. If you read the document, you'll see that each area holder would have a vote and will also act as the law within his or her own territory. There's a provision for selecting a CEO and board to refine it further once our areas are established. You're getting in on the ground floor, Jed! I'm talking to four other people in the next week, so if you don't sign now, I can't guarantee the offer will still exist. Now, what questions do you have?"

"You said `buy-in.' Do you expect compensation?

"That's a turn of phrase. Buy-in as in, you agree to the terms, all for one and one for all, yada, yada, yada. We have specified a payment to a treasury in gold at the end of year two. Finding gold in your territory shouldn't be difficult. We're going to need a currency system, and gold can be used as coin or to secure another form of monetary remuneration once we have a basis for valuation. It's all laid out in the contract. Think of the future, Jed, and of the tremendous opportunity. What do you say?"

"I say . . . I think I could have been Donald Duck when I walked in here and you would have made me the same offer."

For the first time, Scott dropped the slick, faux optimistic expression. He leveled his eyes at Jed and there was humor in them. "Which says to me, you aren't a cartoon character and we could really use your help."

"Look, I'll have to think about it. I suspect you're kidding yourselves about how many people are left. My estimate is somewhere less than 100 in all of California. You may want to consider staying together." Jed held his tongue, wanting to add, *rather than dividing up a kingdom.* "Can I get a copy of the contract to review?"

"Sure can." Scott was back in his sales pitch delirium. But I must warn you, don't wait too long. It's too good a deal and it won't last. You look like a guy that could make a difference. We can wait for you to read the contract now."

"No, I appreciate it, but no." Jed stood up. "I've got some other business in LA and I need to get on the road. Once I'm done, I'll read this and let you know."

"You don't have to rush off. Let's hash this out. Get to know one another."

"Sorry, but no. I want to be moving while there's still daylight."

"Okay then, you have my channel," Scott beamed. Check in if you have any other questions."

They all shook hands, and Millie gave him a sultry kiss on the cheek.

As he jogged back to his van, Jed wondered if the world was too screwed up now to be fixed. Maybe his tech wouldn't make a bit of difference. His initial impression of the LA group—maybe well-meaning but, more likely, bat-shit crazy people. He wouldn't give it a year before they were trying to off each other to get a bigger piece of the nonexistent pie.

Jed knew one thing for certain. A generator weighing less than 100 pounds that could power a city with a freely available energy source called thorium would be a distinct competitive advantage to any group. Also, batteries that quickly stored up to 50 times the energy equivalent of previously existing technologies made all kinds of things possible to its owners. He needed to talk to Mike tonight after he made it safely to Tallmark's corporate headquarters and had the goods.

There were long shadows on the buildings by the time Jed wound through the clogged dead metropolis once known as the City of Angels. A city that was just now living up to its name. His luck had run out when it came to easy access—Tallmark was completely locked down. He pulled the van near the back loading dock, jumped out, and tried the hand-print entry pad just in case back-up power still worked. No luck again. Grabbing one of his special batteries, some connector cables, and a small tool kit, he set to work on the sophisticated mechanism.

Jed was so focused on getting into Tallmark, his first sense that he was no longer alone was an earthy animal smell that didn't fully connect in his synapses to a danger response. When he heard a yip, his internal system went immediately to overload. Heart racing and the hair on the back of his neck springing into action, Jed whipped around to face the source of his fear.

Three coyotes were creeping toward him from the bottom of the loading ramp. Three more were loping into position around his van. He pulled the Colt off his shoulder, trying not to set off a stampede. His hands shook. The closest coyote was big and rangy, and the best description of its countenance was hungry. Jed realized this wasn't normal coyote behavior. They were wary of adult humans. He wondered if these coyotes had already adapted to the radically changed environment and he was simply an opportunity for a good meal.

Jed calculated survival permutations in a flash. His brain was good at that. Running to the safety of another building or his van—nope. Shoot and hit all the predators before they were on him—nope again. His only chance was to take out the closest animal and hope it was the alpha, then fight like hell until maybe, just maybe, the pack determined this human meal wasn't worth the effort. He aimed and shot the lead animal dead on. The remainder didn't stop to grieve their lost pack mate. They raced at him up the ramp in a nanosecond.

He felt jaws grabbing his leg and slammed the stock of his weapon hard on the coyote's head. Another sunk its teeth into his calf muscle from the back. Jed twisted and fired his weapon wildly. He swung the weapon like a club at an animal that was leaping, jaws snapping at his face. They kept coming. Screaming a war cry, Jed kicked at two coyotes lunging again for his lower body. He was beginning to lose hope that he could best five coyotes when they suddenly backed off and turned.

Jed saw what he thought was a German shepherd running, head low, directly into the fray. The dog grabbed an outlying coyote by the neck, ferociously shaking until the animal folded, melting to the ground in a heap of fur. The coyote/dog encounter was worse than the most cringe-worthy National Geographic animal specials. Almost dark, Jed couldn't make sense of the next events. Fur and teeth, snarling, growling, yipping, swirling animals. In his mind he was watching from a distance, and this was all happening to someone else. He stood in shock as the unharmed coyotes scrambled and ran. Two massive, panting German shepherds were all that was left. The lettering from their collars had a strange glow that he could see even from this distance.

Dogs were another thing his parents never wanted in the house. The only thing more terrifying to Jed than a pack of six hungry coyotes was two wolf-like dogs. He thought he heard a whisper, *not hurt*, and knew he was losing his mind. If they hadn't retreated down the ramp and laid near his van, Jed would have shot them too.

Convinced a dog attack was not imminent, he went to work on the hand pad with renewed vigor. After he entered the dark building, he slammed the door and stopped to breathe until his shakes receded. The leg bites were starting to hurt. The sight of blood always made Jed a little light-headed, but he risked a glance at his torn jeans. He put a hand on the door to steady himself as the gloomy scenery surrounding him began to spin. "Bit by coyotes, brave new world," Jed mumbled. "Pull yourself together, dude. No one is going to fix it but you!"

It took a couple of hours to find a first aid kit and tend to the bites and then get the servers on-line by powering them with his battery. He uploaded the important data on a laptop he found in the center. It was fortunate that Jed had written the security protocols for the servers, or he wouldn't have had a chance in hell of retrieving the generator and battery specs.

Jed thought about sleeping on a couch for the night, wondering if his dog saviors would still be waiting. He favored his coyote-bit leg as he ambled to the drink fridge, pulled out two cherry cokes, and thought about the dogs while he drank. They had saved him. Or had they only been using the laws of the jungle, bigger is better, to secure a meal for themselves? Were humans better eating than dead coyotes? One way or another, he couldn't live in the confines of corporate headquarters. That was a guaranteed route to total insanity.

I need to go. I will give them the benefit of the doubt, since they did, after all, save my skin but, I will keep them trained in my rifle sight. If they have more nefarious motives, I think I can hit both dogs before they eat me.

After wrapping the satellite phones in bubble wrap and putting them and the laptop in a heavy garbage bag, Jed used the yellow plastic pulls to sling the ungainly cargo over his shoulder and peeked out the door. The dogs had backed up further from the van and were waiting patiently in the parking lot, watching. Jed could see two pairs of eyes reflecting moonlight as he stepped out. "This is so weird." With the rifle raised in his hands, Jed tried to reason with the animals from just outside the door. "Hey, I appreciate your help, but I have to be on my way. If you could stay very still, I will get in my vehicle and be out of your fur."

Jed moved at a snail's pace. When the dogs didn't do anything other than watch, he bolted for the van. One of them barked, but it didn't ring hostile to Jed's ears. He turned on the vehicle and shot out of the parking lot. Jed saw them running behind him in his side mirror. When his van put some distance between them, the dogs finally stopped chasing. It was curious—they seemed sort of sad.

He drove until the shortwave came to life. He heard Mike's voice. "Jed, do you read me. We need to talk."

Jed locked the doors and then pulled to the side of the road. "I'm here, Mike. What's up?"

"Quite a bit. How about you?"

"Dude, you wouldn't believe me if I told you. Let's just say it was the strangest day of my entire life. I met the LA group, which plans to time-share the city and its environs. I was attacked by coyotes and saved by dogs. Oh, and yeah, I got the plans for technology that's going to help save this sorry world. And yeah, if you've got nothing better going on, I plan to join you."

"Outstanding, Jed! You read my mind. I met another survivor today and you know her. It's Karen from the ranch broadcast."

"Karen from Tacoma! Is she a hard-ass with a sense of humor like she sounds?"

"That might be a partial description," Mike chuckled. "I'm going to try to convince her to stay in Tacoma and we can build a community here, although, I don't think it's going to be a hard sell. She finds Mathias to be off-putting, to say the least."

"Smart lady. Yeah, I can do Tacoma. Seattle would have been better but hey, Tacoma works!"

Chapter 13: A+88, What Do You Want to Do?

Karen woke early. She hurried dog feeding and exercise tasks as she wanted to spend a little time to make herself presentable. No electricity, running water, or other people around had taken a serious bite out of her grooming habits. Running a brush through her hair, Karen marveled at her new set of choppers. "No doubt about it, the canvas I have to work with now is way better."

Ready for breakfast, she strolled nonchalantly to the gate, told her crew to stay there, walked out, and tapped lightly on the screen door of Mike's RV. She could smell the steak. Her mouth started watering.

"Come in, Karen!"

"You shaved your beard!" Karen said as she stepped into the RV.

As he laughed, Karen could see a dimple in Mike's square jaw. "I never had a beard before, and it seemed to make sense in the Alaskan wilderness. To tell you the truth, I don't think it's me."

Karen's eyes shined. "Well, you look good with a beard and even better without."

Mike blushed, thanked her for the compliment, and directed her to the little bench table already set for breakfast. In a glass of water on the table, Mike had placed red and yellow spring tulips he'd plucked from the neighbor's yard. Karen noticed the back wall was reconfigured from a normal RV to accommodate an extra freezer, gun case, radios, and tools. Mike must have built the new wall of cabinets at some point during his trip.

"Wow, everything looks and smells great! I haven't had an egg or a steak in forever."

Working on omelets, Mike eyes grinned. "Make yourself comfortable. I'm almost done. And welcome to my oh-so-humble abode."

Karen sat at the table where orange juice was poured. Mike grabbed the plate with the omelets and sat across from her. "Please, help yourself."

Karen wanted to eat slowly and talk while enjoying a meal, but it was impossible. She chugged the orange juice down in one gulp and then ate a complete T-bone and five-egg omelet in under four minutes. Mike mostly watched with a small smile as Karen inhaled her meal. He thought it was cute the way her jaw worked continuously and she hummed appreciatively after each large bite.

While she was scraping every last bit off her plate, Mike asked, "Karen, have you thought about what you would like to do? I mean about going to Idaho, staying, or moving somewhere else?"

Swallowing one last time, Karen stopped and studied Mike intently. "Yes, I have given it a lot of thought. Until you showed up yesterday, I thought the only way to quit being alone was to make the trip to Idaho and see what happened. More than that, I think we owe it to everyone we loved and the human race in general to survive. I read an article once about a species survival tipping point. Essentially, when numbers get too small in a species, it reaches a tipping point where extinction is likely. They call it critically endangered. I'm fairly sure there are enough humans left, but we're so spread out that the only way to increase our chances individually and also as a species is to find survivors and create communities.

"I mean, I never realized how little I truly knew about basic things. Even finding a shortwave radio was a struggle. Groups of people together sharing information and helping each other out are our best chance. When you think about it, humans are back to the first level of Maslow's hierarchy—simple survival. Sure, we've always desired connection, but I think in the modern world we lost sight of the reason that was so important to the human condition."

"I hadn't thought about it that way, but you're exactly right. The internet probably had a lot to do with it. Don't get me wrong, I would love to have an internet right now, and I'm convinced it did more good than harm. But all that as background. Step back into the now. What do you want to do about your current situation, Karen?"

"Oh, yeah, that," Karen smiled, seeing Mike across the table studying her and realizing she had been talking around the question. "Stay here, find other people, and build a new world. What about you?"

"Ha! That sounds about right to me. We appear to be stronger physically and maybe mentally because of the change, but I doubt the needle has moved much on human nature. If we join a community with a megalomaniac as its leader, our lives could be hell just when we have an opportunity to make the world a different and better place. Maybe I'm dreaming that a better world is possible given how screwed up mankind is, but, I think it's worth giving it our best shot." With that, Mike gave a small shrug and glanced down at his plate. "I trust myself and you more than a guy on a ranch in Idaho."

Mike had a reputation as a smart guy. Don had thought the world of him and was always raving about what a great boss he was and an all-around decent person. What Karen noticed most about Mike was his humility. Sitting in front of her was a humble, accomplished man with a sense of humor, an amazing body, and the decency to ask her opinion first. It probably was dumb luck that he had landed on her doorstep. She was certain she hadn't done enough in life to warrant such good fortune, but hey, when your lottery number comes up, you take the money. Karen reminded herself to stop swooning and asked, "So do you have any ideas or thoughts specifically?"

"Actually yes. I spent some time talking to Jed on the shortwave last night after I left." He held up his hand to forestall Karen's next question. "I've been talking to Jed on a different frequency for about a month. We don't think the ranch has been listening, but we can't be sure. Jed would prefer to come to Washington with us. There's another fellow in Los Angles recruiting survivors, but Jed wasn't impressed. He wants to finish some work he's doing and says he'll join us when we he's done.

"And then there is Bangor, the submarine base. We still don't know if people not exposed to this thing will catch it. There is so much we don't know about the disease. Submarines come into the port in Bangor, so it's possible that after being at sea for extended periods they weren't exposed and can avoid ever becoming sick. If anyone survived at the military bases in the area, we might find someone who would be helpful in a newly formed group. I say we get a siren, set up a perimeter, and then see what happens."

Karen replied, "So you already decided what `we' were going to do?"

"No, I decided what I wanted to do. If, however, you were adamant about going to the ranch, I would have gone with you. I'm glad I won't have to."

"Why, Mike? Why would you go with me to the ranch if you didn't think it was a good idea?"

"I would have tried to talk you out of it," Mike said frankly.

"You didn't answer the question."

Mike gave a slightly irritated sigh. "Karen, Don was my friend! I'm sure he would have wanted me to watch out for you, at least where I could. Besides, I thought we agreed yesterday we were going to hang out. I can hardly do that with you traipsing off to the ranch alone."

Karen looked out the RV window at the empty neighborhood, and then turned back and saw Mike sitting erect, ready for some verbal sparring. "Good points, Mike. So, back to the question of finding survivors . . ." Mike interrupted, "Also, just so you know, I like the fact that you're just a little bit crazy."

Karen smirked and nodded. "You have no idea." They gazed across the small RV table into each other's eyes for a moment and then Karen glanced away, diving back into short-term planning. "We could use the dogs for security while we're looking for survivors. I've been using them effectively during my outings."

"Maybe Jack or Jill would be a good idea."

"No, all of them," Karen said emphatically. "I can't leave them alone in the event something happened to us during long hauls. We need to go to Bend to get Sylvie in four days. I would like to practice with all the dogs before that. When do you want to go to Bangor? I was hoping you could help during the pack training session this morning to get a feel for what they can do. You need to understand the commands, and they need to get used to you giving them."

Mike face showed some skepticism, but he agreed. "Alright, let's plan to go to Joint Base Lewis-McChord this afternoon—it's a quick trip—and then set off early tomorrow for Bangor.

Karen and Mike stepped out of the RV and entered the gate to find six exuberant canines impatiently awaiting their arrival. Mike was surprised and impressed with how the dogs worked together as a team. They went from being boisterous and playful to deadly serious with one command. Mike was a natural with the dogs; it wasn't long before they were all vying for his attention and approval. He could also throw the ball significantly farther than Karen, which Jack and Jill very much appreciated. Mike laughed as Tilley stole the ball, and the entire gaggle chased her around the property, the normal daily end of dog games.

Jack wasn't done. He bounded to the orchard and found his life preserver toy hiding behind a tree. With his neck and ears erect and head held high, he dragged it to Mike and laid it at his feet. "What's this?" Mike asked, confused. Jack was already crouched in a play position.

"Oh, that… It's his favorite toy. He wants you to play tug of war. He tries to get the other dogs to play with him, but only Maple will take him up on the challenge."

"A life preserver?" Mike asked. "Is there a symbolic reference here?"

"Long story," Karen smiled.

Mike heard that male voice again. *Play, man!* What could he do? Mike grabbed the preserver, and Jack clenched the rope in his wide jaw. The dogs stayed and watched the melee, barking approval at the struggle. Jack surprised Mike with a particularly quick, sharp head twist as his body pulled with strong haunches and Mike lost his grip on the preserver. Jack was smiling, his tongue hanging low while his tail beat a win signal. "Okay, Jack, you're the tug-of-war king. Next time I won't be so easy." Karen walked inside feeling a warm glow.

Joint Base Lewis-McChord was their first survivor hunt. They drove around Lakewood until they found a police car parked at a quick stop place. Mike jumped out with his tool chest. After fiddling with the siren for an hour, he managed to get the siren off the police vehicle and wired to Karen's truck.

Karen still couldn't adjust to entering a well-known location that had once been filled with people and activity, now finding it silent and empty. It was a somber reminder of everything that was different and all that was lost. Karen was unnaturally quiet as they drove on the grass around the traffic jam at the JBLM front gate.

This just sucks, Karen thought as she studied empty cars and buildings while Mike set up their first position, a half mile into JBLM proper. Mike ran the siren for three minutes and then they waited a half hour. When there was no response, they moved to two other locations and tried again. Either anyone there was fearful or, more likely, there was no one around. Even local dogs and wildlife stayed away.

"Dammit!" Mike shouted after their third try. "I know I shouldn't have gotten my hopes up, but I thought there would be somebody here".

Karen walked over to Mike standing in a deserted parking lot and lightly grabbed his arm. "Come on, Mike. Let's go home."

He looked at Karen and her own disappointment finally registered. He gently touched her cheek, "Maybe Bangor".

Chapter 14: A+89, Twins

They were loaded and ready to go to Bangor by 9. Jack, Jill, and Tilley were in the covered back of the truck, and the second-string Zoe, Raider, and Maple held the more desired positions in the extended cab. Raider was beside himself to be going on an outing and jumped up on the driver side window, the back window, and then the passenger window over and over while smiling and displaying his best attempt at a big dog bark. The more sedate Zoe sat serenely on a seat trying to remain uninvolved with Raider's machinations. Maple chewed on a large bone like his normal goofy self.

Mike rubbed his eyes as he stood outside the door of the truck waiting for Karen as she made one last trip into the house for something she'd forgotten. He shook his head, wondering how he had become part of this unusual family so quickly. As Karen shut the garage door, Mike asked, "Wait! Did you remember the kitchen sink?"

"Very funny," Karen retorted. She'd packed as if they would never return. Extra food, dog food, weapons, tools, ammunition, gas lamps, and the portable shortwave radio were but a few of the necessary items. "You can never be too prepared."

A mile away from the westbound side of the Gig Harbor Bridge, they sat frowning at a line of cars and trucks bumper to bumper across all lanes stretching as far as they could see. There was no room to maneuver through the traffic to get across.

"Wow," Karen said. "Some of these people probably didn't make it home. So terribly sad." She couldn't help but think of Don out there somewhere trying to get back to her and had to choke back a sob. "Do you think we could find a boat and then locate a truck on the other side?"

"I've got another idea that's a bit easier. The eastbound bridge might be passable. I'm going to back track and enter the highway from the exit side." Doing a careful U-turn, Mike headed back in the direction they'd arrived, drove across the overpass, and entered the left side of the freeway. He weaved around empty cars. Near the western edge of the bridge, a four-car fender bender blocked enough of the road that they couldn't get through.

Karen jumped out of the truck to see if any of the offending cars happened to have keys left in them. No such luck. Turning the truck off, Mike got out and evaluated the situation on the bridge from several angles. "I think I can push that sedan with your truck enough to make space. Why don't you and the dogs wait for me just past this accident? This bridge makes me a bit nervous."

Karen unloaded the gang and put them at heel to walk 50 yards out of the way. Then Jack did something he'd never done: broke the heel command, running to heel at Mike's side. *Help man.* Karen could see a softening in Mike's face as he reached out to rub Jack's head.

"Okay, big man, you can help me out."

Karen yelled back while smiling, "I'm warning you, they aren't very good at assisting with driving tasks!" Jack sat in the passenger seat as Mike backed up, shifted to four-wheel drive, and hit the car midway on the front bumper. With a lot of screeching and grinding, the two vehicles moved forward together until Mike had room to squeak through. The sounds of metal meeting on both sides filled the silent bridge.

Karen walked around the Ford. "Dammit, you screwed up my shiny new truck!"

Mike smiled his best lopsided grin out the driver's side window. "You were right. It was Jack's navigation! The truck has some character now, but if it doesn't please you, I'll buy you a new one as soon as we get back!" Jack barked that he concurred with Mike's assessment.

This time the whole pack made it known they wanted to sit in the cab, and Karen had to push Jack to get him off her seat. The eight of them sat together in the truck on the bridge for a few minutes enjoying the natural beauty of the Puget Sound. An eagle soared over the hanging upper girders against an azure sky. The distant view of snowcapped Olympic Mountains topped by majestic pines was set against the cold, swirling blue waters of the Sound. It was so beautiful Karen felt like weeping—for once, not for the guilt of those now gone. She was happy for this moment, that she was alive and that she was somehow, against tremendous odds, no longer alone.

Normally a half hour drive, it took longer as Mike drove carefully to avoid abandoned cars. They were talking about their favorite foods when Mike mentioned a corn soufflé dish Missy used to make. "How did you meet her, Mike?"

"Oh. I knew of her in high school in Iowa. She was three grades behind me, and I was friends with her brother. All I wanted to do was get away from that small town and not be a farmer. I saved money working at a granary during the summer and left for Iowa State in the fall. I had no idea how I was going to pay for anything more than the first semester. My roommate joined ROTC and it sounded like a good deal, so I did too. Vietnam was mostly wound down by the time I graduated.

"I was 31 when I met Missy. I went home on leave because my dad was sick and ran into her at a local bar where she was working as a waitress. She had two small kids. Her worthless husband had left to find a good construction job in Florida, never to return. We spent the week together. I loved her kids, and after six months of calling and writing, I asked her to marry me."

Karen said, "If you don't mind me asking, did you decide not to have any kids together?"

"Missy had two really difficult pregnancies and didn't want to try it again. Her kids became my kids, and they were mine in every way except genetics."

An extended silence followed. Finally Mike said, "Before you ask, no, our marriage was not a joyful union. Missy had depression problems. We tried everything: all types of drugs, counseling, different diets, and exercise plans—nothing worked. There were days when I would come home and she hadn't even gotten out of bed. She was so sensitive, and I think the world was just too harsh for her. She did what she had to do to help me with my career, so while some people may have sensed how sad she was, they didn't really know for sure. But I could never leave her, and the kids needed me. She was a good person and brave in her own way."

Mike was focused directly ahead. He seemed more wistful than sad. Karen tried to imagine this amazing, vibrant man living with a wounded and sad woman for most of his adult life. "I'm sorry, Mike."

"Don't be. I made my choices, and I had a full life. And now, the powers that be have given me another." He glanced at Karen for a just a second and then back to the road. "What about you and Don?" he asked.

"We had our problems; what Army marriage doesn't? But I loved him, our family, and the life we built."

Mike nodded at Karen's statement while keeping his eyes on the road and then asked, "I've always wondered why you left the Army and got in the demography business?"

Karen's expression morphed into a stoic mask. "My parents weren't around much when I was growing up. When I had Nathan, the last thing I wanted for him was to ever feel abandoned like I did as a child. Don and I were trying to juggle deployments, twelve-hour work days and parenting duties, and it wasn't working out. Don thought we could pull it off, but then, he wasn't the one doing most of the home stuff and the Army. It made the most sense for me to leave.

"Were you bitter about that?"

"No, not really. It was me that struggled with leaving Nathan, so I fixed my life to suit what I needed. Anyway, I wasn't exactly the stay-at-home mom type, so I got a job at the Census Bureau as an analyst. I was certain it would be deadly dull, even though it checked the box on being a stable, 8-to-5 desk job and would give me a needed break from being at home in the world of women and kids. I was so wrong about how dull it would be.

"Every day I worked on one of the world's most complex puzzles. Piecing together economic, cultural and population data to spot trends and what the future might hold got my heart racing! I know, sounds weird."

Mike shrugged his shoulders. "I don't think so. I can see the real life applications, particularly if you know what you're doing. It could save the government a whole lot of grief and money, too."

"Exactly!" Karen beamed. She spotted the entry gate for Bangor and pointed. "There it is."

Joint Base Lewis-McChord had been spooky, but this place was something else entirely. A substantial submarine industrial complex, the buildings felt haunted, all drab, gray, and square with some of the doors standing open. Grass and weeds had grown up around everything, adding to the ghost town feel of the base. Even the beautiful day could not reduce Karen's uneasiness. Driving through the maze of roads toward the water, Karen thought she saw shadows pass by windows. Mike was unfazed. *Maybe he's more used to entering dead towns than I am,* Karen thought to herself.

Mike said, "Let's try to find a headquarters building to see what we can find out."

They pulled in front a rather large building with signs and flagpoles, a military giveaway of some form of command. The pack jumped out with Karen and Mike. Jack and Jill ran to the front, and the rest of the dogs stayed to the rear of the group. Mike pushed the unlocked door open, entering a large atrium foyer with gray concrete steps surrounding each side. A wall of what used to be glass cabinets containing memorabilia faced the entry; the glass was broken and strewn over a good portion of the foyer. "Sit and stay," Karen ordered, not wanting the dogs to cut their paws on all the glass.

Overlooking the foyer was what appeared to be offices, with naval officer names and ranks adorning the front-facing glass doors. Karen and Mike headed up the right staircase with their weapons at the ready while the dogs, in a stay command, remained at the door watching, shivering, and moaning, wanting to be them. Dried blood in the form of footprints and smears on the wall didn't bode well for the chance of survivors. They entered the offices to a terrible stench and the remnants of a battle or struggle. Furniture was pushed around, desks lamps had been knocked on the floor, paper was scattered everywhere, and blood saturated the thick carpet. There were no bodies. Yet.

Mike walked to a tipped-over whiteboard and set it back on its legs. Written in descending order were the times and designations of submarine arrivals. "Karen check this out. All but three of the subs are lined out. Do you think that means they were all in except those three?"

"Could be. Hard to say. Or were all but three lost? What's more concerning is someone has written Idaho in all caps with a question mark on the back side of the white board." Karen turned the whiteboard around so Mike could see.

"What the hell?" Mike muttered. Goosebumps sprinkled Karen's arms. None of it made any sense. Still thinking about what it might mean, she stepped into the next office on the right.

"Come here, Mike," Karen shouted. He leaped to her side, and both stood immobilized in the doorway taking in the sight of a dead captain, still in his uniform, slumped in his desk chair. Blood from bullet holes had soaked into his white uniform. What remained was a crusty red, black shirt in stark contrast to his still-white pants. He certainly didn't die from the plague. Even more significant was that the time of death appeared to be only about three weeks ago.

Shaking her head from side to side with her jaws clenched, Karen asked Mike, "Who did this?! And why? It had to be a survivor that shot the Captain."

Mike surveyed the scene and walked around the desk, rifling through scattered papers to see if there was anything that made sense of the recent murder. He turned to Karen and said, "I think we should leave. Whoever did this may still be around. If that whiteboard is correct, any ships or subs that should have arrived have done so or are lost."

"The dogs are quiet, so they don't hear anything, but yeah, let's get going, check out the port area, and skedaddle home."

Hearing the door to the upstairs office open, all tails were wagging as Karen and Mike double-timed down the stairs. They burst out of the building entry very relieved to bask in the fresh air. They were almost to the truck when Mike heard a husky voice say *female* as Jack rocketed across the street to a small one-story building with Jill following in his wake. Scrambling around a dumpster on the side of the building, Jack and Jill disappeared and then a woman screamed. Running, Mike, Karen, and the rest of the team sprinted to the front of the dumpster and could hear what sounded like a girl shakily repeat, "Don't come any closer or I'll shoot. I mean it. Don't come any closer."

She obviously had a weapon and could be the killer from across the street. Karen pointed to Mike, signaling for him to go around the other side of the dumpster while Karen began talking to the girl in an easy, calm manner. "Hey, I'm Karen. You may have a gun but I doubt you are pointing it at my dogs or they would have tried to take it from you. And believe me, you don't want that. They are two of my very best friends. They won't hurt you if you just keep still. We aren't here to hurt anyone. We were just looking for survivors. What's your name?"

"Rachael. And tell your friends to stay away."

"If I call them off, will you put down your weapon and come talk to us?"

"I don't know who you are. There were some bad men here like a month ago. How do I know you aren't with them?"

Karen sighed. "I understand how afraid you are. Please, we just want to talk. Those two big dogs in front of you are the sweetest things in the world. Their names are Jack and Jill. If you put down your weapon slowly, they might lick you to death but otherwise they won't hurt you. I have four more dogs with me on this side of the dumpster: Raider, Tilley, Zoe, and a crazy puppy named Maple. I'm going to call Jack and Jill to me. Just stay still, please, for both our sakes." Karen paused and then said firmly, "Jack, Jill, heel!"

As Rachael followed the dogs' movements going around the one side of the dumpster, Mike grabbed the girl from behind from the other side with a bear hug and pulled the rifle, still slung on her shoulder, off her arm. "Why did you do that? I wasn't really going to shoot them!" Rachael said in that petulant way of which only teenagers are true masters. She scowled at Mike but couldn't hold onto anger when a wagging mass of fur crowded at her feet. Apologizing for the scare, Jack sat in front of her panting and raised his paw. She squatted her over six-foot-long body to Jack's level. "Very pleased to meet you, shiny knight," taking the offered paw and shaking vigorously. Maple licked her ear and the side of her face, Tilley smelled her hair from the back, and Raider rolled over to hopefully get a belly scratch. Rachael giggled and stood up, wiping the saliva from her forehead.

She reached out her hand to Karen and then Mike and stood uncomfortably waiting for them to make the opening overture. "I'm curious," Karen said. "What did Jack and Jill do?"

"Like, they just appeared and then surrounded me and sat down. They didn't look like they were going to bite me, but then, like, the darker one had this expression on its face that said I'm not messing around. I didn't point my gun at them or anything."

"That's a good thing," Karen said with a grin. "The darker shepherd is Jill by the way. What were you doing behind the dumpster?"

"Watching you. I heard your car while I was at the docks so came up to check it out. What are you doing here?"

"We came from Tacoma looking for survivors. Mike thought people on submarines might not be exposed to whatever thing caused this. Mostly we wanted to gather a group of people to help each other out."

"Like a town of survivors or something?"

"Exactly!"

Mike pointed to the walkie-talkie hanging from Rachael's belt. "Do you have some friends here?"

Rachael looked guilty and scared when Mike mentioned the radio. Karen could see Rachael's mind whirling, trying to decide whether to trust them. Finally Rachael took a deep breath and blurted out, "I use it to stay in contact with my twin sister. We live in base housing and take turns watching the port to see if our dad comes back. Speaking of that, I need to check in with her so she doesn't worry. I told her I thought I heard somebody."

Rachael pulled the radio off her belt and pressed the button on the top. "Katie, are you there?"

Static and a bleep sounded before a voice saying, "Of course I'm here! What's going on?"

"I found some people. They're here with me, and I think they're okay. We're coming to you. They have some awesome dogs with them."

This announcement was greeted with a long silence. In an almost whisper Katie replied, "Are you sure?"

"As sure as I can be in the land of magic and mystery! Be there in five. Over and out!" Placing the radio back on her belt, Rachael looked at Karen. "Can you fit me in your ride? Oh, never mind, like, I'll ride in the back with the dogs. We have a dog and a cat. You'll like them."

With that, Mike shook his head at the thought of more animals, and they ambled off to the truck.

It took several hours to convince Rachael and Katie to come back with them and to wait while they decided what to pack. Even in a post-apocalyptic world, sixteen-year-old girls hadn't changed much: everything they owned had some emotional significance. Most challenging was adding a street savvy Garfield-like cat to the mix of seven dogs. Thor lived up to his name. Nearly twenty pounds with claws intact, he demonstrated the use of his protection system when Tilley, previously unexposed to the feline persuasion, decided Thor might in fact be similar to a very large rabbit or squirrel. Karen had to clean red claw marks on Tillie's snout, and lesson learned: Tilley steered clear of Thor, instead watching him from the other side of the room. Half the size of the cat, Tadpole was an enthusiastic Pomeranian mix that Maple immediately found mesmerizing. The puppy commenced determinedly to lumber behind Tadpole wherever he went.

Katie was standing behind Karen as she surveyed the pictures of castles, fairies, princesses, knights, and hero cartoon characters in Rachael's room. Figurines were haphazardly placed and half covered with clothes and food trappings. "My sister has something of a hero complex," Katie said with a half-smile. "She was always after Dad to take her to one of those medieval festivals. He promised to do it this summer—not going to happen now. Come check out my room; it's a lot more sanitary."

As promised, where Rachael's room was stuffed to the brim with whimsy and mess, Katie's was organized and dealt with practical matters. A "Stop Global Warming" poster hung prominently above her bed. Karen pointed at it and said, "Mission accomplished."

Katie smiled back with a faraway look. "Yeah, I guess you're right."

"So you're into sports, I see." Karen picked up one of the trophies from her dresser and read "2nd Place All State 880." "Wow, you must be really fast."

"I am, and I trained very hard. The girl who got first graduated, so I think I would've taken it this year. We are both athletes, me and Rachael. Rachael prefers team sports, and I like to compete with myself. As you can see, we are very different."

"I can see that. You are identical twins, right?" Karen asked.

"We are. I mean, we look alike and like mostly the same foods, but where Rachael talks, I listen. She acts and I study. Sort of like that."

"I get it. I won't ever forget you are two completely different people." Karen considered what Katie had just said and thought maybe they were an example of a symbiotic relationship where each took on different roles.

Rachael burst in the room all activity and noise. "So, like, is she showing you how clean she is and complaining about how messy I am?" she asked in a good-hearted manner.

Katie shook her head and Karen answered, "No, actually she was just describing how each of you are very much individuals."

"Like, no kidding, sista! Hey, like, Mike asked me to come get you. Tilley got in the trash and, like, won't let go of some feminine hygiene stuff. He's kind of grossed out. He needs your help."

"Coming," Karen winced.

There was a lot of discussion about taking another vehicle after Rachael assured Karen that she and her sister had learner's permits and were very capable drivers. Karen did not have the heart to ask them to leave their abundance of precious possessions, including family photographs, so they found the keys to a small SUV at a neighbor's home. Karen told Rachael she could drive until they reached the bridge. Studying Karen with her eyes narrowed, a confused Rachael announced, "You don't look much older than me, but you sound like my grandma."

Katie wrote a note for their father, placing it on the now-still refrigerator with a Mariners magnet in case he returned home. Mike, uneasy with the decision, asked that she only provide a shortwave frequency, but relented after seeing the desperation in Katie's eyes. "Okay", he offered, "You can put the street name on the note. How about we drive back over here every couple of weeks to check for him?" Katie looked disappointed but nodded acceptance.

Vehicles full to the brim, Mike led with Katie as his navigator, and all the dogs shy of Tadpole and Maple. Now inseparable, they travelled with Rachael and Karen. Rachael was open and talkative and only had to be reminded twice to watch the road. She talked about their life up to the apocalypse and her parents. "My mom passed away when we were nine from breast cancer. Auntie Meagan, my dad's sister, came to live with us so there was an adult in the house when Dad was at sea. Like, we are old enough to take care of ourselves now, but Dad said the Navy had rules about kids under eighteen."

Both girls were great students and athletes; Rachael excelled at volleyball, and Katie chose running as something different than her sister. Rachael proudly announced, "We are seniors and already have a full ride to the University of Washington. Like, we were so big and ahead of the other kids in reading and math they put us ahead a grade right away." Then, remembering it was all gone, Rachael mumbled under her breath, "Well, we *did* have big plans until the world went all, like, kamikaze on us." Rachael turned to Karen. "Tell me the truth: do you think our dad will come back?"

"Watch the road, Rachael!" Karen said in a panicked tone, automatically using her right foot on an imaginary brake.

"Oh, yeah, sorry," Rachael smiled sheepishly.

Karen thought about hedging the truth but didn't think Rachael would believe her. "I don't know. The whiteboard we saw in the base headquarters seemed to indicate all the subs were in, but we can't be sure. It may be unlikely, but it's not impossible."

This time Rachael's eyes stayed focused ahead. "Yeah, that's kind of, like, what I was thinking. I miss him …" Rachael's voiced cracked as she made the simple statement. "He taught us a lot of stuff. How to shoot, ski, and play poker. He was always dragging us out for long runs and bike rides." She smiled shyly. "I think he wanted a boy and got us instead. He used to say the only thing better than a boy is two rooting tooting girls!"

Karen asked as gently as possible, "Did you guys get sick?"

"Yep, just about the same time and before Auntie Meagan. When we woke up, Auntie Meagan was dead."

"I'm really sorry, Rachael."

"Thanks. It sure isn't fair. Did you lose some family too?"

"My husband and two kids" Karen replied.

"Oh no. I'm sorry. This whole thing is so screwed up! I still can't wrap my head around it. What do you think happened?"

"I have no idea." Karen didn't feel like talking about her losses and changed the subject. "If you don't mind me asking, did you change any?"

"Yeah, it was really weird. We were both 5'10" and then we grew three more inches. My hair got a little different." Karen looked over at the green hair shimmering from the sun through the windshield. "Oh, that. I almost forgot. We were so bored one day, Katie and I found some colored hair dyes and we each did a different color. The other thing that happened is stranger. We can hear for, like, miles. It isn't just because it's so quiet. I mean "hearing bugs walking on the porch outside" kind of hearing. It took a while to tune some of it out. Katie freaked out, but she's, like, cool now."

They stopped before the bridge, changed places, and drove in companionable silence the rest of the journey.

Everyone finally settled, the nightly meeting with the ranch was almost over. Karen tuned in and made excuses; she said she had fallen asleep while reading and almost missed it entirely. Katie and Rachael busied themselves carrying their most important belongings from the vehicles and staking out a place in their new home. The dogs were clearly excited about new additions to the pack, hovering near the girls and nipping at each other to encourage the twins to play.

When Mike offered Karen a hot shower using the gas heater in the RV, she jumped at the chance. He pulled the RV inside the gate near the house for the extra protection of the fence and stayed in the house with the twins, giving Karen privacy while she showered.

Karen wore a satisfied expression as she strolled into the kitchen with a towel covering wet air. "Mike, that was absolutely wonderful! If I had thought about it, I would have borrowed an RV a long time ago and parked it here just for the luxury of a shower. Thank you!"

"Welcome. I might be able to rig a shower inside in one of the bathrooms, when we get some time, for you and our new guests," Mike added as he was studying Jack's collar. "Any idea where Jack and Jill came from? These are unusual markings on the dog tags. Even the embroidered names are unique. The thread almost has its own light."

"Not really. They showed up at my car in a commercial district in Tacoma. Police or military dogs, maybe? It doesn't make much sense. The only thing I am certain of is an expert trained them. I've never managed the level of discipline in my dogs that Jack and Jill came with."

Jack, sitting perfectly still to allow Mike to inspect his collar, said, *Hungry Jack.*

Mike nearly jumped off his chair. He frowned at Karen with a startled, perplexed scowl. "What's wrong, Mike?" Karen asked worried.

"Did you hear that?"

"Hear what?"

"Ah, uh, nothing. Never mind. I think I'm going to hit the hay. Would you mind if Jack came with me to the RV tonight? I'd like to test a theory."

Karen signaled an OK. Mike got up, gave Karen a peck on the cheek, mumbling goodnight, and left in a daze, calling Jack on the way out the door. *What was that about?* Karen wondered as she stood watching their backs until they were out of sight.

Chapter 15: A+90, The Gifts

A marine layer moved in during the night, filling outdoor spaces with a white foam curtain and drawing the small survivor group into a separate and seemingly safe world. There was so much to plan. Mike, up early, knocked lightly on Karen's bedroom door. "You up, Karen?"

"I am now. Give me a minute to put on some clothes." Karen performed one long, languid stretch and rubbed the night crumbs out of her eyes.

Mike had to stifle a laugh when Karen opened the door to let him in. She was wearing gray cut-off sweat pants at least two sizes too large and a pink t-shirt with butterflies cascading across the front. Her hair stuck out in every direction. Karen hadn't been kidding when she said that she'd cut it herself. It was a style somewhere between punk rock and apocalypse freak-out.

"Not much of a morning person, huh?" Mike asked.

"No, that be a true statement. Those O-dark-thirty physical training sessions in the Army were a misery! Also, I just can't seem to get enough sleep since the change. That happen to you?"

"A little bit. My thing is no matter how much I eat, I'm still hungry."

"I've been having some pretty bizarre dreams lately. They keep waking me up."

Mike watched Karen's face before he responded. "Bizarre how?"

"I don't know how to explain it. They are so real. Like last night the worst one was a curly-haired guy pointing a gun to my face. I could see his face clear as day."

"Are you thinking that means anything?"

Karen scowled. "I don't know! Maybe."

"Be good to know. If you figure it out or want to talk it through, I'm here. Yeah, well, different subject, the reason I barged in here is because I think we should be on the same sheet of music with Rachael and Katie. They have been through a lot. I know they look almost the same age as us, a very unusual predicament, but they're not. They're up, by the way, cooking pancakes."

'What do you think?"

Mike shrugged, "I think we should share everything we know with them. We are not their parents, and you saw how they adapted to taking care of themselves. For all our sakes, growing up quickly is an imperative in this new world."

"Hmmm," Karen grunted, "I suppose you're right. It's just the judgment thing. We look the same age as the twins but there's a significant difference. We have the experience and judgment of a lifetime of mistakes and near calamity. The fact that we're alive says we never had a total meltdown and learned from our stupidity—or that we were very lucky."

"Or some combination of both," Mike nodded. "So does that mean you agree? I don't want to be the boss or parent of anyone right now, even when it seems almost natural."

"Okay, agreed. Let's go get some coffee and eat pancakes!"

During a long breakfast they told Rachael and Katie everything about their ages, their departed families, the change, and the ranch. They concluded by asking for the girls' help to find Sylvie in Bend and offer her the chance to come to Washington even though it could be dangerous. After a long pause, Mike added, "And… I think Jack communicates with me in my head. I hear him speaking."

"Awesome!" Rachael declared. Katie giggled.

"Oh, so that explains last night's weirdness," Karen added.

"Yeah. I was afraid my cancer was back and I was hearing voices. When Jack spoke his name last night, it spooked me. Watch this." Mike stood up and stared intently at Jack. Jack jumped up and then dropped to the floor. He crawled to Mike and sat again. Then he backed up to his original position, did a 360 turn, sat, and barked twice without a word from Mike.

The ladies all applauded Jack's dog dance routine and then Jack did a deliberate dog bow, gracefully lowering his front end. Karen chimed in, "Wow, Mike, that's pretty cool. Did you tell him to take a bow too?"

"I wasn't sure if he knew that one. He uses simple words, so I don't have a feel for his actual vocabulary. So I take it that means you believe me?"

"Why shouldn't I? After all, I'm having visions in my dreams. Before we went to Bangor, I saw that whiteboard and what was on it."

Mike asked, "Why didn't you say something? That's what you were hinting at earlier."

Pained, Karen responded, "How was I to know the difference between a dream and an actual future event? I've always been very sensitive to patterns and good at predicting future events from those patterns. Also, I dream a lot—or at least I remember my dreams. But nothing had ever been that specific. I saw the whiteboard very clearly in a dream the night before we went to Bangor but thought it was my subconscious making a guess as to what could happen."

"I can see that," Katie replied. "Since we are doing truth or dare here, besides supernatural hearing I can sense people farther away than I can hear them."

All eyes turned to Katie in silence, and Mike stood up, raising his hands to the heavens. "Hallelujah, now *that* is something specific and useful! We must figure out a way to use all these things or gifts or abilities, whatever you want to call them. Katie, do you know how far out you can sense people?"

"Not really. I knew two people were on the sub base before Rachael told me she heard something and was really worried. What's that, about a mile and a half? It may be farther, but I haven't really tested it."

Rachael asked Katie why she hadn't said anything before. "It took me a while to understand. The images I saw in my head were like blips on radar. I wasn't sure until yesterday when you called me and said you had run into Karen and Mike."

Mike, excited, was already planning. "We can use Katie's ability to help find other survivors and warn us, too. We'll start testing the limits of your ability as soon as possible. And Karen, if you see something in your dreams you think is a warning, don't hold back."

"Well, gang, first: Katie and Rachael, are you in with our idea on starting a community here?" Karen asked.

Rachael stood and put her right fist to her heart. "On my honor, I offer my loyalty to your noble quest! I only wish I had super powers too."

Katie rolled her eyes at Rachael. "Yes, I'm in," she said.

"We've got work to do, so let's get at it," Mike announced.

Planning and preparation for a trip to Bend was the order of the day. Mike warmed them up on a makeshift firing range of cans tied to the top of the fence along the back edge of the property. He praised their shooting ability. Dog training consisted of two teams; Jack and Jill were separated so the other dogs could benefit from their skills.

Karen worked with Jill and Maple on the attack command using Kevlar vests tied around foam padding she had sewn together. The attack command was for protection, not for unrestrained violence as the word implied. The dogs were trained to grab the weapon arm of an assailant, disabling their ability to kill, and then bring them to the ground so they could be immobilized. Wishing Jill had learned some command other than "Attack" from her previous owner, every time Karen said the word "Attack," she shuddered as memories of what Jack had done to the crazy man edged into her consciousness.

Maple, a massive dog, thought it a wonderful game. He bulldozed into Karen, easily knocking her to the ground. Jill performed the move with more finesse, using leverage while grabbing the outside of the arm and turning like a martial arts expert. Glad she had padding in her protective suit, Karen was still bruised and slightly beat up after the session. Mike and the twins worked with Jack and Tilley and then Zoe and Raider on spotting, silent commands, and crawling.

Mike wished they had weeks and not just a few days to get ready to go to Bend. When the shit hits the fan and adrenaline surges, the best way to survive is to intuitively know what needs to be done without pausing. The Army trained soldiers until their reactions were muscle memory. Just as a gymnast doesn't think about what the body does to perform a backflip or a pianist knows the exact position of fingers on keys to make a specific sound, the soldier can be trained in the same way. It's not that soldiers don't have to think; rather, they reduce the distraction of rote reactions so the mind can focus on more important matters. Rote reactions also help to keep a soldier moving and alive when fear takes hold.

Mike had to chuckle when he realized he was thinking of two sixteen-year-old girls, a mid-60's woman who appeared much younger, and a ragtag group of household pets as soldiers. Sure, Karen had received basic Army training, but she was in transportation. It takes significantly more skill and experience to be effective in a fight. Other than Jack and Jill, and to some extent him, they were all novices. Unfortunately, they didn't have the luxury of time and needed to be ready to fight to live. Besides, there was something about each of them that assured Mike they had the right stuff.

Most curious to Mike was the reason they were already on some kind of quasi-war footing. There was certainly plenty for everyone. With so few people left, it would be several years before it became necessary to grow their own food or find a way to produce fuel. Whatever happened to them during the change, they appeared to be stronger, healthier, and perhaps smarter, with a dash of something extra. Plainly, the best chance for everyone was to cooperate, using the talents of individuals to get the best result for the whole.

And yet, some part of human nature made it hard to trust the goodwill of others. Was it learned, or embedded in DNA? A survival instinct perhaps? Or maybe, trust is difficult because in our heart of hearts, we sense in others a similar desire for power and control as our own. Isn't that desire an emotional form of the very same survival instinct? He who controls the stuff and people has the best chance to survive. And if so, is it so deeply rooted within us that man's destiny is to recreate that same chaotic and too often cruel world? Was Mike imagining a threat and thereby guaranteeing that outcome? If he could understand what had happened to them and why, maybe that would hold the key. For today, all he could do was protect what was his.

Mike shook his head and watched Karen and the twins joking and laughing about something. *Jeez*, he thought, *in just three days I'm already thinking of them as mine. I'm in pretty deep.*

Chapter 16: A+92, The Ruse

The shortwave sat on the center of the dining table. All eyes focused on Karen as she breathlessly signed into the daily ranch meeting. Mike grabbed Karen's hand, squeezed, and mouthed, "You will do fine."

The small group sat at the dining table every night discussing scenarios and options for safely picking up Sylvie if she wanted to join them. They weren't sure if the ranch and Mathias were a benign group of people gathered to make a better life or whether they were something else. Either way, they agreed it was best to avoid any confrontation with the ranch.

Karen fell squarely on the "something else" side. From the first time she heard Mathias, a sense of foreboding had always accompanied the start of the daily broadcast. She wished there was something she could point to and say, "Aha, this is why I feel this way." Other than a general impression that Mathias was a pompous ass, there was nothing specific said during the meetings that would lead anyone to believe they were other than what they appeared to be.

Mike and the girls trusted Karen's intuition about the group but still held to hope, reasoning that there was no point for the ranch to make life more difficult for the remaining survivors. When Karen raised the issue of the annotation on the whiteboard, Mike pointed out that the Gig Harbor Bridge was blocked. Ranch members would have had to travel on the bridge. The car accident on the bridge was clearly something that had occurred in the initial panic of the illness. Besides, as Mike said, "Anyone with a shortwave radio probably knew about the ranch in Idaho and could have written that on the whiteboard, even the Captain."

Regardless of the deeper psychology of the ranch, they agreed there was a decent chance Mathias or an emissary would show up to greet Sylvie and Karen at the designated meeting place. Two days earlier, Mathias had offered that option, but Karen had demurred, saying it was totally unnecessary. They all agreed it would be safer to simply avoid any physical interaction with the ranch.

Their plan was to go early and use Katie's extra sense to find Sylvie in Bend; just like them, Sylvie had never given her exact location. Testing Katie's ability to sense other people turned into fun game as Karen and Rachael drove to an undisclosed location and sat in the vehicle waiting for Katie and Mike to find them. It was also a great opportunity for the twins to practice their driving skills.

A ten-mile range was about the limit of Katie's ability. As she explained it, "It's like I see a glow at the corner of my eyes. As I get closer, it becomes more intense." The good news was the impression in her peripheral vision gave them a direction. The bad news was within a half mile the impression was diffuse, filling her view, and left only a sense that someone was near. Each time Katie found Rachael and Karen, the dogs in each vehicle gave a boisterous, and "I haven't seen you in forever!" welcome. They shouted barks of glee, hanging their heads out the vehicle window, smiling and panting. Karen watched the dog antics and turned to Rachael. "It never gets old for them, does it?"

The ranch meeting started without fanfare. Mathias addressed Karen halfway through to ask if she was ready to go. He provided a highway intersection where they could meet and be escorted to his "estate." "Mathias, Sylvie," Karen said, "I'm afraid I'm going to have to postpone for one day. There is something wrong with my truck. I keep getting an engine light. After I find some other reliable transportation, I have to reload everything."

Mathias responded, "There must be plenty of other vehicles available. That shouldn't take a whole day, should it?"

"Maybe not, but rather than have everyone waiting out in the open, I think it's better to just plan for the extra day."

Sylvie chimed in, "Hey, Karen, that's okay by me. I've waited this long; another day won't matter."

"Thanks, Sylvie, it's settled then," Karen quickly added.

"Well, hmm," Mathias relented. "Alright then. Karen, you haven't you come across any other people in your area, have you?"

Raising her eyebrows, seeing Mike and the twins with full knowledge she had omitted the mention of their presence, Karen pressed the transmit button and used her well-honed obfuscation ability. "Interesting you should ask, Mathias. About two weeks ago, I did run into another of the damaged people while looking for gas. She came out of a drug store grunting and screeching. She was filthy and huge. I jumped in my truck and pulled out, just barely getting in front of her. Can you believe she ran after my car for a half-mile? It was so pathetic I thought about going back to see . . ."

Mathias cut her off. "Well, I see. Thanks, Karen. We may need to evaluate the danger of these unfortunate individuals at a later time. We have a lot to get through, so let's move on. In the event you have problems with your travel, what is the route you are taking to Sylvie's location?" Karen's intuition suggested that he was trying to get information that she might be better off not giving.

"Thought I would drive straight down the I-5 and cut across at Eugene."

"Yes, as you might recall, Bill came through Portland and said the southbound bridge over the Columbia is passable, but you will need to take some side roads as you enter Portland."

"Good info, thanks, Mathias. I can handle it."

After apologizing to Sylvie about the delay at the end of the hour, Karen signed off.

"What do you think?" Karen asked the assembled group at the table.

Vigorously shaking her head, Rachael responded, "Good job, Karen. You are a master of deceit!"

"Thank you, I think?"

Mike said, "I think they bought it. So we leave tomorrow morning?" He waited until Karen, Katie and Rachael, each, shook their head in agreement.

Chapter 17: A+93, Sylvie

It's rare that a group of individuals departing on an adventure, much less a mission, shares equal priorities. For the four human survivors, decisions on whether to take one car or two and which, if any, of the furry friends should be left at home became emotional and at times heated. In the end, compromise meant no one won and no one lost, euphemistically called win/win in the now extinct world of organized institutions.

All the animals except the cat would be travelling in two vehicles. Mike and Tilley seemed overly satisfied with the decision to leave Thor to guard the homestead. The trade-off, to make room for the dog contingent, was a limited amount of food and water. Rachael and Katie pouted after Mike demanded that he and Karen drive. Everyone agreed when Jack dragged his life preserver toy to his assigned vehicle that the toy would not make the trip. They were only 45 minutes late from their stated departure time.

It was already warm at six in the morning. Katie and Mike were in their element, quiet during the drive, delighting in the simple observation of the world around them. They enjoyed quiet introspection time as opposed to Karen and Rachael who preferred to talk about it.

Karen wanted Rachael's perspective on how she and Katie were so different given they were identical twins. Also, talking helped avoid constant fretting about the possibility of running into someone from the ranch.

"Rachael, I can't tell you and Katie apart from a distance, other than the green and orange hair, but the minute one of you opens her mouth, I know. Why is that?

"You know that's a good question. Being an identical twin is wonderful and a big pain all rolled into one. I have a built-in friend. I mean a friend who can almost finish my thoughts. It's like a mind-meld almost."

But everyone wants to be unique and special. Hard for that to happen when you have a clone by your side. As soon as we were able, we demanded that we wear something different. Even the same outfits in different colors wasn't acceptable. And then as we started to get older, we purposefully chose different things. If I wanted to play soccer Katie would choose something else. If she saved her money, I would spend mine. It took a lot of effort on my dad's part to let us do what we wanted. But he did. He was a great dad." Rachael's voice cracked on the last statement.

"By nature, I think we are both independent and stubborn. So we stubbornly chose different things to be independent. And like, now we are different sides to the same coin. Weird, huh?"

"Not at all. Makes total sense. I think you're both delightful young ladies. And very perceptive, too."

"Aw shucks, Karen. You're kind of cool yourself for a grandma who could pass for twenty." While Karen drove, Rachael sang songs, counted overturned vehicles and accidents, and talked about imaginary battles with bad guys where she was the hero, saving all from calamity. Karen joined in on the songs she knew and kept a running tally of the crashes. The animals slept.

Their route was not the one Karen had described to Mathias; instead, they would go west from I-5 at Longview, crossing the Columbia at a smaller and hopefully less crowded bridge, and then follow the Oregon coast to Newport. Only then would they cut east to Bend. It was a longer route with the advantage of avoiding congested areas, seeing beautiful coastline, and not being a route ranch folk would guess they would travel.

At Cannon Beach, Karen radioed Mike that she was ready for a break. Concentrating on not running into stalled and empty vehicles was tiring. Besides, she wanted to see the famed Oregon Coast, Haystack Rock. They parked in the middle of town under a tree close to the beach, grabbed their weapons, and piled out of the trucks. The wind off the ocean was sandblasting Karen's face as she yelled to Mike, "Look, the tide is out! Let's go!!" Kicking off her shoes, she ran madly toward the haystack with the rifle beating against her right side as the rest of the human/dog pack dashed to be first.

With long, powerful strides Katie and Rachael passed Karen and ran jubilantly to tide pools surrounding the massive rock just offshore, home to a variety of birds and abundant marine life. Normally on a day like today there could be hundreds of visitors carefully exploring on the sand bridges between tide pools taking pictures of the massive starfish clenched against black rock or peering into the pools at sea anomies.

Today, the emptiness magnified the grandeur of now completely wild Oregon coastline. Karen could feel her neck muscles relax as she took in the expansive beach and tuned into the energy produced from the roar of waves, wind, and cacophony of sea bird calls. Mike came up behind her and gave a back, bear hug, wrapping his arms around her waist while lifting her off the ground, and whispered "Thank you" into her ear. She turned her head slightly and was just about to return the surprise by planting a kiss on his mouth when Katie screamed.

Tilley was jumping and spinning in panic with a crab she tried to smell latched onto her jowls. Mike ran over and freed Tilley from the offending crustacean while Rachael doubled over in laughter. After Tilley received adequate sympathy from the twins, she quit crying, and Rachael and Katie went into full picture taking mode. The used cell phones that were no longer communication devices to record each other and the scene around them. Karen and Mike oohed and aahed at the wildlife and put their feet in the surf, gazing out at the Pacific Ocean until Mike quietly said, "We probably need to get going."

Slogging through the sand with a stiff wind at her back, Karen noticed other dogs watching them at a distance from sea grass bluffs separating the beach from hotels and businesses. The small artsy community of Cannon Beach was known for its pet-friendly approach to commerce. In the high tourist season, there were almost as many dogs as owners walking along the sidewalks or enjoying the expansive beach. Some of them were still here. Karen thought she shouldn't ascribe human feelings to the animals, even though she did so on a regular basis, but their watching was almost wistful, as if longing for a life that had also ended for them.

Mike and Karen stopped in a restaurant tucked away from the main street and found bottled water, pickles, and canned soup. "One last stop, and then we go see if we can find Sylvie," Karen pointed to the pet store across the street. She asked the twins to help her gather as much dry dog food as they could carry. They opened the bags and left them along the sidewalk. It wasn't much, but Karen hoped it made life a little better for the abandoned dogs, at least for a time.

Stopping only once to siphon gas, the drive to Bend was quiet as the reality of possible trouble permeated the overall mood. In the center of the state and at higher elevation than coastal Oregon, the weather warmed to the mid-80s as they drew closer to the small city. Once a logging community, Bend, nestled between plateaus and mountains, had survived the downturn of the lumber industry by focusing instead on outdoor enthusiasts and people wanting to get away from the hustle and bustle. Many of its recent residents were high tech escapees who chose to toil from the comfort of a home office; one that offered soaring vistas and high tech amenities.

Katie was leaning forward and staring straight ahead. "Wait, wait, I've got something." Mike and Katie, in the lead truck slowed to give Katie a chance to get a bead on the impression in her vision. She pointed northeast and said, "Go that way." Mike drove a half-mile north and then a half-mile east for four iterations with Katie nodding. "We're getting close, Mike; turn right here." They turned onto a winding circular road in an upscale residential neighborhood. "I can't get us any closer. Someone is near. We should stop and look on foot."

Mike pulled to the side of the road, blocking a driveway filled with a Lexus and BMW. Karen stopped behind Mike. They got out of the vehicles after donning weapons and gathered at the hood of Karen's truck. Mike said, "Let's keep the same teams. Katie and I will knock on doors from this side of the street and Karen, you and . . ."

Jack began to bark and growl. The rest of the pack followed suit. In unison, the human heads swiveled as Mike yelled. "Everyone, get down!"

A long-haired woman with white blonde hair, had stepped out of the door from the house across the street onto a covered front porch. She was trying, without success to hide her body behind a support post. She wouldn't have been scary if not for the M-15 lodged in her shoulder pointing in their direction. "Who are you and what are you doing here?"

"Sylvie?" Karen yelled across the street. Jack was snarling on the ground beside Karen, his front incisors in full view. She whispered to him. "Jack stay. Calm down."

"Karen? Who are these other people?"

"If you will quit pointing that thing at us I will tell you." Sylvie hesitantly lowered the weapon. "These are my friends, Mike and the twins Rachael and Katie. The dog friends are Jack, Jill, Maple, Tilley, Zoe, Raider, and Tadpole."

Sylvie stepped down to the washed stone path but stopped at the driveway. "I thought you were coming the day after tomorrow. You scared the hell out of me!"

Karen moved across the street to Sylvie after telling the rest of the assembled crew to stay put. "I know I did, and I'm sorry. I decided to stay in Washington after I found other survivors only a week or so ago. I, er, we wanted to give you a choice of coming with us or going to the ranch. I thought I owed you at least that much after telling you I would pick you up."

Sylvie hesitated, checking out Karen first and then the gaggle on the street, finally shouldering her M-15. She stepped to Karen, wrapped her arms around her, and started laughing. "Oh, thank the Lord, and thank you, Karen! I've been so alone." After she released Karen, Sylvie stepped back and inspected her from head to foot. "My, my, my, you're stunning and so are that hunk of a man and those princesses across the street."

Karen could only mutter after noticing Sylvie's clear blue eyes, perfect complexion, full lips, and a body that men would desire and women might covet, "You aren't too bad yourself, lady. But, I didn't picture you as a blonde."

Laughing again, Sylvie said, "Oh, that. I did it! I always wanted white blonde hair, but my husband thought it was trashy so I obliged him. After he was gone and my hair started turning, I decided, what the hell, and found the strongest dye on the market. Do you like?" Sylvie said, running her hand through her hair and flipping it while batting her eyes.

"Super sexy, Sylvie; the guys will be falling all over you."

"I think you're right; now if I could just find one." Both ladies started in a fit of giggles as Mike and the girls looked on, feeling a bit left out.

Sylvie and Karen, now holding each other at the waist, turned to the others while Sylvie waved at them and said, "Come on in, you crazy kids!"

After hugging each of them and introducing herself to the animals, they filed into Sylvie's large, modern home. Photos of her lost family were everywhere, taped to the walls and glass in windows, in frames over every surface, and completely covering the refrigerator. Noticing that her guests were studying the displays, Sylvie appeared vulnerable and a little embarrassed. "Uh, well, that. When I finally realized my family was really, truly gone, I thought I would go crazy without them. I printed a lifetime of photos from my computer and surrounded myself with their memories.

"I had a lot of food and water in the house and didn't go out for almost a month except to visit their graves in the backyard. We have power outages all the time around here so my husband had a back-up generator already wired to the house. I think I woke up when I drank my last bottle of water and realized I smelled like old, damp exercise clothes. I remembered one of our neighbors played around with a shortwave, so I went and got it. When I walked back in, the photos seemed a teensy bit crazy, but I didn't have the heart to take them down. Who would know, anyway? So sit down already and tell me why you're here early after saying something else."

Rachael, Katie, and Karen sat on the sofa, and Mike and Sylvie shared a loveseat. Karen thought Sylvie was sitting awfully close to Mike. Feeling heat behind her ears, Karen couldn't help noticing how Sylvie gave Mike long looks with her baby blues and had playfully touched him on the arm and the closest leg several times. Damn, she thought to herself, this is high school shit—I'm older and wiser than that.

Karen loudly cleared her throat to get everyone's attention, especially Mike's, back to the subject at hand. She leaned forward with her elbows on her knees and explained, "As I said, Mike came to my gate and we found Katie and Rachael in Bangor just recently. We've decided to stay put and try to find others to join us. I know Mathias probably wouldn't be happy with that decision, but we need to do what's best for us. We're here to offer you the choice to come with us to Washington. Or, you can wait for someone from the ranch to pick you up. I won't assume to know what will make you happiest, Sylvie.

What I feel certain of, deep in my bones, is since the ranch has a time and place, they'll be there to meet you. Or should I say "us" if I was going with you to the ranch— which I'm not. We—and I think I can speak for my friends—only want to have the peace and freedom to start a new life of our own choosing."

"So how long do I have to decide?"

Karen looked straight into Sylvie's eyes. "Depends on how long it takes you to pack if you decide to go with us. The longer we stay here the greater the chance that the ranch people will find us. Best to avoid any misunderstandings with ranch folk if they happen to show up early. We want to be a couple hours away from Bend by the time it gets dark."

"Kind of thought that's what you were going to say," Sylvie sighed. "Are you and Mike a couple? What's the chance that these beautiful twins and I will live out our lives without finding a partner? They *do* have men on the ranch, you know."

Flabbergasted, Karen and Mike looked at each other not knowing how to answer. The twin's heads swiveled from Karen to Mike also interested in the answer. Even Jack appeared to be waiting for a response. A pregnant pause would be an ungenerous description of the intervening silence, but finally Mike spoke up. "Well, uh, we haven't had a whole lot of time to be called a couple. I was rather hoping at the appropriate time, we could explore that possibility. For now, the best description is apocalypse colleagues or team members and..."

Mike wore the cornered expression of a man about to stick his foot in his mouth and was beginning to blush so Karen saved him. "Jed has decided to join us. Other than that, I can't give any guarantees."

Mike looked like he wanted to say more when Karen gave him a small headshake. He remained silent. Sylvie got up and gazed out the front window then put her hands behind her head and stretched. She reached in her pocket, took out a piece of gum, popped it in her mouth, and started chewing vigorously. She rubbed her forehead. Jack padded up and sat beside Sylvie, glancing up at her, sensing her indecision. She reached down and patted him behind his ears and ruff, both woman and dog studying the neighborhood before them.

Karen was just about to recommend they get going when Sylvie turned around and said, "I need a few minutes alone. I'm going upstairs to my room. Why don't you find something to eat? There's peanut butter and tuna around. Do you think we'll drive straight through to your home?"

Mike answered, "No, we're going to find somewhere to stay for the evening; with all the abandoned cars on the road, it's better to drive during the day."

"Okay then. Be back in a few. I need a few minutes alone to think about it." With that she flipped her hair, turned, and headed purposefully up the stairs.

Mike scratched his head and shrugged. The twins gave each other a curious glance and then Rachael said, "Like, tuna sounds good to me."

They had just finished raiding Sylvie's pantry when she reappeared, dragging a suitcase down the stairs. "Everyone full? Better the devil you know I guess," she chuckled.

Mike and Karen shared a look and Mike added, "I'm not at all clear on why I'm so often associated with the devil."

"My stuff is packed. I'm going to say goodbye in the backyard, and then I'll be ready to leave."

Sylvie attempted to steer her suitcase to the car Mike was driving. Rachael noticed the strange expression on Karen's face and jumped in. "Sylvie ride with us! Like, Karen has told me about your refashioned garment business. I want to hear all about it." Sylvie gave a half-hearted shrug and climbed in the back of Karen's vehicle, gently pushing Zoe out of the way to make space.

With dry eyes, Sylvie stared out the window, quietly watching her home until Karen pulled out of the driveway. They stopped in a small town on the east side of I-5 and found a deserted house with an empty garage to park the trucks and sleep for the evening.

In the moonlight, Mike and Karen sat on their borrowed home's deck, drinking warm beers the previous owners had graciously left for their arrival. They clinked their beers together. Mike said, "That went okay. I don't think we're out of the woods yet, but I'm happy we're away from Bend without incident."

Karen nodded and continued to look up at the star filled sky. "They're beautiful, you know. It's amazing. Those stars were always out there—I just couldn't see them against all the background lights with my aging vision. Do you think we need youth to really see the wonder of life?"

"No. I suppose the better vision and hearing helps. I think it's more about the ability to tune out distractions and responsibility and our personal worries. Like you said, it was always there. We simply didn't often take the time to look. What's up? You seem quiet and reflective tonight.

"Nothing really."

"Karen, I may not have a talent for saying the right thing at the right time but, I have lived long enough to understand when a woman says *nothing really* what she means is *something really*."

Karen chuckled and met Mike's gaze. "Just thinking about what you said to Sylvie's question earlier."

"Did I screw it up?"

"No, you didn't. I want to take you up on your offer to *explore our relationship at the appropriate time*. I do. But today when Sylvie was fawning all over you, I got jealous and I haven't had that feeling, not really, in a very long time. At first, I thought I was just being small and insecure. Then when I looked at it tonight, I realized it was unmitigated fear. I've lost everything important to me, three times: my parents, my grandfather, and then my husband and kids. If I care about you and the twins, will I lose you too? How much loss can a woman withstand until her soul shatters into a thousand different pieces?"

Mike grabbed Karen's hand and leaned in front of her to see her face. "First, she wasn't fawning and secondly, I don't know how much any given person can lose before it becomes too much."

"She was fawning."

"If you say so, but let me finish. I've watched you with the dogs and the girls, and it's too late, Karen. You care already. I'm hopeful about the way you feel about me even though I can't be totally objective. But I think I get you. You won't shatter into a million pieces, not ever. You're like the energizer bunny."

Tears started to roll down her cheeks even as Karen laughed. "You have such a way with words Mike. And thank you."

"I'm glad you approve. And one other thing, strength isn't about how macho you are or whether you can harden yourself to loss. Real strength of character is continuing to love deeply even knowing it can all be gone in an instant."

She saw his sincere, frank expression as he leaned in further to kiss her tears and then her mouth. She wrapped her arms around his back savoring his smell and scratchy day old whiskers.

Most of the dog pack was snoring nearby on the deck. As one, they sat up alert when Sylvie came through the door to the deck. "Oh, oh, I'm sorry. Bad timing. I'll just drink my beer in my room."

Mike stumbled back to his chair and Karen, a little breathless said, "Sylvie, please join us."

"If you mean join us as in *join us*, I would love to. Somehow, I don't think that's what you meant, so I will take my leave. You two just carry on. See you in the morning." The door whooshed shut and Karen and Mike began a healing belly laugh session.

"Look at us Mike," Karen said holding her stomach. "Like a couple of embarrassed teenagers caught necking by their parents."

"I know, feels pretty great, huh."

"What we should be doing is talking about how to build our new community."

"Oh, hmmm, you mean like how to build a community from the ground up in the most efficient way, since we won't have many people? What can we grow, do we need livestock, how we'll govern ourselves so everyone has a say, how we'll protect ourselves… that sort of thing? Don't worry, we'll have time."

Mike gave Karen another soft kiss and said, "Long day tomorrow, we'd better get some rest."

Chapter 18: A+94, Gas Station

A brighter mood surrounded the band of survivors. An early morning marine layer pushed inward from the coast, and enveloped their journey in a gauzy shroud, lending an illusion of safety. Karen, in the lead, spent the morning trying to pay attention to the road while listening as Sylvie regaled them with funny stories of her hippie parents and a brief stint as an exotic dancer.

"I had five older brothers and came along when my mother was 42. My parents opened an outdoor shop, renting equipment and that sort of thing at the Gorge before the windsurfing craze. Then all those young men and women heard about the wind on the Columbia River, well, my folks did quite well for hippies. My brothers worked at the shop, but I didn't want to. My parents got tough on me and cut me off financially when I decided attending college wasn't part of my plan. Just because I was a good student didn't mean I wanted to sit behind a desk somewhere working my ass off. Sort of weird for hippies to force college on someone, don't you think?

"I needed money, so the exotic dancer stint gave me plenty of cash. I was sick of my parents and older brothers trying to run my life. They were really pissed about the dancing. Anyway, I met my husband Todd at the Diva Retreat. He was loaded and they liked him pretty well, so it all worked out." Sylvie gave a huge, boisterous laugh. "Do you know what my real name is?"

"Like, it isn't Sylvie?" Rachael responded.

"No, it's actually Sunshine. Can you believe that shit? What were my parents thinking? Probably so high when my mom conceived me they thought that was a good idea. I changed it legally as soon as I could. At eight, I told them never to call me Sunshine again. They tried some derivatives, but nothing came out right, and finally I consented to Sylvie. It sounded cute."

Karen was beginning to feel sorry for Sylvie's parents. They sounded like good, hardworking people who only wanted the best for their children. It wasn't surprising that Sylvie's parents had wanted their bright daughter to attend college when they had not. Most parents know all too well the mistakes or missed chances in their own lives and hope to steer their kids in a different direction. Sylvie seemed not to appreciate, or even acknowledge, her parent's love. *Boo-hoo*, Karen thought, *your parents were protective, wanted you to go to college and didn't want you to work at a strip club.* Her in-head counselor reminded Karen that she didn't know about Sylvie's life and was probably being small because of Mike. *Yeah, well, even so, Sylvie's old enough to know better. She sounds like a spoiled brat to me.*

They crossed the Columbia at the same Longview Bridge, drove through town, and then turned back onto the I-5 for the final leg of the trip. The sun filtered through the clouds as their journey took them inland from the coast.

"Hey, where are we anyway?" Sylvie asked. "I'm hungry and have to pee."

Karen, still watching the road, said, "We're about 20 miles north of Longview."

"There's a good truck stop a few miles up ahead. Could you stop there? I really have to go."

"Sure Sylvie. Rachael call Mike and let him know where to stop."

Mike heard the radio bleats and Katie picked up. "Hey, sista and Mr. Mike, we need to stop. Karen says that truck stop just ahead should be a good place."

"Why do you call me Sista?" Katie asked, shook her head and rolled her eyes. "I'm going to make up a name for you too, as soon as I can think of one. We read you and are slowing our rate of approach."

As they crested the exit ramp, a full and horrific view of a blackened truck stop came into focus. Trucks, cars, pumps, and a restaurant had been blown up or burned to the ground, with bits of metal and unidentifiable debris strewn across the blacktop. A small, untouched, and abandoned gas station sat forlornly across the street; undoubtedly the owners or caretakers had left in fear of the spread of fire and never returned. Pulling both vehicles into the gas station, Karen jumped out of the truck and walked to Mike's window. There was a sooty, chemical smell permeating the air, and Karen wrinkled her nose as she said, "Damn, wonder how this happened. I have plenty of gas to make it the rest of the way but Sylvie's got to go."

"I have less than an eighth of a tank," Mike replied. He looked at the winding road heading eastward from where they sat. "I'm betting this station has some food in there. Why don't you guys sit tight and scavenge what you can from the station? I'm going to drive down that road a piece and see if I can find a vehicle with some gas to siphon." Karen nodded and considered the desolate area with a concerned expression. "Don't worry. It shouldn't take long. Just keep your radio and weapons with you. I'll be back before you know it." He started the truck and took off while Karen stood watching him until he was out of sight.

The gas station reeked of a hurried departure since old, moldy hot dogs were lying still in the metal grooves where normally they would be turning and roasting to a golden brown. With a normal complement of candy and crunchy snacks, Rachael breathlessly remarked, "I hope they have trash bags somewhere because I'm taking some of this back with me! Oh my God, there are even some Monster drinks in the cooler!"

Karen laughed and pointed. "Hey, they have Twinkies and Sno Balls. I heard they had sold the rights to someone but I haven't seen any for a long time. I love Sno Balls! Save a trash bag for me, Rachael!" After placing their favorite high-calorie snacks and beverages in reusable shopping bags sold for only $2.99, they sat waiting for Mike at a small table behind the cashier station slurping and crunching like small children with their cache of goodies at Halloween. Even the dogs scored a few potato chips and a dish of bottled water.

Karen plucked the bathroom key hanging in front of the counter from its hook and said, "I have some business to attend to—be right back."

"It's nasty in there," Sylvie mumbled, her mouth full of cheddar crackers. "Might want to use the bushes."

Sylvie was right. The outside door led to a bathroom so offensive she decided the bushes behind the station were a better option. She grabbed toilet paper from inside the restroom and walked a few yards into the vegetation. As she was pulling up her pants she heard the clack of a rifle being pumped behind her. Adrenaline flooded her system so quickly she almost fell over as her heart pounded hard in her chest.

"Drop your weapon and turn around very slowly if you want to live," said a deep male voice. She shakily laid her rifle on the ground and turned around. He was like everyone else in this new land—tall, handsome, and strong. His curly hair and fair complexion gave him an almost angelic countenance, if not for the very cold blue eyes. "You must be Karen. I am Brian David, but you can call me Dave. No need to make this an ugly situation. I am here to escort you to the ranch."

Oh holy hell, it's the man from my dream. Taking a deep breath to steady herself, she almost laughed thinking how useless prescient dreams were if she couldn't connect them to actual events or times. With as much confidence as she could muster, Karen said, "I changed my mind about joining your group. Why don't you just put down that weapon and we can talk about it?"

"Nice try, Ms. Karen." He came around behind her and pointed the gun at her head. "We need to go get your friends. I'm really looking forward to meeting them." Karen noticed another man standing watch near a tree at the edge of the parking lot. "That's Bill. Now move along."

Karen walked slowly with Dave behind her. As she entered the station, Sylvie and Rachael glanced at the door and Maple growled a serious warning, moving around the counter so quickly Karen did not have time to say anything. As he jumped for Dave's weapon arm, Tilley leaped from the other direction. Karen turned with an elbow up to hit Dave's windpipe but missed. Maple had already dragged Dave to the ground. Karen pulled the rifle out of Dave's hands and pointed it at his head. "Release!" Karen screamed. Both dogs, panting with bloody snouts, obeyed her command.

Keeping her eyes on Dave, she glanced at the man by the tree. She doubted he could see inside because of the reflection of sun on the tinted exterior glass doors. "Rachael, go see if there is a back exit," Karen ordered.

Before Rachael could move, Sylvie pulled a Glock from her side holster and said, "Not so fast, Rachael." Karen backed up slowly while the dogs sat watching Dave. She looked over her shoulder and saw Sylvie pointing a weapon at Rachael. "Karen, it's over. We're going to the ranch. Drop your weapon or, as much as I hate to do it, I will shoot Rachael in the knee. And, get your dogs under control or I swear, I'll shoot them too."

Karen was more pissed than scared. "Maple, Tilley, heel!" After they came to her side, she threw her weapon to the ground and yelled, "Shit, Sylvie, how can a place that sends someone to kidnap people be a good place?"

"Calm down, Karen, or someone is going to get hurt. Dave, get up. I will tend to your arms later, but first put the handcuffs on Karen and Rachael." Dave did as told, blood dripping from his arms while Maple and Tilley eyed his every move.

"I say we shoot these beasts, Sylvie," he said.

"No need for that. They were just doing as they were trained to do. I keep telling Mathias that dogs are handy to have around, but he won't listen. Karen, tell them to stay and we'll leave them here. Mike will find them. Now, we need to get going quick because Mike will be back any time. Even though he seems mild mannered, there's something about him that screams danger to me. Where are you parked, Dave?"

"We need to go after this Mike, too," Dave huffed. "We don't need them following us later and making trouble. I'll take care of him."

Karen and Rachael looked fearfully at each other. Karen spoke up. "They don't have any idea where the ranch is located. Idaho is a big place. Why take the chance of this all going bad? You have us."

Sylvie studied Karen, wondering if she was up to something. She tilted her head, deciding Karen was simply trying to protect Mike and Katie. "She's right, Dave. We have what we came for. By the time they find the ranch, *if* they find it, we'll have enough people and it won't matter. You have our transportation ready, right?"

"Just on the exit ramp out of sight. The helicopter is down the road," Dave said.

"Then let's get moving. No need for this to get ugly."

Dave might not have agreed if his arms weren't bloody and hurting. He reluctantly nodded. "We'll probably regret this later."

Sylvie and Dave pushed Karen and Rachael out the door. The dogs, frantically whining, were left inside the gas station. Bill helped push an enraged Karen along to the car.

Chapter 19: Mike and Katie

Mike and Katie drove along a tree-lined road for a couple of miles before they saw any homes or businesses. Katie was scouting to the left and right for easily accessible older vehicles to siphon gas.

"There's one to your right, Mike!" Katie pointed. Mike pulled down a gravel driveway alongside a red SUV, stopped the truck, and reached into the backseat for the siphon gear.

"Just hang in the truck, guys," Mike said. "I want to get back as quick as possible."

He used a crowbar to pry open the flush gas gap and inserted the siphon tube. The SUV was almost empty. Mike deliberately gathered his crowbar and siphon gear and stepped back into the truck. "Next victim," he called to Katie.

Two vehicles later and a mile down the road, Mike had all the gas he needed for the remaining 80 miles of their trip. As he pulled onto the road, the tire warning light flashed on, just as the vehicle tugged right. Mike heard a *thunk* sound on his right front side. Groaning, he stopped, got out, and walked around the vehicle. The front right tire was nearly flat. Examining the rest of the tires, it appeared the back left was low as well.

Katie was leaning out of her open window with a dog nose by her ear. "We have a flat tire?" she asked.

"Yep, probably ran over some debris near the truck stop fire. I have to change the front tire. The back one looks low too. Hopefully it's a slow leak, because I only have one spare. I'm going to change the front and then go back and get everyone else before we look for another tire. Just stay in the truck, and I'll do this as fast as I can. Could you hand me the owner's manual in the glove compartment?" Katie nodded and rifled through old registrations, insurance cards, maintenance receipts, and food wrappers left during their trip.

"I can't find it, Mike," she said in a frustrated tone. He opened her door, leaned in, and confirmed Katie's assessment.

Jack and Jill were trying to climb out through the truck windows. Katie clicked the window button until they were partially up.

"Just need to find the jack, and I'm not certain where the manufacturer stores it in this vehicle," Mike said more to himself than anyone else. Before leaving Washington, Mike had removed the spare tire bracketed under the truck and put it in the truck bed for just this eventuality; he had, however, left the better jack at home because of space constraints.

After moving around some of their abundant travel supplies and pushing helpful dog snouts out of his way, he found the jack in a back, side panel. He was just about to place the jack in the slot when Katie began screaming. Pulling the rifle off his shoulder and into a shooting position, Mike stood up, turned around and noticed that the dogs weren't barking.

"Mike, I feel something! More than one!!" Katie wailed.

"Where, Katie? Where do you feel them?"

"The gas station…" she said, pointing straight ahead.

Mike chewed on his lower lip and calmed his voice. "Don't worry, Katie, this won't take long." Swallowing his own panic, Mike focused on the job at hand. He quickly and deftly lifted the truck, threw the old tire out of his way, and hefted the spare while grabbing the lug wrench. Mike madly pumped the jack to lower the truck to the ground, tightened the nuts again and grabbed the tools, running to the driver side while throwing everything in the back seat. Even knowing there was a leak in the back tire, Mike drove as fast as he could the three miles to the station with little regard for their safety. Katie sat stoically clenching her hands, tears leaking out the sides of her eyes.

The second the gas station came into view, Mike knew something was wrong. He pulled directly in front of the door and bounded from the truck. Tilley and Maple were crying and jumping at the glass door; their paws bloody. Blood streaks coated the inside of the glass. Mike could feel bile creep up the back of his throat as he entered to see if the women were hurt.

As he swung the door open, Tilley and Maple raced around him toward the highway and Katie, already out of the truck, ran after them. Tadpole and Zoe were hiding behind a snack display, frightened but still wagging their tails. Tadpole jumped, begging for Mike to pick him up. He grabbed the small dog while moving into the service area. Mike made short work of the search. Carrying Tadpole in one arm like a football and Raider clinging to his heels, he jumped back in the truck. Katie was yelling and pointing from the side of the road near the exit overpass.

Mike slammed the truck into gear and swung in beside Katie. "Get in!" he yelled and floored the gas at the exit ramp, trying to increase his speed as he merged onto the highway. They passed Maple and Tilley heading in the same direction, running along on the grassy shoulder, and caught sight of a vehicle cresting a high area before it went out of sight. Mike ignored the sound of the left rear tire, instead concentrating on moving around any obstacles in the road. He pushed the accelerator to almost 90 before he heard the beating of a helicopter.

Katie pointed a shaky finger up and said, "That's them."

"Katie, this is important. Think, think about what direction they're heading."

She closed her eyes, hesitated for a moment, and then pointed. Mike knew immediately she pointed to the southwest toward Idaho and helplessly slowed to a stop.

Katie's face, devastated and in shock, was drained of color as Mike leaned over and grabbed her face with strong and tender hands. "Listen to me, Katie. Are you listening to me?" She nodded her head as Mike met her eyes with an intensity that almost scared her. "We will get them back. There…is… NO…question about that. I promise you—and I keep my promises—we will find them and bring them home." Realizing that Katie needed his strength, Mike inhaled deeply to keep the emotional release at bay. "Right now, what we must do is walk back to the other truck and pick up Tilley and Maple on the way. I can't go any farther on this flat tire. Grab some water and your weapons."

"Then will we go get them?" Katie asked in a voice so young it nearly broke Mike's heart.

"Not yet, Katie. We need a plan and some help." Katie wordlessly reached over and hugged Mike, trembling with fear and resignation. He patted her on the back, letting her vent some of the pain, and finally whispered, "We need to get going."

Katie opened the door to the truck. Jack and Jill pushed around Katie and leapt to the road, shooting down the highway and running like guided missiles. She was just able to catch Raider as he was preparing to follow Jack and Jill. Mike turned just in time to see the running dogs and barely caught Jill in a body block, grabbing her by the collar. She squirmed and whined.

Mike yelled in a loud, hoarse scream, "Jack, Come!!"

It was enough to make Jack hesitate. He stopped and turned to look at Mike. Even from a distance, Mike saw sorrow in the dog's eyes. Jack swung his regal head back in the direction of Karen's kidnappers. He sniffed the air and tried to divine where she had gone.

Pleading now, "Jack, we'll get her back. Come!"

One last time, Jack glanced at Mike. Mike knew, without a doubt, that the dog would move heaven and earth and give his life if he had to, to find Karen. Jack said, *Duty* and began to run. Mike watched as Jack ran for a hundred yards on the eastern shoulder, and then cut across the trimmed gully along the side of the road before disappearing into the forest.

Jill continued to cry in a warbling mewl. "Katie, get a lead for me. She'll take off too if I let her go."

The corners of Katie's mouth turned down. She pushed back the agitated dogs that were trying to escape the captivity of the truck and dug under her seat for a chain. She begged as she handed Mike the lead. "We have to go get him Mike, now! Before he's too far away!" Right now, please…" Mike didn't answer. He studied the landscape, his face a steel mask. "We'll never catch him, Katie. He's going to try to find Karen and there is nothing we can do about it."

"Can he do that?"

"I have absolutely no idea. I hope so."

Katie dropped to the pavement, sobbing. Mike waited as she cried.

Neither man nor dog had a further desire to say anything. Tilley and Maple were loping in their direction. Two loyal companions, the fastest long-distance land mammals on the face of the earth, had arrived to join them in their grief. The first word spoken was by Jill when they were almost back to the exit ramp. Mike heard another voice, this time a feminine one. *Jill talks, too.*

Chapter 20: A+94, Ranch Style Welcome

Enraged, Karen sat ramrod straight staring at one captor and the next. She saved her most penetrating appraisal for Sylvie, who refused to meet her eyes. Bill reached over to Karen and put a water bottle by her lips. She glared at him and then took a sip. This helicopter was not nearly as loud as the green birds in Karen's Army experience. The whining sound from the rotors had the effect of making her drowsy when dammit, she wanted to stay angry and alert in case an escape attempt became possible. It was counterintuitive, but Karen knew that sometimes in extreme stress, the body's response is to sleep and completely withdraw. That was happening to her now and she had to fight it. Rachael, clearly in shock, leaned against her harness straps, blinking to hold back tears.

Karen couldn't see anything until they swung around preparing to land. She noticed low hills, dry grass, and a mixture of pines and deciduous trees frosting higher elevations. The throbbing and whine increased until a small bump, like a fast elevator coming to a stop, signaled their landing in Idaho. Still handcuffed with plastic ties that were starting to cut into their wrists, Karen and Rachael were prodded out of the helicopter and into a van awaiting their arrival.

The driver looked over her shoulder to study the two new survivors. Sylvie, pushing herself into the passenger seat, said, "The gorgeous piece of womanhood is Karen, and the gazelle-like creature is Rachael. Drop me off at the awareness center and then take Karen to the stables and Rachael to the guest house. Bill will stay with you to help out, but I have to get Dave some medical attention right away. Their dogs attacked him. Karen and Rachael, meet Mabel. Mathias found her wandering around in an old folks' home. Hard to believe, but she is 98 years old."

"You called them, Sylvie, didn't you, when you went upstairs. How could you?" Karen hissed to Sylvie.

"Just get over yourself, Karen. Like I said, this is a good place. Did you think I would wait forever for you to show up and escort me to the ranch? Bill came and got me three weeks ago in the helicopter while you were making up your confused mind. Mathias thought you would feel more comfortable coming if you had someone along. I didn't expect you to bring the others. I mean, you lied to us, too! So just spare me the theatrics."

On the opposite side of the van, Karen viewed Mabel's profile and the disgusted scowl she gave Sylvie. Mabel had a freckled, pert little nose and wide-set, kind brown eyes; amazingly, she looked, like everyone else, to be in her early 20s. Nothing more was said until Sylvie and Dave jumped out at a one-story white ranch house, fronted end to end with a wide covered porch. Rocking chairs and a hanging swing chair gave the picturesque ranch home the perfect balance of charm and function.

"Bill, does it have to be like this?" Mabel asked.

"Be quiet, Mabel," he returned.

The van drove over a combination of crumbling blacktop and gravel to the guest house, once a place where migrant workers or farmhands had stayed to help during busy months. A low-slung metal roof sat on a wood building. "This is your stop, dear," Mabel said to Rachael. "I will bring you a nice warm meal later, so just take some time and rest."

Rachael turned to look at Karen, eyes wide in indignation and fear. "We want to stay together!" she demanded. Bill sat in the middle between the two ladies and tried to calm her, but Rachael would have none of it. Using her strong legs, she started kicking Bill and head butted him in the chest. He reached around Rachael, opened the sliding door, and pushed Rachael out to the ground. While Rachael scrambled to get up from the hard packed dirt, Karen scooted on the seat to the open door, pushing Bill out after Rachael. She yelled, "Don't you dare hurt her, you asshole!"

Bill rolled over, jumped up, stepped back, and pointed a taser at Rachael, who was now preparing to charge him with her head as a battering ram. "Enough!" Bill shouted.

Realizing the futility of fighting this battle, Karen forcefully said, "She's only sixteen! For God's sake, let me give her a hug before you separate us so she'll know I will be alright." With her eyes narrowed, Karen stared at Bill, daring him to contradict her or do anything more to Rachael.

Relenting, Bill nodded, "Just don't try anything."

Karen slid out of the van, stepped up to Rachael, and with her hands still behind her back, stood on her toes, leaning her head next to Rachael's beautiful cheek, and gave her a kiss while whispering, "Don't worry, they'll come for us. Be ready."

Waiting in the van with Mabel, Karen tried to talk to with her. "How did you end up here, Mabel?"

"Sylvie had it about right, except the wandering around part. There wasn't anyone to care for me after I fell and broke my hip two years ago. My granddaughter found a nice old folks home in Salt Lake City for me to stay. One of my daughters was killed in an auto accident in '92, and my son passed a few years ago from cancer, so all I have—well, I mean *had* left is some grandbabies who didn't have the time or wherewithal to be bothered by an old fossil like me.

"You can imagine my surprise when I woke up from the sickness. I just hung around at the empty old folks' home, enjoying the peace and quiet and the fact that my legs worked again." Mabel turned and beamed at Karen. "It felt so good to be released from that decrepit body. I was sitting out front in a lawn chair enjoying the sunshine when Mathias drove by and spied me. He stopped, turned on the charm, and I got in his car and came with him. Me and Carlotta were the first ones here. You'll meet Carlotta later. Mean as a snake, that one. If I had known who she was at the time, I probably would have told Mathias to keep on moving down the road."

"And you are—were—98 years old?" Karen asked.

"Born and raised in the hills of Tennessee. They called us hillbillies, but not like that ridiculous TV show. We weren't stupid, just poor!"

Karen could tell Mabel had a lot more to say, but she quit talking and turned her head back to the front when she saw Bill exiting the guest house. He didn't look happy. Yanking the passenger door open, he ordered Mabel to get to the stables. Turning and pointing at Karen, he said, "And if you give me any trouble I will tase you—no question."

The stable was a beautifully renovated red brick building with finished pine woodwork and arched ceiling. There were no horses Karen could see as they moved to the middle to what would be Karen's stall.

Someone had fashioned cages out of several of the stalls using green metal fencing material welded to steel supports. It had a ceiling to make it impossible to climb out. Karen's anger simmered as she saw a cot, chair, portable toilet, and a bucket of water in the corner. As the swinging gate clanged shut, locking her inside, she shouted, "You know this is truly fucked up! When am I going to meet the great and wonderful Mathias?"

In a hushed voice, Mabel said, "I will bring you some food later." Then they were gone.

Chapter 21: A+ 96, Home Base

Mike and Katie sat on one side of the dining table, the shortwave in front of them. Mike pressed the transmit button on the microphone, excited to finally reach Jed. "Hey, buddy, I was getting worried. I've been trying to reach you for a couple of days."

"Mike, what's up? I've been busy getting ready to come your way."

"I'm glad to hear that, but first, we have a big problem. The ranch kidnapped Karen, Rachael, and Sylvie when we were driving back from Bend." Mike's voice caught as he said Karen's name.

"NO!! How did it happen?! Damn, I'm so sorry, man. I knew that guy Mathias was an asshole."

"It's a long story. They got them at a gas station when I left to look for fuel."

"But how did they find you or even know you were there? Are you sure it was the ranch?"

Mike paused and then said, "I've thought about that a lot. My instincts tell me Sylvie was in on it. She was all alone in Bend and not that far from Idaho. The way they got in and out so quickly with a car and then a helicopter tells me it was planned."

Jed responded, "But it could have been, like, anybody. I don't want to frighten you more than you already are, but there may be other groups clandestinely listening to the ranch's New Age-y broadcast."

"It's possible, but I don't believe it. The helicopter headed in the right direction. I don't want to tell you in the open how we, Katie and I, know the bird was heading to Idaho, but we're pretty sure. Jed, will you consider coming to Washington right away? We're making a plan to get them back—it would sure be great to have your help."

"Whew," Jed said quietly. "You know I'm a tech nerd, right? I never even used a weapon until the stuff hit the fan."

"By the time you arrive, we'll have a plan. It's the tech support where I was thinking you could lend a hand. Please, Jed, I know it's asking a lot given you don't even really know us. "

Katie chimed in, "Please! They have my sister."

Katie and Mike gave Jed some time to think. "Well, as it turns out, other than some IT fellows in foreign lands, you are the only people I feel like I can trust. So yeah, I'm in. It will probably take at least two days on the road. How will I find you?"

"We will find you, "Mike said as he nodded at Katie. "Just let us know the day and stop anywhere in Tacoma."

Jed laughed as he said, "Alrighty then!"

Mike signed off and turned to Katie, "Tonight I plan to crash the ranch's party."

Better collect the dogs, Katie said to herself, and yelled out the door for the fur children to come in for dinner. Since the kidnapping, the dogs had spent an inordinate amount of time sitting and pacing at the gate, waiting for Karen, Rachael, and Jack's return. Tilley, Jill, and Raider appeared to be the most crestfallen; sleeping under a tree with some shade and a good view of the road, they bounded for the gate at every noise or smell.

Katie was glad for Mike's total conviction that they would find them. It helped her to keep a positive focus. Rachael was her mouthpiece, her other half. Always together, they'd often fantasized about finding careers and husbands, living separate lives, but they knew they would never, *could* never, be completely separate. After losing their mom and dad, the tendrils that bound them to each other had multiplied, winding together their individual selves into a strengthened whole. Katie could not lose Rachael.

Katie watched the animals eating in their designated places, seven food bowls ranging in size and shape to fit its owner. Their devotion to each other and their human family was so uncomplicated, so true, it filled her with courage, something she would surely need in the coming days. Even the cat, now surrounded by canines, was getting into the groove.

Mike sat still, waiting at the table for an opportunity to speak to Mathias, looking angry, focused, and determined. Katie didn't know what he was going to say. They'd talked earlier about warning anyone listening of the real intentions of the group. Whatever happened, she couldn't wait to out that pile of crap.

Mathias's dulcet voice signaled the start of their broadcast as Mike waved Katie over.

"Welcome, everyone. So glad you could join us this evening. We have quite a bit of business to cover, so I ask your forbearance while I deviate from our normal proceedings. I have tried to the utmost of my ability to offer a sanctuary, a safe place where the pitiful few survivors could live and work in a community of harmony. I wish it were not so, but the world is still not a safe place. Even now, when we need each other more than ever before, there are nefarious individuals afoot seeking only to do us harm. As many of you know, Karen and Sylvie decided to join us. Unfortunately, we were unaware that an angry and powerful man found Karen at her home and forced her to be his slave. He also coerced Karen to take part in a plot to kidnap Sylvie. If not for Sylvie's quick thinking and her growing relationship with me, this diabolical scheme would have succeeded. I am proud to say I was able to marshal the honest, hardworking men and women of the ranch to foil this attempt and successfully rescue these lovely women from their captor.

"My concern about the viability of the ranch has become paramount. Any of those listening who wish to join us must do so immediately. It is with a heavy heart that I must shut my doors to guarantee the safety of the innocent survivors who have sought my protection. I want to thank each of you for your friendship to the ranch and your participation in our effort to make the world a more enlightened place. Is there anyone who would like to make final plans to join us?"

Katie was speechless as she witnessed Mike, by force of will, unclench his fists and become deadly calm. He put the mic to his mouth, whistled, and said, "I've heard some tall tales before, but that one, *that one*, Mathias, was an Academy Award-winning performance. Listen up, sports fans, and use your good judgment to decide who is telling the truth. It was Mathias and his thugs who kidnapped my partner Karen and the twin sister of my friend Katie halfway between Portland and Tacoma. My guess is Mathias is a narcissistic control freak who believes his motives are pure and the rest of the world just doesn't get it. He will lure you in by his promises of a good life and will take your freedom, dignity, and individuality to use for his own purposes. He will use every trick in the book to bend you into someone you never wanted to be, and you will thank him along the way because he tells you what you most want to hear, no matter that a voice inside tells you it isn't true. By the time you figure out you have been hoodwinked, you will be in so deep it will be hard to get out. Listen to that voice now! If what you say is true, Mathias, I would like to hear it from Karen. Let your listeners decide the truth for themselves."

There was nothing but the sound of an open-air frequency for over a minute. Finally, a shriller Mathias came on. "You only need listen to the joy and peace of those individuals living here. And who qualifies you to psychoanalyze me? I will not force Karen, who has been deeply traumatized by your actions, to face her tormentor. That would be cruel. If you have no need of a safe haven with good people then make your own way, but do not castigate those of us who choose a different path. I have been told you were a soldier, someone who makes his life by violence. It is to be expected that you would see our path differently."

Mike said, "There you have it, folks. Karen can't talk because she's probably confined, gagged, or drugged. I am a violent man because I spent a lifetime in service, willing to put my life on the line because I believe in my country. It's the same choice we were left with before the virus destroyed our civilization. Who do you trust? A self-important academic with a wonderful speaking voice who lived in a safe, cloistered world of theories and ideas never concerning himself much with actual results and all too often bolstered by adoring teenagers and early twenties acolytes? Or a soldier, an individual required to navigate the real world, willing to stand against some truly evil people, forced to see and accept responsibility for the consequences of his decisions? In all honesty, there are good and bad people in both camps. Just ask yourself one question: who would you have standing next to you when things go bad? It's your choice."

Mike's voice was a low growl as he made one last comment. "Mathias, do not harm either Karen or Rachael, or I give you my word, this soldier will make sure you pay."

Mike was nearly quivering with anger. He only hoped he was as convincing as Mathias.

Clearly shaken, Mathias sputtered, "Enough of this! I will not continue to be insulted. Karen is in our loving embrace. We are signing off for the evening and welcome any last minute additions to the ranch."

Mike sighed as he turned to Katie, and she took his hand. "I hope anyone listening believed me. Mathias talks a good game. He's certainly very persuasive. But the facts are the facts. He stole Karen's and Rachael's freedom and then made it sound like he saved them. I don't need to know anything else to know who he is. And the worst part of all," Mike said, as his eyes bored into Katie's, "is people listen to what others say instead of watching what they do, never realizing evil is just on the other side of the door. They close their eyes to what they see because they want to believe."

"You did well, Mike," Katie said after they signed off. "That's all you can do."

Chapter 22: A+97, Home Base Gathers Friends

Up early, Mike was ready to search for weapons and equipment at Joint Base Lewis-McChord. Finding the ranch in the whole state of Idaho was going to be like finding a needle in the proverbial haystack. He had pinned his hopes on Jed's ability to help them find that needle. Once the ranch was located, there was the more important issue of getting Karen and Rachael out alive. He had been on the periphery of operations like the one he intended but was by no means an expert.

Tilley, Raider and Tadpole were dig-scratching the front door from the inside after Mike shut it. He had closed them inside the house because he wanted to limit dog passengers for this trip to only Maple and Jill. Katie glanced over her shoulder at Mike with some disdain. He shrugged and smiled sheepishly. "I can't control a group of dogs as well as Karen." He sighed. "But I guess there's no time to learn but the present." Mike opened the door and they charged out, wagging and yipping joyously as if no slight was intended.

Mike took back roads to avoid I-5, jammed with lifeless cars from north of Tacoma to just past DuPont. As they were winding their way along the Puget Sound, past the quaint community of Steilacoom, Katie sat up straight, looking to her left in total concentration. "Mike, I feel somebody. No, wait, it seems like two."

"Can you tell how far away?" Mike asked, concerned.

"Not too far, maybe a few miles."

"Any idea why you didn't feel them sooner?"

Katie responded, "I'm not sure. It could be I just wasn't trying to look for anyone."

"Okay, no worries, Katie. Keep them in your focus and let me know if we are getting closer. I think we need to do what we need to do and then figure out if we should find them."

"Got it," Katie said.

Entering the back gate, Mike wound his way through the western section, crossing over I-5, through the main gate and then into the heart of the sprawling 200 square mile complex. During his last trip to JBLM with Karen, she had pointed out the Special Forces Headquarters as they drove by, and that was where Mike wanted to start. Special Forces units always had the latest technology and best equipment for covert operations requiring stealth and deadly force. "How we doing, Katie?" Mike asked.

Katie was sitting erect with her eyes closed in complete concentration. "We are getting closer."

They turned left toward the hospital, passing rows of plain gray soldier barracks, office buildings, and the requisite supporting gas station and fast food establishments. "How about now, Katie?" Mike asked.

"We're getting closer. Seems as if they're moving our way. Maybe they heard the truck."

"Well, darn." Mike shook his head. "We're almost there, so stay alert. May have to meet them sooner rather than later."

Sensing the anticipation, the dogs covered all the windows on the left, front, and back. Mike saw the Special Forces sign and headed to the headquarters building. He parked quickly at the front door and barked at Katie to get out and inside the building. All of the dogs except Jill, followed Katie inside. Mike backed to the door with his rifle ready, scanning the buildings and vegetation for any signs of movement. Jill was on Mike's left, intuitively duplicating Mike's posture.

Mike felt rather than heard the rumble of a low growl from Jill as he heard her say, *Man, woman, dog.* Mike followed the direction of Jill's focus and could just make out someone peeking from behind a concrete façade sign that was surrounded by small pines and rhododendrons.

Mike yelled, "I see you! Why don't you come out slowly and we can talk?"

A bullet whistled over his head and Mike dropped to the ground, signaling Jill to do the same. He had the strange feeling the bullet was purposely aimed high; a hopeful sign.

"What are you doing here?" a deep male voice called out.

"Hard to yell on my belly," Mike replied in a loud, calm tone. "Some freaks in Idaho kidnapped my girlfriend and a friend. I was hoping to find some nice toys in there to help me get her back."

Mike heard roaring laughter and a dog barking in tune with its master. "Well, I'll be damned. You're the guy on the radio last night! That was awesome, man, truly. We are going to come out. Don't freaking shoot me!"

Remaining still with Jill alert by his side, Mike gave the command for stay and quiet. A giant of a man with a gleaming ebony head stepped slowly from his hiding place with a brindle cattle dog and tall, lean Asian woman. He picked up the pace as he walked across the parking lot with his hands up and a huge grin on his face. Finally, mostly sure he wasn't going to get his head blown off, Mike stood up, slung his rifle, and reached out to grab the giant's offered hand.

"Warrant Officer Thomas Fleming at your service. This is Sara and my dog Ghost."

"Mike McCollough. Glad to meet you, I think." Mike looked down at the size of the man's hand clasping his own.

Thomas bellowed another belly laugh, recognizing Mike's trepidation. "Yeah, I was big before, about 6'2". Hell, now I'm so big it's hard to find a bed that fits. We've been listening to that ranch for a few weeks as entertainment. Yesterday I stood up and cheered when you tore that jerk-off a new one. We knew you were around the area somewhere, but I didn't know how to find you."

Relaxing, Mike asked, "So what are you doing here?"

"At this very spot, this very moment? We heard your vehicle and came to investigate. I used to live over in Yelm and met Sara being chased by a crazy, hairy, humanoid thing in Seattle. Sara loved American Lake when we came down on one of our scavenging missions, so we set up our base of operations at the recreation center. I believe I can help you find what you need in there. You might even be able to talk me into helping you rescue your friends. This new world can get a bit boring." Sara stayed silent and watched the interaction of the two soldiers with a small smile, still learning the rituals of this interesting club.

"Music to my ears," Mike smiled. "You wouldn't happen to be Special Forces?"

"As a matter of fact, that is exactly my brand of mayhem!"

Chapter 23: A+95, Nothing Looks Better at the Ranch

Rachael slept on the top bunk in a room with two other women on her first night at the ranch. Carlotta, obviously not happy about either the accommodations or Rachael's tossing and turning during the evening, was bunking underneath Rachael as her minder. Jan slept on the other side of the austere room with her back to the new arrival, while Carlotta pretended to be impervious to the emotions emanating from the other beds.

At daylight, as Rachael swung her legs over the side to jump down, Carlotta said in a groggy morning voice, "Where do you think you're going?"

"I have to go to the bathroom. I thought you said I wasn't a prisoner."

"You're not, but that doesn't mean we trust you. As I told you last night, I have to stay with you everywhere, and that includes using the facilities." Carlotta sprang out of bed completely naked. Rachael watched as she grabbed a cattle prod thing she must have been sleeping with, pointed it at Rachael, and ordered her to go first.

As Carlotta wedged in after Rachael in the tiny one stall bathroom and leaned her bare behind against the sink, Rachael said, "You are kidding me, right? You want to watch me pee?"

Carlotta gritted her teeth and said, "Just shut up. I hate chatter in the morning."

Returning to the room, Carlotta told Rachael to get dressed, pointing to clothes placed on a chair. Rachael dressed in the humiliating outfit provided by the ranch: a beige tank top, no bra provided, and some baggy green shorts. "Where are my shoes?"

"You'll get some when you work. Until then, it discourages attempts at making a run for it."

"Oh, yeah, but I'm no prisoner," Rachael said with as much scorn as she could muster.

"Move it, girlie. We are going to visit the boss."

Walking to the main house, Carlotta didn't say a word, staying a couple paces back, giving Rachael a chance to surreptitiously study the surrounding area. It reminded her a bit of Spokane without the city. To the east, a snow crested mountain range stood sentinel on the slopes of a high desert valley where the ranch sat. Wondering what type of ranch this was, Rachael could see fencing in the distance without any accompanying livestock. The natural grass, mostly dry and bleached, blew eastward with a steady, humidity-free breeze helping to make an otherwise cloudless warm day comfortable. Treading on a gravel road barefoot was no easy matter, especially with Carlotta frequently demanding that she hurry up. Rachael resolved to toughen her feet so that when the time was right she could escape with or without shoes.

Spotting the top of a far distant building to her left, Rachael wondered if that was where Karen was staying. It broke her heart to be so cruelly taken just when she believed things were going to get better. To be separated from Karen, too—now that was just too much. It surprised her how much she had grown to love and respect Karen in the short time they had been together. Karen was a friend, a mother, and a grandmother all rolled into one. "I will not let this stand!" Rachael whispered to herself. She pictured herself ripping Carlotta's weapon off her shoulder. Then she could subdue Carlotta and take the ranch house; killing Mathias and his sidekicks to save the day.

Carlotta gave Rachael a sidelong glance and said. "Don't even consider it."

Rachael's bare feet were sore by the time they reached a charming ranch house. Carlotta pointed to an office at the far side of the huge formal sitting room with the baton she carried. "Go on in and be respectful," Carlotta grunted.

Rachael entered a spacious, almost feminine office. A brown wavy-haired man sat behind a desk with his back to her, reading by the light of a window. She stood and cleared her throat, knowing the man was aware of her presence. Without turning, he said, "Rachael, thanks for coming," as if she had a choice. He closed the book he was reading and placed it in the group flanked by elaborate bookends.

As he stood and turned, Rachael could see Mathias was taller than the normally height-advantaged survivors of this new world at maybe 6 feet 6 inches. A handsome but somehow doughy face surveyed Rachael from her bare feet, stopping for a moment at her barely covered breasts, and then, appraising her with his eyes, he asked, "How old were you when the change occurred?"

Feeling small and determined to be strong, Rachael stepped back slightly as if she was afraid, settling on an "I'm not a threat" strategy and boldly told a lie hoping Mathias was not a pedophile. "I just turned 12."

"Hmmm, that's very interesting. I was wondering what would happen to children or if children could even survive the change. Please sit down."

Rachael sat with her hands between her knees, clearly uncomfortable. "I don't want you to be afraid, Rachael. We truly mean you no harm. As they say, desperate times call for desperate measures. You already know I've assigned Carlotta as your watcher until we decide you are all in and dedicated to the group. The quicker you settle in and accept this place as your home, the sooner you'll be free to express your own will and talents.

"This place really is for your own good. It will be wonderful for me to watch a young person flourish while learning to know themselves and know others through an enlightened approach to bonding and trust—so sad that our old world could never provide that opportunity in pedantic schools and places of worship. But I digress. You will be assigned some work duties, as everyone here must work. I am thinking the greenhouse, where we grow our food, would be a good start; Carlotta works there, so she will show you the ropes. We have a nightly meeting to discuss our relationships and, as you may know, engage the world at large. This is where the real magic of our close group happens. I expect you to attend and hopefully engage openly and honestly. Do you have any questions for me?"

"When can I see Karen?"

"Oh, my dear. Well, I suppose you have grown fond of her. I felt she might need some additional adjustment time. I am not at all sure she will work out; in fact, I am doubtful. Nevertheless, we will give her the same chance we give all of our members. I am afraid you will have to wait until she is ready to approach the group with interest and curiosity."

"What does that mean?" Rachael asked in a voice wracked with panic.

"Once you understand what we are doing here, you will know. Now, my dear, I have some work to do. Carlotta is, I am sure, waiting for you outside the door, so see yourself out. I look forward to seeing you again this evening. And Rachael, as soon as we feel you are one of us, we will give you back your shoes." Mathias gave a smile that did not extend to his eyes and he turned, dismissing Rachael.

Meanwhile, in the stable, Karen's arms hung loosely to her side as she sat on her cot in a lotus position trying to remember her dreams. If this new ability was going to be any use at all, she had to decipher the difference between dreams that were the product of previous events from those that could be a window into the future. With almost no leverage other than her wits, Karen needed every advantage to have any hope of escaping this cell. That morning she determined the best approach would be to create a mental catalog of each of her dreams and then separate the ones that came true. Frustrated, she whispered to herself, "There must be a way to tell the difference!"

Being caged like an animal was as bad as it gets. Locked up for less than a day, Karen was already feeling crazy, or at least, crazier than normal. When Mabel brought breakfast that morning Karen tried to talk to her, asking about Rachael's status and when she would meet Mathias. She received only a cursory "Good morning; I'm in a hurry" from Mabel. If Karen focused on the residual smell of horses, it helped to calm her—at least until the man across the way would scream from his cage, shattering any inward peace she had created. Karen guessed he might be like the man she met in Tacoma, somehow damaged from the change instead of improved.

When she attempted to talk to him from her cell, he gave excited grunts and he became agitated as she continued the one-way conversation, demonstrating his antipathy by releasing blood-curdling shrieks. He did appear to appreciate singing, no matter how bad the voice. Earlier a song had wedged itself into Karen's mind, and as she began to sing the tune at low volume, her fellow captive said "uh huh, uh huh" in time with her singing. *Now that's interesting,* Karen said to herself.

By the time Mabel showed up for lunch, Karen had already completed three sets of 75 pushups, hundreds of sit-ups, stretched every muscle in her body, and had run in place by lifting her knees to her waist for a continuous hour. She had memorized every dream by picture and content, cleaned her cell, and relived an incredibly fun-filled summer in her college years. Starting this time with more benign conversation from behind her cage, Karen asked how Mabel's day was going.

"Nothing much changes around here," Mabel replied. "They treat me like a servant while that psychopath Carlotta gets easy duty following your girl around."

"You know, Mabel, it isn't very comforting knowing a psychopath is following around Rachael, my friend and a wonderful young woman."

"Oh, I'm sorry; that wasn't very kind. Don't you worry, though—Mathias won't let anything happen to her. I don't know for sure, but I think he believes females are important to creating his new kingdom. They can have babies, after all."

Less than reassured, Karen pressed on. "So you must have had an amazing life, Mabel. How did you end up in Salt Lake from Tennessee?"

"Now that is a long story. I have a few minutes and will tell a little. So as I was saying, my daddy was a mean drunk. My mamma came from a strict religious German family in North Carolina that believed education was important, even for girls. A more loving, stronger woman than my mamma has never been born. Every day after chores, while my daddy was out hunting or drinking, my momma would sit us kids down at the table and teach us reading, writing, and math. We were so poor. There was a school a few miles away but we couldn't get our work done if we went, and no one checked to make sure you went anyway."

"At 18, my older brother and sister ran off. I figured between my daddy's beatings and the all too frequent hungry winters they just up and left. When I turned 18 my mamma pulled me aside and handed me enough money for a train ticket. Not sure where she got the money. She sold homemade apple butter to other hill people so she must have scraped together every extra cent." Mabel's voice broke as she continued the story. "It happens every time I tell it… She told me she loved me and to get out of these hills and make a life for myself. She said I had everything I needed: an education, good morals, and a strong work ethic."

"But Mamma, why don't you come with me?' I asked."

"Sweet child, you know that's not possible. I still have to raise up your younger brothers and sisters."

"I viewed my worn, skinny mamma and knew what life had in store for me if I stayed. She couldn't have been barely more than 40 at the time, and I just wanted to die thinking about leaving her. But leave I did. I walked to the train station and bought a ticket to Memphis. When I got off that train, I stopped at a corner store to buy a drink with the few pennies left over in my pocket from the train ride. The establishment proprietor was working the cash register while trying to mind three children under six. When I stepped up to the counter, I asked if he needed help with watching the youngins. He eyed my ragged clothes and worn shoes, but I just gave it right back straight in the eye, and I told him I might not look like much but I was strong, smart, and he wouldn't find a better girl to care for his children."

"Mr. Howard was desperate. His wife dead from blood poisoning, the sister he enlisted to help left just the week before to marry a farmer. So he said yes, and I moved into his place above the store as a nanny. He treated me very well; after a few years he remarried and agreed to help me get nurse training. When WWII started, I picked up and went as a nurse. Best move I ever made since I met my husband Willie, from Utah, in Italy when I cared for him after he fell from a ladder and broke his leg. After the war, that's where we went: Utah."

"Wow," Karen said. "What happened to your mom?"

"Well, she outlived that mean son of a bitch we called a father and came to live with me for a short while before she passed. She missed Tennessee like crazy, but I was sure glad to have the time with her."

Wanting to transition the conversation, Karen asked if Mathias was also from Utah.

"Nope. Think he grew up on the East Coast somewhere and then moved to Idaho. I get the impression something bad happened, something about his credentials, but couldn't say what. He sure is an odd duck." Mabel stopped talking and then said, "Well, I got to run. See you at dinner."

"Hey, Mabel," Karen said, "two quick things. I was wondering whether you started your period after the change? You are the only other woman I know over 50 when it happened."

"Oh, good Lord, girl" Mabel chuckled. "I sure as heck did! I couldn't believe it when I saw that blood running—thought maybe I was dying of cancer."

"Do you think we can have children again?"

"Can't say for sure, but it sure feels like the real thing, cramps and all. I wouldn't mind another baby at some point."

"Yeah, that would be something," Karen sighed. "The other thing: do you think you could find me a toothbrush? My teeth feel like they're covered in fur."

"Sure, I can probably find one."

Once again, Mabel seemed to simply vanish. Disappointed she didn't learn more about the ranch but glad for the opportunity to build some rapport with Mabel, Karen thought allowing Mabel to talk might be the key to persuading her to help her escape. Besides, Mabel's story was interesting.

"How're you doing over there, Uh Huh?" Karen asked in a loud voice to no reply. "One way or another we're going to get out of here."

Chapter 24: A+98, The Tribe at Home Base

Thomas and Sara agreed to move into Mike's RV for the time being until they successfully rescued Rachael and Karen; after that they would decide as a group what to do next. Ghost was a little intimidated by the rapidly expanding pack of dogs but allowed each of her new friends to sniff and smell and then returned the pleasantry. Attempting a herding maneuver with Jill, Jill let Ghost know by her posture, tail position, and steely glare that she would be calling the shots. Once Ghost acquiesced to the alpha, the two dogs found a natural affinity, and she became Jill's ghost, quietly following her every move.

Thomas laughed at the dogs' interaction. "She's the most silent dog I've ever owned. Rarely even barks and can sneak up on you in a heartbeat. For a dude that's supposed to be a herder, Ghost makes an awesome hunting dog. She knows how to track a scent and alerts me without making a sound."

Mike stood still, watching, surprised at his growing connection to the animals. How did it happen? Even though he liked watching their agility and boundless enthusiasm, in the past he'd had little patience for the fur, smell, drool, and shit that accompanied dog ownership. Spending so much time in the company of canines made Mike realize and fully appreciate the uniqueness of each dog. Like people, they had their own personalities, strengths, and weaknesses. To get the good, he knew he had to live with, accept, and learn to love some of the bad. Maybe it was his special bond to Jack and Jill, but even the dog smell was starting to grow on him, although he'd never admit that to anyone.

"Well, we don't have a lot of time to waste. Jed is going to arrive in a couple of days and I want to be ready with a tentative plan so he can help with the technical portion. I have some ideas, but so much depends on the location and layout of the ranch. We need to start training and preparing for those types of actions that we can be reasonably certain we will need. I'm hoping Jed can help us find the ranch."

"I hear you," Thomas replied. "We have to be able to sneak in, locate Rachael and Karen, and then extract them without raising an alarm. That takes a specific set of skills, and it will be important to be able to reliably use the dogs to make it happen. We can train on that. Wish we had a mock-up of the area," Thomas sighed wistfully.

Mike asked Sara if she could shoot. "Thomas has been working with me. I have gone from terrible to terribly average. "

"Don't sell yourself short, Sara. Besides, as the group's only doctor, we'll want you to stay in reserve to help with any wounded," Thomas added.

At that comment Sara noticeably paled. "It becomes so much more real when you say that."

Mike wondered about Sara. He'd talked with her that morning after breakfast while Thomas went out to help Katie refuel the generators. Sara said she was in her mid-30s and was regretful that up to that point her whole life had been about school and work. Never married, she had not even made time for close relationships. Thomas was her first boyfriend in years.

Laughing, Sara had explained Thomas was far different than her normal circle of peers and acquaintances.

"Sara, I want to make sure you understand: no one is forcing you to do this. We need you. We could absolutely use your help, but in this group, no one will be forced to do anything, and we won't hold it against you if you choose not to participate. This isn't your fight."

Katie nodded her head in agreement. "I hope you'll help us, Sara. You'll love Karen and Rachael. Either way, I understand. You don't know either of them."

Sara listened stoically but turned away from Katie's pleading eyes. "I need to think about it. In the meantime, I don't see the harm in training and planning."

They set up a game of seek and find for the dogs. Using two sets of unwashed clothes from Karen's departed family, the dogs, confined in a room in the house, were commanded to "find" and were presented with the scented clothes. Katie hid the the second bundle in the yard.

Poor Maple was the very last to understand the desired result. At the day's final attempt, he stepped on the front porch, put his nose in the air, taking in all the air his lungs would hold, and loped directly to the hidden bundle while the rest of the dogs ran this way and that. Katie smiled, "He may not be the sharpest knife in the drawer, but the big fella has a great nose!" Maple was so happy to receive a reward; he put his forepaws on Katie's chest to give her a kiss and nearly sent her tumbling.

Sitting around the dinner table, the group was cheerful and excited with the progress they'd made in just one day. "Tomorrow we should make it harder," Mike commented as he looked to the others for suggestions on how to incrementally train the dogs for what they needed from them. With a chart displayed on a computer monitor, Mike prepared a training plan for the next few days.

Thomas said, "We need to set aside at least one block a day to familiarize everyone with the equipment. The ladies have never used night vision devices, and it takes some getting used to. Optimally all of us should be able to use all of the equipment no matter what each of us is carrying."

"Good idea," Mike replied. "That make sense to you, Katie and Sara?"

Sara added, "Just one thing, I don't know much about this stuff, but it seems like the dogs have to know how to be sneaky. I mean, they can't just run into the ranch and expect no one will see them, can they? Don't they have to know how to keep out of sight while they are searching?"

Thomas smiled at Sara, "See, I knew you'd be a natural at this stuff! It's merely a function of planning, training, and common sense, with a heavy dollop of intelligence gathering and a dash of good luck. "

Sara rolled her eyes. "Anything you say, Thomas."

"Just don't want you to sell yourself short Sara. If I can do this with my pea brain, anyone can."

"Well there is that," Sara chuckled with a wry smile.

"Moving on," Mike added wanting to get back on task. He completed the training and preparation calendar then switched to director mode. "We still need to check in with Jed. After that I think we should turn in. We have a busy few days ahead."

Thomas stayed behind to talk with Mike as the women headed to bed. He pulled out a chair with the back facing Mike and straddled it. "Hey, Mike, so what do you think?"

"I think I wish I knew where they were in Idaho and that we knew more about the ranch. As for the training, we'll get there"

"Roger. I wanted to warn you that Sara's very uncomfortable about all this. She doesn't understand. Her whole life has been about school. From what she's told me, her parents gave her everything she ever wanted. Not that she isn't a good person, because she is, but she can't imagine placing herself in harm's way for someone she doesn't even know."

"I'll try not to pressure her, Thomas, and I won't go until we can get in and out with minimal risk. At least, I won't allow anyone else to go if it's too dangerous," Mike stated without hesitation.

"Man, you got me regardless. I live for this shit!" Thomas laughed. "When I heard that mealy mouth MF say he didn't kidnap your friends, all I could think about was finding that asshole and shoving his words where the sun don't shine. We are in the same club, Mike; I knew that when I heard your take-down. It's a matter of honor for us and protecting the things that are ours. That's just what we do. But we don't do stupid. Hell, if there aren't too many, I can probably do it myself." Thomas clapped Mike on the shoulder as he got up to leave.

Mike looked at Thomas and nodded his head. "Thanks, friend."

Jill was sitting next to Mike, taking in the conversation. She put her head on Mike's knee as Mike studied the training schedule and rubbed her delicate ears. "So what do you think, sweet girl?" Mike asked Jill. He was surprised how quickly, Jill, always the quiet dog, had stepped up to lead the pack and get close to Mike. She was a better conversationalist, too, using more words than Jack—just like a woman. Jill looked directly in Mike's eyes to respond to his question: *Mike go, Jill go. Find friends.*

Chapter 25: A+97, The Ranch

Karen walked around her tiny cell trying to remember each dream after a restless night. She was surprised at the mishmash of flashes, partial conversations, running, activity, and emotion that comprised her dreams. Two stood out. In one, Rachael sat on the floor in corner, hair and clothes askew, crying silently into her hands. Karen hoped this dream was not prophetic. In the other she saw a small room with electronic equipment and multiple monitors like an elaborate security system. A man sat in front of the monitors with his back to Rachael. She asked what he was doing, to which he replied, "Watching."

You don't think? Karen said to herself. There weren't many places in her cage to hide a camera or microphone. She started with the cot, pulled the bedding off, and ran her hand over the entire surface—nothing. Putting everything back, she sat on the portable toilet pretending to stretch and felt around the bottom of the small toilet as she surveyed the rest of the cell. The original function of the door was to keep in horses. A wood lip was flat on the bottom half of the gate, allowing the top portion to open separately. Karen walked to the door and ran her hand under the lip, finding a wireless device on one side hooked with a tiny bracket. She popped it out easily with pressure then immediately put it back. This could be useful, particularly if they didn't know she knew.

Mabel was late with breakfast. Uh Huh, restless in his jail, was sighing, moaning, and occasionally yelling gibberish, probably as hungry as Karen. After what seemed like an endless morning, Karen heard footsteps and called good morning to Mabel. Dave's voice answered, "It's cleaning day, princess. Mabel is busy with something else. I want you to step to the far corner of your cage and face the back. If you give me any trouble, I have a nifty, fully-charged cattle prod that will ruin your day."

Karen stepped to the back, doing as Dave demanded, and heard the gate open. He entered quickly, roughly smashing Karen against the back wall and forcing handcuffs over her hands. He reached around, grabbed one of her breasts, still leaning against her, and smugly whispered in her ear, "Life will be better for you if you cooperate. Now move slowly out of the cell."

Dave guided Karen to a metal ring in the center of the stable by pushing and prodding. An ankle iron and a chain was attached to the ring. He ordered Karen to sit and locked one of her legs in the iron. "Don't move." Dave yanked a hose off the wall, and moved to her cell, hosing everything. Done with the cell, he pointed the water blast at Karen. She squeezed her eyes shut and clenched her teeth. Then the rage at being taken and treated like an animal took control of her. With water dripping from her hair into her eyes, she forced herself to open them and direct her hostility at Dave. She sat trembling with anger, heat flaring behind her ears, and then she went still.

"Listen, pervert: don't expect me to go all wobbly for the likes of you," Karen said. "I'll bet you were a fat little piss-ant before the change, right?"

Dave wheeled around, dropped the hose, picked up the cattle prod, and zapped Karen on the arm. She bit the inside of her mouth, her whole body racked with pain, but she didn't scream. From a fetal position on the ground, with blood on her lips, Karen said with all the strength she could gather, "Well, I guess that proves it."

Dave inspected her, clearly wanting to do it again, but he just shook his head. "I have known lots of bitches like you. You think you're so smart and special. Well, we'll see, won't we? Now zip it."

He took the cattle prod and walked to Uh Huh's cage. "Get back!" Dave yelled. With the prod forward, Dave opened the gate and began to zap Uh Huh. Misery pealed from the cage as Uh Huh screamed in a high-pitch keening. "You stupid beast. Why can't you at least learn to use the toilet?! This is disgusting." Uh Huh began a gurgling cry as Karen heard the electricity spark again and again. Dave backed out, grabbed the hose, and sprayed into the cage at Uh Huh. Finally, he slammed it shut.

He unlocked Karen, threw her in the cell, and stomped out. Uh Huh was still crying, so Karen began her rendition of "Moon River." It seemed to soothe him. Karen wished Dave had left some food—she was really hungry.

At the other side of the ranch, Rachael was milling around barefoot waiting for the start of her fourth group session. *Nothing like being psychoanalyzed by a bunch of fools*, Rachael thought to herself. At least they gave her a hoodie sweatshirt to wear over the see-through tank top.

Mathias walked in and asked everyone to sit in chairs arranged in a circle. In each of the other meetings, the whole group attended except for one or two; most likely they rotated as ranch security. Carlotta said she would get her chance to perform guard duty as soon as they thought they could trust her—in other words, as soon as Mathias trusted her.

The only option Rachael could see was to play along with their weird mind games. Mathias called it "enlightenment through honest feedback and interpersonal bonding." By shedding their own walls built from hurt and pain, experienced in this life or a previous life, they could know others in a truer way and create relationships that could sustain a civil and peaceful society. Mathias reminded the group daily that it was hard but necessary work if they wished to join and be part of a better world.

Mathias gave his henchmen, Carlotta, Dave and Eric—rotational responsibility for group facilitation, and today was Eric's turn. "Ahem, let's get started with self-discovery," Eric, a fussy man with a razor-sharp, pointy nose, began. "Jan, can you tell us what you've learned about yourself?"

Jan twisted on her chair and near her lap, wound her shirt around her hand. In a soft, quivering voice she said, "I have learned that I am deathly afraid of rats."

"Okay," Eric replied. "Why do think you have such fear?"

"They have beady eyes," Jan said.

"What experience did you have with rats previous to the ranch?" Eric asked Jan.

"None other than books and TV."

At this point Carlotta interrupted, "Jan, you know the whole point of this exercise. It isn't just about fear, but learning where it came from so that you can get rid of those irrational thoughts. A rat is a creature, just like you. Where do you think the fear comes from?" Carlotta demanded.

Even more anxious, eyes wide, Jan looked up toward the ceiling, perhaps hoping the answer was written on the ceiling tiles. She fidgeted and grimaced until Eric blurted, "Oh, good lord," and moved on to the next person.

At her turn, Rachael explained she had learned how important shoes were to almost everything you do. Eric's red face gave notice his temper was rising. "That's not the point of this exercise! We aren't dealing with physical issues; we need emotional insights. What issues have you had to deal with in your life that prevented you from becoming everything you want to be?" He stared intently at Rachael.

"Well, like, I always wanted to be a knight, but there weren't, like, any clubs at school where you could do knightly things. I'm only 12," Rachael responded in her best girlie voice.

"Oh, good grief; this is hopeless. Think about it and come up with something for tomorrow," Eric said between clenched teeth.

They continued around the circle with fears, self-doubt, back patting, and a couple of sincere insights.

Rachael sat up straight in her chair. This next part, now that's where it really got going. The feedback rules established by Mathias were that since all feedback is a gift, you shouldn't respond to it other than to take it in and see if it's helpful. It didn't appear to matter how accurate, underhanded, reprehensible, or downright mean the feedback might be; in this crazy place, it was all a gift.

Today was Bill's turn to be in the hopper. After only four sessions, Rachael recognized a pattern of using the vulnerability expressed by certain people during the first part of the session to really dig in when it came time for feedback. Essentially, if you were in the in-crowd, everything you said was met with praise and compassion. If you were not part of the in-crowd, prepare to be crucified. It reminded Rachael a lot of high school.

Dave told Bill his attitude about the ranch seemed insincere. Bill, surprised, responded, "Why would you say that? I do everything asked of me."

"You roll your eyes when I mention it's almost time for the group meeting," Carlotta added.

"Well, I didn't realize I did that," Bill said, crossing his arms.

Jim jumped in, "The other day when you were given the honor to pick up Sylvie and the other ladies, you said you weren't sure if what we are doing is right."

Clearly frustrated, Bill said through tight lips, "I was afraid Sylvie might get hurt."

Sylvie, wanting to defend Bill, blurted, "It was a legitimate concern. Everyone had guns!"

Mathias stopped the interaction with a heavy sigh. "Bill, you need to stop defending yourself, and Sylvie, you know that saving Bill from his own enlightenment is self-defeating. Bill, take the feedback and say thank you. Go back to your quarters tonight and reflect over what was said. I want to remind each of you no one must stay. If you are not completely bought in to what we are doing here and the progress for humanity we are about to make, it would be better if you leave."

Bill knew Sylvie hoped to stay, so he said, "Thank you" and nothing more; his hands remained in white fingered fists.

Rachael, a recent ranch kidnap victim, wanted to jump up and wrap her hands around Mathias's neck; she quaked internally from the force of will it took to constrain her mouth and body. Jan, sitting next to Rachael, continued to look at her hands while her shoulders shook. Rachael wasn't sure whether Jan was laughing or crying.

The session concluded with Mathias talking interminably, describing how he had reached a greater level of enlightenment. He explained his childhood in which some of the kids picked on him because he was a smart, sensitive, shy boy. "At some point I realized their taunts were not about me. I had to change my perception of myself, that I was somehow less, and realize the qualities that made me a target were actually my strengths. I was the better person because of my sensitivity."

Dave and Carlotta nodded their heads in total thrall. Mathias made it easy to read between the lines that the freedom offered at the ranch could only be enjoyed by those who had reached a heightened state of awareness. Rachael was pretty sure "a heightened state of awareness" was the same thing as "total obedience to Mathias" and the only real gateway to freedom. Of course once you gave your free will to Mathias, there could be no freedom. Rachael thought she may only be sixteen, but she knew a con when she heard one.

"So ends another episode of The Game of Enlightenment," Mabel whispered to Rachael on their way out. Carlotta gave Mabel a stern look, not knowing exactly what was said to Rachael. She escorted Rachael back to the bunkhouse and handcuffed her to her bed. "I'm going out for the night, so you stay here."

"What if I have to go to the bathroom?" Rachael pleaded.

Carlotta threw an adult diaper at her. "Use this." She skipped out of building, ecstatic to be free for the moment from babysitting duty, but not before she slammed the door for effect, making Rachael jump.

Jan returned from the bathroom in a zombie haze, glanced at Rachael, lay on the bed, and rolled over to the wall.

"You wouldn't happen to have a bobby pin, would you?" Rachael asked Jan.

Without turning over Jan said, "No, but I have a key."

Rachael waited for Jan to scurry over and release her. After she didn't move from her wall-facing position, Rachael asked, "Well?"

"Well what?" Jan responded.

"Are you going to let me use the key?"

"Okay."

Slowly Jan sat up. Furtively glancing at the door, she moved to a short dresser and pulled the top drawer completely out. She carefully placed meager belongings on the bed and turned the drawer over, revealing a key taped to the bottom.

"How did you get it?" Rachael asked as Jan moved silently to Rachael, key in hand.

As she put the key in the lock Jan answered, "Carlotta left it in the bathroom. I picked it up."

"Did they lock you up, too?"

"Yes."

Rachael wondered if Jan was drugged, confused, or simple. "Jan, I really appreciate this. I have one more big favor to ask that would be a great help. Can I borrow your shoes? If I run around barefoot, Carlotta might suspect I've been out."

"Are you coming back?" Jan asked.

"I promise I will. I need to find my friend."

"I suppose. Just don't get them dirty."

Jan hadn't looked at Rachael during their stunted conversation, so Rachael asked, "Jan, are you okay?"

"Yes. I was mildly autistic before I changed. I am different now but don't know what to call it. I really like music but they won't give me a violin or let me use the piano."

Rachael grabbed her hand and Jan gently pulled it back. "I am so sorry, Jan. They have treated you badly. My friends and I will get you out of here and take you with us. We will get you whatever you need to make you feel better. Just don't tell anyone about me going out. I'll be back as soon as I can. You are really going to like my friends. We have great knights and beautiful damsels!"

For the first time, Jan looked directly at Rachael with a sweet, innocent smile. "I would like that."

Rachael pulled on her dark gray hoodie, stuffed her feet into too-small shoes, and flew out the door, stopping just at the front entrance. Thinking they probably had cameras somewhere, she moved along the edge of the building to the dark side and then took off running toward the building she'd spied earlier. Karen must be there.

It was dark; hazy clouds filled the moonless sky. In the distance she heard the long, wailing calls of wolves. *Guess we'll need some weapons if we make a run for it*, Rachael thought as her breathing regulated from the hard-running pace she set.

As the building came into view she slowed her speed and darted to a clump of trees to get her bearings. The front was lit with spotlights, and the rest of the building was in darkness. Avoiding the illuminated front, she made a wide berth to the side, looking for another door. She found one, locked, in the back. "Don't know why they bothered to lock it," she mumbled to herself, climbing in the half-open window next to the door.

The smell of animals permeated the tiny office Rachael entered. Slowly opening the office door, she looked out to see stalls lining each side of a spacious stable. She didn't see anyone. Rachael whispered "Karen, are you here?"

Rachael flinched when Uh Huh screamed, announcing his presence. Karen yelled out a semi-loud, "Shush." Not sure whether the silence command was meant for her or the screaming guy, Rachael moved to the cage she guessed housed her friend.

Karen, already moving, popped out the monitoring device and folded her blanket around it. "Rachael, keep your voice down. There's a camera with a microphone in my cell. I took it out, but they may still be able to hear us."

In hushed voices, Karen and Rachael's mouths whispered from through the stall door. "That guy over there isn't helping us out. I can barely hear you through the screeching. What's wrong with him, anyway?" Rachael asked.

Karen answered, "That's Uh Huh, and I'm not sure. How are you, Rachael? Are they treating you alright?"

"I'm okay. What about you? I've been so worried." Rachael tried to hide the emotion in her voice. "You may be locked up, but at least you don't have to participate in their brain-whacking sessions—and don't ask."

"Are you free to come and go?" Karen asked.

"Nope. Long story, and I can't stay too long. They took my shoes. I've made a friend, though, Jan. She's different and not doing too well here. I don't know what to do, Karen."

"You're doing the very best you can, and you've already found me! I'm sure Mike and Katie will come for us, so if we could escape, I think we could find a hiding place with a view of that entry road and intercept them when they get here. These fools don't have any dogs, so I don't think they could track us."

Rachael thought about that. "Unless they have someone who can sense people like Katie … I will do what I can to steal and hide food and water. They watch me all the time, so it won't be easy. Save what you can too. Is there anything in your cell that might work as a weapon? There are wolves in the hills and God knows what else."

"If there was anything in here, I would have tried to use it already. And Rachael, the food is hit or miss. I'm hungry right now. They finally gave us a little bit this evening."

"Those jerks!" Rachael hissed.

"Among other things," Karen replied. "I might be able to convince Mabel, the lady who watches us, to help. I'm not sure. Do what you can, Rachael; just don't risk getting caught. Do you think you'll be able to come back before we make an escape?"

"Probably. Carlotta is my minder, and she hates the job. Oh, and I promised Jan she could go with us when we escaped."

"Hmmm," Karen murmured. "It's harder to hide with more people. Let me think about it."

"Alright, but if she doesn't come with us we'll have to come back to get her with Mike. She really needs a different place. I have to get going. I need to search for a key to your cell in the office before I leave."

Rachael put her hand on the door and after an extended silence said, "Karen, I'm sorry you're here, but I'm glad it's you here with me."

Karen had cried for weeks after she'd lost the world she knew and everyone in it. Since Mike and the twins had walked into her life, she was so busy, the moments when she thought about lost family and friends were far fewer than before. And then, here was this young woman, right behind her cell door, whom she felt bound to in mere days. Karen thought the heart was truly an amazingly resilient organ. "I love you, Rachael. Don't do anything to get yourself hurt."

Chapter 26: A+99, Oregon

Mike was worried. There'd been no word from Jed in three days. Katie and Thomas had just returned from hunting, bringing home a couple of rabbits to augment their canned and bagged food supply. With increased numbers, Mike's RV freezer stock was already getting low. The smell of fresh cooked meat meant their fur friends were alert around the table for any inadvertent drops or generous human donations. Jill said, *Me hungry* to Mike repeatedly. In some ways, Mike thought, Jack and Jill were an awful lot alike. For the thousandth time, Mike wondered where Jack had gone and whether he was safe. *Are you looking for Karen, Jack? Can you find her?*

Already frustrated by Jack's departure and Jed's missing status, he told Jill in a stern voice, "Pipe down" out loud, resulting in laughter all around the table. To the others, Jill sat still as a church mouse next to Mike's chair. It broke the tension enough for Mike to laugh at himself.

"If we don't hear from Jed by tomorrow, maybe we should take a drive down the I-5, at least into northern California."

"Dangerous," Thomas replied.

"I know, you're right. Two things: he wouldn't be headed this way if he hadn't agreed to help us, and he had equipment essential to finding the ranch. Not to mention some gear that will make it easier to get in and out."

"Pay now or pay later, I guess," Thomas added, finishing the last bite of his rabbit.

"That's about the size of it. This is taking too long! Who knows what's happening to Karen and Rachael? I'm going to sleep in here and monitor the shortwave all night."

Katie looked at Mike, concern on her face. "I can do the radio tonight."

Mike shook his head and calmly told Katie, "Naw, you get some sleep. If we do go looking for Jed, I need your radar in tip top condition."

Sara sat in the adjoining living room, Thor purring on her lap. Listening to the conversation and Mike's growing apprehension she turned to look at him and added, "Mike, we don't have any reason to believe the ranch people would hurt them. I mean, what would be the purpose of kidnapping them other than to add to their numbers? If we get in a rush because we've made incorrect assumptions, someone could be needlessly hurt."

Standing, Mike rubbed his face with both hands. "You may be right, Sara—I hope you are. I would just ask: what would you have us do if the situation was reversed and you or someone you cared deeply about were taken against their will? If we're going to be a community, a family of sorts, these things have to matter. Everyone needs confidence that each person is important to the whole. But you're right; going off half-cocked isn't the answer. I promise you, I will try not to do that, and if I try, I've got Thomas around to tell me I'm being stupid."

"Absolutely, my man!" Thomas shouted from the kitchen with his mouth full of peanut butter.

It was still dark when Mike banged on the RV door, waking Sara and Thomas. Years of training evident, Thomas opened the door fully alert and ready to go. Sara was still in bed.

"I just heard from Jed. He was shot in the leg by someone, probably from long distance. He doesn't know who or how many and is holed up somewhere along I-5 in Oregon; couldn't tell me where and risk someone hearing. He said he's okay for now, but he can't drive. Luckily, Jed brought antibiotics and coagulating powder with him. Can you ask Sara to come too? He needs medical attention ASAP."

"Sure. Start getting everything ready. Let me deal with Sara."

Mike, Katie, dogs, and assembled gear were waiting near the trucks when Sara and Thomas exited the RV. The sky was lighter as sunrise approached. Sara carried her bag of medical equipment and an ice chest, which Mike took as a good sign. She nodded to the assembled group and climbed in the passenger seat of Thomas's truck, asking only which animals were riding with them.

The drive to Portland was easy but stalled empty vehicles in the city itself made passage maddening. Not wanting to get too far from I-5, they wound through city streets, also clogged, and had to pull up on sidewalks and backtrack. The river that ran through Portland and the accompanying bridge system further complicated an already difficult journey. At one point they were left with only one option—push cars out of the way.

Nearly three hours after entering Portland, they were on the southern boundary of the city when Katie alerted on a person due west. Mike stopped the truck and walked back to Thomas and Sara. Maple and Ghost stuck noses out the back window in greeting. "Katie just felt something. She says they're west and would have to be about ten miles from here. What do you think? Pretty far off the I-5."

"My gut says no. If he was hurt, I can't see him heading through the city. He did say he was near I-5, right?"

"Yeah, my thinking as well. Let's take a quick break and head south. We can check out the other person on our way home, if they're still around."

Moving on the I-5 south of Portland, Mike kept his speed down so Katie could focus. He worried Jed hadn't made it as they neared the California border when Katie yelled, "I got something! Actually I have three: two on the east side and one on the west."

"How far off the freeway is the group of two?" Mike asked.

"Hard to tell. Could you drive a little farther?"

As they passed a sign stating "26 miles to California," Katie held that dreamy-eyed stare she used when tracking people and signaled to Mike to slow down. "The two people are almost directly ahead. Maybe just off the freeway on the east side."

Mike stopped for another group meeting along the shoulder of the road. Explaining to Thomas that two unknowns were on or near the highway and Jed most likely somewhere to the west. Thomas nodded and said, "I'll draw them off. There's an exit a mile up, so I'll head east and south. I'm sure they'll hear my truck if they haven't heard us already. You wait here until Katie senses they're moving and then find Jed. We can't risk an ambush."

Horrified at the prospect of Thomas setting out on his own, Sara grabbed Thomas's hand. "But there are two of them!"

With a huge grin showing all his pearly whites, Thomas replied, "I know. Great odds for me!"

"Assuming you can lead them on a chase, how will you find us?" Sara asked indignantly.

"Easy peasy, Sara. Meet me at 2100 near mile marker 15. If I'm not there, try again at 0600 tomorrow morning. All else fails, we'll use a different shortwave frequency with updates every 6 hours starting at 2400. And Mike, think I could borrow Jill?"

Mike looked at Jill, shocked at the strong emotion Thomas's request engendered. On one hand, Jill was now the best-trained dog; it made sense for her to be by Thomas's side in the event everything went to hell. No question Jill was a strong, capable, independent being. But somehow, he felt Jill, and Jack before her, were *his* dogs. He was still hurting from losing Jack, and the bond with the shepherds was nearly as strong as the bond for a child in his charge. The desire to protect them measured in equal proportion to their willingness to risk their safety for him. Mike decided he would put the question to his friend. "What do you say, girl? Will you go with Thomas and keep him safe?"

Jill nodded her head, dog tag tinkling, yawned, and then trotted to Thomas's truck ready to do what needed to be done. She didn't respond to Mike's question with a verbal answer; she merely demonstrated her loyalty to the cause.

They ate apples, cheese, and granola mix on the gravel shoulder while waiting for Katie to sense movement from the two people ahead. Old habits die hard: there wasn't a single moving vehicle within hundreds or perhaps thousands of miles from where they sat, but for some reason they continued to pull to the side of the road as if someone would come along incensed, filled with road rage over the temerity of a driver purposely sitting in the middle of a major highway.

Katie spoke. "It must be working; they're moving. Going east."

"Let's give it a little time," Mike replied

Finally, Katie, still crunching granola, stated, "I've lost them."

"Good news. Let's get going."

Katie zeroed in on the single individual's location, guiding them off the interstate to a two-lane, winding road. When they were close enough for Katie to lose a sense of what was hopefully Jed's location, there were only two lonely houses within view. They checked the first, an older farmhouse, and found the remains of a family in the master bedroom, but nothing else. The second home, a compact 60's style limestone rock-fronted ranch, sat on the crest of a hill surrounded by a huge concrete driveway taking up most of the front yard.

"This has to be it. Keep away from the house. No telling what Jed has jerry-rigged to protect himself," Mike said. The group got out of the truck and from across the street yelled Jed's name at the top of their lungs. Tilley, Maple, and Raider joined in barking with the group. But nothing.

"Okay, the hard way then. You guys stay here." Mike tentatively walked down the driveway. A few feet from the door he heard a soft beeping sound. "Shit." He leaped for the front door as some sort of chain reaction on an electrical grid spread over the driveway where he had recently stood. Mike knocked at the door, relieved he was not electrocuted in the driveway. Nothing again. Opening the door and stepping inside, he saw Jed lying on the couch in the front room either dead or unconscious, hopefully unconscious. Folded on his stomach, Jed's hands held a device. Mike wrested it from his fingers and flipped the switch to disable the grid outside. There was blood everywhere. Placing his fingers to Jed's neck, he felt for a pulse.

He ran to the door, double checked that the humming of Jed's electrical grid was silenced, and yelled to Sara, "Hurry, and bring your stuff!"

Sara pulled the blanket off Jed and carefully removed gauze. She peered, pressed, and squeezed around the wound. It must have hurt. Jed whispered expletives, confirming he wasn't completely out. Sara turned to concerned faces. "He's lost a lot of blood. I put some blood in the cooler behind the seat—Katie, if you could please go get it.

"Where did you get blood, Sara?" Katie asked.

"I'm an O, the universal donor, and so is Thomas. We donated last night. Hurry, please, Katie; the bullet is still in his leg. Fortunately there's only a little bit of infection. Unless I can get that bullet out, antibiotics won't be enough, and the wound may not heal. Mike, I need you to clean the dinner table, find some clean sheets and towels, and see if you can find a way to boil water."

Sara spent a minute studying Jed's colorless face. He had a largish nose, a strong chin, and soft brown eyes. He reminded her of years spent in medical school with many similar young men. Something about him screamed, "I have spent most of my life indoors in a book or behind a computer." Even clammy and pale, his overall countenance was kind.

Katie, Mike, and Sara lifted Jed from the couch to the sheet-covered table. He screamed out. Mike was impressed with the quantity of pharmaceuticals Sara had stuffed in her bag and was glad she knew how to use them. After testing Jed's blood, Sara said to herself, "He's an O positive too, which is excellent news. Katie, did you see what I just did to test his blood?"

"Yes."

"Please test yourself and Mike in the event we need more than I brought."

An IV was hanging from a coat tree Katie found in an add-on vestibule between the garage and kitchen. Almost ready to start, Sara asked Mike to confine the animals to one of the bedrooms. "We need as sterile an environment as we can manage," she said apologetically.

When Mike returned from dog confinement duties, not a task he enjoyed, the IV was attached to Jed. "Just curious, Sara, not that it matters, but have you ever done anything like this before?"

Without looking up, Sara replied, "Yes and no. At one point I wanted to be a surgeon and started in a program. It didn't take long to realize I'm temperamentally not suited for it. Mechanically, I have gifted hands, but I never possessed the passion or competitive spirit to be a great surgeon. Bottom line: I've helped with surgery, but this is my first time to fly solo."

"Good enough for me," Mike smiled encouragingly.

For three grueling hours, Sara worked meticulously at a painstakingly slow pace. It would not have taken nearly so long except the bullet, located close to bone and nerves, needed to be extracted without causing more damage. One of his tendons was nearly severed, so Sara did what she could to repair it. After putting in the last stitches, she smiled up at Mike and Katie. "By George, I think I did it! I can't be sure, but I believe he'll make a complete recovery. There was a lot of muscle damage, but it will heal. We need to keep him immobile for at least three days."

Katie and Mike glanced at each other with concern etched on their faces. Sensing their chagrin, Sara said, "I know you want to get out of here as soon as possible and save your friends. I for one would like to see Jed walk again and don't want to take the chance that movement will pull something loose. If you must, leave me here with Jed, and I will follow you back when he is able to go."

"We can talk about it later," Mike stated. "Right now I have to get out and meet Thomas."

"Can I go with you? I need some fresh air," Katie asked.

"You guys go. I'll be fine," Sara said, still looking at Jed's face.

When released, the dogs stampeded through the door in a surge. Tilley spun in circles while Maple jumped on Katie, trying to lick her face in thanks. Raider did amazing air leaps, coming completely off the floor at least twice his body height. Even calm Zoe spun in circles in front of Mike. "Let's go, boys and girls," Mike said with a smile in his voice. Hearing the word "go," the dogs were at the door and out waiting by the truck before Katie could even pick up her weapon.

A moonless night, the only illumination was Mike's truck lights as they drove the back roads toward the highway and south for a few miles to the designated meeting place. He pulled under the trees and turned off the engine. The phrase "long lonely highway" couldn't begin to capture the scene before them. In just over three months, with summer in full bloom, vegetation from the side of the highway had begun its inevitable encroachment on man-made structures. The only sounds were an occasional hooting owl and the low, almost imperceptible murmur of insects and small animals. As the night darkened, the road was hardly recognizable except for a change in the darkness of shapes and forms.

"Mike, do you really think we'll find them?" Katie asked.

In her voice, Mike heard fear. He knew he would do everything he could, risk his life if necessary, to find them and bring them back. Still, it took discipline to push aside his own doubts. He ached for the loss of a woman he had only just met and was already falling for. It was a tough pill to swallow. More so, because of everything already lost.

Mike saw Katie, her vulnerable and sincere face looking to him for reassurance. A child at moments and a quiet, confident young woman the next, the Katie looking at him now was most of all a frightened teenager forced to grow up quickly. He remembered once entering his daughter's room after she left for college and noticing stuffed animals arranged on bed pillows patiently awaiting the arrival of a more adult benefactor. For parents, that part of their children always lives in the heart, even when they demand to be seen differently. Katie and Mike looked almost the same age, but they weren't.

"You are damn right we are going to get them back!" Mike responded. "Nothing on God's now green earth will stop us."

She nodded her beautiful head in agreement. "Yeah, Mike, darn straight!"

After nearly two hours of waiting in the vast silence of a six-lane highway, Katie yawned. "I'm not sensing anyone, Mike."

Mike rubbed his eyes. "Yeah, let's head back and try him again on the shortwave at midnight. I could use some coffee."

Jed was awake and talking to Sara when they came in. He smiled a tired grin and lifted his hand to shake Mike's as he stood next to the makeshift hospital bed.

"Hey, buddy, how're you doing?" Mike asked as he grasped Jed's clammy, pale hand.

"Better now, thanks to Sara. Wasn't sure I was going to make it. Can't thank you enough for coming to find me—I owe you one. Sara told me about Katie's extra gift—totally awesome!" Jed looked over at Katie, and she beamed with pride.

"The way I figure it, you wouldn't be in this mess if it wasn't for us—maybe some other mess, but not this one. We're just glad you're here," Mike said.

"I brought an extended van full of goodies; it's in the garage. First thing, look just behind the passenger seat; there are eight long range secure satellite radios. Since satellites are still operational, and I found the connectivity software, you should be in business just by turning them on. The rest of the stuff is pretty technical, so you'll have to wait until I can at least sit up."

Sara thought Mike might break into song upon learning about the secure radios. He was already racing to the garage as she said to his back, "You need to let Jed get some rest."

Mike and Katie laid the radios on the coffee table. Dying to play with them, Mike stopped to try to raise Thomas on the shortwave at midnight with no luck. He was starting to get a little worried and reminded himself Thomas was a big boy accustomed to operating alone, then went to back to inspecting the new equipment. Sara, exhausted from surgery, left to sleep in one of bedrooms, ordering Mike to keep an eye on Jed as she walked out of the room. Wanting to be part of everything, Katie was fast asleep sitting on the couch. Mike covered her with a blanket, put a pillow behind her head, and turned his complete attention to the new radios.

Mike nudged Katie when it was almost time to leave for the second scheduled meeting with Thomas. Sara, already up, was puttering around, checking on Jed and looking for edible food in the kitchen. She was fully briefed on how to use the new satellite radios, and one sat prominently on the end table in the family room. "I have turned it up, Sara. You should be able to hear it all over the house."

"Thanks, Mike. Could you call if Thomas is there so I can quit worrying?"

Mike nodded, picked up his gear from an overstuffed easy chair, and they were off again to mile marker 15. Days are long in the Northwest during summer. The sun was already over the horizon on what felt like a scorcher day in waiting. Katie said, "There is someone out there" as soon as they got in the truck.

"Let's hope it's Thomas," Mike mumbled. When they reached the mile marker Mike motioned Katie to get out. He exited the truck ready for an ambush just in case the person Katie sensed was not friendly. The dogs jumped out after Katie and headed into the woods without even pausing to say, *Hey, we'll be back in a minute.*

"Great," Mike said, "I hope they aren't after deer." He was just about to follow when Thomas loped out of the woods, eating an apple and surrounded by a whirling pack of welcoming canines.

Jill proudly led the procession coming to a sit in front of Mike, her tail waving back and forth, scraping dirt on the ground. "That's my good girl," Mike said in doggy baby talk as he reached down and rubbed Jill's head, as relieved to see his dog as he was to see Thomas. "Well?" Mike asked as he glanced up at Thomas.

Thomas laughed a big, booming laugh. "It's cool. I'll tell you when we get back so I don't have to tell it twice. It will be in my memoir as one of my choice war stories. Lost my truck, though—we'll have to get another. That's sort of why it took so long. Did you find Jed? Is he okay?"

"Yes and yes," Mike replied. "Heads up!" Mike said as he threw the sat phone in Thomas's direction. "You need to call Sara; she's worried."

Thomas grabbed the phone from the air with his catcher mitt hand. He gave a low whistle. "Yo, Mike. Cool toy. Jed is my new BFF."

Katie eyed Thomas, walked over, and gave him a hug as he was studying the phone. Interesting, Mike thought. With three good-sized humans and eight canines of varied sizes, the truck was crowded and comfortable at the same time. The smaller dogs rode on laps while the big dogs sat in a row on the extended cab back seat, refusing to ride in the covered truck bed. Mike put all the windows down and gasped, "Jesus, we have got to start brushing their teeth; the dog breath is killing me." Katie and Thomas laughed most of the way to their new hideout.

They whooshed in and, after new greetings all around, gathered near Jed's table bed. Mike introduced Thomas to Jed and Jed to Jack and Ghost.

"So tell it, Thomas," Mike stated.

With center stage, a place Thomas enjoyed, he began: "After scoping the area, I drove just outside the small town next to I-5 where I thought they might be and waited. It didn't take too long to hear a vehicle coming my way. I had a pre-planned route to a perfect hidey-hole. In a chase, when they think they've lost you, most people will double back using the same route. I would be lying in wait when that happened.

"Ha! Best laid plans. What I didn't expect was their ride: a canary yellow Porsche Carrere GT. Damn, that thing was fast! I couldn't put enough distance between us, even knowing where I was going. Had to pass my stop-off point and did a quick turn onto a side road, almost rolling and slid into a ditch at just the wrong angle—couldn't drive out. We jumped out of the truck and scrambled up a bluff as the Porsche smoothly made the turn.

"The dogs and I found a tree for cover, and I had them in my sights. You wouldn't believe it. The two stepped out of the Porsche, guns blazing, and started walking up the hill like they were in a gangster movie—idiots. They were shooting willy-nilly in my general direction. Decided I didn't want them too close, and since I had a clear shot, I landed a few rounds near their feet. They turned and ran down the hill lickety-split and hid behind the Porsche. I kiddingly said, 'Jill, why don't you guys go around behind?'"

Thomas stopped and looked frankly at Mike. "Damn, Mike, that dog is something else. She understood! She took off with Ghost through the trees on the ridge to the east. I was just going to wait 'til dark and do it myself. I sat there eating a candy bar while our Mexican standoff continued. I half expected one of those dumb shits to get up and try something stupid—I was getting impatient so probably would have done something I regretted later.

"When I saw Jill and Ghost running low and fast across a field behind the Porsche, I started moving. I could hear screaming and growling as I came around the car. Jill had the man on the ground with his right arm in a vice grip and Ghost held the woman. I didn't even know Ghost could actually do it! The man started pleading for to me to get them off.

"I used some twist ties to truss them up. Wish you could have seen them. He was dressed up like a *Mad Max* character and she had on a Cat

Woman outfit. They introduced themselves as Bonnie and Clyde." Thomas started a low, rumbling laughter just thinking about the two in their doomsday outfits. "So I ask, 'Who the hell are you two numb nuts thinking of robbing? Seems to me all the people are gone—just take the hell what you want!'"

Katie was grabbing her gut, and Sara was laughing so hard tears were leaking out of her eyes.

Thomas continued, "I didn't want to kill them. They didn't seem evil, just a bit whacked, but whacked people can cause a lot of problems. Look at poor Jed over there. I asked if they'd shot Jed, and Clyde denied it. Jill walked over to Bonnie, put her snout near, and growled. Thought Bonnie might lose it. She was crying her little cat heart out and finally fessed up, at least sort of. Said they were hunting and she thought Jed was a deer. Not sure I believed them, but you never know. I stood there and made pleasant conversation while Jill continued to give them the evil eye. Best good cop, bad cop routine ever. They were very forthcoming. Found out they were just kids. Clyde said he was 19 and Bonnie 15 at the change. Only thing they didn't give up was their real names.

"I warned them if they followed me or bothered my friends again I would kill them—no questions asked. After taking their weapons and leaving some water, I set them loose. Then, the girls and I went on a joy ride in that beautiful piece of machinery. That's what took so long. We drove the hell out of it until the Porsche ran out of gas and made our way back to the meeting place."

Mike asked, "Do you think they'll be back, Thomas? It was risky to leave them."

"No, I don't think so. They might even rethink their approach to the new world. Getting a huge dose of reality after being roughed up has a way of changing your perspective—what I call a boatload of paradigm shift."

"If they weren't so bad, maybe you should have asked them if they wanted to join us," Katie said.

Thomas met Katie's sincere gaze. "You are a very decent person, Katie, but I'm not at all sure we need Mad Max on our team. Nevertheless,

I offered. Told them if they cleaned up their act and wanted to join the real world, or what's left of it, all they had to do was make their way to Tacoma and we would find them. At that moment they didn't seem interested. Never know; they might change their minds if they get tired of romping around the countryside."

Mike steered the conversation back to the present. He filled Thomas in on Jed's status and the need for him to stay put for a couple more days. Sara reiterated her offer to join them later when Jed could be moved.

Thomas said, "We still don't know where the ranch is located. I'm not sure what rushing back to Washington does for us anyway."

In a weak voice, Jed asked Sara if she could prop him up. With Mike's help, they gathered pillows from around the house and arranged them so his head was comfortably raised and he could talk more easily.

"I think what I brought with me will help you find them." Jed had the group's attention. "I have some very special drones. They have a heat finding radar embedded that can identify any warm-blooded mammals of approximately 100 pounds or more, in a three-square mile radius. That technology has been around and is in use now. What makes these drones special is the power source. Drones are small and don't need large fuel tanks or batteries, but range is still constrained by energy requirements.

"Most good scientists understand we'll never be able to reliably use renewable energy sources on a practical basis until we can efficiently capture and store that energy. I worked for a cutting edge, privately funded, and very secretive company that was taking out-of-the-box approaches to the most vexing energy problems. I still don't know who funded the research; I only know we didn't have to worry about being the shiny new penny to pursue pure science.

"Anyway, in the last year we made two earth shaking breakthroughs: one regarding batteries and another in energy production. I won't bore you with all the details other than to say the battery we developed can store enough energy to move an automobile nearly 1000 miles and it weighs just a little over a pound. The energy source is a thorium reactor generator, which I might add is no larger than your average household generator. You can recharge the battery in ten minutes using a process fueled by a tiny amount of thorium. Thorium is safer than uranium and in abundant supply around the world. The U.S. supply alone would power the country for a thousand years. As the population is now, well, let's just say indefinitely."

Each of the survivors, totally mesmerized by Jed's amazing news, sat silently. "You are the first people outside the company I was able to tell. We were testing the new technology using drones because they're a lot easier to hide—thus the drones I brought with me. We were almost ready to fast track our discoveries for commercial use. The plan was to revolutionize energy in ten years. But alas, the world ended before we had that chance.

"I have three of these drones. They will fly for approximately 15,000 miles before they must be recharged. I can hook up satellite-connected laptops to view infrared heat signatures, but someone must watch. Idaho is a pretty big state. I recommend we decide the most likely places to search first in a grid pattern. It may still take some time."

Mike said, "Can I kiss you?"

Sara added, "No, I will do it" and gave Jed and soft peck on the cheek, to which he blushed.

"I still have a lot of questions. Isn't thorium radioactive—dangerous? And do you have any of it with you?" Mike asked.

"It is radioactive, but far less than uranium. The process used in the generator/reactor I brought with me renders the radioactive materials inert, and the generator is small enough to fit in the van. That's the beauty of it—remarkable, really."

Not done with questioning, Mike rubbed his chin and inquired, "So did you build the generator, can you fix it if it breaks, and/or replicate it? I thought you were an IT kind of guy."

Jed was either pulling their numerous legs or amazingly humble. "Actually, I was hired because of a grouping of disciplines. That was the key to our success. The company recruited individuals with a greater range rather than deep focus in any one scientific field. They thought it made for increased problem-solving and, looking at results, they were right. I have undergraduate degrees in physics and electrical engineering and received advanced degrees in energy and information technology.

"I didn't build the generator but lent a hand to solve one of many complex issues in the development. I do have complete specifications and diagrams. With enough time, we can build another. But don't worry, we won't need to for some time. This little jewel will power a small city."

Thomas yelled, "God damn! It's a good thing we saved your skinny ass!"

Jed looked at Thomas with the most earnest expression Sara could remember. "And I will always be eternally grateful. The worst part, when I thought I might die, was that I would take that technology with me to the grave. It is considered in the scientific world a generational leap in technology."

The dogs were getting restless—it was dinnertime. Sara and Thomas went to the kitchen to look for something to eat. Katie could hear the two stridently whispering through the door. She tried not to listen to the unfolding drama, but curiosity won the day.

"Thomas, the least you could have done was called on the radio—I was totally worried. And you went on a joy ride in a hot car as we were concerned about your safety? That's just juvenile."

"Looks to me like you were very busy taking care of my man Jed," Thomas responded.

"What are you insinuating? Jed was unconscious when we got here. If it hadn't been for me, he might not have survived," Sara indignantly sputtered.

Thomas's shoulders relaxed as he considered Sara and all they had shared about their previous lives. Being a doctor, able to make sick people well, made Sara feel important and worthwhile. She had told Thomas before everything crashed and burned that her friend Dan had volunteered for Doctors without Borders and left to help in Ethiopia. For a long time, she couldn't understand why he would voluntarily put himself at risk only to live in an inhospitable environment. His spotty emails described horrible conditions, and yet the work drew him in. Sara was doubtful she could survive living in a dusty tent and saw people everywhere that could benefit from a good general practice doctor; you didn't have to travel to the far ends of the earth to be of service. Nevertheless, she dreamed about doing something substantial and respected doctors with the courage to help people in the way her friend Dan had chosen.

"It's an amazing thing you did for Jed. I trusted that if anyone could help him, it would be you. But I need you to trust me, too. This is who I am. When I was a kid in school the teachers were always telling my parents I had ADHD. It wasn't that I couldn't sit and be quiet. I just didn't want to. I found a home when I joined the Army. For once, all that energy was put to good use, and like you and your ability to heal, it gave me a purpose. I'm good at it, Sara, and accustomed to operating on my own or in a small team for long stretches. The truth is, I get off on the challenge."

"I'm not saying you aren't good at what you do. But seriously, you couldn't have taken two minutes to check in with Mike? I thought that was part of the discipline!"

Thomas looked down, realizing she had a point. "I don't think I can change, Sara. Yes, I should have checked in, but I thought you all would trust me to get back to you safely. This is the reason I was only married for six months…Sara, if you can't handle it, I understand. You don't owe me anything. I'll always care about you."

"You saved my life in Seattle, you thick-headed ass! I owe you that."

"What I do… and Sara, like it or not, the whole world is now doctors without borders."

Since the dinner table was occupied, the close-knit group sat on chairs near the table with plates in their laps as they discussed their next move. Jed's sudden escalation as a person of great importance won the day. The vote was four to zero to stay and wait until Jed was well enough to travel. Jed recused himself from the vote, justifying his lack of participation as bias due to personal benefit.

Chapter 27: A+101, Karen Meets Enlightenment

"I'm going stir crazy!" Karen said to the wall of her cage. "You would think I'd be accustomed to isolation." No dogs or volleyballs to talk to, no work tasks to be accomplished, and with little ability to plan, Karen leaned into a world of her mind. She practiced conversations in Spanish, worked on her breathing while shooting an imaginary rifle and gently applying pressure to the trigger pull, and relived a hot, muggy day in Florida at Disney World with her family. As the texture and richness of imaginings improved, so did Karen's clarity about her dreams.

A pattern had emerged from disorder, as Karen hoped—no—*knew* it would. The universe was a mirror-filled funhouse; look straight on and a distorted view of a bulbous or stick-thin replica is the only reward. But find the sweet spot. That place where the reflection stretches to eternity, and that place will reveals chaos-free sameness.

Dreams of the future were flashes or detailed pictures, while normal dreams moved in hazy, undefined circles. In normal dreams she often knew where she was or who she was with without actually seeing it. After recounting night dreams quickly, she sorted and categorized until she was sure which ones might foretell events to come. Even better, she was having flashes while awake. This morning, after making love to Mike in his RV, she saw Mathias standing behind a desk and knew she would meet him today.

Mabel had been less talkative lately, obviously warned or threatened not to become involved with the prisoner. It didn't stop Karen from trying. When she heard Mabel's footsteps bringing breakfast, she yelled out, "Good morning, Mabel. How's it going?"

"Not bad, and thanks for asking. You'll have to eat fast. We need to get you looking decent so you can visit 'the one,'" Mabel replied sarcastically while pushing Karen's breakfast through the small hole in the gate. She shoved some clothes in after the food. "Wash up and put those clothes on. I'll have to handcuff you before we go, and I'm hoping you won't give me no trouble."

Overjoyed she had nailed the prescient dream, Karen gave a resounding, "No trouble from me, Mabel. I can't wait to get out of this cage!"

Karen found herself standing in front of Mathias's desk, shoeless, with a tight fitting tee, biker shorts, and hair sprouting from her scalp in clumps created by her very own self-styled haircut. She knew this was all part of Mathias's plan to make her feel small and weak to gain a larger measure of control, as if locking her in a cage for a week wasn't enough.

Mathias continued working on a document, pretending he was unaware or unconcerned with her presence. Karen stared at him, prepared to stand in silence for as long as it took. He was not exactly as she'd pictured him in this morning's flash. The mental image of Mathias she saw in her dream state was the man before the change. That man had soft, fleshy features, a weak chin, and puffy dark circles under his eyes. Mathias raised his eyes and pointed to a chair directly beside his desk that was positioned like a grade school classroom, facing forward in a teacher/student arrangement. "Sit down, Karen."

The change could not totally ameliorate an unremarkable face, but Mathias's eyes were a different matter. They were the same intelligent, intense, and startlingly pale gray witnessed in her vision. "You aren't what I expected," Mathias stated as he assessed her body from Karen's breasts to her bare feet.

"I've been so busy I haven't had time for my beauty routine. And you are," Karen replied, sitting straight in the hard metal folding chair.

"I am what?"

"What I expected."

"Hmmm well…" Mathias paused, analyzing how to direct the conversation. "I don't think it's in your best interest to antagonize me. Clearly that's your modus operandi. It was obvious to me, even during short conversations over the radio, that you have little appreciation for any approach other than your own. There really is no need to be adversarial. What I'm prepared to offer is a little bit of freedom so that you can build relationships and trust within our community. All I ask is that you set aside previous experiences for a little while and give our way some consideration. Learn something new, Karen, and open your mind to different possibilities. If it doesn't fit for you, we will look at other alternatives. I would love nothing better than to see you as a thriving, integral part of our new system for improved enlightened living."

Damn, he's good, Karen thought, *so convinced and persuasive. His smooth conversational tone in a pitch-perfect tenor and just the hint of a threat… what harm could come in submitting my will to this narcissistic asshole? What could possibly go wrong?* Karen wanted to get out of her cage and try to escape. She swallowed the bile in her mouth and answered, "I'm ready to try. I'm also very curious about this new approach. And I love learning something new and really appreciate the chance to earn your trust. Thanks for the opportunity, Mathias." All true, she thought, but not exactly in the way that it sounded.

Mathias stared at her, trying to divine any underlying meaning as she looked back with an angelic expression. "Well, good then, I do hope you'll give our community a sincere effort." Mathias said, his forehead furrowed.

Karen was aware that the best thing to do now was walk-out and leave well enough alone. However, she needed more information and had a feeling one-on-one time with Mathias wasn't part of his plan. "I just have one question. Why did you bring me here?"

Mathias exhaled and raised his chin, irritated to have to explain to the unworthy. "Whatever do you mean, Karen?"

"I mean, you know I don't want to be here. And, I don't believe you hold me in high regard. Why would you force someone to be part of a community that, as you say, is a new way to achieve strong bonds and relationships?"

"You may have difficulty understanding this concept, but not everything I do is about what I personally desire. I have a vision. A long-term vision that entails a strong community of families, and we need an equal representation of both men and women."

Oh great, Karen thought. *Add another "ist" to the pile. He's also a misogynist*, which given everything, she could have expected. "But, wouldn't someone like me just be a thorn in your side? Wouldn't achieving your vision be easier if you found people who were more, shall we say, receptive to your vision?"

"I never anticipated this would be easy! It will take hard work. And I also know, when families form and children are born, it's the cement that binds; particularly for the fairer sex."

Karen's face paled, realizing her worst fear. She was merely breeding stock he planned to keep in his zoo by capitalizing on her maternal instincts. There was a strange gleam in Mathias's eyes with the recognition of a direct hit to Karen's fears. He pressed an intercom button on his phone, and Karen could hear his voice echoing in the room outside the door. "Mabel, come in and escort our guest back to her lodgings."

Karen was allowed to attend the nightly session, albeit with handcuffs and still barefoot, clad in her humiliating outfit. The other ranch members besides Rachael, were dressed in normal casual apparel. The meeting was everything she'd imagined and more. Clearly the true path to enlightenment in this group of dingbats was total fealty to their leader and his henchmen. Karen always believed she would not be vulnerable to brainwashing. As the session unfolded, she had a sense that most people, in the right circumstance, could fall prey to this insidious mind-screwing style. A basic human instinct, most likely one of survival, is to belong and be loved or at minimum accepted by the community in which you are a part. Sitting among the assorted ranch members, even an unabashedly stubborn individual like her could feel the pull to form bonds and somehow mold to the culture.

The horrid beauty of Mathias's brand of enlightenment was that it didn't rely on beatings and significant violence—merely on the threat. Karen was pretty sure she understood Mathias's "vision" and process. Begin by isolating already vulnerable new recruits, taking control over even basic needs like hygiene and clothing. The ranch would then offer salvation from the fear through a misguided and religious notion of enlightenment. All the while, convince recruits that they're bad or broken but you have the answer. Convince them that the world would be a beautiful place if only they would do yada, yada, yada.

And every cult needs an enemy—nothing binds a group together like a common enemy or more than one, if possible. That was the last phase.

Mathias would create enemies and villains to blame for the pain while reinforcing the tribe identity and loyalty. Toss in a few enforcers to dole out rewards and punishments, and voila! A small cult or the Third Reich or ISIS is born. Size and scope are only dependent upon circumstance, the evil force of egotistic leaders and people willing to follow them. More repeating patterns from funhouse mirrors.

Karen still remembered a fragile young woman named Amelia Draper. Almost as petite as Karen and stick thin, her eyes fluttered sideways or down whenever she was noticed. Her body rigid and withdrawn during even short conversations, she seemed to be prepared for a beating at any given moment. Karen wondered how in the world she had ever made it through basic training.

She had come to Karen's unit as a Private First Class when Karen was a Company Commander. In her concern for PFC Draper, she asked the First Sergeant to assign her as a company clerk. "We need to keep an eye on her, First Sergeant. I'm not sure how she'll do. Maybe we can help her get started."

The First Sergeant, not the mothering type but always short-staffed of clerical help, tightened his lips and nodded. "Another project, huh? Hope she can type."

Millie was a good worker, an amazing athlete for someone so slight, and never a behavior problem. But she was always so alone. Over the course of a year, Karen was able to earn some trust. One day she came out of her office and Millie was bent over her desk crying. Karen pulled a chair up to her desk, sat and asked, "Are you okay, PFC Draper. Can I help?"

Her soft brown bangs were plastered to her forehead as she glanced up sadly with red, swollen eyes. "I was just remembering something, ma'am."

"Do you want to talk about it?"

"You and the First Sergeant are awful nice to me, but it's just hard to talk about."

"Okay. You know, sometimes it helps to share. But, if you don't want to share with me, why don't we get you in to see a counselor?"

"You'll think I am crazy."

"No, I don't think you're crazy. I think something has hurt you very badly." Of all the things Karen expected, the thing that came out of the Private's mouth was the last thing she would have guessed.

"I was raised in a cult with my family. I ran away. My parents and brother are still there."

With little understanding of cults, Karen was dumbfounded. They got PFC Draper in to see a psychiatrist immediately. Little Millie seemed to be improving and even smiled with her eyes on occasion. Then one weekend she was found in the barracks bathroom, on the floor with her wrists slit. She didn't survive.

Karen read everything she could get her hands on about cults to understand. She felt like she had failed this young woman and needed to know more. And so Karen became a self-taught expert on cults.

Karen read that most cults eventually crumbled under the weight of their own unhinged foundations, but only after tearing the fabric of humanity from all too many souls. Inevitably questions regarding the new order would mount as offenders were made into examples or eliminated. Punishments escalate, resistance mobilizes, chaos reigns, and then, normally too late, the evil is conquered.

This new world was a veritable breeding ground for cult leaders like Mathias or worse, and the ranch was an example of the early stages of cult formation. Karen wanted to be long gone before it hit the skids. Lost in thought about how to avoid this phenomenon in the new world, Karen heard her name called. She looked up with a deer in the headlights expression and asked, "Uh, I'm sorry, what was the question?"

Carlotta, exasperated, said, "You need to get with the program if you want to continue to attend these meetings." All eyes were turned to Karen. "I asked what you had learned about yourself."

"Ah, yes, that. It's exactly what I was thinking about and then got lost in my head. I haven't been sleeping well, and the isolation has me a little off. I've spent so much time alone the last few months, and all the voices and back and forth make it difficult to focus. And I was thinking about my dogs, whom I truly miss…"

"Just get to the point!" Carlotta huffed as Mathias leaned back in his chair, rubbing his chin and pretending to give a damn about what Karen might say next.

"Okay, yes. What I've learned about myself is that for me, autonomy is more important than membership."

There was silence as the group tried to decide what the hell that meant. Karen wasn't sure either, but she was ready to defend the statement regardless.

"Please expand on that, Karen, so the group can benefit from your insights," Mathias said.

"It's about freedom versus acceptance. I have a greater need for freedom."

The group became even more quiet with the knowledge this discussion could become contentious.

"Tell me more, Karen," Mathias prodded.

"Well, alright. I see it as a sliding scale, with total individual autonomy on one side and adherence to a group on the other. As you become more immersed in what is good for the group or belonging to that group, your individual choices and needs are limited. I think on that scale, I prefer to sit closer to the autonomous side; some call it freedom."

"Interesting. It sounds like you believe freedom and group membership are diametrically opposed. Can't those two things exist in harmony and benefit both the group and the individual?"

Karen was sitting forward in her chair, actually enjoying the intellectual exchange. "Sure they can, but that's the challenge. Without laws or a system to keep things balanced, I think the tendency is to subvert individual will. I know what's good for me better than anyone else. I don't trust a group to know."

"So it is your need for control that is at issue? Where do you think that comes from?"

Karen stifled a laugh at Mathias's statement. "From life, Mathias. Perhaps it would be easier if it came from one cathartic incident in my past. That would be oh so much less effort to isolate and extract from my value system. My total life experience taught me those groups that yell loudest from the rooftops about only wanting to do good for all, be they religious or educational or political, are often the same groups led by individuals that actually have only their own best interests at heart, not mine." Karen glared at the Mathias, and he looked angrily back.

"Well, this is getting us nowhere. What you propose sounds like chaos to me. A large part of the human experience involves bonding with others for the welfare of the whole. Without that, we are nothing more than wild animals. I am simply trying to improve upon the techniques that strengthen those relationships. I would like you to consider your feelings about control for the next group meeting." Mathias looked at Carlotta and nodded, indicating she should move on to someone else.

Karen held her tongue rather than point out to Mathias and his minions that kidnapping and jailing someone in a stable was proof positive that their brand of enlightenment had already gone off the rails. Luckily, it was too early to eject Karen from the group, so they moved on to Mabel.

Carlotta tore into Mabel with a viciousness that surprised Karen. Carlotta and Dave took turns pointing out all of Mabel's perceived failures, from being sarcastic to the way in which she refused to fully participate in ranch activities, demanding she identify the root of those behaviors so she could atone to the group. Mabel sat silent, her hands locked tight in fists, nodding at their accusations and thanking them for the feedback.

Karen wondered how long it would be before psychological flogging was inadequate and power lust demanded something more visceral. After Mabel's verbal bloodletting, Karen looked across the room at Rachael, who was staring straight ahead repeatedly placing her left hand underneath her chair. It took a minute for Karen to realize it was a signal and not a nervous tick. She would take that chair tomorrow.

Rachael avoided Karen on her way out, glancing back only once with a half-smile and moving in a different direction. *Very disappointing*, Karen thought, *but understandable if you want to keep up appearances.* At least she hoped it was a ruse and these people weren't getting to her.

Walking with Mabel to the stable, Karen was chilled by a cooler evening breeze as goosebumps rose on her uncovered skin. Mabel, scowling, looked straight ahead as they walked over the gravel path in near total dark. Certain now was the time, Karen formed her question. Mabel had lived for a very long time; long-winded explanations, subtle introductions, or BS would be unwelcome, so Karen came straight to the point. "Do you want to leave, Mabel?"

Mabel kept walking for a time then abruptly stopped. Turning to Karen, she replied, "Yes."

"Keep walking," Karen motioned.

"He wasn't always like this, you know. When we first met he was excited and wanted to create something better; 'truer' is how he explained it. I got all caught up in Mathias's enthusiasm. And why the heck not? For all the joy in my life, there was at least as much pain and loss, and I wanted to believe. He would tell me stories about how our new lives would look and feel, those eyes flashing and him all smart and confident."

"He said his reputation had been maligned by some jealous tenured professors at the small private university in New York where he was teaching. Something about the originality of a paper he published, I'm not really sure. All I know is he moved out to Idaho with his family not long after he bought the property. Mathias said he found the ranch accidentally when he was looking for a secluded place to start a retreat. He just drove up to the door and said he wanted to buy the place. The owner didn't have any family or friends and finally agreed to sell for the right price.

His wife left him not long after they moved to Idaho. She took their two kids back to the East Coast. Before the sickness came, he was already planning to make the ranch a retreat for people searching for a better way.

"Well anyhow, then Carlotta and Dave came along. She was always sashaying around him swinging those hips and pouting like a damn girl. And she ain't no girl! I know what she is, and my momma told me not to talk bad, so I won't say. Dave is an opportunist, plain and simple. He saw someone who could do what he couldn't and latched on for all he was worth. Having them around let open the floodgates of bad juju. We all have a dark side, but most of us try to fight it and keep it locked up nice and tight. Those three, well… I think they was just lookin' for an excuse to let it out."

None of this surprised Karen. Evil is a chameleon. So often disguised as good intentions, the road to hell and all that stuff, it wraps tentacles around the unaware and open hearted. She whispered to Mabel, "Keep your office window unlocked and see if you can find and hide a weapon. And all that stuff they said to you earlier, that's all just bullshit to make you feel small and weak. Stay ready."

Mabel looked at Karen. "Thank you, and I'll be ready."

Chapter 28: Jack

Hungry. Jack needs the partner. Small animals are fast. Good when Jill flushes and Jack catches. Together we are strong. Jack is alone.

Must find the woman Karen. She is Jack's duty. Find the humans, bond with them, and protect and defend. The bond is strong. Jack feels where she is a long way away. The girl Katie feels too but not as strong. Jack is stronger. Jack knows where to go.

Jack hears the forest. Jack smells the creatures big and small. Jack feels others like him. They are far away. Jack smells the wild dogs—must keep away, go around. They know duty only to pack. Many territories in this place. Their scent marks the boundary. Jack must go around. Jack is alone.

Jack smells big animals, not a pack but many. Jack will hide and wait. They are coming. Jack is smart. He rolls in grass and mud with their scent. Jack hides until they come. Jacks finds the place where they can't run. Humans call it path. He waits until they are almost gone then jumps. He takes the smallest as his. Jack drags his prize to a safe place. Jack eats.

The stream is wide and fast. Jack can swim. Fear from the last swim makes Jack look for a better place. The water caught Jack in the last swim. He was carried too far from Karen by the water. Jack is smart. There will be a better place. Jack looks into the distance and goes the way to the woman. He finds a place to cross. A wild dog boundary is on the other side. Jack goes back. He will find another place.

The dark is not safe. Predators hunt. The wild dogs are like him but not. Jack does not know their language. He listens to their howls to understand. Jack needs to understand. The man Mike would understand and tell Jack. Jack is alone.

Jack finds another place and rests for the dark. He hides under rocks where a big animal rests too. The big animal has not been in this place for a time. Jack is safe. He hears the wild dogs in the distance and wants to hunt with them. He feels the woman's fear and longs to make her safe. The man is far away. Jack whimpers. A memory of their smells, fills him.

Jack doesn't understand. He ate the animal. He still needs. He is still empty. Something changed. The bond that is duty is changed. It is more. The dog part of him needs more. He hurts for them—the man, the woman, the young females, Jill and his pack. He yearns for their touch. Jack is alone. Jack is duty.

Chapter 29: A+103, The Home Team

Circling his finger above his head, Mike yelled, "Load em up." Jed, having been judged well enough to travel by Sara, lounged on the back seat of Thomas's new extra-large SUV procured from a local grocery store. Dog excitement had reached a crescendo as they set off north, straight up the I-5, while Thomas wondered how it was dogs always seemed to know when the direction was home.

With three vehicles including Jed's extended van, the convoy travel slowed an otherwise quick trip. In the lead vehicle, Katie shifted her position to scan for the presence of other survivors. As before, just outside Portland she sensed someone in the area. "Mike, I feel someone. Maybe the same person as before when we came down here. It seems like they're straight ahead."

Wanting to keep Katie on task, Mike fumbled with the secure radio as he drove. "Thomas, Sara, just ahead, Katie found someone. I'm going to go more slowly until Katie gets a better lock and then stop."

It wasn't long before they were huddled next to the highway. Jed was talking out the window while Tilley, standing over him, perfectly aligned her head to Jed as if she was speaking for him. "Let's use the drones. If you will please hand me my laptop under the seat and get a drone out of the van. No time like the present."

Back in southern Oregon, Jed had barely finished explaining the equipment and drones he'd brought with him before Mike bolted to the garage to retrieve them. Under protest from Sara, Mike had perched the laptop on Jed's lap and asked for a demonstration. Mike and Katie had tried to fly one in the backyard, but Mike, on the high end of the Baby Boomer population and not particularly adept at computer controls, cursed as he crashed it twice into the ground. Katie took over when he lodged the drone in a tree. Katie was better than Mike, but today she had a job to do scouting for other people. That left a mostly immobilized Jed to fly the sleek bird-like contraption.

Sitting with his back against the side of the van, his wounded legs lying lengthwise on the seat, Jed's fingers flew across the laptop keyboard as Mike, outside of the van, placed the drone on the ground on top of a hard launching platform. As it lifted into the air, it was off and flying along the highway with oohs and ahs from the gathered observers. Tilley, Raider, and Zoe started barking and gave chase, following the drone down the road until Katie and Mike simultaneously yelled, "Come!"

They huddled outside the van peering through the open window at the laptop screen as Jed adjusted the viewing angles. Sara, excited, squealed, "Look straight ahead on the right of the highway. Is that a person?"

Jed closed in, aiming the controls at the speck in the distance, and said, "Definitely a person." Not wanting to risk his bird being shot down, Jed raised the drone's elevation and focused the camera. "Yep, it's a guy. Must have seen the drone. He's holding a sign up to the sky and smiling. Looks like a dog lying behind him in the grass. "

Thomas, not able to get a clear view, asked, "What does the sign say?"

Jed answered perplexed, "Will work for food? No, that can't be right."

"Does he have any weapons?" Mike wanted to know as he tried to nudge Sara to get a better view of the screen.

"Don't see any. He has a big pack over there. See it?" Jed pointed with the cursor.

"Keep it flying, Jed, and pay attention. Only one way to do this. Thomas, get your gear; Jill, Tilley and Ghost, you're coming with us. Katie, you stay on the radio." Mike, reverting to commander mode, ordered the rest of the group to remain vigilant.

Thomas and Mike made quick work of the distance, jogging three miles up the highway. When they could see the man, Mike called back to Katie to ensure he hadn't acquired any weapons and was reassured that the man was still holding the sign. Mike told Jill to go along the vegetation to the man's rear, and Ghost, already moving, followed Jill's lead. Tilley stayed by Mike's side.

"Well, Thomas, what do you think? You're the expert."

"Wish there was some cover so we could have a conversation with the guy without being shot, but I'm not seeing any. I say we yell at each other. Worked pretty well for you and me."

Road man didn't give them a chance. When he saw the two men and dogs he slowly placed the sign on the ground, raised his arms above his head, and yelled first, "Hey, man, I'm no threat. Heard you a few days ago and been waiting. Come closer so we can talk."

Guns drawn, Thomas, Mike, and Tilley edged within better yelling distance, wary of any quick movements. The man's dog finally convinced them it was safe. Obviously old with a silver snout and rheumy eyes, the dog, sensing Ghost and Jill behind him, pushed off the ground with that time-honored infirmity of stiff joints and wagged his tail.

Mike looked at Thomas. "How bad can he be?"

"I was thinking the same thing," Thomas rejoined.

Mike closed the distance while Thomas and Tilley stayed alert, Thomas's rifle at the ready.

The man reached his hand out to Mike. "I am Manuel. So very good to meet you."

Mike hesitated for a moment, watching the man's eyes, then clasped his hand and replied, "I'm Mike. What are you doing here?"

Manuel's shoulders sagged as he released a breath, relieved he had lived to tell his story. "You and your friend over there are the first people I've seen since everything went bad. I heard you, or someone, pass by a few days ago, but by the time I got to the interstate you were gone. Was it you?"

"Probably, or at least I hope so, or someone is following us." Mike stooped down to pick up the sign on the ground. "Will work for food? Really?"

Manuel's dark eyes flashed with humor. "That was a joke. Perhaps not a good one, eh? I hoped you would come back this way. Henry and I camped out in a little house over there." Manuel pointed to an old farmhouse set back from the highway. Hearing his name, Henry slowly moved to Manuel's side then plopped down on the gravelly shoulder, resting his head on Manuel's feet. "What does one write on a sign to express a sincere desire for friendship? NO WORRIES, I AM NOT A ZOMBIE?"

"Kind of a dangerous play, Manuel, don't you think?" Mike said, intently assessing the man.

"Yes, Mike, not a doubt. I was very lonely. I had to take the chance." Manuel smiled down at Henry. "He was my son's dog. I brought him home as a pup when Enrique was six. My boy loved this dog." Manuel paused, shaking his head to push aside the memories. "I am a good cook and a great builder. I can build anything you want. My family had a small construction business and Jessie, my oldest son, got a degree in architecture. He taught me everything he learned at school." Manuel looked at Mike proudly.

Mike, still wearing his stern expression, shouted, "Jill, Ghost, come! Put away your gun, Thomas. This man says he's a good cook!"

Jill and Ghost flew out of the shadows. Jill slowly walked to the old dog, displaying appropriate respect, and then stood in front of Manuel wagging her tail as Manuel got in a crouch to pet her ruff. Jill's head swung in Mike's direction and Mike heard her say, "Good man."

Manuel smiled with pleasure as Thomas introduced himself and shook Manuel's hand with his own mitt-sized version. "So Manuel, what gear are you packing?"

"I have a truck with some tools and food over at the farmhouse. If you will wait, I'll carry Henry over there—he can't walk very well—and meet you back here."

"No need," Mike said. He unlatched the radio from his belt and called Katie. "Can you drive up? We have a new team member." He put the radio back and gave his attention to Manuel. "We'll give you a ride to the farmhouse and then you can follow us back home."

"Thank you so much, Mike. You won't regret it. And if you don't mind me asking, where are we going?"

"Oh yeah: Tacoma. It's only fair to tell you we have a few issues we're dealing with. Two women from our group were kidnapped and taken to Idaho. We're in the process right now of trying to figure out where they are and come up with a plan to get them back. Sorry to drag you into it, but we can use all the help we can get."

"It would be my pleasure to assist in any way I can. Yes, I know of the ranch from my radio. I decided to take my chances on strangers on the freeway rather than join them in Idaho. This man Mathias, he seems a little weird to me," Manuel responded, raising his chest and smiling. "And so you know, cooking and building are just my specialties. I am what they call a renaissance man."

Manuel lived up to his self-proclaimed expertise as a cook. The first night back in Tacoma he made the best Chile relleno Katie had ever eaten. Demolishing the food, a cacophony of moans and smacking had the dog pack circling the table in curiosity. Sara asked Manuel how old he was and where he grew up, learning just the week before he'd celebrated a lonely 48th birthday. He said his parents had a farm in the Salinas Valley in California and they'd lived there until he was almost thirty. Eyeing Manuel's thick, dark, slightly wavy hair, matching eyes, chiseled nose, and square chin, Sara cautiously inquired, "I hope this isn't impertinent, but were you this male model good looking before the change?"

The chewing stopped. Thomas and Mike wore surprised expressions while Katie glanced down at her plate giggling. Manuel, seemingly as unaware as the other men, took a few seconds to process Sara's question. "Sara, I greatly appreciate the compliment, but I think the answer to that question is most definitely no. I was known, as they say, as roly-poly. My brothers were very surprised my beautiful Hannah agreed to marry me." Mike shook his head and rolled his eyes as the rest of the small tribe laughed and enjoyed the camaraderie.

Up early the next morning, Manuel was out scouting the neighborhood, arriving just in time for the morning's training session. He tugged at Mike's elbow as they were getting ready to practice using cameras and microphones on the dogs, another tech gadget Jed had brought with him. "Mike, I think it is getting very crowded here with me and my dog. I looked at the immediate neighborhood outside the gate. I think it would be easy to fence the entire area when we return from our important mission. The ridge behind the homes makes it easy to protect if others find us. Also, I could wire the homes together and use Jed's amazing generator to power everyone. It will give us room to grow."

Mike nodded. "That's a great idea, Manuel. I haven't even had a chance to think much about the community we can build. I've been so focused on saving my friends, I haven't done much else."

Manuel appraised Mike, "These two women are more to you than just friends, I think."

Mike nodded and looked forlornly at the sky. "Karen and I talked about how we would go about creating a good place to restart just before she was taken. It is important to me and to her and will be important to everyone who stays in our group. Would you be willing to take responsibility for developing our physical community once we get back? Everyone would need to be included in any final plans, and of course we'll all have to help with the labor."

"Yes, Mike, thank you! I would be very proud to do it, and don't worry, I will create an oasis of our new town." Mike smiled at Manuel's excitement, glad to know Manuel was willing to share the burden for building their new community. He just prayed Karen would be there to share it with them.

Manuel noticed Jill was almost always at Mike's side. It seemed that Mike was barely aware that he continually touched and stroked Jill's ears and head as she stood looking up at Mike as if listening. "It is a wonderful thing to have a friend like your Jill, is it not?"

Startled out of his thoughts, Mike glanced at his canine buddy, panting and waiting for any interaction. Jill's eyes said play would be good but so would work, which to Jill was also a form of play. "To tell you the truth, Manuel, and you may find this difficult to believe… Jill talks to me in my mind."

"Of course she does, Mike. When you find that bond with a dog, it is possible."

Katie strolled up to the two men before Mike had a chance to explain further that he could hear and talk to Jill. "I'm beat already," she sighed. "For the most part, the computer flies the drones, but you have to watch for heat signatures, and it makes me tired. Sara just took over for me. Jed thinks we can get another drone up and going tomorrow, but we'll need two watchers all the time."

"We'll just have to make due, Katie. Finding the ranch is the priority," Mike answered, hiding his frustration about the time it was taking to find Karen and Rachael.

Chapter 30: A+110, Bad Meets Worse at the Ranch

Karen sat in the seat occupied by Rachael the day before. She slid her hand underneath the chair to retrieve Rachael's missive. After cupping it in her palm for a time, she searched the little pocket inside her biker shorts for a tissue and slid the note in.

Not happy with the psychological progress made by fellow ranch dwellers, tonight Mathias would be leading the group on a journey to discover emotional events preventing everyone from realizing their full potential. Once such an event was identified, all they had to do was pluck it out and forever be free from the fears and neurosis associated with it. In other words, Karen surmised, after revealing your vulnerabilities, they would use them to lampoon you later. What utter nonsense.

Soothing music played over an intercom system as Mathias guided them on their personal journey. With eyes closed, Karen visualized Mike, the twins, and the dogs, the only things in this new world sure to calm her. She wore a joyous expression and hoped it would earn brownie points from her deranged captors. When it was her turn to speak, Karen made up a gruesome story. "At an early age, I was forcibly dragged by the hair from my bedroom. I screamed the entire time as my older stepbrother beat me until I was bloody! Now… I can finally let it go…" Karen wailed.

The assembled ranchers tsk-tsked and viewed Karen with the appropriately feigned horror and compassion. Mathias didn't seem to mind at all that Karen never had an older stepbrother. His eyes gleamed as he breathlessly shared with his acolytes, "This is exactly what we are looking for: raw emotion. You have just been witness to Karen making her first real step toward enlightenment. Good job, Karen."

"Thank you, Mathias," Karen said as she looked down at her clasped hands. Karen was pretty sure Mathias didn't believe a word that came out of her mouth and that he also didn't care—that wasn't the point. The point after all was to make people feel more vulnerable. No pain, no gain, as they say.

Not to be outdone, fellow ranch members seeking Mathias's approval upped the ante on harrowing stories of cruelty and humiliation.

There was barely a dry eye in the house. By the time the session was near an end, Karen wondered if Kool-Aid refreshments would be offered. Fortunately, the big triad of Mathias, Carlotta, and Dave, rejuvenated from the quagmire of pain, literally skipped out of the room early to do whatever it was they did.

Walking back to the cage, Mabel eyed Karen with a half-smile on her lips. "Well played Karen, well played."

"Yes, I know. My real emotional event was getting sick on tryout day for the school play, missing my chance for a career in acting. It forever changed the course of my life."

Both women had to calm each other to keep from being heard as they laughed and created stories about imagined emotional events in their lives. Wanting to read Rachael's note, Karen quickened the pace as they drew closer to the stable.

She turned her back to the camera in her cell and read the Post-It note. "I know where they keep some extra weapons, and I will see you tonight, my queen!" A heart was drawn on the bottom encircling a sketch of a warrior princess. *Boy, oh boy, I love that girl,* Karen thought. Karen decided to take a nap so she would be awake later when Rachael arrived.

Karen awoke groggy after bad dreams. It seemed awfully late—Rachael should be here by now. "Might as well sort my dreams while I wait," Karen said out loud. Uh Huh's snoring at unimaginable decibels made it difficult to concentrate, so Karen had a hard time getting her arms around some of the more troubling flashes. With dread, she forced her mind to look directly at the most frightening picture; it was the same dream about Rachael she'd had earlier. Terror gripped her heart as she witnessed Rachael beaten and bloody sitting against a corner, hands covering her face while she cried.

Before succumbing to total panic, she focused on Rachael's surroundings. She was sitting on straw, and chain link covered the upper wall portion—the stable… "Oh my God," Karen moaned. Hoping and praying she was wrong, Karen sat on her cot, now wide awake, her heart pounding in her ears. Time slowed.

Night reached the tipping point before day, when all creatures, human and otherwise, slumber. The wolves' plaintive howls subsided, and owls, with their carrion feasts captured, slept quietly from the evening's activities. Even Uh Huh was soundlessly, blissfully peaceful. Karen almost drifted off sitting cross-legged when she heard footsteps outside, the stable door banging an entrance.

Sure there was more than one person, Karen heard stumbling and a grunt as someone was shoved or fell against a stall door.

"Don't move, bitch," said Dave's voice.

"Who's with you, Dave? What are you doing?"

"Oh, shut up, you stupid cow, or I'll come in and have some fun with you," Dave responded to Karen's plea.

Uh Huh woke and began a high, pitched wail. Karen heard Rachael's voice cry out, "That hurts! Stop!"

Over the piercing sound of Uh Huh's fear, Karen yelled to Dave, "You pathetic son of a bitch! Did you hurt her? You are so small—did your mommy not love you or did the girls make fun of you? Does hurting someone else make you feel better, you little shit!!"

Dave didn't answer. Karen heard and felt a stall door swing forcefully open, more grunting, and then a ferocious clang as it was shut. It seemed impossible, but the volume of Uh Huh's screams increased. Karen pressed her ear against her door to hear what was happening and was greeted by a loud slap on the wood. She jumped back.

Dave was standing just outside her cage. "Listen up, little filly. Your time is coming. Just for fun I'll do to you what your step bro did and then some."

The time for pretending was over. Karen planted her feet and with determined menace spoke through clenched teeth. "Lucky for me I didn't have a stepbrother. And write this down, Dave, so your small little mind can remember: if you hurt her, I will kill you. You are a dead man if you harmed a hair on her head."

"Oh, really? We'll just see about that. Looks to me like you're the one in a cage."

Karen didn't answer. Dave stood at the door for a time and then turned and walked out. Maternal rage, a most powerful force in the last world and this new one, flowed through Karen's body. Willing her mind to think, she had to do something about Uh Huh so she could talk to Rachael. Karen started a shaky delivery of "Silent Night," since it was the first song that came to mind that was calming, and she knew most of the words. When Uh Huh was finally repeating his name to the rhythm she quit singing.

"Rachael, please, please tell me: is that you?"

In a small voice Rachael answered, "It's me."

"Are you okay?"

"Noooo…" Rachael replied, crying softly

The adrenaline effect draining, Karen had never felt so powerless. It's one thing to be locked in a cage like an animal and entirely another to watch as a child you love is hurt and demeaned; strong, independent, creative, and willful Rachael. Wanting to cry while knowing it was the last thing Rachael needed, Karen tried again.

"Listen, sweetie. First, are any of your injuries bad? Are you bleeding?"

"No, I don't think so."

"Do you want to talk about it?" Karen asked.

"Not now," Rachael answered, her voice shaky. "I just want to sleep."

"I understand. No matter how much it hurts right now, know this: Mike and Katie are coming for us." Karen didn't want to lie to Rachael, but a bit of embellishment was called for. "I had a dream about them tonight. It won't be too long until they're here. All the dogs are coming too, and they will heal you with their happy faces and wet sloppy kisses. Just don't give up, Rachael. I'm so sorry he hurt you. I wish I could hold you."

"Okay," was all Rachael could manage.

Sitting vigil all night, Karen couldn't tell whether she slept or not. A horrible hangover feeling clouded everything as her head pounded. Thankfully, Mabel came to bring breakfast early.

"Mabel, you have to check on Rachael now!"

"So that's where she is. I knew something was up. Mathias and Carlotta were arguing this morning, and Jan was driving them crazy 'cause Rachael was missing. Where are you, girl?"

"Over here," a tired voice responded.

Mabel opened the cage, set down the tray with food, and sat on her knees in front of Rachael. She brushed the hair out of her eyes. Other than a few bruises and scrapes, the young woman didn't look too bad. However, Rachael's dead eyes told a different story.

"Who did this, Rachael?" Mabel asked in a soothing voice.

Rachael looked away and sank into herself. "Dave. He caught me last night when I escaped the bunkhouse. He came up behind me. I didn't even hear him, and I can hear everything!"

"Well darlin', it isn't your fault. Why don't we just get you cleaned up and then you need to try and eat something."

Mabel led Rachael to her office. She pulled out some clean clothes, a large bowl of warm water, soap, and some towels. "Do you need my help?"

"No!" Rachael shouted.

"Well, okay. I'm going to leave you in here to tend to yourself. Don't go nowhere, I'll be just outside. I'm going to go talk to Karen. Let me know if you need anything else."

"Okay. Sorry I yelled at you."

"Now, don't you worry about that," Mabel answered.

Rachael took off her shoes and handed them to Mabel. "These are Jan's and she'll be worrying about them. Could you make sure she gets them back?"

"I'll do that. You're a good friend."

Mabel opened Karen's cage, put her finger to her lips for quiet, and signaled Karen to follow.

She whispered to Karen as they hustled to the office. "She needs you right now. Just be quiet or they'll throw me in here with the two of you. Heck, won't be long before most of us end up here…"

Karen knocked on the door. "It's me, Rachael. Can I come in?"

"Yes," a tired voice responded.

Karen entered, then ran to Rachael and put her arms around her. Rachael sobbed as Karen cooed that it would be alright, even as she knew things for Rachael might look forever different.

At the ranch executive headquarters, another drama was playing out. Jan, inconsolable, sat outside Mathias's office and asked everyone who passed, "Where is Rachael and where are my shoes?" Inside the office, exasperated voices struggled with how to keep control of wayward ranch dwellers.

"It's like herding cats," Mathias mused. "Why can't they simply let go of archaic notions and be in the moment of what we're doing here?"

Since she was largely responsible for Rachael's night roaming, Carlotta sat in the chair of honor by the desk. "Mathias, I can't spend my whole life watching that girl. I think we need to crack down on everyone we can't trust."

Mathias concentrated on Carlotta and asked, "Who can we trust other than ourselves?"

"Eric is on board. Sylvie is coming along, and Jim won't give us any problem. You know what I think about Mabel, Mathias. She is bad news, and sooner or later you'll regret having her around. I'm not at all sure about Bill either. And then there's Jan. Bringing those two new women back was a huge mistake."

Dave chimed in, "Our biggest problem is Karen. She's just playing you, Mathias. She'll fight us no matter what we do. I say we just get rid of her. And I have to ask: what are you planning to do with that gorilla in the stable?"

"If I could wave a magic wand and make them understand, I would. It takes time. We have to make the best of the people here and try to bring them around," Mathias lectured. "As for the deranged man, I want to study him. We don't know what happened with the change to make him the way he is. It may help us better understand ourselves. And Dave, please explain to me one more time what happened last night."

Uncomfortable with being interrogated again, Dave began, "After we finished last night, I stopped by the control room to see what was happening. Eric saw something by the greenhouse, so I went out to check. When I didn't see anything, I decided to head to the stable and look around. I saw someone running from near the bunkhouse, so I waited behind a tree until they passed and then jumped out and tackled them.

"It was Rachael. She tried to gouge my eyes out." Dave pointed to his black eye. "She fought me the whole way to the stable, kicking and scratching. I had to backhand her to get her to stop. Then I put her in a stall, figuring it was the safest place until we could talk about it today."

"Hmmm. Yes, I agree that was for the best." Mathias rubbed his chin.

Carlotta spoke up. "I say we leave the two women down at the stable. Let's give Sylvie a chance to demonstrate how much she's learned. There's a lot of hard physical work to be done around here. Let her lead Karen, Rachael, Mabel, Jan, and Bill on a work crew of sorts. If they are tired, they won't cause us as much trouble. We've talked about reinforcing the fencing and improving our security. It frees Dave and me to fly with Jim to look for better people during the day. Eric can stay and guard the ranch."

"That makes a lot of sense, Carlotta. Please advise Sylvie to ensure they don't conspire against us as they work." Then Mathias added, "And tell her harsh punishment is allowed if it is warranted."

"Gotcha, Mathias," Carlotta smiled. "I say we cancel the daily meeting tonight and let things settle down."

"Yes, that would be wise. I am so disheartened. I thought we made real progress last night... Well, we must continue our journey nevertheless. I would like to go with you on searching expeditions. With one conversation, I'll be better able to determine who would fit here."

Dave and Carlotta looked at each other, absorbing the slight on their instincts. Carlotta said, "Mathias, you are welcome to ride along. But prepare yourself for the reality. It is difficult to find anyone, much less someone willing to go with strangers."

Mathias waved them off. "We just need to be persuasive." Looking down at work on his desk, whatever that might be, he added, "Oh, and Carlotta, please do something with Jan. Her incessant whining is driving me crazy."

Sylvie was nervous as she drove the van to the stable the next morning. No one had ever put her in charge of anyone, and she wanted to show Mathias she was worthy of greater responsibility. Besides, it would be nice not to be under Carlotta and Dave's thumb. Bill sat in the front seat next to her. Mabel and Jan sat solemnly in the back.

"Don't forget, Bill, I expect you to have my back. You are my second."

"Yeah, that's why Dave informed me I was a worker…" Bill answered.

Sylvie barked orders. "Mabel, get the food and clothes from the back of the van, and Jan, you stay put." They tumbled out and could hear the helicopter flying over.

Bill's eyes followed the white and blue aircraft across the horizon. "Off to find more victims, I suppose."

"Stop talking like that! We need to build membership if we're to succeed; you know that." Sylvie spat.

Bill gave a disgusted headshake and entered the stable. Since breakfast was late, the natives were restless. Uh Huh grunting and intermittently screeching was accompanied by Rachael and Karen singing "We Shall Overcome." *This doesn't bode well*, Bill thought.

They spent too much of the morning searching for tools and materials to repair and rebuild the ranch fencing. It didn't help that neither Bill nor Sylvie had ever built a fence before—or even a birdhouse for that matter. Sylvie had once pounded nails in the wall to hang pictures while Bill's expertise was watching the building of a bridge over the River Kwai during repeated viewings of a movie his father loved. Mabel refused to lend a hand, stating unequivocally that it wasn't her job, while Jan sat chewing her nails.

Mabel rushed food to Uh Huh to calm him and then pushed food in through the slots to the women. Sylvie stood in the center of the stable, her dyed white blonde hair styled in a very managerial bun, and said to the masses, "Listen up. It has been decided that some of our members have not been pulling their weight. I have been asked to lead you in an effort to improve ranch security. You will go willingly and work hard. You will not talk to each other about anything other than the work. I have a gun and a cattle prod with me and am not afraid to use them."

With the motivational speech concluded, Karen yelled through her gate, "Lovely. I have been dying for a walk in the wilderness." And with that auspicious start, the work began. Or at least it was attempted. Arriving at the outskirts of the ranch, it didn't take long to realize digging in dirt the consistency of concrete required a posthole digger, which Mabel recommended only after using one of the two shovels for nearly an hour and making little headway.

Nearly lunch and with only two posts implanted in miles of fencing, Jan asked casually, "What did you bring to cut the wire?" This request was met with resounding silence from Sylvie and Bill. Not wanting to admit defeat, after eating their box lunches, Sylvie made a command decision to wait out the afternoon by discussing "how you build a fence," hoping to encourage participation by her crew.

As could have been expected, the work crew was in no mood to assist their loathsome foreman. After sitting in the sun for most of the day, Karen finally sighed and then provided a long list of construction items needed to build a fence. Sylvie was dutifully writing these recommendations down in a little notebook she brought along until she heard Karen mention hairpins and tweezers. "Not at all funny, Karen! Do it again and I will cut your rations."

"Oh my," Karen said with mock sincerity. "I was just trying to help."

Bill, sitting a little back from Sylvie, tried to laugh silently but couldn't hold it in. Sylvie turned and pointed the cattle prod at Bill. "That goes for you too, asshole!" Karen noticed the look Bill gave Sylvie and thought he might be interested in breaking that prod over her head. Jan and Rachael were lying prone in the grass sleeping while Mabel sat studying the surrounding wilderness. Sylvie finally gave up and loaded them all in the van to return to their lodging. "Be ready for an early start tomorrow," Sylvie admonished as Karen and Rachael were shuttled to their cells.

Determined to show her worth to the ranch while wowing Mathias with her leadership skill, Sylvie had all the materials they would need in the van for day two of work crew duties. They were out bright and early by 9 AM and finished almost 25 yards of fencing during the day. "At this rate," Mabel sighed as they were driving back, "we should be done before the next apocalypse."

Day three was a scorcher. Nearing the end of August, the normally humidity-free higher elevations took a breather. Not a breeze or even a slight waft of air could be felt. The sun was killer before noon, and since no one had sunscreen or bug spray, the chain gang was in a surly mood.

Karen, worried about heat exhaustion or stroke, especially for Jan, who was flushed and clammy. She needed to convince Sylvie in the most unthreatening way she could muster for more frequent water breaks. She also had to make her suggestion Sylvie's idea so she wouldn't become defensive. Karen had watched newbies without leadership experience try to lead a group of unwilling followers; the results went from hard feelings to unmitigated disasters. "Sylvie, could I offer a suggestion that might improve productivity?" she said at last.

"What now, Karen?" Sylvie responded in a hard voice.

"Uh, well, one of the techniques the Army uses to avoid heat injuries is to enforce water breaks. Sometimes people don't drink enough water, and they can get very sick. If you make us stop every hour and drink, you won't have to stop work later to care for someone ill. Besides, we'll be able to get more done."

"Hmmmpf. You were in the Army?"

"Yes, I was."

"I'll consider it," Sylvie responded as she turned away and surveyed the work crew.

"Thank you, Sylvie. And if I might mention, Jan looks like she isn't doing well. Would you mind allowing me to try to get her to drink something?"

"It's about time for lunch. Do it then." Sylvie climbed on the trailer hook-up attached to van, drew up the girls, and in her most commanding voice barked, "Okay everybody, listen-up. You have twenty minutes for lunch. And be sure you drink plenty of water."

The four women and Bill sat on brown grass in a circle, eyes almost closed due to the unrelenting sun overhead, and tried to eat their peanut butter sandwiches. Sylvie wouldn't let them sit in the van or stray to the shade of trees in the distance. Karen positioned herself next to Jan and offered her an orange Gatorade. "I don't like orange," Jan responded petulantly, with a disgusted look on her face.

"Well what kind do you like?" Karen calmly asked.

"Grape."

"Hey, Bill, mind trading me your grape for my orange bottle so Jan can have something she likes to drink?"

Bill half dozing in place, was startled by Karen's question. He picked up the bottle next to him, read the label, and threw it to Karen. "I don't care. I can't believe I got myself into this fucking mess," he muttered.

Sylvie blew an ear-piercing whistle to let the five workers know lunch was over. "Is she *trying* to piss us off, or does it just come naturally?" Rachael whispered to Karen as they were hoisting themselves up to discard lunch wrappings and get back to work. Jan remained seated. "Come on, Jan," Rachael said, offering her hand to pull her up.

"No!" Jan screamed as she wrapped her arms around her body.

Sylvie noticed the angst from Jan and came striding over, the cattle prod swinging in her hand as she purposefully moved to the small group. "Get up," Sylvie directed.

"No," Jan said in a small voice.

Karen tried to put herself between Jan and Sylvie. "We got it, Sylvie; just give her a second."

Sylvie poked the cattle prod at Karen's foot as she jumped back, narrowly escaping a shock. "Just shut up and stay out of it, Karen! I'm sick of everyone babying her."

Leaning down to yell in Jan's ear, Sylvie repeated, "I said get up!"

Jan gave an even louder response. "NO!"

Rachael put her hands under Jan's arms and whispered, "Come on, Jan. I'll help you."

Tightening her crossed her arms and falling over in a fetal position, she screamed, "NO, NO, NOOO!"

Sylvie loomed over Jan and commanded again, spitting through clenched teeth, "I… said… get… up," which only served to make Jan curl tighter and close her eyes, ready for the backlash to come.

Mabel moved softly to Sylvie and implored, "Please, Sylvie, let the girl be. She told me this morning she didn't feel well. Just let her sit in the shade until she cools off."

Sylvie surprised Mabel with the cattle prod, poking Mabel's shoulder and sending her sprawling to the ground as she pulled a revolver from her waistband and pointed it at Jan. She kicked Jan in the knees and yelled, "One last chance, now get up." Sylvie stepped over Jan's curled body so she could see the rest of the crew. Sylvie's face, distorted in rage, held a shaky revolver in one hand and the cattle prod in the other. She kicked Jan again, this time in the back, uttering, "Get to work! I said get up, now." When the kicking had no impact she shocked Jan with the cattle prod.

Bill responded, "What the fuck, Sylvie?! Stop it NOW before you really hurt her!"

Karen inched forward toward Sylvie as Bill yelled. Sylvie noticed the movement from the corner of her eye and pointed the gun directly at her. "If you take one more step, Karen, I'll shoot you. I swear I will."

"Really, Sylvie?" Karen said. "Is this who you really are—is this what enlightenment looks like? You going to shoot me and Jan? Will Mathias be happy with your performance then?"

"Shut the fuck up, Karen." Sylvie said while sweat dripped off her nose, eyes doing a lifelike imitation of a cornered wild animal.

Rachael started inching forward to Sylvie as well. "You can't shoot us all. Only one. Make it me. And Karen, when she shoots me you get this whacked up bitch!"

"Stop, Rachael!" Karen screamed.

No one noticed Jan as the work crew team did a less than bang-up job de-escalating a bad situation. She untethered her curled body, jumped up in a flash, and began sprinting toward the woods faster than a jack rabbit flushed by an excited dog. Sylvie turned and fired twice as Jan was almost to the tree line. Jan went down just before Bill tackled Sylvie. He wrested the gun from her hands and punched her in the face while the remainder of the women sprinted to Jan.

Karen landed on her knees next to Jan and could see she was conscious and very pale. Mabel pulled at Jan's clothes and looked for the source of the bleeding. "She got shot in the ass. No vital organs there, which is a good thing. We need to get her some help quick though, because she's bleeding pretty well."

"I'll put pressure on the wound. You go get Bill and tell him to drive the van over here," Karen said to Mabel.

Jan looked dazed. "She shot me."

Cradling Jan's head, Rachael smiled while sweat made tracks down her dusty face. "She sure did, you silly girl. You just lay still. We're going to fix you right up—nothing to worry about."

"No more digging," Jan said as she closed her eyes.

With leftover rope, Bill tied Sylvie's feet and hands then threw her in the van, none too gently. Sylvie, cursing and crying, screamed at Bill, "How can you do this to me? I didn't have a choice. You know I had to do it. I didn't have a choice."

"Haven't they been telling us you always have a choice? I don't know what the hell happened to us, but this has gone too far. I am done with you and with Mathias. I never signed up for this shit."

Bill was already in the van turning on the engine when Mabel reached him and jumped in the passenger seat. "Hurry. Pick up Jan and the others. We may have time to gather medical supplies and what we need to get the heck out of Dodge before the helicopter comes back. The only one left at the ranch is Eric."

"Great minds think alike, Mabel," Bill responded and floored the accelerator, kicking up dust. He parked the vehicle next to Jan and leaped out. Bill and Rachael gently carried her to the van while Karen walked next to them trying to keep pressure on the bullet wound. With a satisfying thump, Mabel rolled Sylvie off the seat onto the floor to make room for Jan.

Karen and Rachael hovered over Jan as they drove. Karen asked, "Are we going to make a run for it?"

"That's the plan," Bill responded.

Everyone except Sylvie was silent as they willed the van to go faster over treacherous dirt back roads. "You'll be sorry if you do this," Sylvie muttered. When threats didn't get a positive response, Sylvie tried another approach. "Look, let me go and I will help you. I know where they keep the key to the weapons shack. I'm tired of this place anyway. Please, take me with you."

Rachael took off her shirt and sat in her bra ripping the bottom edge of the garment with her teeth. When she had enough fabric, she reached under Sylvie's head and wrapped the torn shirt portion across her mouth, and then tied a tight knot. "There. That's better. The wicked witch is silenced."

Rachael was slipping into what was left of her mangled shirt when her extraordinary hearing picked up the sound of a helicopter. "Bill, can you go faster? I hear them coming."

"Shit, shit, shit!" Bill responded, stepping on the accelerator and fishtailing on the gravel. "I thought they went out for the whole day." He glanced panicked at Mabel. "We could just leave now," he offered.

Rachael snapped at Bill, "Jan will bleed to death or die of infection if we don't get her some help. Not an option."

All eyes turned to the southeast as the helicopter came into sight, making its final loop to the landing pad located directly in front of ranch headquarters. "We aren't going to make it," Mabel sighed.

"Bill, stop the van. We need to let Sylvie out," Karen barked.

Why, Karen? What good will that do? Revenge won't make anything better."

"Just trust me here, Bill. Please, do it now," Karen said. Sylvie grunted a protest from under her gag as Bill pulled to a stop. Karen looked at Rachael. "You do it." Nodding, Rachael swung her legs over the side of the seat, yanked on the sliding door, and stepped out. She pulled under Sylvie's arms and yanked her through the door, easily dumping her on the ground even as Sylvie struggled.

"Should I untie her?" Rachael questioned.

"No, we can't take the chance. They will eventually find her when they go looking for the van."

Bill drove more slowly, listening to Karen as she leaned forward, talking to the back of his head. "I didn't want Sylvie to hear. Not all of us can make it out. Mabel, will you stay with me to take care of Jan? I need you to convince them we left the work site in a hurry to get Jan help, and the rest of crew had to drive back to pick up the supplies we left. By the time they figure it out, Bill and Rachael will be long gone. Bill, drop us off and head in the direction we just came then keep on going. Rachael, as soon as you can, find a shortwave and call Mike. Come back when you can get us the hell out of here."

"I can't leave you, Karen!" Rachael replied indignantly.

"You can and you will." Karen glared at Rachael. "It's not safe for you here, and besides, I want to be absolutely sure Mike gets the information he needs to find us. I trust you to do that."

"This just isn't fair," Rachael replied, sounding more like the teenager she was.

Karen grabbed Rachael's hand. The thought of losing another child, this time to a power crazy cult, well, she couldn't let that happen. At this moment, the only thing that mattered to Karen was the survival of this one young woman. But how to make Rachael listen to her? Then it came to her as she said in a powerful voice, "I am the queen, my princess, and I command that you do this!"

Rachael looked back at Karen, tears welling in her eyes. "As it shall be, my liege. And fear not, I shall return with white knights and furry steeds!"

"So what say you, Mabel—you in?"

"Oh, sure," Mabel responded. "I want this nice young lady to get the heck out of here—you too, Bill. Just make sure you come back for us if you can. I think we can fool 'em. Mathias and his worshipers don't use the brains they was born with."

Bill made sure the returning people hunters were inside the ranch house before pulling to the front. Mabel and Karen moved quickly to carry Jan inside. Before the women reached the front door, Bill drove away from ranch craziness at a normal speed. Karen wanted to look back at Rachael, possibly one last time, but stopped herself, knowing any unusual actions might give away their deceit. When ranch leaders found Sylvie tied and gagged, the jig would be up, and then she and Mabel would have a lot of explaining to do.

"We're back and we got trouble!" Mabel yelled as she pushed open the front door. Eric, doubling as ranch doctor since he'd received a paramedic license while living in Montana, came running. Jan was whisked away to the doctor's office, aka the formal dining room, leaving Mabel to tell the tale. Carlotta looked skeptical, but the others appeared to buy it. They were otherwise preoccupied with a new guy, a bear of a man named Sam, with a full dark beard and shifty eyes. Finding a new victim most likely precipitated their early return. He gave Karen and Mabel the once over with his eyes. Perfect, Karen thought.

Nervously sitting on the hallway floor outside the operating room, Karen and Mabel tried to remain calm. At just under an hour, Eric came out and brusquely explained, "She'll be fine. The bullet didn't hit anything important—I got it out. We need to keep her here for a little while."

"Can we see her?" Mabel asked.

"Nope, she's still under. Take Karen back to her building."

"I think the van is gone," Mabel returned with something less than conviction.

"Not my problem. Go ask Carlotta if you can use something else."

Eric walked back in the dining room and shut the door. The two women gave each other a "what now" look, and Mabel suggested they go to the kitchen and get a snack. As Mabel was looking through the refrigerator, Carlotta swung in, dressed mostly in black, resembling a ninja with poor taste, and asked, "Where are they?"

Without taking her head from the cool confines of the ice box, Mabel nonchalantly replied, "Aren't they back yet?"

Moving in behind Mabel, violating personal space decorum, she hissed in Mabel's ear, "I know you're up to something."

Karen had never seen Mabel angry; sometimes a little bitter or stressed, but not truly angry. Mabel stood up, turned around, and without stepping back looked directly in Carlotta's eyes, only inches away; they were breast to breast. Karen, very impressed with Mabel's bravado, held her breath and prepared to enter the fray if needed. A little taller than Carlotta, Mabel used her height drawing herself up and then… started laughing.

"As my granddaughter used to say, you want a piece of this, Carlotta? Is that what this is about, huh? Well, here I am." The two women stared, each threatening some level of violence. Carlotta broke off the contest first and walked out, glaring at Karen and muttering before her final exit, "Karen come with me—I'll take you back to the stable."

Dave was waiting in a black car with the engine running. Karen climbed in the back seat and Carlotta pushed in beside her holding a very large .45. Dave's face made Karen sick to her stomach, so she gazed out the window. Karen was almost happy to be back to the safety of her cell— well, almost. She prayed for Rachael, Bill, Jan, Mabel, and her other family in Washington while waiting for the ax to drop. As the night wore on and dinner never came, she sang inspirational songs to Uh Huh.

Chapter 31: A+114, Home Base Gets Some News

Rubbing her eyes, Sara sat in total concentration in front of a computer screen. "Anything interesting on your side, Katie?"

"Nothing. Well, that's not entirely true. There's a surprising number of wolves in my search area. I'm getting better at identifying large animals."

"I know what you mean; I may have enough data to write a book describing the nocturnal wanderings of wolves… when this is all over, of course," Sara replied.

Manuel entered the extra bedroom, now housing their drone equipment, carrying two large cups of steaming coffee. "I thought you two could use a nice cup of java. I can take over for one of you if you need a break."

"Aww, Manuel. That's sweet, but no thanks. I'm good 'til the end of my shift," Katie said with her eyes still on the screen.

"Me too. But you can sit and keep us company," Sara added.

Manuel peered at the screen with Sara. "Anything?"

"Afraid not. Did Mike finally go to bed? He isn't getting enough sleep and gets shorter tempered every day. I thought he would bite Jed's head off yesterday when he tried to reassure him that it would happen, that we would find the ranch."

"Probably didn't help that Jed told him to be patient," Katie chuckled.

"Yes," Manuel added, "Mike is very worried. He tries to hide his feelings and keep a positive attitude, but I know each extra day is painful for him. I just wish there—""

Jed yelled from the dining room, "Wake up, Mike! Wake Mike up. Somebody get Mike!"

"I'll do it." A concerned Manuel moved quickly out of the room down the hall and opened Mike's bedroom. "Mike, wake up. Jed needs you now."

Groggy, Mike asked with a croak, "Did he find them?"

"I don't know. Please come now."

Mike leaped from the bed wearing last night's shorts and tee shirt. Jill, Tilley, and Zoe were already at the door, ready to follow Mike wherever he went. "Tilley, could you move out of my way, please?" Mike growled.

As he stepped in the dining room, Jed turned, a big grin on his face. Raider, Thor, and Tadpole sat on the table by the shortwave wagging, purring, and smiling at Mike's entry. "Is that Rachael's voice? Jed, is it Rachael?" Mike asked and was rewarded with an affirmative nod. Mike looked up, said a silent prayer of thanks, and took the microphone from Jed's hand. He steadied his voice and pressed send, saying, "Rachael, it's Mike. Where are you?"

"Hi, Mike. I don't want to say where I am. You need to come right away. I've given the location of the ranch to Jed. Karen is still there, and so are our friends Jan and Mabel. They are in trouble, Mike. You have to hurry."

"How are you, Rachael? Are you OK?"

"I'm doing OK. I have someone with me; his name is Bill. Thanks to Karen, we got away. Please don't worry about me. I will join up with you when you pass by. Remember that day we were driving around looking for chickens and, like, we shared stories about childhood trips? I mentioned one that I loved and Katie hated. If you can remember that, you will know which way to go."

"I don't remember what you're talking about, Rachael," Mike said with a perplexed expression.

As soon as Manuel learned Rachael was on the shortwave he'd replaced Katie so she could talk to her twin. She was standing behind Mike and tapped him on the shoulder. "I know!" Katie said, vibrating with happiness.

Mike breathed a sigh of relief. "Rachael, we have it. We'll leave as soon as it's light. I should be near you by tomorrow evening, but just in case something slows us down, check in with us again at the same time. Take care of yourselves and be safe. I can't wait to see you. Now, I think your sister would like to speak to you."

Mike handed the microphone to Katie, and as Rachael cried, they spoke in a foreign language only they seemed to understand. Mike asked Jed to wake Thomas and yelled for Sara and Manuel to drop what they were doing. With the whole team gathered, Mike gave instructions so they would be ready to go in six hours. The animals, sensing something big was in the works, milled about, poking their noses in gear to be packed and followed their human companions back and forth from the house to vehicles.

Get woman? Jill asked, looking up from Mike's side.

"Yes, Jill, we'll get our woman back."

Get Jack?

Mike lips drew into a thin line. "I don't know, Jill. I hope so."

The drive to Coeur d'Alene, Idaho, progressed nicely until just after the Snoqualmie Pass on I-90. Coeur d'Alene, Idaho, was their interim destination. After Rachael's call for help only ten hours ago, Katie recounted a childhood trip with their father to the Silverwood Theme Park. "It had these really huge wooden roller coasters. Rachael and I were tall for our age or we wouldn't have even been able to ride them, which would have been fine by me. She was so excited. She bugged my dad until he bought us holsters and toy squirt guns, which she used to surprise me with face squirts the whole day—so annoying.

"Anyway, she couldn't wait to ride the roller coasters. I told her I didn't want to, but she laughed at me and called me a coward. When I still said no, she begged. Dad said he would ride with her but noooo—Katie had to go. She wore me down. I hated it and started feeling sick the minute we were looking over the top plunging to our death. I was done with roller coasters after the first ride, but there were two more. Rachael promised to let me use her iPod, which she'd bought with her own money, whenever I wanted, if I would just ride each roller coaster once. On the third one, I puked all over her; it was disgusting.

"Dad and I cleaned her up as best we could with bottled water and paper towels then went back to the motel to swim. When we find Rachael, and if there's ever a working roller coaster again, I will ride them with her until… well, until forever."

The theme park was just north of Couer de'Alene. Mike's decision to take the most direct route to reach Rachael seemed the best choice given the urgency. Best laid plans, Mike thought to himself as they stopped just east of the Snoqualmie Pass on I-90 looking eastward at wall-to-wall cars for several miles, culminating with two jack-knifed semi-trucks and a massive pile-up. The westbound lanes were similarly clogged from the truck accident in the other direction. It had been spring in the mountains when the sickness came. In March and April, the mountain passes, still prone to sleet and snow, made it all too easy to imagine the resulting chaos from untended, slippery roads and panic stricken drivers trying to make their way home.

Thomas whistled, "I do believe that's the biggest accident I have ever seen. And I've seen some pretty ugly snarls in the Middle East."

"Awful, isn't it?" Sara said sadly. "All those people and no one to help."

"Want to hear something almost as sad?" Mike lamented. "We're going to have to turn around, go back, and use another pass."

Jed scowled, "Damn, I didn't think to use the drones to check out the highways."

"Not your fault, Jed. I was so anxious to get going to find Karen and Rachael, I didn't give you the time. Let's try the southern pass on 410 by Mount Rainier. Jed, can you send one of your drones that direction so we can at least have more warning to make directional changes?"

"You got it, Mike," Jed said as he pulled out his laptop. After man and beast took a break, they saddled up and were on their way. Mike and the group called Rachael at the appointed evening time to let her know it would be almost noon the next day before they arrived. "Hurry, Mike," was all she could say.

Chapter 32: A+114, The Ranch and I Hate Snakes

Her stomach rumbling, Karen sat on her cot after a restless night. Cataloging dreams came easily, as one stood out with vivid clarity. Like a 3D, super HD, and curved screen rolled into one, she stood in a natural forest. Karen slowly turned, taking in the scenery. On one side, a group of three large trees stood sentinel by themselves. Other pines, interspersed at regular intervals, provided near full shade, making what would be a very hot day bearable.

In the opposite direction, a small path rose slightly to a clearing with a view of the other side of something, a gully or maybe a cliff. Light from the path hurt her eyes after staring at the gloom of the forest. Karen tried to walk along the path to see what lay beyond the edge, but her feet were lodged in place and would not move no matter how hard she tried; she could only turn. The ground was rocky and mostly barren with only dry grass and an occasional succulent or small bush to add color.

It was so quiet. She listened for sounds of life and could hear the rattle of a snake probably behind rock a mere twenty feet away. Terrified of snakes, Karen tried again to move her feet and add distance between herself and the snake. Falling to her knees, both feet remained planted. She woke up, heart pounding and sweating. The dream terrified her in ways she could not explain. But what did it mean and how could it help her?

Mabel did not show up with breakfast. Karen had squirreled away two energy bars yesterday when she and Mabel were in the kitchen, so things could have been worse. She only wished she could give one to Uh Huh, hungry and restless in his cell. Afraid to fall asleep again and repeat the dream but knowing she should try anyway, she lay on her cot looking at the stable ceiling through the chain link of her cage, willing herself to sleep and hoping to learn more. Karen heard a vehicle approaching, followed quickly by the sound of Sylvie's voice talking to someone else. *Uh oh*.

They wasted no time moving to her cell and swinging the door open. Dave and Sylvie stood just outside, daring Karen to make an aggressive move. "Good morning, bitch," Dave gleefully sneered. He grabbed Karen by the shoulders and hurled her through the opening face forward. Karen landed on her face. She was stunned. After shaking off the unexpected violence, she pulled to her knees trying to stand. A pulsing shock to her back sent her reeling to the ground again. Sylvie loomed over Karen holding her favorite weapon, the cattle prod. "Don't move, Karen," Sylvie said.

Dave stepped forward and leered down at Karen. He was smiling— yet his cherubic face was twisted in some form of primal bloodlust. Karen was panting from the fear and adrenaline surging through her body.

She watched Dave as Sylvie talked. He was the one most likely to kill her. "Karen, you'll be happy to know your time on the ranch has come to an end. Mathias gave us permission last night to set you free. He wanted us to make sure we left you far enough away that you wouldn't come back for any of your friends. Dave and I put our heads together and came up a perfect plan. And let's just say, karma can be a bitch. Dave, will you please do the honors?"

Dave actually moaned. He's actually moaning from the pleasure of this, Karen thought as her fear spiked. She shrieked as Dave yanked her from the floor by an arm. Uh Huh sensed something was up and very wrong. Screaming a battle cry as loud as any Karen had heard since her stay at the world's worst bed and breakfast had begun, he pounded his body into the door of his cell, shaking the entire row of cages. Dave glanced over to make sure Uh Huh was still safely in his cage.

Dave stepped behind Karen and roughly pulled her hands behind her back. He snapped two zip ties on Karen's wrists and then placed three around her ankles. Karen remembered watching a TV show where a character drew up, making themselves as big as possible as they were tied and bound. When relaxed, there was slack in the bindings. She tried, but Dave cinched them tight. Karen wasn't sure it would make any difference.

Uh Huh continued to ram his door with an urgent frequency and intensity. "Think I should I do anything with him?" Dave asked Sylvie.

"No, we don't have time. Maybe he'll beat himself to death," Sylvie giggled. She pulled a blue bandana from her pocket, twisted it a few times, and tied it tightly over Karen's eyes. Patting Karen on the head, she said,

"There, that'll do it. It was a really bad idea to dump me on the road like garbage. That wasn't very nice, especially since I've always been supportive of you."

The normal Karen would have been angry, livid, enraged; instead, all she felt was calm. It was a surreal sensation. She'd always known, somehow, her time at the ranch would come to this, and this morning's dream was merely a reminder. It was almost a relief to get it over with. Needing all her resources to survive, she would not waste another ounce on these people.

"I'm disappointed she didn't put up more of a fight," Dave said, looking at their handiwork. "Any last words, Karen?"

"Could you please feed Uh Huh before we leave? It will quiet him," Karen stated.

"Who's Uh Huh? Oh, you mean the beast." Dave took a couple of candy bars from a small fanny pack around his hips and slid them through the floor level passage in the stall door. Uh Huh viscously screamed and growled when Dave came near. "It's beyond me why Mathias keeps this animal."

Karen stood waiting, and she heard Uh Huh scramble for the candy. She let out a grunt as she was hefted on Dave's shoulder and then again when she was carelessly dumped in the bed of a truck. Thanks to her dream, she at least knew where they were headed.

When they arrived at their destination, Dave hoisted her over his shoulder again, carrying her a distance before dropping her on the ground. He and Sylvie got in a good kick each, their parting gift before leaving Karen in the forest in the spot she'd seen in her dream. Still blindfolded, she heard the truck drive away. She waited until she was certain the truck was gone, struggling to calm her heart and rapid breathing. "Don't panic," she ordered herself.

First thing: figure out which direction was which and get to those sentinel trees. Karen pushed herself on her knees and listened. No snake rattle, which was both a good and a bad thing. Good because she didn't want to add catastrophe to misery via snake encounters of the third kind;

bad because it was the most convenient way to orient her position to the terrain.

She scooted on her knees in a full circle, hoping to feel or maybe see the sun through the blindfold. No luck. Sylvie had wound it just tight enough to block residual light. Maybe if I stand, she thought. She quickly figured out that getting to her feet with hands behind her back and feet firmly tied together was more difficult than one would think. She tried rocking from a sitting position. She rolled back on her upper back and then pushed up to her feet when she rocked forward. On the second attempt, after falling face forward once and adjusting the momentum, eureka, she was erect! Karen had to smile as she thought of her 60+ pre-apocalypse self attempting that maneuver.

She did the 360 again, using the balls of her feet to make teeny tiny movements and thought she could feel warmth from the sun in one direction. She hopped and turned to the opposite direction. If she was wrong about the direction, she would hop or move with teeny tiny steps aimlessly through the forest becoming hopelessly lost. Karen didn't want to fully commit to the hop approach. That was a quicker route to her demise if she was going in the wrong way. With little bitty steps, she moved over rocks and small objects in exposed feet, rapidly scraping the skin raw on her heels and balls of her feet. When foot discomfort became too much, she huffed, "Okay, hop technique then". On the second hop, Karen's left foot hit a sharp rock that was large enough to twist her ankle and went down with a whoosh.

"Well, fuck me!" Karen shouted, and then, predictably, she heard the rattle. Good news again, she thought; I am headed in the right direction. Then, the really bad news: the rattling had stopped. Karen wasn't sure, but she could swear she could hear the snake moving. She spent a few reflective moments convincing herself rattle snakes weren't aggressive if left alone. "Hopping and tiny steps are out. Rolling it is!"

She carefully slid to the ground, all her senses alert for any sign of the snake. Turning her body perpendicular to the estimated location of the trees, Karen rolled first on her back and then stomach. The gravel and forest floor scraped her entire body but with far less force than using only her feet. Karen's ankle only hurt when she made the turning movement. She should be just about there…

"Oh my God… I do hear that snake." Everyone has an Achilles heel, although Karen felt she had several, but snakes reigned as the big dog of all phobias. It didn't make any sense. Growing up mostly in the northern U.S. where the limited number and variety of snakes makes seeing a one in the wild unlikely, her only first-hand experience was zoos and the occasional kid who, finding one, wanted to carry it around to scare unwary friends. Even that filled her with revulsion and sent Karen running. It had to be the DNA thing. One of Karen's long lost ancestors experienced a near death experience with a snake, forever changing inherited fear. Or maybe it was the Adam and Eve story.

Whatever the reason, Karen's heart lost the battle with her mind. Pulse rocketing, sweating profusely, she lay there knowing to blindly move meant she might roll over the damn thing. *Was there anything worse than rolling over a hissing rattler?* She tried to control her panting, panicked breathing as she lay on her back alone in the dirt of a silent forest, bruised and scraped, waiting to be bit by a venomous snake. She felt the flick of its tongue on the side of her knee. Karen swallowed the bile in the back of her throat to keep from vomiting. Pleading with her maker, she begged, *Oh, no… God please, anything but this, please. It's crawling over my leg!!!*

The edge of Karen's consciousness darkened. As if in one of her dreams, Karen felt the snake's belly slither over one leg and test the inside of her other thigh with its demented forked tongue. Finding nothing of interest, it moved on to the other leg. At one point both thighs held the weight of a good sized and poisonous snake endowed with what could only be large fangs.

Time slows when we least desire it, particularly when waiting for something. Karen remembered as a small child sitting in a bathing suit on a hot summer day, waiting for her parents to hurry up so she could finally, finally dive into that lake they promised. It seemed to take forever. And then there was the time she watched slow motion events from the driver's seat of her car during an automobile accident. Unable to react quickly enough to move away from a van careening toward her door, she sat powerless observing her probable death. Like now, time shifted into a slow gear as a type of self-imposed torture.

And so it was. Karen waited as seconds stretched to infinity, the weight of the snake slithering against her skin as a lifetime passed hoping for the serpent to move to greener pastures. *I don't care what all the snake lovers say—it does slither.* And leave it did. Thankfully, it was warm and the snake had no reason to stay and cuddle. She remained still for an indeterminate amount of time until her muscles quivered with the effort. Expelling stale breath and breathing deeply she steadied her quivering body. "Well then, back to plan C." Karen resumed rolling and yelled "Hallelujah" as she bumped into a tree.

Sitting beside the tree, her legs stretched in front of her body, Karen rubbed her face against bark, trying to pull the blindfold up enough to see. At first, the rubbing was merely unpleasant against tender skin. She tried several different techniques, each increasing face discomfort until she wanted to scream from the fire that was now her face. After much cursing, varying face angles, and moving to different positions on the tree, the blindfold snagged something. Gently, gently she pulled upward until regaining partial vision in one eye. Rocking to her feet again, wincing with pain in her ankle, Karen spied a broken branch low enough to allow its use to lever the bandana completely off her eyes. After another fifteen minutes of careful effort she felt the bandana catch and pulled the blindfold high on her forehead until both eyes were free. At last Karen could see the place in her dreams. Now the twist ties.

Snake rock looked most promising. If there was a sharp edge somewhere on the rock face, maybe she could saw off her bindings. Karen inch walked to a safe distance, eyeing the rock formation. "Okay, disgusting snake creatures, if there any cousins hiding about, I strongly recommend you move to another location. I am in no mood to be trifled with!!" Karen listened. No rattles. "I am coming in!" Using her minute gait, all that was allowed with bound feet, she moved around the rock. It was about four feet wide and only two-plus feet high. Most of it looked to be lodged under the ground. On the back right side it had one pointed edge; like a piece had been sheared off during some other apocalyptic cataclysm. It would have to do.

"Hands or feet?" Karen asked the wilderness. They always do the hands first in the movies, she thought. Even so, every part of Karen was screaming, "You have to get the hell out of here before Dave or the snake or some other really shitty, scary, bloodthirsty thing comes along." Karen needed to be able to move, preferably faster than an inch walk. "Feet it is,"

Karen answered herself. She sat on her butt facing the rock, opposite the side with the sheared edge. Draping her legs over the rock, she placed her ankles on either side of the sharp rock face and moved her legs up and down in a saw-like motion. She sawed, sawed some more, pulled, twisted and cursed for the better part of the afternoon and into the early evening. When she felt the last tie give and pop, tears filled her eyes. "When I write my memoir, I'm including this in a list of recommended post-apocalyptic training exercises," Karen commented to the rock. "My lower back and abs are killing me."

Assessing her physical condition, thirst was Karen's most pressing priority. Sweating and peeing herself during the snake visitation and the physical exertion used to battle zip ties and the blindfold had left her... *well*, she thought, *high and dry*. Karen manically giggled at that expression. She couldn't see her inflamed face, but if it looked anything like her feet and ankles it was better not to see. The ankle was just a little swollen, probably a strain rather than a full-blown sprain; it would support her weight, albeit with some pain. The snap tie war had produced bloody strips and scrapes over the entire area. "So enough of the pity party," Karen said to the quiet woods.

She wanted very badly to stay and free her hands, but the risk was too great. In just a few hours, predators would be frolicking in the moonlight. Karen stretched and then moved to check out what was below the clearing. The drop off, an easy climb on a good day with full use of feet and hands, was a mere 30 or 40 feet and not too steep—difficult but doable. She could clearly visualize normal water flow by the pattern of rocks and grooves in the earth of a dry creek bed at the bottom of the drop.

Traversing back the way she came, Karen looked for tire tracks and any sign of a road or path. They had to get the truck up here some way, but it was so dry. Before dropping her on the ground, Dave had carried Karen over his shoulder, but she couldn't estimate how far. She peered at the gloom. "Well damn, why couldn't my dream include a picture of a map with a 'you are here' arrow?"

Forty years ago, at a long-ago Army training camp, Karen vaguely remembered an instructor saying, "Follow the water." At least she thought that's what he'd said. She turned to make the climb to the creek bed. It was challenging without hands. Using her body for leverage as a third point of contact, she slid on her butt down the embankment, scraping heretofore untouched skin in the process. Once she reached bottom, the flat area of the dry stream bed was easily maneuverable; she limped quickly along, looking for any telltale signs of civilization.

The shadows of the day grew long. Karen couldn't see the sun on the horizon and only felt its surrender to the night. She'd reasoned by the position of sun during the last sighting that she was traveling west. Not that it mattered. She was still lost. No water, no houses, no roads; nothing in at least 10 miles. She needed to find a safe resting place soon. To the north, storm clouds were gathering; the calm day gave way to warm gusts, blowing grit into Karen's eyes she could not remove without the use of her hands.

Karen hoped to find a tree with branches low enough to allow climbing. She thought she could use a use a caterpillar-type movement over a branch, standing and then doing it again. Lightning changed her mind. The stream embankment was smaller now and allowed Karen to easily climb the loamy face and search for a rock formation that might provide protection during the night.

Raindrops plunking on bone-dry ground followed her ascent. When she reached the top, rain mixed with hail battered her head and shoulders. She limped/ran to the nearest pine tree for safety from pelting ice bullets. The temperature change was dramatic, and huge goosebumps pulled Karen's wounded skin as her teeth chattered a protest. Barefoot with only a t-shirt and shorts, hypothermia was added to a growing list of life-threatening possibilities. Karen waited for her eyes to adjust to the darkness, only to be disappointed; the forest and storm left no light. She could barely see a few feet in any direction.

The rain was now a pervasive roar. Exhausted, thirsty, hungry, sore, lost, alone, frightened, and extremely cold, Karen had reached her limit. Using her feet to scrape nearby pine needles, leaves and debris to make a natural blanket, Karen huddled on the ground next to the tree, her mouth up and open to catch rain trickling from the branches above.

She saw Mike's worried face as he stood beside the twins, hugging each other and screaming for joy. Jill sat at Mike's feet while Tilley and

Maple rose on hind legs, front paws extended to join the hugging girls. Mike commanded "Get down," and the dogs reluctantly obeyed. *Where is Jack*, Karen wondered? With the knowledge that Rachael was safe, Karen slept a dreamless sleep.

Chapter 33: Jack and the Wild Dogs

Jack is close now. Jack can feel the woman. She is alone. Like Jack. Jack tried to go around the wild dog territory but it is too big. To find the woman, Jack must cross their place. She is in their place. Jack will cross in the day when the wild dogs sleep.

Jack moves quickly with all his senses alert. It is higher here and the day is not hot like before. There is no water. Jack is thirsty. Jack smells rain from far away and knows it will come here. That is good. The wild dogs will rest when the rain comes. Jack will not rest. He will find the woman.

The shadows grow. The night and the rain are close now. Jack feels the wild dogs. They are awake and restless. The Alpha howls to warn and the others join his song. He warns Jack he runs in the wild dog place. Jack reaches his mind to the Alpha. Jack does not know their language. The Alpha does not understand. The Alpha and his pack will come for Jack.

Jack knows he will not reach the woman. The pack will come for him and leave the woman. The woman will be safe. Jack leads the pack away from the woman, to a place where he can fight. He reaches his mind to the Alpha again. Jack sees what the Alpha sees. The Alpha pushes Jack's mind away. Jack tries another wild dog, a young female. She tries to speak to Jack. Jack waits.

The Alpha is here. He is big like Jack. The wild dogs are big like Jack and Jill. They look like Jill but are different. They do not smell like Jill or my pack. Their eyes are light and shine in the dark. They are different. Jack is not scared. Jack has duty. The pack surrounds Jack. They bend and move. Their heads are low. They are showing teeth and growling.

Jack sends his mind to all the wild dogs as loud as he can speak. *Jack is no threat. Jack looks for his pack.* The wild dogs stop. The male in front whimpers and shakes his head. The Alpha will not stop. He will fight Jack.

The Alpha moves to the front, each step slow. Jack sees the Alpha is intelligent and strong. Jack has duty. He will fight the Alpha if he must.

Jack is alone. The Alpha has pack. Jack may not win but the woman will be safe.

Jack looks away from the Alpha. He lowers his head in deference to Alpha's strength. He does not lower his tail. He tells the Alpha by his body position, Jack is also strong. Jack also has pack and must find them. Jack is no threat to the Alpha or the Alpha's pack.

The young female moves next to the Alpha. She does not look at him but mewls at his side. The Alpha snaps at her. The Alpha is ready. His fur is raised and his tail is straight out. His muzzle is furrowed and his teeth are flashing on all sides. The Alpha snarls.

Jack thinks of the word the woman uses many times. *Shit!* Jack tries to speak with all his mind to the pack again. *LEAVE ME!* The young female echoes his words in her language, *LEAVE HIM!* Jack understands the strange language now. With his chest up he looks at the Alpha and heaves the command in the wild dog way. *LEAVE!*

Chapter 34: A+116, White Knights to the Rescue

Rachael cried on Katie's shoulder as she greeted her with a huge hug. After acknowledging dogs and people, Rachael pulled Katie's hand and led her into another room and shut the door. Quizzical faces turned to Bill.

Bill wore a concerned expression. "I'm not sure what happened with Rachael. She wouldn't talk about it. One minute she would be fine, excited about seeing all of you, and the next she was almost unresponsive. I thought she was just worried about Karen." He shrugged his shoulders.

Mike scowled and rubbed his head. "Katie will fill me in later. In the meantime, let me introduce the crew and find out more about you."

They sat around the dining table as Mike filled Bill in on their plans. A murmuring of female voices could be heard behind the closed door for the better part of an hour. The dogs waited for the twins just outside the shut room. They were the first to respond to Rachael's and Katie's return, dancing and whining with joy as soon as they heard the metallic sliding of a doorknob.

Both girls had red-rimmed, puffy eyes. Rachael was the first to speak. "Wow, Mike, I never expected so many people. I'm, like, glad though. And who are these cute furry additions?" she asked.

"We can get to that all later, but first, are you okay to talk about what you know about the ranch? Bill's been sharing what he knows and I would also like to hear your perspective. I know this is quick, but Karen is still in danger."

"Yeah, sure, of course." Rachael said, becoming more serious. "But what took you so long?"

Thomas looked at a highly tense Mike. He was like a dog straining on the leash. "You had to ask. Do you want to tell her or shall I?"

Mike scowled, "I have no desire to relive it."

Each member of the newly formed group knew the seriousness of what they were about to do as well as Mike's total dedication to saving Karen. But even in dire circumstances, and maybe even more so when fate deals one the absurd, they had to laugh. The team did their best to hide amusement as Thomas told a quick version of the story.

"Let's just say, my friend and constant companion Murphy's Law was in fine form. Among the more notable events: a completely blocked mountain pass, a pass partially blocked from sliding rock, one over-heated engine, two flat tires, an elk crossing, a dog escape to herd said elks, a satellite radio left at the herding melee, and a partridge and a pear tree."

Mike closed his eyes and shook his head at the retelling with a smile sneaking on his lips while the rest of the group, holding their stomachs, shook from laughter. It was the first time since their frustrating journey anyone had a chance to let off steam.

"Moving on," Mike said, trying hard not to laugh. "The ranch, Rachael, please."

Rachael and Bill were holed up in a small motel on the outskirts of Coeur d'Alene in the owner's apartment above the office. The group was crowded around the dining table already filling with soda cans and snack debris. Rachael found some paper to drawn on, and she and Bill described the ranch layout and people. Bill knew a little more about the ranch's security and described the location of monitoring cameras and sensors along the perimeter.

Thomas mapped out a possible approach plan. "I will take the ranch house with Bill, Ghost, and Jill. Mike, you and Katie can use Maple and Tilley to find and retrieve Karen from the stable. Rachael and Manuel, your responsibility is the ranch hand billets. Hopefully, Jan will be there. Get her back to the vehicles as soon as you can and then stay put. You may want to take Zoe. She can be an early warning system for anyone roving between the three buildings."

"Jed and Sara, you stay with the rest of the animals at the vehicles. I need Jed to man the drone and camera feeds and relay information." Everyone knew, but didn't say, that Jed was too important to their long-term survival to risk. Sara, the group's doctor, was to be ready in case anyone got hurt.

"In and out quickly," Mike said, happy with the plan.

Thomas responded, "Yep, and just one question: rules of engagement? I know we aren't a U.S.-sponsored Army anymore, but from a 'live with yourself later' perspective, I think it's a good idea to decide ahead of time."

"Good point. What do you think, Mike?" Manuel joined in.

"First, I say we don't bring any prisoners with us back to Washington. If Rachael says they're okay and they want to come with us, fine. I don't see any utility in having to jail someone long term—we're going to have enough to do once this is over. We leave anyone we don't want to bring back in place, and we make sure it takes them a long time to become a threat to anyone again. If they offer resistance or get in our way, we do what we must do," Mike replied flatly.

Bill's brow furrowed with concern. "Problem is, my bet from knowing these cowardly nut jobs is something in between. Carlotta and Dave will put up a fight, but I don't see Mathias, Sylvie, Eric, or Jim doing that. If they see it going bad, they'll try to convince us to take them along, and that wouldn't be a good idea. Don't see these cats changing their spots. Also, I think Dave may have an extra gift. Now that Rachael has explained Katie's finding ability, it makes sense. Dave was always prowling around in the dark and would sneak up on you just for fun. In hindsight, I think he either had a sense like Katie's or some unusual night vision. Anyway he is strong and fast, so be wary of him."

Everyone was quiet, thinking about real life and death questions and the responsibility they entailed. Making those judgments after listening to a news report from the safety of the living room made it all seem so simple.

Rachael was sitting in a lounge chair behind the table with Maple and Tadpole lying on her lap. Maple's weight prevented any movement, while Raider perched next to the head rest. The rest of the dog gang vied for space near her feet. "Leave everyone except Dave in place. We can take their weapons, vehicles, and radios and decide on the helicopter later. I will deal with Dave… if there's a need."

Questioning eyes turned to Rachael. "No, I won't talk about it."

"Sounds like a plan to me!" Thomas bellowed.

Mike leaned down and drew two "A"s on the road map spread on the table. "This is where we'll stop and dismount. Katie and I will go further to the south since it's closer to the stable. I want to get Karen out to the truck quickly. I'll join up with you after she's safe. These locations should be far enough away that they won't see or hear us. Do what you have to do and load up. Sleep when you can and switch drivers if you get tired. Please ride with the team you've been assigned and talk through what you will do once we are on-site. Jed, I want eyes on the ranch after it gets dark, so have a drone flying and ready. We need to be there no later than 2 AM, so let's just pray our friend Murphy had enough fun with us on the first part of the trip."

Mike stopped, taking in each person as he viewed the unusual band of warriors. "I know I've been a bear to live with recently, and I can't adequately express my gratitude to each of you for helping me save a most amazing woman. I am honored to call you my friends and grateful, truly grateful, we found each other."

Always hovering somewhere near Mike, Jill stood up, tail in the air, giving two full throated barks as Thomas shouted, "Hooah," Army slang for "hell yes." In only ten minutes, seven human souls and seven hero canines sat in a small four truck convoy, engines running, for a last radio check.

Rachael talked Manuel into letting her drive for at least the first part of the trip. Manuel relented easily, having an ulterior motive. It made him happy to simply sit next to her watching Rachael's erect posture and proud raised chin. He could imagine her in a Viking headdress with painted face, part of some long-ago raiding party. Even so, it was difficult to get around the knowledge that he was very recently a pudgy middle-aged man and Rachael was a gorgeous young woman, even if they looked the same age. *Better to bide my time*, he thought.

Rachael for her part, mostly preoccupied with thoughts of Karen, couldn't help noticing Manuel's eyes when he smiled and how he listened to her every word— and he was hot too. After they walked through the plan three times, Manuel asked Rachael about her life before the change and shared some of his much longer story.

Manuel had a deep sense Rachael was wounded, even though she never mentioned anything traumatic or otherwise that had happened at the ranch. In fact, she seemed to be avoiding the subject entirely. Could this Dave person have done something horrible to Rachael? He was filled with indignation at the thought of it. "Are you tired, Rachael? Would you like me to drive now?"

Keeping both hands on the steering wheel, Rachael glanced at Manuel's sensitive face. "No, thanks. It feels good to be doing something productive."

"I understand. Please do say if you get tired. And Rachael, also, please keep your eyes on the road." Startled, Rachael swerved back on the road from the shoulder. She raised her eyebrows, eyes wide, and said "Oops" as she locked both hands on the wheel and concentrated on the highway ahead.

Sara, in a truck with Jed, thought the secret to an introvert's social clumsiness might be long drives in the middle of the night when there was nothing to do but sleep or communicate. Jed was operating the drone computer while she drove, and, multitasking, sharing his favorite nerd stories. Sara had plenty of those too. She didn't think she'd ever laughed this much. Jed for his part couldn't help but notice Sara's long, lean frame and her big brown eyes that always held a hint of something going on behind her cool exterior.

In the car with Bill, Thomas listened to Bill's apologies for most of the trip. "I'm just an accountant from a small town in Montana. When I met Mathias, Carlotta, and Mabel, they seemed like okay people, and hey, I didn't have anything better to do. It was Sylvie who really turned my head. I was never the kind of guy that people noticed and man oh man, did she turn it on to me. At first, I thought Mathias's weird nightly séance was benign, but then Sylvie asked me to help her pick up Karen and things started heading in a bad direction. I had no idea they were going to lock her up in a stable."

"Should have been a clue," Thomas replied.

"Yeah, man, I know. I kept making excuses for their shenanigans, 'oh it isn't so bad' and 'they mean well,' that sort of thing. Mostly I ignored what was going on because I wanted Sylvie. Then she morphed into a

Gestapo guard and shot Jan. Anyway, I'll do whatever I can to make it right. I feel like a total fool."

"Thing is," Thomas said, eyes on the road, "sitting on the sidelines and doing nothing is still doing something."

Bill closed his eyes and sighed. "Unless you're tired, I think I'll get a little sleep."

"Before you do, I'm wondering about this enlightenment stuff Mathias was always talking about. What was it?"

"Hell if I know. Looking back, I guess it was something like the guy in a tent who says he heals people, although this might be an even better con. When a faith healer yells, `Alleluia, you can walk,' and a severed spine victim stands, at least there's something to check. Maybe the guy or gal walked into the tent on their own anyway. Something or someone almost always gives away the truth. Mathias was trying to help us fix our minds, not all of us willingly I might add, and who's to say it didn't work? If you believe it, maybe it does.

"All I know, from my perspective, is that for all the talk about building strong relationships and self-reflection and discovery, the whole group was a dysfunctional bunch of selfish assholes. Maybe too much self-reflection becomes narcissism, or maybe the whole thing was a con from the start by a narcissist who wanted to control the world. When I figure it out, I'll let you know. Can I sleep now, because I get headache thinking about it?"

"Sounds about like what I expected. And nope not quite yet. Before you sleep, I need you to give me a good physical description of everyone on the ranch. Also, anything else you know about them that could be important. The more intelligence I have, the better I'll be able to take them down. After that, you can catch a few winks. Also, I'll need you to take over driving an hour before we arrive so I can get a nap, too."

Bill gazed out the window, wondering one last time how he got sucked in by the ranch and then began by talking about Sylvie.

Mike, in convoy lead, enjoyed companionable silence with Jill curled in the passenger seat and Katie snoring in the back. He tried to imagine what Karen was doing at this very moment and willed her to know he was almost there.

He remembered watching Karen's animated face during a long-ago dinner with her husband and his wife. She had been so full of life: quirky, smart, and confident. Something about her had made him want to stay and know more. He was married and so was she; it had been all he could do to keep his mind in the right place and stop himself from looking at her too frequently. Instead, like a teenager, he'd stolen glances when no one was watching and felt embarrassed later, thinking someone might have noticed.

Mike liked to nail down logical explanations for things. This attraction, this need, had defied easy answers. He didn't believe in stuff like love at first sight; lust at first sight, yeah sure. He didn't think in terms of only one true soul mate and thought it took a lifetime of work to make that happen. Yes, Karen was gorgeous, and yes, he was battling the sometimes-all-consuming hormonal rages of a young adult male; it had been a very long time since his body had responded in this way. But all the women of the new world looked pretty damned good. It was more than that. He wanted her, and he had wanted her from the very first time they met. With no effort at all she had lodged herself in his consciousness and refused to leave—no one had ever excited him like Karen.

Mike heard the quiet buzz of the Satellite phone. "Katie, wake up and get that."

"Huh, okay," Katie sat up dazed from her nap.

Thomas's loud voice was easy for Mike to hear from the back seat. "Jed just saw two people doing something on our entry road a klick away from the first dismount point."

"Could he tell what they were doing?"

"No, could be setting up an ambush or a roadside bomb. Can't say for sure. It looks like something is up or they know we're coming. There appears to be no one in the ranch hand building or the stable. At least we haven't seen any activity all evening. We need to stop five clicks away and make a new plan. I'm going to pass to you to pick a stop point."

"So much for in and out quickly."

"I'm just glad we have all the intel from the drones. Nothing to worry about, Mike. I'll come up with something."

"Thanks, Thomas. Glad you're with us."

Chapter 35: A+115, Bugs and Bodies

"Oh no, I'm itching—is my skin peeling off again?" Looking down, Karen saw her skin, completely covered in scales, molting and sliding off her feet. As Karen thrashed on the ground trying to scratch her legs, she remained in that half-asleep, half-awake world where dreams grab external reality and meld a visceral thing to whatever interests the unconscious. She awoke breathing heavily, heart racing from a piercing and lonely howl that sounded all too much like Uh Huh.

Sitting up, confused, Karen didn't know where she was or how she got there. Light was filtering through the pine forest. "Oh, that's right, how could I forget? I'm lost in the middle of Nowhere, Idaho." Karen attempted to reach down and scratch her knee as the full impact of her tenuous situation resulted in a shriek of her own making. Her hands, still bolted behind her back with a snap tie, couldn't reach the inflamed skin. An army of unnamed marauding insects had obviously feasted on her tired body during the night, covering her legs and arms with red welts.

"Get up and get going, Karen!" she ordered herself. At least it had quit raining. The temperature was cool but not so cold. Early morning light filtered through the trees. She could hear yesterday's dry creek bed, filled with the fruits of an evening thunderstorm, whooshing its way down the mountain. She stood up, walked to the embankment edge, and realized she could no longer travel in the mostly level creek floor and instead had to move along the edge of gully in the forest in her bare feet. "Shit, shit, shit, and son of a bitch! I would kick a tree if my feet didn't hurt so much."

She didn't even stop to do a physical assessment because, in the immortal words of one prominent and likely dead politician, really, at this point what difference did it make? After getting a long drink from the newborn stream, Karen climbed back up the bank and walked, and walked, tripped, got up, and walked some more. A nurse friend had once told Karen that at a certain point your pain highway, the nerves carrying pain signals to the brain, is filled, meaning there was an outer limit of pain one could experience. Karen thought she had now tested this theory and found it wanting. Everything hurt at the same time: her swollen ankle, scraped skin, bloody ankles, bruised body, near skinless blister-encrusted feet, and the all-consuming itch of insect bites. The itching may have been the worst of it.

Morning bled into afternoon and then into early evening. Karen sat on a boulder to rest and forced her mind to make a plan for the night. She was bone-tired and hungry, having not eaten for two full days. On the glass half full barometer, at least she hadn't run afoul of bears or mountain lions, so far. And she'd found water to drink. She didn't know what to do. Last night, the rain had given her a measure of protection from predators. The clear blue skies transitioning to hues of pink and orange made clear that she would not have that luxury for the night bearing down on her now.

With her hands still affixed behind her back and the aching from her bruises and swollen ankle only worse when she sat, Karen didn't think she could climb a tree. Even if she could, it would only help with wolves. As she recalled, bears and mountain lions can climb trees. The best bet was to find a rock cubby that didn't house a snake nest and snuggle in with a hope and a prayer the predators didn't find her. If they did, all she had to fight with was her feet. Not an entirely promising strategy.

Karen hauled her weary, stiff body to its feet. Now that she had a plan, scant though it might be, she needed to start looking for a place to hide for the night. As if on cue from a badly written science fiction novel, Karen heard the scuffling noises of a large animal breaking branches from a nearby outcropping of bushes. A giant black head peaked above the din and glared at Karen now standing near her resting boulder. Karen was surprised there was enough adrenaline left in her body to react to the predictable sight of a bear, but it did. Her heart immediately started pumping blood to her limbs and brain, forgetting for the moment the body's long list of injuries.

Since she couldn't outrun it, Karen hopped on the boulder to make herself appear bigger. She scowled and yelled at the bear, "You don't want to mess with me!"

The bear wasn't convinced of her sincerity. It raised up to its full height and yelled back in a growl-roar something that sounded like, "You aren't shit!"

Karen's bravado considered flight. She looked with only her eyes, left and right to see if there might be a reasonable escape route. There wasn't. Only one thing left to do. She had to be all in. Karen shook her head back and forth like a crazy woman and screamed at the top of her lungs to the bear. She screamed all the stored anger and frustration she had packed away for the ranch and her lost world. "Fuck you! If I gotta go, I will go fighting, you stinking pile of mangy fur!"

The insult was perhaps harder for the black beast to bear than Karen imagined. It clacked its teeth, huffed and then dropped back to four legs preparing to charge. Resigned, Karen whispered under her breath, "Well, that's it then." Karen thought she had read you fought back against black bears and curled in a ball for Grizzlies, or was it the other way around? *Does it matter? I can't really fight without hands and curling in a ball would only result in a slower death.*

As Karen was contemplating her imminent demise again, a dark, furry creature flashed between her and the bear. *Is that a wolf? Are they going to fight over my broken body? How strange.* Still on the rock, Karen slid off and started to back away. Before she turned to dash into the forest, Karen took stock of the animal at her front assuming it would be her next nemesis. Oh, my God, that's not a wolf, that's Jack. "Jaaack!"

He glanced at her with his growl on and then turned his attention back to the bear. Mesmerized, Karen watched Jack badger the bear, intimidating it with snarls and alternating forward movement. Karen had managed to piss it off, but Jack was having a different effect. The bear gave one last snarl and hustled in the opposite direction.

Karen was already crying as Jack leaped to her. "You saved me again…you amazing dog." She lowered to her knees and laid her head against his neck as Jack tried to lick the tears from her face. "How did you get here? She looked around for any signs of Mike, but it seemed Jack was in the wilderness alone.

Jack loved behind-the-ear scratching and when Karen didn't comply, he trotted behind Karen and stuck his cool wet nose between the zip ties and her hands. Karen whined, "Please Jack, get it off," as he nibbled at the hard plastic. Using sharp incisors, Jack made short work of Karen's bindings. She stood and stretched her arms. "Oh, thank God! And even more, thank you Jack." Karen twisted her torso stretching her shoulders and then hugged Jack and scratched behind his ears some more.

If Karen could have heard Jack as Mike could, she would have known his pride at fulfilling his duty. She would have heard him say, *woman is safe now. Jack is here. Jack has pack.* She might have also heard him say he was no longer empty. He was filled with something he could not describe.

Jack would have explained that when the Alpha wild-dog heard Jack's last command in the wild-dog way, he finally understood. The command was so powerful, so strong, the Alpha sensed something different and did as Jack asked. The young female stayed. She did not have a mate and wanted Jack. They stayed together during the storm and then he chased her away so she would return to her pack. The wild dog was not meant for Jack's pack.

Jack signaled to Karen that he wanted her to follow by tugging on her shorts and then scooting forward. After two tries, she got the idea. "So you want me to follow you?" Jack yipped. "Alrighty then. I was kind of out of ideas anyway."

Jack led Karen through the dry brush to a higher elevation. They reached a rocky outcropping where a small cave was inset into the rock face. It was a tiny entry. "Do you promise there are no snakes in there?" Karen asked.

Jack didn't know what she asked but climbed inside the cave to demonstrate what he wanted. Karen crawled on her belly finding a roomy little cave where she could stand. Jack picked up a dead rabbit from a pile of what appeared to be several small fur bags and presented one to Karen. "Hmmm, I'm not sure I'm dead, cold, rabbit hungry, yet."

Jack stood in front of her, his eyes gleaming, wagging his tail madly at Karen. She didn't have the heart to refuse his gift. Karen took the rabbit and sat cross-legged, with the carcass in her lap. She tepidly pulled on fur trying not to gag at the exposed flesh. Biting down she nearly choked. It was not cold. Taking a bite with a grimace, Karen chewed and provided as close to a smile as she could manage in Jack's direction. Satisfied, Jack began tearing into the rest of the pile.

By the time Jack finished his meal, Karen was already in the fetal position, snoring on hard, packed ground. Jack twirled around twice, reversed course once and then plopped next to her, sighing happiness as he rested his head on her knee.

*   *   *

Karen and Jack headed back to the stream the next morning and started walking. As they were nearing the hot part of the day, Karen glimpsed a rough-hewn cabin through the trees on the other side of the creek as the creek made a southerly dogleg. "If I had any energy left I would break into song," Karen shouted to Jack with a huge smile cracking her sunburned lips. The water looked to be only knee deep at the turn. She scrambled over the rocky edge and rushed into the water, careful not to slip. The cold water gave momentary relief to her lower body.

The cabin looked habitable. It was a basic log cabin, probably one of those kits, with a square porch, large windows on both sides of the door, and one window on each side of the rectangular building. Sitting on a grassy rutted path behind the cabin was a rusted and dented Chevy SUV. Karen stepped up to an anachronistic elaborate wood door and turned the handle, smiling that it was unlocked.

The ever-present apocalyptic smell of decomposition flooder her nose at the entry. As she moved slowly into one large room, leaving the door open behind her for Jack, Karen waited for her eyes to adjust to indoor shadows. Nicely outfitted, the cabin was more than just a hunter's stopover. Someone had lived here full time, and what little was left of him or her was on a bed in the far corner of the room.

Karen was starving. Rifling through the cabinets, she found a plentiful assortment of canned and bagged goods. "Good grief, I'm salivating over canned ravioli and Oreos," she chuckled to Jack. "Oh what the hell. I would love a Coke right now." She inhaled before she opened the refrigerator. It wasn't as stinky as she imagined, and she snagged bottled water, warm beer, and Cherry Coke (not her all-time favorite but good enough) from inside the moldy metal box.

Sitting outside on the stoop to get away from the aroma, with her dog at her side, Karen enjoyed a glorious meal, ecstatic to be alive and survive once again. She fed Jack some ravioli even though he was begging for the cookies as she planned her next move and listened to the surrounding forest. "Tend to my wounds and drive off into the sunset. Yep, that sounds about right." After frantically searching for SUV keys, Karen learned Mr. Cabin kept them in his pants pocket that he happened to be wearing. Yuck! The Chevy battery was as dead as the cabin's inhabitant. Karen would have to stay the night and walk out. She folded slimy sheets around the almost bare bones of Mr. Cabin and covered him with extra blankets. She would bury him tomorrow before she left. For now, she desperately needed rest.

Karen made a bed for the night in an old lazy boy chair. On Jack's third attempt to wedge in next to Karen on the chair, he finally took the hint that there wasn't enough room for the two of them. Karen nudged him gently to the floor. "I love you, boy, but I am not sharing this chair."

Jack looked back at her, only a little hurt, and finally settled on a small rug in front of the door. Jack could hear the wild dogs during the dark of night. He sniffed under the door to catch their scent. He lifted his head once and returned a plaintive howl in the wild dog way. Fearing he had woken the woman, he glanced at her to find she was still sleeping. With a small whine, Jack laid his head on his paws. He twitched as he dreamed he was hunting with the wild dogs.

Karen found everything she needed in the cabin to finish her trek out of the wilderness—a fully stocked medicine cabinet contained antibiotics, anti-inflammatories, and anti-itch crème. There were all the anti-'s one needed to combat wilderness living. There was also plenty of gauze to cover the mess that was her feet. She had her choice of three rifles and ammo and located a decent hiking pack. Boots were still a problem. The owner was a man with sized 10's but with enough gauze and a couple of pairs of socks, she would fill them.

Karen woke the next morning to Jack's whining at the door after a dreamless sleep. She wondered if no dreams meant nothing horrible would happen to her during the next day. *Wouldn't that be a refreshing change?*

After finishing burial duty she cared for her feet, put on the too-large boots and hefted a stuffed backpack on her shoulders. A loaded rifle was slung over her other shoulder. Karen closed the door to the cabin and called, "Let's go, Jack," as they walked to the path that would lead them out of the woods.

Chapter 36: A+116, The Ranch Meets a Hard Place

"Mathias, you need to get your head out of your ass!" Carlotta, standing and glaring at the ranch's supposed leader, pounded the table with her fist, hoping to elicit a reaction.

"Carlotta, sit down. Theatrics are not helpful in our current situation. You may need to spend some time self-reflecting to decide where this unseemly anger has its roots."

Carlotta looked up in frustration and then plopped into a chair. With a steadier tone she tried again. "Mathias, I don't know how many ways to put this to you. We are in trouble here. Rachael and Bill have undoubtedly contacted Karen's friends. If what Sylvie says is true, they will be coming, along with attack dogs and anyone else they've found to help. We have to be ready!"

"Hmm, well, yes, of course we need to be ready. I'm simply not as concerned about the invincible force you believe will arrive at our doorstep. Does anyone know what Mabel is making for dinner? I'm famished."

Dave shook his head at Carlotta's rigid and red-faced stare. "Mathias, let's assume for a moment, they attack us tonight and they have enough people and weapons to launch an assault in multiple locations. Then what? We are spread out here and sitting ducks in these buildings. I think it's time to consider leaving the ranch and looking for a better location, at least for a time. One that is more defensible. We can come back later when we have more people to build a real defense system.

"Thank you, Dave." Mathias opened a desk drawer, put his hand on something, and slammed a hammer on the top of the desk with an ear-piercing bang, shattering the unbreakable glass covering the surface of the desk. "Never speak again about leaving our home." Wide, shocked eyes viewed Mathias's. He was standing now, radiating authority with feral intensity.

In a normal voice, that was more frightening than if he had chosen to yell at his acolytes, Mathias continued. "The next person that mentions leaving our home will not live to speak about it again. You could have asked the correct question instead of acting like a bunch of frightened girls, running for your lives. Someone please show me you have learned something here and ask the right question!" Mathias, loomed over the small group, taking in each member with a penetrating stare.

Eric was the first to intuit Mathias's meaning. "Mathias, can you please explain why you are not afraid?"

"At last. Thank you Eric. I am not afraid because I have prepared for this eventuality. The gentleman that sold the ranch to me was something of an eccentric. He believed the government had plans to seize all private property. He accumulated a treasure trove of equipment to prevent that eventuality. You will find particularly effective mines and other weaponry painstakingly preserved in an underground shelter."

In the groove now, Dave asked, "And where is this shelter, Mathias?"

"It is behind the house. The in-ground door is covered by the birdbath. Now isn't that a better way to communicate? Rather than make all kinds of assumptions about my perceived ineptitude, simply ask. Oh, and Dave, the man who agreed to sell me the ranch is also in the shelter. Please don't disturb his final resting place. If you could please see to our defense in an expeditious manner, I am going to dine and then will retire to do some reading. Please inform me when we are ready for visitors. Also, bring Jan and Mabel here and secure them. They may be useful." Mathias strode slowly to the door, all eyes following his movement. He turned back around to ask a question as he was almost through the threshold. "Dave, are you sure the creature is gone and not lurking around somewhere on the ranch?"

"I'm sure, Mathias. After he broke down the door in the stable cell, I tracked his movements. He took off toward the east. He's long gone. We had no idea he was that strong. We're probably lucky he didn't hurt anyone."

"Most unfortunate," Mathias mumbled. "We could have learned so much. Perhaps Karen and the strange man will meet up in the wilderness. They did seem to build an unusual relationship."

"I doubt it, Mathias," Dave replied, his eyes on Sylvie.

At the sound of the door closing, Eric said, "What was that! And you two: what did you do with Karen?" Eric saw Dave and Sylvie exchange guilty glances. "Just what I thought. You had to get your piece of revenge, didn't you, guaranteeing that her friends would come looking for her. If you had given her a car she would have left, never to return, her or her buddies. But no!"

Sylvie, ignoring Eric's accusations, implored, "I say we leave. This place is too big and spread out to defend, even with mines and stuff. I don't want to be up all night every night waiting to be attacked. Mathias is getting scary, Jan and Mabel will work against us, and that only leaves the six of us. We could load what we need and take the helicopter—start over somewhere else."

"Why are you so afraid of them?" Dave asked. "You make it sound like they're supernatural soldiers."

Sylvie hesitated, thinking about her answer. "I don't know how I know. This Mike character doesn't look like a badass, but he is. Rachael is a tough hombre, and my guess is her twin is, too. More than anything, it's the dogs. That German shepherd, Jack, can read minds—I swear it. He tells the other dogs what to do."

Dave laughed, "Sure, Sylvie, anything you say."

Sam, the new guy, cut in before a building fight between Dave and Sylvie got rolling. "I think she's right, Dave. This place isn't going to cut it for the long haul without more people. We don't have enough time tonight before it gets dark to load the helicopter and leave. I say we set up a defense for this evening and go tomorrow. Just leave Mathias, Mabel, and Jan. Let them fend for themselves."

Jim added, "I would prefer not to fly at night anyway. I agree with Sam."

Dave, pouting with his arms crossed in front of him, said, "Shut up, Sam! Who the hell are you to tell us what to do? You just got here. And Carlotta, just give up? That's all you got?"

Carlotta, now calm, put her hand on Dave's arm. "Not giving up, Dave. Just starting again somewhere we have room to build and still protect ourselves. Why don't we vote?"

"How many vote we leave?" Eric asked. All hands except Dave's went up. "The 'get the hell out of Dodge' vote wins. We'll set up to defend for tonight and then load what we need to leave first thing in the morning."

Chapter 37: The Ranch, Before Dawn

Leaning over the hood of Mike's truck, Thomas pointed at a map he'd drawn with Jed's input. Covered in camouflage paint, Thomas' face was a mask of muted colors. Mike and the other unlikely warriors clustered around Thomas taking in the new plan. "I don't know if they have any more directional mines. Someone had the wherewithal to deploy one with a sensor switch, which doesn't bode well for the good guys. If Jed hadn't picked up someone doing something on the road with the drones, we would've driven right into it. Our drone sensors show a perimeter of four people surrounding the main house."

"One person—Bill said it's probably Dave—is continuously moving around the property doing what looks like a roving patrol. That's what we know. What we don't know is why Jed's drones are also seeing one person to the east in the hills and another group of two further south and east. Sara is convinced the group of two is a person and a wolf, which doesn't make any sense. Also, the roving patrol has moved to the south away from the ranch. I am thinking he may be covering the southerly road entry. What we can't see and don't know is who's left in the buildings."

"I don't want to give up the initiative and wait until light. Now is the best time to approach. They'll be tired. Given all the unknowns, I think it's best for me to go alone with Ghost and disarm any other mines. It might be possible to use them to our advantage, and it gives me a chance to see what's what. When I call, Mike, Bill, and Jill need to position themselves forward at this location." Thomas marked the spot with a circle on the map. "Katie, Rachael, Manuel, and the other dogs will be reserves."

Rachael jumped in, "I want to help, Thomas. I think I've earned the right. Please don't leave me here. Three people doesn't sound like enough. There are at least six of them!"

"No doubt you have earned the right, Rachael, and I know you want to be a part of this. But the best way to do this and get your friends out alive is stealth and not overwhelming force. Besides, any plan is better with reserves. That way I can use you where and when you'll have the greatest impact."

Rachael didn't appear happy but nodded agreement. "Is everyone clear on the plan?" Thomas waited until all he heard a yes from each person. "Mike, could I talk to you for a sec before I leave?"

The two men strolled down the road out of earshot from people with some extraordinary hearing. Thomas leaned in, talking low. "If you hear a big-assed explosion, that's your cue to take over. I think I can find any mines but if something goes wrong, just move through the area where the explosion occurred. You know my route. There won't be two of them in the same place."

"Are you that worried about it?"

"No, not really. There are only a few places where you could effectively use anti-personnel mines. But shit happens. Also, don't use the twins and Manuel unless it's absolutely necessary. Too many people without firing discipline are as likely to shoot each other. One last thing, have Jed keep a hawk eye on roving Dave and update me. I don't want to get flanked."

"Yeah, I got that. Happy hunting, Thomas," Mike said with a knowing smile and slapped him on the shoulder.

"Like fish in a barrel Mike," Thomas returned, seating his night vision device over his eyes and then sliding into the night.

* * *

After travelling all day from a path to a gravel road to a paved two-lane, Karen had been walking uphill for several miles. As the road crested, the ranch came into view below; serendipity. Somehow, she'd wandered through the woods and ended up back where she started. She'd decided not to stop when it got dark. With Jack by her side, she felt safer to just keep trudging all night. Karen's first instinct when she viewed the topography of the ranch was to keep moving in a different direction, but Mabel and Jan were still trapped and she wanted to get them away. *Hell, I've got a rifle,* she thought. *I can sneak in when everyone is asleep and get them out. With any luck, I can take out some of those bastards too.*

Jack stood at attention sniffing the air and whined. "What's up, Jack boy?" He became restless and began to bark and whine. Turning in Karen's direction and then toward the ranch, he trotted off the paved road and spun in a circle, then came back to Karen and barked again. "I'm guessing it's my turn to follow. Is that what you want?" Jack stood poised and excited, wagging his tail. Karen barely got out, "Your lead, Jack," before he was running downhill toward the ranch. Karen scrambled to follow.

* * *

Mike was watching the computer screen, following Thomas's movements with Jed. Three laptop computers lit the nearly moonless night and sat on an open truck tailgate tracking each of the drone feeds. Jed said, "Oh, shoot, look at that. That pair is moving in our direction."

Wide-eyed, Mike called quickly to the twins and Manuel. "Everybody needs to come with me. Put on your night vision and turn on your communications. I'll show you where to set up a firing position. Looks like we may have company. And hold your fire until I tell you otherwise."

Agitated, Tilley was running around the vehicles. She stopped and stared into the distance and then released a long sing song howl. Jill joined in. Mike was so busy getting everyone in position he wasn't listening to Jill's insistent plea, *Jack, Jack, Jack*.

Jill knew her duty to her humans. She tried to stay with them. Finally, the unrelenting pull of her companion was more than the dog side of her could withstand and she bolted into the distance. Tilley smelled Jack, too, and used Jill's defiance as an excuse to follow. Rachael saw Jill and Tilley pass her and yelled out with no result. Raider was the last of the dog pack to run by, following Jill's lead.

Karen stopped running, braced herself, and waited for Tilley. She could almost see Tilley's weird dog smile from this distance. Skidding to a stop, Tilley jumped, both paws on Karen's chest, frantically licking and moaning with joy.

"Oh, Tilley, I've missed you so much, you silly girl!" Karen laughed as she sat on the ground and hugged her dog. As Karen talked in a high, sing-song voice reserved for babies and beloved pets, Tilley wiggled and squirmed, tried to sit on her lap, and mouthed a rock and offered it to Karen while grunting in pleasure. Tilley had always provided greeting gifts, often a shoe located near a door, which Karen accepted graciously with sincere thanks.

"I love you too, Tilley. Calm down, sweetie pie." Raider reached Karen next. Like Tilley, he launched himself at her and nearly knocked both her and Tilley over. He pushed Tilley to the side, crawling on Karen's lap and began licking her face and neck as fast as his little tongue allowed. He whined his own, unique greeting song.

Karen cried and laughed. She could barely catch her breath from the shaking sobs of joy. Her loyal friends were here, and somewhere in the distance must be her human friends. She was found and she was alive. She had never felt such unrestrained bliss. It occurred to her in that moment that only profound loss provides the context for to know euphoric happiness.

Jack was performing his own greeting dance with Jill. They playfully charged and jumped at each other, circling and smelling while their tails beating madly, expressing their own glee. Jack repeated to Jill in the language that they had been provided, *I am full. I have duty. I have pack.*

Karen was the first to start moving to where she thought she might find Mike and the twins. The dogs immediately ran to the lead, pointing her in the right direction. Mike was directing his group over a communication device, "Hold your fire, I hear them. Hold your fire!"

Mike held the night-vision binoculars in front of his eyes, "It's Karen! And, and, I think I see Jack! Well, I'll be damned." He let the binoculars drop and started running. Seeing Mike's response, the twins glanced at each other, smiled and then pushed to keep up with Mike's blistering pace, following him up the hill. Katie had to laugh. *Maybe dogs and humans have more in common than some might think.*

Karen jumped into Mike's arms and Jack stood and looked at Mike, expectant and proud. "You found her, Jack," Mike said as he hugged Karen to him. Rachael and Katie took over hugging Karen when they arrived, and Mike gave Jack well deserved attention. He crouched down and put his arms around Jack's strong neck massaging his ruff with his hands. He choked back tears of relief as he whispered in Jack's ear. "I am so proud of you. You are the best dog anyone could ever hope to call a friend." Jack gave a large "You are welcome" lick from Mike's mouth to his forehead.

Mike stood and looked back in the direction of their trucks. "Okay, guys, we have to cut this short. Thomas is in harm's way and we have to get back. I can tell him to call off his attack now that we have Karen and Jack."

"What are you talking about?"

"We had a plan to rescue you, Karen. Thomas is my new Special Forces friend I met on Joint Base Lewis McChord. He is on the ranch as we speak, trying to scope it out and disarm any mines."

Karen looked at Rachael, "Mines? Do you have Mabel and Jan, too?"

"No. They're still with the ranchers as far as we know."

"Well, then, no way we can call it off! Mabel helped Rachael escape, and Jan won't survive here. We have to get them out! And what about Uh Huh?" Karen was indignant. "You can't just leave him in a cage."

Mike viewed Karen's determination. As messed up as she appeared with her wild matted hair, bites, scrapes and bruises covering her face and exposed skin, limping on one leg, he didn't think she'd ever looked more crazy beautiful. "Okey-dokey, then. Still, we have to get back to the group."

Mike introduced Karen to his team. Zoe, Maple, and Tadpole were running about doing their own hello's to Karen and Jack. Jed looked over his shoulder and said in an uncharacteristically stern voice, "Everyone needs to settle down. I just heard from Thomas. He found one mine and has disabled it. He wants Bill and Mike forward to their position in five minutes." Then Jed saw the shepherds together and his jaw dropped open. "I saw them…"

"Saw who?" Sara asked.

"Those dogs. They were in L.A. when I was attacked by coyotes and those exact dogs ran them off."

"That's impossible. Jill has been with us the entire time and Jack was in central Washington when Karen was kidnapped and he chased after her. No way Jack was in Los Angeles unless he also knows how to fly."

"I thought Jill was just like one of the dogs I saw and convinced myself it was a coincidence. But both, the exact same markings and size, not to mention they act like they know more than any regular dog. They also have the same glowing collars. Very weird." Jed did an impression of the X-Files theme. He was shaking his head in confusion as Mike walked up.

"Where is Dave, Jed?" Mike asked.

"If you mean the roving individual, he moved off the grid to the south. Maybe he decided to take off. The other unknown to the east is still moving in the direction of the stable."

Karen was frustrated realizing she had just walked into the middle of an ongoing operation to save her. She was safe, but now Mike and Bill were heading into danger. Mike's new buddy Thomas was already out there. I want to go with you and Bill, Mike. It's my responsibility. You came here for me and I made it about Mabel and Jan. I have to go with you."

Everyone looked at Mike concerned and he returned a sad smile. "Karen, give me a minute, will you?"

Karen huffed and then strode into the distance, Mike hustling to follow. She stopped and stared at him with narrowed eyes. "What?"

Mike pushed around dirt with the toe of his boot, collecting his thoughts. "I know you don't want me to be patronizing, so I won't. You are in no shape to do this. I need you to stay put with the twins so that they don't get involved unless absolutely necessary and to make sure Jed and Sara stay focused."

"What do you mean, no shape to do this?"

"When was the last time you slept, Karen? How is that ankle you're limping on? I have no idea how you ended up in the wilderness with Jack and it's a story I really want to hear—but we don't have time right now. While we've been discussing our plan and training, you've been held captive or out in the woods. Not your fault—just the facts. I totally get you want to help. You have more reason than any of us except maybe Rachael. Just wait until we have everything under control. You know these people and can help then. Please. Thomas is good. He'll get it done."

Mike's speech took the wind out of Karen. She shook her head and exhaled. "Yeah, I suppose you're right, but I don't have to like it."

"Didn't expect that you would." Mike said with a half-smile.

Karen laughed and gave him a light punch to the shoulder. "Smart-ass."

"Two minutes until you need to move forward, Mike," Jed yelled out, "Thomas needs you and Bill forward."

Mike gave Karen a kiss on the forehead as he whispered, "I would like to take Jack with me. He is in considerably better condition than you."

"Go, Mike, before I change my mind!"

* * *

Thomas was improvising his butt off. After disabling the old-style claymore mine, he crept within forty meters of the ranch house perimeter. Thus far, they were not aware of his presence. He could hear two people in the front of the house laughing and talking. One of them lit a cigarette. Thomas was glad they didn't have noise or light discipline but that wasn't going to help. Dug-in to a firing position, an M60 machine gun was manned by a guy who looked like he might know how to use it.

Thomas low-crawled to the back side of the house. His heart was beating hard as he realized that if he was heard, that machine gun had an effective range of about 1100 meters and would tear him to shreds. There were trees on this side that helped hide his movements. Thomas climbed one to get a better perspective. Two more positions were located at the back, one of them, with another M60. *Where did they get all this military stuff*, he wondered, *and what else do they have?* Thomas used his night vision device and binoculars to study the dark-haired woman holding the second 7.62 caliber tripod mounted machine gun. *That must be Carlotta*, he thought. She matched Bill's description and she appeared to be asleep. Thomas mulled his limited options and then had an idea. He snuck out of the tree and backed way off to make a whispered call.

"Mike, this is Tee. Are you in position? Over."

"In position, Tee. Over"

"We have a tiny problem. Two M60's, one in front north corner and one behind ranch house on the south side. Need you to move to secondary position Bravo. Stay covered and silent. I need a distraction and maybe the dogs. Relay to Jed to have drones ready to make an aerial attack on my order. Over."

"Tiny problem you say? Two machine guns? And the drones don't carry ordnance…oh, they are the distraction. Roger."

"I need you and Bill to draw fire from your position when I call for the drones or if you hear any firing. In that case, you tell Jed to bring in the drones. There is an old trailer and some trees at position Bravo. Not much, so stay low. You have four minutes starting now."

"Roger, Tee. You should know, Karen was one of the unknowns. She and Jack are safe with the reserve force. Our new mission is to get Mabel and Jan out alive. They will not be on the perimeter."

"Jack, he found her? That's beyond amazing. And these other two ladies, are they worth risking our necks, big time?"

"Karen guarantees it."

"Saving damsels in distress is after all one of my specialties. Out."

Thomas crawled back into position and checked to see if the woman was still soundly sleeping. She was. The man was awake but playing a game on a tablet and not paying attention. He had to get to that M60 before the woman woke up and make sure the man couldn't react quickly enough to shoot him. Ghost was at Thomas's side. Thomas waited until the four minutes he had given Mike elapsed. He pointed to the man and whispered, "Ready, Ghost?" Her eyes followed from his hand forward to the correct position. Ghost looked at him like she understood. He hoped the hell she did. Thomas thought if you had told him a year ago that he could use a dog like a soldier, he would have said it was crazy talk. Mike had said Jack had done something to the other dogs. Thomas wouldn't have believed it if he hadn't seen it for himself with Jill. He didn't know how or what or why, but he was sure as shit glad.

His muscles tensed as he pushed himself into a sprinter's position. Thomas looked at his bestie one last time, nodded, and softly gave the attack command as he sprung forward, willing the woman not to hear him too soon. Thomas hurled his massive body at the woman in a leaping tackle just as she was grabbing the machine gun. It wouldn't do her any good now; he was too close. She grunted when Thomas landed on her. The man in the next position noticed Thomas. He was taking aim at the two wrestling bodies just as Ghost reached him from his blind side and locked on to his right arm, savagely twisting. The man screamed in pain.

The woman fought harder than Thomas expected. She was face down trying to roll him off her when she pulled a knife from a sheath on her waist. He reached for the arm with the blade. He was too late to prevent some damage. He felt the knife slide along his leg and draw blood. He crushed her arm with his strong hand until she tried to pull her arm free and in doing so, dropped the knife. The man in the position in the position fifteen feet away screamed. Thomas only had seconds. His original plan to knock the woman out wasn't going to happen. He locked his huge arm around her neck and twisted. This was probably Carlotta, and she was gone.

Thomas jumped toward the screaming man and simultaneously commanded, "Release!" to Ghost. He shot the man in the head as soon as Ghost moved out of the way. From Bill's description, he was the helicopter pilot, Jim. Still in motion, Thomas dipped for the machine gun and grabbed it as he ran by. He heard Mike and Bill firing when he reached the tree line behind the house.

*   *   *

Karen had barely let Mike and Bill get out of sight before she announced, "I'm going to take a run over to the stable to see if I can figure out what happened to Uh Huh."

Rachael wasn't having it. "Karen, it's not safe. Stay here with us."

"Rachael, please don't order me around. I've had enough from Mike for the time being. I'll take Tilley, and I have a weapon."

"Then I'm going with you."

"You can't. You know the plan and the people, and you're in reserve if things don't go well. I need to check, and I can't just stand around here doing nothing."

Jed and Sara frowned at each other wondering who would do the honors. It was Jed who broke first. "Karen, I don't think that's a good idea. Mike was very specific about our responsibilities. And, there is an unknown out there moving in the direction of the stable. Mike will…"

Karen cut him off. "Lucky for me, Mike is not my boss. I am quite capable of taking care of myself. After all, I freed myself from a blindfold and zip ties in the wilderness and survived both a poisonous snake and a bear to make my way here. I will hurry. Give me one of those communication devices so you can warn me if that unknown gets too close. Or don't, but I'm still going. Tilley, come!"

Karen grabbed a head set and night vision goggles from the hood of the truck, turned and ran with a painful looking, limping gait. "Mike is going to be pissed!" Jed called after her.

The five reserve forces were arguing about what to do about Karen when Mike's voice came over the head-set. "Are you going to tell him?" Sara asked.

Jed held up a finger for Sara to wait. They could all hear Mike's voice explaining about using the drones as a diversion at the ranch house. "I read you, Mike. Will do. It should only take two minutes to get them in the general vicinity. Shouldn't we keep one drone available for tracking the unknown signatures?"

"We're dealing with two machine guns and need to keep one of them occupied. Send them all. We'll worry about the roving patrol that is probably Dave as soon as we have this locked down. He isn't anywhere near our location, is he?"

"Okay, Mike. You got it. And no, he's still out to the south somewhere."

Manuel stepped next to Jed his eyebrows raised. "You decided not to mention Karen going to the stable then?"

"Not much he can do from where he is, and he was in a hurry. If she isn't back in twenty minutes one of you can go look for her."

Mike and Bill were single file, inching forward to their alternate position. Jack and Jill silently followed behind the two men. Mike could see the trailer ahead. Thomas was right, it didn't look like much cover, especially when an M60 was pointed in your direction. A drainage ditch cut parallel to the white trailer and lay just behind it. They wouldn't be able to see anything, but that wasn't important. They could fire in the general direction, at least enough to draw return fire from the machine gun at them instead of Thomas.

Mike pointed to Jack and Jill and gave them the command of down and stay. They lay side by side in the too small depression, looking to Mike for further direction. Bill kept moving forward. He was bent over at the waist but still offered a full silhouette to anyone who happened to be looking in his direction. Mike frantically spoke low into the headset. "Bill, Bill, wake up man and get down on your belly now!"

Mike heard a machine gun burst and Bill's scream. He was already prone as he called over the communication device. "Jed, bring the drones now!" And then, holy hell broke loose around them.

The M60 gunner saw Bill and aimed in his direction. Bill jerked and fell to the ground. Mike wanted to go get him, but it was impossible. Bullets were ripping the dirt at the crest of the ditch and zinging over his head. He glanced at the dogs. They were totally flat to the ground and safe for the time being. Mike reached his arm up to point his M4 over the top of their cover and fired in the direction of the ranch house.

He was talking as he fired. "Bill, what's your status?"

A weak voice replied. "They got me in the shoulder and the leg. I can't move…"

"Hang in there buddy. One way or another this won't last too long."

Mike thought he heard the high buzzing of a drone but it was hard to tell. When he peeked over the top of the ditch, he saw one swooping toward the machine gun position. He could still hear the M60 but it was no longer firing in his direction. Now's my chance, Mike thought. He told the dogs to stay and scrambled out to Bill. Grabbing him under the arms, Mike dragged him with every ounce of strength and speed he could muster. He barely made it back to cover before the maelstrom of bullets began again.

In the trees, Thomas moved wide around the back of ranch house and could now see the M60 firing at Mike and Bill. He watched as the first drone dove toward the man who was ably handling the powerful weapon. The gunner changed his direction of fire and hit the drone straight on. There were a couple of sparks and a puff of smoke just before the drone fell from the sky. Too quickly, the man transitioned from firing at the drone back to position Bravo: Mike and Bill. Thomas was glad Jed was a smart guy. He didn't bring the drones in all at once.

Also, there wasn't much fire coming from Mike and Bill. He hoped they were okay. Thomas needed to implement the second part of his plan and it wasn't going to be easy. He gestured to Ghost to back off into the woods. At first Ghost didn't understand. "Go back, Ghost," Thomas motioned with a sweeping gesture. "Move back." Ghost eyed him and then something clicked. She turned and ran into the forest.

Thomas whispered into the headset. "Mike, can you move your dogs back?"

"Not without getting one or both of them hurt. It's crazy here. Bill's hit."

"Roger. When you hear `Now,' you have fifteen seconds to cover their ears and yours."

"Roger, Tee."

Mike placed the special ear muffs Thomas had made him bring at the ready and then dug out Bill's from a pocket. "Bill, you need to help, man. Can you cover Jill's ears with your arms?"

Bill, white-faced, nodded and crawled closer to Jill. Mike smiled at him and said, "Won't be long now. Hang in there." Mike had used some coagulation powder on Bill's wounds when he dragged him back to the ditch, but he didn't look good. After placing the ear muffs over Bill's ears, Mike began firing again over the meager berm of their drainage ditch.

Thomas moved to the closest position with cover where he could see and had unobstructed room to throw. It was still almost thirty-five meters. *I can do this*, he told himself. He waited in the shadows for the next drone.

Mike heard the drone fly directly over him and tensed. Thomas saw the drone at as Mike heard it. As the big man pointed the M60 at the flying object, Thomas stood. He said "Now!" into the microphone and placed hearing protection over his ears.

This was Thomas's World Series. It was the last game of the series and his team was one up in the bottom of the ninth. The bases were loaded. The other team's best hitter was up to bat with two strikes and three balls. This had to be a good throw. In the case of a world series, he could lose an important game. Here and now, they could lose lives. This is why he did what he did. He was the right guy to handle the pressure.

Thomas thought about baseball all while counting off fifteen seconds. At zero, he armed the stun grenade and set the timer. Standing to the side, he saw a woman with white-blonde hair, probably Sylvie, in the perimeter position next to the machine gun. Her rifle was moving to her shoulder. Their eyes met. Thomas nodded at the blonde as he heaved the grenade at the M60 gunner. The woman took her shot.

The *whommpf* from the blast could be felt in the ground as far as Mike and Bill. They were cuddling the shepherds' sensitive ears as the blast hit. Thomas's throw was true. The grenade hit the machine gunner at knee level with only a tap and fell to the ground. Sylvie wasn't as proficient. Her shot missed Thomas. Game over.

Thomas checked in with Mike while moving to secure the stunned blonde and machine gunner. He still had a buzz in his ears. The hearing protection was good, but stun grenades packed a significant concussion. "Mike, can you move forward now?"

"No can do, Thomas. I have to get help for Bill. Sara is coming my way with Rachael now. I will send Jack and Jill."

"That'll work. Get your ass here as soon as you can."

"Roger, Out."

Thomas whistled for Ghost and looked at the blonde and the man. The big man came to his knees totally disoriented, holding his head and screaming. Blood was oozing out of both ears. The blonde woman zombie-stumbled on hands and knees to the front door of the ranch house. Thomas smiled as Ghost nudged him on the leg and the shepherds bounded to him, smiling back. "You have the honors. Jack, Jill, Ghost, bring them down!" The dogs were on them like greased lightning. After pulling the man to the ground, Jack sensed the man had no game, released his arm, and stood over him barking and growling. The white-haired lady, whom Thomas thought must be Sylvie, wasn't so lucky. She struggled against Ghost, which caused Ghost to bite harder on her arm.

Thomas ran to Ghost and yelled to release, pointing his pistol at the blonde now curled in the fetal position. He pulled zip ties from one of his numerous pockets. Thomas yanked her arms behind her back and quickly bound them with the ties. "Don't move!" Thomas ordered. Sylvie didn't respond. He leaned down to put his face in front of hers and repeated the command after realizing she couldn't hear a thing. Sylvie's eyes, wide and terrified, looked at Thomas. "If you move," Thomas pointed at the dogs, "One or more of these dogs will attack you again. Best just stay very still. Do you understand?" Sylvie nodded a yes. Jill and Ghost crouched in front of her growling with malice.

Thomas moved quickly to the big man who'd handled the M60 like a pro. He tied his hands and feet with twist ties even though he probably wasn't going anywhere. He had some nasty burns on the back of his legs. "No need to take the chance," Thomas said to Jack, still on guard. Thomas didn't know who this guy was. Bill had not described anyone like this. He was pretty good with the M60 so probably had some training. A shot zinged over Thomas's head as he was dragging the big guy from the house to tree line. He dropped behind the wounded man for cover. The man stared at Thomas with pleading eyes. "Sorry, dude. We didn't ask for this fight."

When Jack heard the shot, he did his magic with Ghost and Jill. All three dogs jigged and jagged out of the line of fire to the trees. Sylvie, still on her knees in front of the house, clamped her eyes shut and screamed.

"Mike, I could really use some help here," Thomas said calmly into his headset.

"Roger, Tee. Sara is just pulling up. I can hear you have another problem."

"There's a shooter in the southwest corner window. Can you move to the tree cover near there ASAP and take them out or at least keep them occupied? And make sure the ladies keep down. Don't think there's a real live sniper in there. He missed me."

"On it now. Where are the dogs?"

"They are probably in those trees hiding somewhere. Smart SOB's. Didn't even have to tell them what to do."

"Moving now. Out.

Whoever was in the window didn't want to shoot one of their own. High shots rang out sporadically but they weren't close. Thomas wanted to learn who was in the house. "Okay, big man, here's your chance to earn some brownie points while we lounge here. Who's left in the house?"

The man pointed to his ears to signal he couldn't hear. "Don't give me that BS." Thomas responded. He gestured at the house and said slowly so the man could watch his mouth. "Who is in the house?"

Defeated and in pain, the man mumbled, "Mathias, Jan, Mabel and Eric. I am Sam. Got roped in. Not even sure what we're fighting about."

"Looks to me you're plenty involved." Thomas heard the retort from a rifle in the wooded fringe. "That would be my man Mike." A CS canister flew from the woods through the window. Thomas whistled. "Nice throw! We be playing some baseball when we get home. If you'll excuse me, I have some business to attend to." Thomas leaped over the man and ran to the opposite side of the house from where Mike was. He broke out the glass in another window and threw a second tear gas canister into the building.

"Mike, my man, outstanding throwmanship. Now if you could please move to the rear of the building and cover it for fleeing rats, I will take the front. Please leave me a dog or two."

"Roger, Tee. Ghost and Jill coming your way!"

While Thomas waited for the tear gas to do its work, he called Jed. "I need someone here ASAP to help with a prisoner. I appear to have lost one prisoner as well. Sylvie crawled away when I was pinned down by a shooter and her dog guards had to flee. Have them drive to Position B."

"I can send Katie and Manuel. Rachael and Sara are still trying to stabilize Bill before they move him. They want to bring him to the ranch house as soon as it's safe."

"No can do. There's CS gas in there, and it will take a while to clear. Tell them to head to the ranch hand building. Also, everyone needs to keep an eye out for Sylvie. Her hands are tied and she's probably disoriented and almost deaf so not a threat. And where's Karen? Mike said she was back."

"Uh.., uh, she's occupied at the moment."

"Occupied? Hey, gotta go, the front door is opening."

A woman burst out of the front door. Her eyes were bright red and tears covered her face. She was waving her arms and coughing as she ran. She fit the description of Jan. Thomas yelled to her as she passed him. "Keep running. Don't rub your eyes. The wind will eventually clear it. Rachael is over by that white trailer. Head in that direction." Thomas wasn't sure if she understood his instructions. She kept running anyway.

At last, the great and powerful Mathias was coming to him. That Machiavelli of psychological well-being, humanity's answer to conflict and chaos, didn't look to be "all that" to Thomas. His tomato red eyes flitted back and forth. He had his arm around a fine-looking woman and a pistol pointed at her head. She seemed calm, all things considered, while she coughed and wheezed from the CS. Must be Mabel.

Ghost slid in front of the man and darted at him snarling. Jill had taken a similar stance from behind, nipping at his heels as she growled and looked for way to get at his gun arm.

"Get those beasts away from me or I'll shoot them and then this woman. I need an automobile here now, fully fueled. Only then will I release her."

Thomas stood and pointed his M4 at Mathias. "Isn't going to happen. Here's the thing, Mathias. If you shoot my dogs or that woman, you are a dead man, period. There is over a 90% chance I could shoot you right now without harming a hair on that woman's head. I would much prefer you just lay down your weapon, now. You even flinch like you are going to shoot and you are a dead man. So bottom line, if you want to live, you put down that gun. You can thank me now for the feedback."

"You must not have had any training in negotiation. You are supposed to be concerned with the life of an innocent."

"I have a different kind of training. One that tells me a man of your ilk only cares about one thing—his own skin. Now put down that weapon before I get to three or I'll shoot." Thomas watched the entire scene as he counted. The woman Mathias was holding was, unbelievably, smiling through CS-generated tears. Jill was backing into position to leap at Mathias's gun hand. "One."

Thomas aimed at Mathias's head. He studied Mathias's eyes and movements. At two, Thomas took a relaxing breath and lightly readied his finger on the trigger. Thomas saw Mathias's hand move to drop the pistol as Jill leaped. She landed on his back and her momentum pushed Mathias forward to the ground. Already in motion, Mabel grabbed the gun that had fallen from his hand.

"Well played, soldier man," Mabel said as she covered Mathias with the weapon he was recently holding. "I was beginning to get just a wee bit nervous. Would you have actually shot him with my head inches away?"

"Yes, but it would have been at been at two and a half and you didn't have to worry. It depended on what his eyes told me. In a negotiation, the important thing is that your adversary believes you'll do what you say you will do. He believed it, and that's all that's important. So right now we have Carlotta and Jim out of commission, Sylvie crawling around the property somewhere, a surprise character trussed up over by the tree line being guarded by my dog, Jan probably in Rachael's capable hands, Mathias subdued, and you ably watching his carcass. So where are Eric and Dave?"

*   *   *

Mike and Jack stood a distance away from the back entry of the ranch house, watching. Mike was listening to Thomas on the headset explain that Eric and Dave were still missing. He didn't notice the ground level storm cellar entry only twenty feet from their location. One wood-planked side opened slowly. It was pushed open by a rifle barrel held in Eric's arms. Jack came into Eric's view first. Eric saw the massive dog's head swing toward him. Jack and Eric moved simultaneously in a dance to see who would survive the night. Eric shoved out of the ground aiming his rifle while Jack, harnessing powerful haunches, took two long strides and a heroic leap. A shot reverberated, piercing the silence.

Chapter 38: Stable Reunions

Tilley stayed by Karen's side as she jogged the distance to the stable. Karen moved first to the dark side of the building and along the back to the open office window. She paused to listen for people inside. *It sounds quiet.* Karen gave Tilley the signal for silence, and then pointed and said, "Go." She had to help lift the dog's backside through the window and climbed in behind her dog.

"Doesn't sound like anyone is here," Karen breathed to Tilley, cracking the office door for another sound check. "Coast is clear." She moved out to the center aisle with the hunting rifle she'd found at the cabin leading the way. A medium sized sedan sat in the middle of the stable. "Hmm, wonder what that's about."

Eyebrows raised, Karen glanced around the room. "Where the hell did everybody go?" Uh Huh's stall was empty. She entered his cell and examined the gate that had been torn apart from the inside. Tilley darted around the small space, smelling and snuffling. "He must have rammed it with his body until it shattered. Utterly amazing the strength that took," Karen said and shook her head.

Tilley stopped suddenly. Her head, tail, and neck fur raised, she went still. "What is it, girl?" Karen whispered as she heard running footsteps from the front entry. A man mumbling and dragging something was entering the stable. Karen put her finger to her lips at Tilley and flattened herself against the front-facing jail wall.

"I told them this would happen. Those stupid fucking morons! If I had the time, I would go back and wring Mathias's neck. I'd love to see the expression on that pretentious prick's face as my hands pressed down on his windpipe."

Dave. Karen would know his voice anywhere. But who's he talking to she wondered? She stood stock still, listening. He continued his tirade against everyone on the ranch. He even had a few choice words for her. It took a minute to realize he was talking to himself.

Be patient, Karen, she warned herself, and waited until he passed to step from her hiding spot.

"Speaking of pricks," Karen hissed as she jumped behind Dave. "Stop right where you are now!"

Dave stopped, but Karen could see him tensing to make a move. "Don't move, asshole. I'll blow a hole a mile wide in your back. Drop your pistol and rifle on the floor in front of you. You're probably wondering about now whether I can or will use this pump action rifle to shoot you before you make your move. In the immortal words of one of my favorite action heroes: go ahead, make my day."

He unslung his rifle and threw it in front of him. Slowly he unholstered the pistol and set it down too close to his feet.

"Nice try, asshole," Karen said as she fired just behind Dave, not really caring the shot ricocheted and hit him in the back of the legs. Dave jumped at the sound but remained in place. "Now kick it further away. Put your hands over your head and get down on your knees. No fast movements or the next shot is all yours."

Dave was pissed. He kicked the pistol forward and then did as Karen asked. Crossing the fifteen-foot distance, Karen poked the back of his head with the rifle.

"Not so brave now, are you, Dave? You like to pick on unarmed women and children—makes you feel powerful, doesn't it? I have two simple questions for you. If you answer them, I may let you live. Of course, that's conditional on whether I believe you."

Tilley had moved in front of Dave in a crouch, growling and baring her teeth. "First, was it your group who killed the captain at the submarine base?"

"I don't know what the hell you're talking about, Karen. What submarine base? Whoever did that, it wasn't us. We were looking for survivors to take to the ranch, remember? There wasn't any need to go out looking for people to kill."

Considering his answer, Karen nodded. "Okay, I'll give you a go on that one. It was just a warm-up question anyway. Second question: did you rape Rachael?"

"Karen, you don't want to do this. You aren't the kind of person who kills a man in cold blood. I think you—"

"Answer the Goddamn question, Dave!" Karen spat at the back of his head.

"It wasn't rape. She wanted it, Karen. She'd been looking at me and following me around since she got here. You think you know her but you—"

"Wrong answer, asshole!" Karen yelled. She hesitated for a moment of moral reflection, wondering if she could in fact kill this guy in cold blood. He certainly deserved it.

The momentary hesitation was all Dave needed. He was fast. He whipped around and landed his elbow hard to the side of her knee. With a weak ankle, Karen lost her balance, crumpling to the side and rolling while gripping the rifle in both hands. She sprung back to her feet. Dave was charging at her. Backing up, she attempted to sidestep his momentum. She stuck at him with the butt end of the weapon as he passed.

Karen knew she shouldn't have been that close. Her anger and pride sometimes overwhelmed better judgment. Dave stepped in and grabbed the rifle with both of his hands before Karen could use it on him. He lifted and twisted the weapon. They were grunting and fighting over the rifle. Tilley jumped for Dave's forearm and missed, only ripping some skin. He staggered from the impact and then launched a hard side kick at Tilley. He didn't release his grip on the rifle. Karen saw Tilley's eyes flash pain and confusion. She limped off, then fell over panting.

Karen was losing the struggle. She was strong, but Dave was stronger. She tried kneeing him in the groin, but he turned slightly. All she managed was a knee butt in his thigh. If she could hold the rifle with one hand she would poke one of his eyes or use her palm to crush his nose. *Think, Karen, think!*

Dave began pushing forward, using their locked arms like a battering ram. As he picked up speed, Karen scrambled backward. She stumbled and fell, maintaining her hold on the rifle and carrying Dave with her. *Why do they always end up on top?* Karen cursed to herself, trying to regain her breath. Dave, red-faced, grunted as he pushed down with his weight on the weapon to crush Karen's windpipe. Her arms were trembling. She was using every bit of strength she had left to keep the rifle above her neck. She couldn't hold on much longer. Karen screamed, "Help! Help me!" with the vain hope someone might be near.

"ArrrrEEEE!" Uh Huh shrieked a war cry from the open doors, running full out. With only time to lift his head slightly and turn to look, Dave was lifted off the ground and launched fifteen-feet in the air. He came to the ground in an unnatural pile with a resounding thud. Uh Huh grabbed Dave's head in his powerful hands and twisted. If he wasn't dead from the fall there was no doubt about it now. His anger not satiated, Uh Huh pulled and turned Dave's arms and legs until broken. He began to pull them from Dave's dead body. Karen closed her eyes to the carnage. The squishing, cracking sounds Uh Huh made as he went about his grisly work would give her nightmares for a very long time.

She only opened her eyes when she heard Uh Huh sigh. He was sitting in the middle of a bloody mess; body parts piled next to him. Karen didn't know if he recognized her; their communication had always been behind closed doors. He sure as hell recognized Dave, though. The poor, huge man thing had a long beard, wild hair, and short, dark fur all over his body. Dirt and debris from the forest clung to his beard and head, now liberally coated with Dave's blood. He definitely favored re-imagined pictures Karen had seen of Neanderthals. A pronounced bony ridge on his forehead shadowed his eyes. Karen's eyes watered from Uh Huh's pungent smell.

Karen was steadily scooting backwards away from Uh Huh. *Sing, dammit, sing,* Karen thought. With a shaky voice, Karen began "Bad Moon Rising," gaining strength and conviction in the song at the chorus. Uh Huh's eyes followed her movement. As she was nearing the stable door, he bobbed his head. "Uh huh, uh huh," he grunted in a high, nasally pitch with the rhythm. Three verses in and almost out of the stable, Karen panicked when Uh Huh started to crawl toward Tilley.

She stopped singing. "Please Uh Huh, that's my friend. Please let her be!" Uh Huh made a humming sound and touched Tilley's fur. He leaned over to sniff her. Karen could see Tilley was still breathing. She couldn't take the chance he might hurt her. She scrambled back to Tilley and inserted herself between Tilley and Uh Huh, laying her body across the dog and pleaded. "No Uh Huh. Please no."

He tilted his head and growled. The only thing Karen knew to do was sing. She started another song, "The Lion Sleeps Tonight," while cradling Tilley, who was panting on her side. Uh Huh sat back and watched as Karen ran her hand along Tilley to feel for any injuries, all while still singing. Karen could see Tilley's tail wagging. She inserted encouraging words to Tilley into the Song. "In the jungle, the mighty jungle, Tilley is a lovely girl. In the jungle, she's fine and dandy, and going to be mighty cool." Even though the words only marginally rhymed, Tilley lifted her head in approval after hearing her name.

Tilley licked at Karen's arm and then rolled over to make her stomach available for petting. "Oh my God Tilley, you are such a little wuss." Karen glanced cautiously at Uh Huh as Tilley got up and wagged her tail. Uh Huh, was studying Tilley curiously but without aggression.

Karen hung her head and continued to rub Tilley as she talked. "I don't know about you, Uh Huh, but I've had about all the excitement I can handle. I mean, look at you! What the hell happened during the change that made you like this—no offense intended. Thanks, by the way, for helping me out a few minutes ago." Karen glanced up, and her eyes met Uh Huh's. She was pretty sure he understood what she was saying… well, mostly sure.

"Do you want to go back with me and my friends to Washington? I don't know how we'll work it out, but you'll be free to leave if you decide it isn't your cup of tea."

They stared at each other until Uh Huh fumbled, using giant hands to reach into his shirt pocket. Carefully, with a thumb and finger holding the retrieved object, he extended a hairy arm to Karen and handed her a laminated card. She got up and gingerly pulled the plastic thing from his grasp. Karen hid her shock. A good-looking 38-year-old man named Jeffrey Kline, partially obscured by bloody fingerprints, was smiling at her from a Wyoming driver's license.

"Is this you?" Karen asked.

Uh Huh, aka Jeff, closed his eyes and gave an almost imperceptible nod.

"So Jeff… uh, really sorry about that made up name." His eyes crinkled in what might have been a smile. "Look, I have to go find my friends. If you want to come with me, why don't you use the water in my old cage to clean up a bit and I'll come back to pick you up? Hate to say it, but you smell pretty darn bad. And I saw some boots in the office that might work for you since they were a size huge; that is, if you want something for your feet. I'll help you put them on if you need help when I get back." Karen put her hand softly on his cheek and looked searchingly in his eyes. "And thank you, Jeff, from the bottom of my heart. You saved my life. I owe you." This time, she was almost positive his eyes smiled back. "Come on, Tilley, get off your ass! Let's go find the others."

They jogged from the stable, heading to the ranch house. The sun was coming up behind the eastern hills. A truck rumbled toward them. Karen stopped fast, wondering if she should hide as Tilley ran into the back of her legs. She heard the truck door open, and Thomas's camouflaged head popped out. "Karen, is that you? I'm Thomas, Mike's buddy. I know you don't know me, but he needs you now."

Karen stood, shielding her eyes from the sunrise glare on the truck windshield. "Hey Thomas, Mike mentioned you. Is he okay?" She swung the truck door open and jumped in with Tilley, trying not to become hysterical. "Is he okay, Thomas? Tell me he's okay."

"He's fine. We have things about wrapped up, but Bill and Jack were shot. Sara is with them now at the ranch-hand building."

"Oh no, not Jack. Poor Bill. Please hurry."

"Sara is a fantastic doctor. They couldn't be in better hands."

"People doctor, not a vet, I assume."

"Roger that, Karen. But she's been studying canine anatomy and physiology so she'd be prepared if one of the dogs was hurt. She's doing her best." Thomas squinted at Karen's strong profile as she peered straight ahead, her hands clasped tightly in her lap. "What the hell happened to you? You look like shit."

"Thanks, Thomas, I needed that. I decided to take a barefoot stroll in the mountains for a couple of days; just needed a little fresh air and sunshine to get this awesome look. I was also attacked by a monster and saved by another. Otherwise, same old, same old, different day."

Thomas chuckled, "Mike said I would like you," then he focused on the gravel road and drove like hell as Karen leaned forward, willing him to go faster.

"By the way, I have an unusual friend, Jeff, in the stables. Please tell everyone not to bother him. He's easily frightened. And take my word for it, you don't want to get him agitated. Dave is dead, thanks to Jeff."

"That explains all the unknowns then."

"What are you talking about?"

"Jed, another of our newest members, is a tech guru, scientist, and all-around brainiac. He brought some drones along with some other very cool technology. You can see heat signatures for people on a laptop. We knew Dave was out there somewhere and there was one other unknown, but we lost all but one drone when we used them as a diversion. When we found out you went rogue and galloped off to the stables, Mike sent me to find you."

"I wouldn't call it rogue. And yeah, I remember Jed from the original ranch meetings. I met him briefly when I came out of the wilderness. Glad you came to check me out, even if you were slightly late," Karen grimaced as she pushed the Dave mutilation out of her mind.

Surrounded by trucks, the ranch-hand building came into view. Karen jumped out, leaving the door open for Tilley. Rachael, Katie, Mabel, and Manuel were standing near the entry nervously waiting. Rachael screamed first, followed closely by Katie. Both girls surrounded Karen, hugging and crying. Karen looked over Rachael's shoulder at Mabel, who remained seated on the steps but gave Karen a beautiful, knowing smile.

"Where's Mike?"

"Inside," Katie said as she pointed.

Karen took a deep, steadying breath and strode to the door, opening it slowly. She saw Mike first in the corner of the room. He looked up then rubbed his eyes, trying not to cry. Karen stepped around Sara in the center of the room tending to Jack and Jill lying on their sides on one table. Both dogs were connected to tubes and a bag of blood, and Karen figured Jill must be giving blood to Jack. Must be pretty bad, Karen thought. Bill lay on another table. She stood next to Mike and grabbed one of his hands with both of hers. They leaned against each other, squeezing hands for comfort and support.

During the wait, Karen learned about the perils of having only one doctor to care for both people and dogs. Even though Jack was seriously hurt, Bill had to come first. Mike had grudgingly agreed that Jack had to wait. Sara said that Bill would survive. Jack's fate was uncertain.

Daylight was filtering through the windows as Sara announced to the rest of the team in the room, "I've done all I can do; all we can do now is wait. I got the bullet out of Jack, but it bounced around and did a good deal of damage. I hope I fixed everything, but I can't be sure. Jill's transfusion should help. By the way, I think Jill's pregnant."

Mike and Karen were sitting on the floor leaning against the wall. Mike said, "I want to stay with him, Sara. Could you ask if someone could find some coffee and maybe something to eat? And thank you, Sara, for everything."

She gave a sad nod. "Sure, Mike. I'll be right outside if he needs anything. I'm going to try to take a nap."

As the door shut Mike stood up, pulled Karen up too, and they circled next to Jack's head. As he rubbed his ears and ruff, watching Jack's labored breathing, Mike said, "He saved me, you know. I screwed up and didn't see the door in the ground. Eric came out and Jack just, well, he just leaped at him." Tears welled in Mike's eyes as he swallowed hard.

Karen hugged Mike as he buried his head in her shoulder. "He saved me too, more than once. In a way, and I know it sounds weird, I always felt like he was sent to save all of us. In a world brimming with special dogs, he is something, well, I think you could say magical. He drew us together, dogs and people, in a way that I can't comprehend or explain."

"Eric is gone," Mike said flatly.

Rachael came in the door with coffee and energy bars followed by the rest of the crew, including the dogs. They remained with Jack in a vigil, willing him to be alright.

At almost noon, Mike heard Jack's soft voice. *Man, woman come, man come.*

Mike jumped up, followed by Karen, who didn't understand Mike's sudden movement as he leaned over Jack, whispering, "I'm here, boy; I'm here."

Sorry… man, Mike. Jack not fast enough. Jack has… pack, family.

Still touching Jack's fur, Mike noticed it was unusually warm. A soft luminescent glow covered the dog's body. His hands penetrating the soothing light, Mike felt overwhelmed with joy and love. In his next breath, he inhaled a miasma of smells, as distinct as the colors in an elaborate painting, from the mice in the walls to the different grasses and wildflowers outside. Mike's perspective shifted again. Colors are not as vivid. He views the world from only 30 inches off the ground.

I am running effortlessly on four perfectly coordinated legs through an orchard, chasing a ball. I stop for a moment to leap at a butterfly flying by. A man and a woman call to me. The woman, Karen, scratches behind my ears. At her touch, I feel her as part of me. Her scent fills me, engendering loyalty and unbreakable trust. It is a bond so strong I will gladly dedicate myself to her protection above my own life.

I can see the big round toy they call life preserver. I drag it to the man, Mike, to play. The man is my equal in strength. He will protect me as I protect him. What he asks of me, I will do. We play the games that together make us whole and full. I am his partner. With him and the woman we are pack, family, and we are strong. I take the round toy in my jaws and savagely pull.

"Everybody, quick, touch him," Mike smiled as tears streamed down his rough cheek. They gathered around, hands and paws pressed to his beautiful black and tan fur, filling with Jack's true essence. The glow intensified and then lifted from his body. It became a white mist and then was gone. The dogs in the room began to bark wildly as birds stopped to listen, and wolves, sleeping from their nightly hunt, woke and sniffed the air.

"What was that, Mike?" Karen asked.

Mike shook his head. "Jack magic, I think."

Jack's eyes blinked opened. He whined and panted like any other dog. Mike leaned down and snuggled his head. "That's my good boy."

It was a busy but quiet afternoon. Thomas, Mike and Rachael, dug graves for the Ranchers killed during the attack. Manuel and Jed found some lumber and tarps to make stretchers to take the wounded back to Washington. Sara demanded they wait at least until the next morning before traveling to Washington. She was determined to ensure her patients were stable. No one protested. Everyone was tired and needed hard earned sleep. Karen and Rachael didn't want to stay on the ranch any longer than absolutely necessary, but they also didn't want to leave Bill or, more importantly, Jack.

The new guy, who introduced himself as Sam, still couldn't hear from the concussion grenade. He convinced Mike and Karen he had no idea what the ranchers were up to and went along only so he wouldn't be alone anymore. They agreed to give him a probationary try.

After they loaded everything they needed for the trip home, Thomas and Jed rigged explosives at the ranch house and farm hand building. Mike gave Rachael and Katie instructions to disable vehicles to be left behind and emptied ranch gas tanks into their own.

Sam showed Mike the storage location of ranch weapons and ammunition. It was in the same outside storm cellar Eric had used to make his escape. Along with the weaponry, they found four nearly desiccated skeletons. They were wrapped in a bulky tarp lying in front of a gun rack. No one could be sure who they were or why they were left in the underground room. There was general agreement Mathias probably had something to do with the bodies, and that it was most likely nefarious doings. "You don't suppose it could be Mathias's wife and kids, do you?" Mabel asked.

For his part, Mathias refused to talk about it. Thomas volunteered to get the information out of him and in unison Karen and Mike yelled, "Oh, hell no." The grave they dug for the tarp covered bones was marked, "Unknown Victims of the Ranch."

Neither Sylvie nor Mathias could fly a helicopter so it was left in place.

Rachael and Sara found Sylvie in a ditch that she'd stumbled into the night before. They might not have found her at all except for her plaintive wailing. She begged for them to bring her along. "I will be loyal to you guys, I swear it. I've been so confused since I lost my family. I can cut hair, and I'll do whatever you want. Pleeasse take me with you!" Her pleas were sad to hear, but no one wanted someone like her in the group.

For Mathias's part, he was completely indignant, accusing the group of becoming an imperial force and threatening any number of disastrous outcomes as their probable fate. Mabel tried to talk to him, but he sneered at her and spat in her face. Mabel wanted to clobber him, but she decided he was too pathetic to bother lowering herself to his level.

A startlingly bright morning welcomed their departure from the ranch. Together as a group, they transferred Jack and Bill onto Manuel's stretcher contraptions and placed them gently in the covered back of one of the trucks. Sara would ride with the wounded and her medical equipment. The entire dog contingent was solicitous toward Jack, sniffing him and pacing anxiously. They did their best to jump in and ride along, but Sara glared at the canines and forced them back.

They left Mathias and Sylvie a little food and water. Rachael finally relented and let them keep their shoes. She told Katie later, "Like, they didn't even appreciate how important shoes actually are!"

Karen had one more task to accomplish before they could ride home. She waited the night to give Jeff/Uh Huh time to think about her proposal. And, if truth be told, she wasn't sure how she was going to make good on her offer to take him along. Karen made everyone wait with the loaded convoy near the stable as she and Mike walked into her jail one last time, hand in hand. Karen explained to Mike, "He was intelligent, just different. Uh Huh, I mean Jeff, was the first person who ever loved my singing."

It was quickly obvious Jeff was gone. Only a hint of his acrid smell lingered in the stable. The driver's license Jeff had handed Karen was left in the middle of Jeff's stall, the gate still smashed open. "Interesting, don't you think, Mike? He always had the ability to get out," Karen said as she leaned against his hard shoulder. The boots in the office were gone as were, curiously, Dave's body parts.

As Mike hugged Karen he whispered in her ear, "I don't think he's coming back."

She bit her lip, nodded, and looked one last time at the strange place she'd come to know as the ranch. They strolled from the stable together to join their new community of friends. With his finger, Mike gave a circling signal above his head to start moving home.

Epilogue

I just read Geronimo's story. He did a fine job and got most of it about right. I mentioned to him I thought it would be important to add something about what happened to the people in the story, and we had an artistic difference of opinion. I don't know where he gets his stubbornness, LOL. He said it was "good enough" and has already moved on to another project. I am old but still not so feeble that I can't add a few words. He'll appreciate it when I finish.

After the New Washington founders returned to Tacoma, life was good for a while, though never easy. There simply aren't enough people to do everything we would like or need to do. For some time, our culture was very much like the early American agrarian experience—we spent all our time working to survive. Feeding and housing humans and their dog companions is a full-time enterprise. The infrastructure of the old world has crumbled and decayed and road networks are nearly useless. Communication satellites died long ago.

Luckily these improved bodies are improved in many ways. We hardly ever get sick; cancer has been eradicated (at least that we know); and pregnancies only last six months. The last item is a saving grace. We need all the people we can get, so everyone is encouraged to go forth and multiply. I had twelve children, fourteen counting my departed babies from before the change. To this day, I still miss Nathan and Ann. It's a loss you never get over.

Right now the New Washington Enclave accounts for almost 6000 human souls. We wouldn't have that many, but the "big one," a huge earthquake, hit California in 2066, and the survivors migrated to our Enclave. They brought along a geneticist, an aeronautical engineer, and Clint Eastwood of all people. Damn, that man is handsome. I've heard rumors he's a bit of a womanizer—I can see why he'd be successful. Jed and the California engineer have created some very interesting flying machines. I won't go into it here, but our enclave is known as the most advanced in the U.S.—perhaps the world. I am very proud of that.

Even so, our existence is still a struggle and not assured. The Virginia Enclave has been making trouble for the other six U.S. Enclaves.

UFOs have been spotted to the north in Canada regularly for the last twenty years. No, I'm not crazy—it's been verified by the Rainier Station. We don't know what they want or why they've come, but there's little we can do about it except watch, wait, and pray.

We still don't know why the human race died and changed but we have some clues on the how. Sara and the geneticist said our DNA is different. As they explained it, it's different enough that the survivors of the change could be classified as a separate branch of humanoids. Jack and Jill's DNA was different, too. Not only were they not completely canine, their blood carried nanites, as do their offspring (both pure and mixed with other dogs). Mark, our resident geneticist, believes humans were infected with a retrovirus loaded inside a common virus that everyone carries within their bodies. He theorizes that something external switched on this mutant so that our species essentially died in two weeks. If his theory is correct, he believes this was done to us purposefully. It remains a mystery.

We have extra sense gifts. Mine is known as a seer gift, just like shamans of old lore. It was why my dreams gave me hints of what was to come. Our children inherited these gifts in a more refined way. My fourth daughter, Amelia, is scarily good at predicting future events. She's so scary that most people shy away from her, poor thing. Quite the burden to carry, I think. Others have sensors like Katie or acute hearing, scent, and night vision. Some of our grandchildren possess all of these gifts and most of them can communicate telepathically with Jack and Jill's offspring.

The politics of our enclave become more complex every year. In the beginning, with so few people, it was relatively easy to include everyone on major decisions. Also, the requirement to scratch out an existence doesn't leave as much time for squabbling about bullshit. We are moving into a different phase now, one where we'll have to make decisions on how to govern a more diverse group. It's a treacherous path. Our bodies and minds are stronger, but human temperaments are little changed.

And back to the reason I wanted to write this. Manuel, truly a renaissance man, followed Rachael around for five years. When she got frustrated and made comments to the effect that she might marry Bill, Manuel finally asked her to be his wife. They are very happy and proud parents of fifteen children and a boatload of grandkids and great-grandkids. Rachael served as the Enclave sheriff and justice of the peace for many years. Manuel created a lot of things for us, but the most important of them was his art. He just finished a bronze statue that sits in the middle of the town square. It's beautiful.

It may be obvious from Geronimo's story that Katie ended up with Thomas, and Jed and Sara were a much better match. Both couples had some marriage problems. If you think it's hard to be married to one person for 30 or 40 years, try doing it for 100. But that's an issue for another time. Thomas is the Enclave Chief of the Forces. He does an amazing job. Katie was our region's animal tender, also an important position. She retired the job to one of her sons a few years ago and works part-time with Sara and her two daughters at the clinic as a vet.

Animals have a very important place in our society, especially dogs, which are honored. They have been our helpers and friends since the beginning. Because of Jack and Jill, we know definitively that animals are complex emotional beings. To hurt an animal needlessly is treated as seriously in our society as purposely harming our human counterparts. Everyone is encouraged to have a dog and/or cat of their own since we believe it makes for healthier, happier humans.

We do have livestock; we need them for survival, but the laws dictate they must be treated humanely throughout their lives and during the harvesting ceremony—no small cages for our animals! Many of our members choose to only eat fish and other protein sources, which is a fine way to pay respects to our mammal relatives.

One of our biggest problems is wild dog packs. We no longer call them dogs, as they've evolved and look like a cross between canines, coyotes and wolves. They're known as Rangers, and they can be as vicious as they are smart. I could spend a considerable time discussing what we have done to mitigate the problem, but that's also an issue for another time.

Jan is our Enclave music teacher. She loves doing it and plays concerts every quarter with her students.

Bill and Mabel hang out together but have never officially married, even though they have five children together. Don't ask me. They are what we call free agents, and both love farming.

Josh and Mei, aka Bonnie and Clyde, came to the enclave about six months after we returned. They were good kids but wild. Still are for that matter, even in older age.

The ranch new guy, Sam, wandered off to parts unknown after twenty years when a huge argument with him and Thomas turned physical. That happens around here. People decide they're better off somewhere else and leave—we never stop them. Likewise, others join our enclave, which has a reputation for being mostly peaceful and civilized.

I don't know what happened to Sylvie or Mathias. Good riddance to them. Likewise, I don't know what happened to Jeff, whom I'm afraid I'll always think of as Uh Huh. There are rumors that a group of strangely mutated humanoids live in the wilds of Montana and Idaho. I can't say if they're true, but I hope so.

As for Mike and me, I am as in love with the man as I was that first day when he showed up at my gate. I believe he's as happy and content as I am. Maybe you must suffer to appreciate what you have, or maybe we practiced being married for so long we just got good at it. Don't know and don't care. We've had so many wonderful years together, I'm simply grateful. Mike always craved a simple family life after the change and didn't want the mantle of leadership. But you are what you are born to be. When things get truly off balance, people always turn to Mike for advice and guidance. He's helped everyone, especially Manuel, to plan and build our enclave and has been involved in every aspect of the New Washington settlement.

Once we came home, I was excited to have a house full of kids and dogs. Mike said he liked dogs, but after almost losing Jack, he couldn't get so close to another again. If dog ownership meant losing them over and over because of their shorter lives, he wanted a pass. (I have to add, this was all before we knew that Jack and Jill and their bloodline would live for 50 to 60 years.) He also commented rather loudly on those occasions when we would squabble about taking in more abandoned dogs that the care and feeding of so many animals would be a problem. Jack and Jill remained his constant companions as did our other dogs, Tilley, Raider, Maple, and Zoe, but he didn't want to love anymore.

I know that feeling after the loss of a truly loved animal. What I also know is the only way to move beyond fear is to love another—so Rachael and I tricked the sweet man. Jill had puppies not long after we returned, but Mike refused to go see them. He has a stubborn side. They were obviously Jack's progeny through and through.

Rachael and I moved them from the new garage to a shed and asked Mike to fetch a tool for us. He walked into the shed on a cool, damp, fall Washington day and nine pairs of sleeping brown eyes woke to his entry. They whirled around him, biting and jumping, yipping for attention. We heard him laugh. He got the feisty fur children back in the fenced enclosure and turned to leave.

Man, man, play, play, man.

"Who said that?" Mike replied, startled as he turned again and saw a dark male looking hopeful back at him.

Well, you know what happened. Mike named him Heart, which means the same thing in German as it does in English.

Thanks!

I had no idea when I started this project how long it would take, or the process for bringing an idea to life. I probably should have done some research before I began but my way is generally to just jump in. The most important lesson is that like almost everything else in life, it takes a team.

First I want to thank my cousin Bonny Burns for saying those magic words, "Why don't you write it?" So simple and yet, for some reason, it was the nudge I needed. I also want to thank my cousin Caren Ruffner for reading my entire rough/messy draft and making comments. I will be forever grateful to you both.

I used two editors: a company and an individual. Both were extremely professional and helpful. Kevin Anderson and Associates did the first review. Reading between the lines from their comments forced me to rethink the storyline and do a major rewrite. When I was done, I wanted another perspective. Also, I felt like it would be helpful to have someone willing to talk to me about the characters, the story, life, kids, grammar and everything in-between. That person was Christel Taylor, an English professor living in Wisconsin. I don't believe she had ever edited a fiction book before, so we learned together. I was fortunate to have her help and her ear. Thank you!

For the cover I found a young woman fresh out of the Seattle Art Institute. She sent me an email over LinkedIn looking for business. I like hiring people with initiative. She did a bang up job for a very particular client, and she did it with great patience and humor. Thank you Heather Diamond!

Jeanmarie Kautzman, dog trainer extraordinaire, made some suggestions on dog behavior and dog training methods. She trains service dogs for wounded warriors and her advice was invaluable. Thanks Jean!

My unending gratitude to my family for all of their support. I know they thought I was crazy, but they went with it anyway. My husband suffered through a bazillion out-loud readings and an untold number of questions like, "Does this make sense?" I hope they'll be happy to know I have already started the next one.

Finally, to any readers who have made it all the way to this very last paragraph, my sincere gratitude. I hope you enjoyed **Critically Endangered** and would greatly appreciate your feedback.

If you liked the characters, give Beyond the Great Dying, Book 2 of the Endangered Series a try. The third novel in the series will be released in the spring, 2019. Check out my website at **nsaustinwrites.com** for information about the next release or send me and note and I'll add you to my email list.

Many Thanks! Nancy